FORCE OF GRAVITY

FORCE OF GRAVITY

R. S. JONES

VIKING

VIKING
Published by the Penguin Group
Viking Penguin, a division of Penguin Books USA Inc.,
375 Hudson Street, New York, New York 10014, U.S.A.
Penguin Books Ltd, 27 Wrights Lane, London W8 5TZ, England
Penguin Books Australia Ltd, Ringwood, Victoria, Australia
Penguin Books Canada Ltd, 2801 John Street, Markham, Ontario, Canada L3R 1B4
Penguin Books (N.Z.) Ltd, 182–190 Wairau Road, Auckland 10, New Zealand

Penguin Books Ltd, Registered Offices: Harmondsworth, Middlesex, England

First published in 1991 by Viking Penguin,
a division of Penguin Books USA Inc.

10 9 8 7 6 5 4 3 2 1

PUBLISHER'S NOTE
This is a work of fiction. Names, characters, places, and incidents either are the product
of the author's imagination or are used fictitiously, and any resemblance to actual persons,
living or dead, events, or locales is entirely coincidental.

Page 321 constitutes an extension of this copyright page.

LIBRARY OF CONGRESS CATALOGING IN PUBLICATION DATA
Jones, Robert S.
Force of gravity / Robert S. Jones.
p.   cm.
ISBN 0-670-83591-9
I. Title.
PS3560.O5249F67   1991
813'.54–dc20   90-50576

Printed in the United States of America
Set in Granjon
Designed by Fritz Metsch

This book is dedicated to
David Tracy and Caroline Blackwood

Suppose you go the other way, all the way down to the center of the earth. There, surrounded on all sides by the matter of the earth pulling evenly from all directions, you weigh . . . nothing! You are weightless because all the gravitational forces are evenly balanced around you.

—Herman Schneider and Leo Schneider,
Science in Everyday Language

CONTENTS

PART ONE
SHELTER

Everything exists; nothing exists. Either formula affords a like serenity. The man of anxiety, to his misfortune, remains between them, trembling and perplexed, forever at the mercy of a nuance, incapable of gaining a foothold in the security of being or in the absence of being.

—E. M. Cioran

CHAPTER ONE

"I am getting small," Emmet noted with pleasure as he reached for the keys to his apartment.

The pocket of his jeans was so roomy, he could rotate his hand a full circle within the lining.

"It's big as a muff," he marveled as he pulled out the keys.

The pressure of his hand caused his pants to dip over his cheeks. Emmet made a mental note to buy a new belt so that he could cinch his clothes more snugly against his waist. He slipped his hand under his shirt and petted the taut skin.

As he turned away from the door to the street, the sun blinded him. It had become his habit to keep his apartment dark even in the day: partly to cool it against the summer heat, partly to shadow the walls so that they gleamed less brightly once he was locked inside. For an instant, the light made his neighborhood thin and black as an X-ray transparency. He blinked patiently until the shapes reassembled.

Emmet paused for a moment at the bottom of the stoop. He zipped his jacket so that the metal hook pinched his neck. The cloth draped loosely over his back. When he hunched his shoulders, the sleeves fluttered like wings.

"Smaller every day," he thought, happily.

Emmet looked both ways before he stepped onto the sidewalk. In the morning, there were never many people about, but he wanted to be certain that a neighbor did not loiter outside to follow his movements. He wanted to be certain his landlord was not watching from behind a bush in the next yard. When he saw that the way was clear, he adjusted his sunglasses over his eyes and settled into the sea-green haze.

Already the cloth of his T-shirt grew damp with sweat. It stuck under his armpit to the blue flannel shirt he wore layered over it.

"Imagine that it is cold. Imagine that it is winter and you are shivering helplessly," he told himself as he turned the corner to hail a cab. With each step, sweat leaked from the pores. Puddles collected in the seat of his pants so that his jeans grew heavy and thick.

"Harder," he said aloud and clenched his teeth. "Imagine skiing on a glacier with no coat. Imagine sleeping naked in six feet of drifts."

In his mind, Emmet saw a mountain slope packed with skiers. He blinked once to narrow his range of vision. Up close, he saw a face ruddy with frost. He held the image in his mind while he shuddered as if overcome by a chill. "Come on," he said. "Cold. Cold. White. White."

The face froze before him. Below it, the wings of a blue nylon collar flapped against its whiskers. He could hear the clatter of skis as they edged across the moguls at the bottom of the slope, the *shoosh* of speed as the ice propelled the skier against the wind. Emmet urged himself on as if he were racing. "Cold, cold, cold," he repeated, until he became dizzy from the steady beat of perspiration dripping from his brow.

He kicked the metal rail that ran along the steps to his house. "The least you can do is make your body feel cold," he berated himself as he recalled the many miracles he had heard.

Emmet had read about people who levitated themselves at will or slept dreamlessly on beds of broken glass or swallowed steel swords as effortlessly as water. Some had made tumors shrink inside their bodies by picturing beams of light attacking the lump of cells. He wanted to believe he could train his mind so that he could wield it against his body, even teach himself to defy the natural elements, if he concentrated resolutely. None of it had worked. Day after day, his brain failed him.

Before he reached the end of his block, Emmet felt thirsty. His clothes drooped over his body as if he had soaked them in the bath before stepping outside. "Imagine it is silk," he thought halfheartedly, but already the heat weighed upon him too miserably to imagine himself another way. He checked his watch to see if he had time to slip into the delicatessen on the corner for something to drink.

For the past month, all Emmet had wanted was carbonated water. He had got it into his head that the water would cleanse him. As he swallowed, he imagined each bubble scrubbing against his soul. He traced its path as it caught in his throat and abraded his lungs. If he had not eaten, he could feel it drop coolly into his stomach before it disappeared. With time, he wanted to sense it pop all the way down to his toes. He hoped that if he drank enough, and only that type of water, he might become pure.

His dog still required food. He was trying to change her. He offered her carbonated water from a bowl set neatly on a mat on the floor. At first, she crinkled her nose at the bubbles, as if they were made of pepper instead of air; but she grew used to them when she realized it was all she was going to get to drink. When she begged Emmet to feed her, he covered his face with a surgical mask so that he did not smell the fumes.

He never felt hungry. At home, he ate nothing but carrots. He spent hours whittling their skins with a knife so that nothing remained but the unblemished, orange flesh. Sometimes he ate them chopped into one-inch pieces. Sometimes he pulped them in his juicer and drank them like soup from a bowl. Sometimes he served them long and sliced on a platter. Sometimes he shaved them into mounds and shook them onto his dish like strands of hair.

Emmet always set a fork and a spoon next to his plate. He folded a napkin in a rectangle under his knife. He lit two beeswax candles in the silver candlesticks his mother had bequeathed him. Although he rarely went into the sun, his skin was acquiring a pale orange blush, like a faded tan.

Emmet's body had adjusted. It felt simpler now. He admired the way his flesh tugged against his bones, tightly, so that he could feel himself every way he moved. The smaller he became, the more secure he felt, as if he were able to maneuver more easily through space. He believed he was on the way to something. He believed he needed patience to learn every part of his anatomy from the inside out before he could hope to change simply by thinking. Already he could track every rhythm his body made. Already he could feel every cell alive down to the last tick.

Emmet had shared none of his new ideas with his psychiatrist. He had learned long ago how to dupe him. But to cover himself, he carefully padded his clothes so that he might keep his thinness secret. He wanted to appear collected when he entered the office, as if there were nothing unusual about the jacket he wore on that summer's day.

Emmet spent part of every session detailing the meals he pretended he had cooked. He described the elaborate ingredients and preparations required for every dish. He told the doctor that he had started giving dinner parties for all of his friends. "I'm getting quite a reputation," he bragged. He added that he was considering taking cooking lessons at a food institute. He planned to change careers and become a chef now that he had conquered his dread of food.

As he walked, Emmet rehearsed what he would tell the doctor

that afternoon. He recited the recipe for a chocolate soufflé he had memorized the night before, letting his tongue trip over the ingredients so that he might seem to savor them.

"Egg whites bubbling with air. Granulated sugar. Four spoonfuls of whipped butter. Eight melted semisweet squares." He pictured himself licking the bowl. He held the image there until a wave of revulsion passed. Then in his mind he sucked every finger clean.

As he rounded the corner by the delicatessen, his attention was diverted by the overloaded dumpster parked halfway out onto the sidewalk. "16-20, Section C," he thought to himself. "Refuse and ashes must be kept within the building or in the rear of the premises until time for removal." Emmet knew the garbagemen were not due on this block for days. Until then, the trash would cook in the heat, drawing rats to the door of every store.

He wished he had brought his camera so that he could record the dumpster's hazard. He had a file of photographs from every part of the city locked in the top drawer of his desk. He had memorized every code in the city's library of violations. He had written away for pamphlets sent free from government agencies. He felt compelled to document everything that was wrong in the city. He believed that people were not sufficiently aware, although sometimes now he grew overburdened by all he had learned. He found evidence of lawlessness every time he left his apartment. Even when he opened the back door to shake lint from a rug into the neighborhood's air, he knew from his pamphlets that he was committing a crime.

Emmet raised an arm to hail a cab. An odor stunned him, heavy as a sick room's. "The poisons leave me," he thought, happily, as he imagined the residue of a lifetime's food escape from his body like exhaust. He waved his sleeve to loosen the cloth from his skin. His clothes clung to him like hair.

As the cab slowed at the curb, Emmet removed his sunglasses

and smiled broadly to assure the driver that he was not dangerous.

The driver lowered the window an inch. "Where you goin'?" he barked from the wheel before he unlocked the door.

"Code 202-A," Emmet noted silently. "He can't ask me that. I can make him take me anywhere I want." Emmet angled to see the number of the driver's license through the windshield. Once he had got safely inside, he considered missing his doctor's appointment to make the man transport him to the city's most distant border. If he refused, he would report him.

The driver turned, carefully studying the seams of Emmet's jeans through the glass. Emmet pressed the pockets smooth against his legs to show that he did not hide a weapon's bulge. Suddenly, he was ashamed that a person would think him guilty before he had uttered a word.

"Eighty-eighth and Fifth," he whispered through the crack in the window. The door lock popped open and he slunk into the backseat.

The driver slapped the meter. Red numbers jumped to life. "Hurry, hurry. You're letting out all the cold air. What's the matter with you? You sick or somethin' wearin' all those clothes?"

"I'm going to the doctor," Emmet replied vaguely.

He unzipped his jacket. He shuddered in the frigid air. "This is how it feels," he told himself. "Cold." He concentrated on every blast from the vent, hoping to store the sensation somewhere in his memory so that he might draw upon it later.

"So what's the story? You a tourist or something? You looked weird standing there. I get it—you live in Alaska and brought all the wrong clothes. Or you got some other problem. Maybe you got more than one, huh?" As the driver laughed, his throat rumbled with phlegm. He spit a glistening pink ball into a handkerchief.

Emmet punched a fist into his mouth to calm his nausea. "Pretend it is gum," he thought. He made himself gaze boldly into the driver's eyes through the rearview mirror. "Thanks for picking me up," he said, as if it had been a favor. "I've always toyed with the idea of driving a cab myself, but I don't know how I'd ever decide who's safe and who isn't just by seeing them."

"The point is you can't," the driver said. He pulled a knife from a sheath and chipped at the dashboard with its tip. "This is my weirdo insurance, so nobody goes gettin' any bright ideas." He stabbed the knife into a hole near the radio and gave it a thwack so that it vibrated like a diving board.

"I can't blame you," Emmet said. "It's hard enough to trust your friends in a city like this."

His foot kicked a beige plastic sack wadded against the door. He could see the corner of a brown paper parcel bundled inside. He scooted to the edge of the seat and cupped his index finger around the arched, fluttery handles. As he drew it towards him, the bag rattled so loudly that he was afraid the driver would hear and claim it as his own. He would remember how Emmet had stood empty-handed on the street.

"What's your name?" Emmet asked to divert him. He peered at the license through the plastic partition separating the seats. "Lincoln? Is that what it says? Is that a first name?"

"First or last, what's the difference?"

"Oh, none. There's just no reason for us to be strangers." As he spoke, Emmet reached down to the floorboard. He coughed loudly and lifted the bag to his lap in one movement. It swung heavily between his legs.

"Hey, what's goin' on?" the driver shouted excitedly.

"What do you mean?" Emmet stuttered. The bag thumped onto the floor. He slipped his hands under his thighs.

Emmet checked to make sure the door was unlocked. "I can grab the bag and jump," he decided, if the driver challenged him. All around them, he saw traffic stalled on both sides of the avenue. Their car had not moved for eighty cents' worth of time.

"Over there," the driver said, swinging halfway out of the cab. "Why d'ya think nobody's movin'?"

A crowd had gathered on the opposite sidewalk. Their faces nodded up the side of the building and down to the ground repeatedly, as if mesmerized by the path of a bouncing ball. A white cloth spread at their feet like a net.

The driver swooped excitedly back into the cab. "I bet it's a jumper," he cried. He gave the knife a nudge for emphasis. It clanked loudly against the radio.

"Jumper?" Emmet asked, confused.

"You know, a dry diver, a moonbeam gone for a space walk. When the unemployment check stops, out the window they go. Let's go take a look," he said, but the traffic began to move forward.

Emmet stared straight ahead. "The other cars . . ." he muttered. "We must go."

"You're the boss, buddy," the driver shrugged, easing the cab into the center lane.

"Did you see a body? Just now, I mean," Emmet asked, after a moment.

"Nah. Just a sheet and a dent in the roof of a car. Better luck next time, whatdyasay, buddy?"

At a red light, the driver unstuck the knife from the dashboard and began cleaning his fingernails with the tip. "Lucky for her it was an old building. Some of the new ones, the windows don't open no matter what you do. No place to be in a fire."

"How do you know it was a woman?"

"It's always broads that jump. Not enough of 'em got guns. Pills or the flight deck, that's the way they go."

In his mind, Emmet saw a woman balanced on her toes on a ledge outside a window. Chips of mortar blew into the air from where her fingernails dug into the bricks, showering the street below with dust. "I wonder if she hung there a long time, deciding," he said.

"Well, not long enough for somebody to get a net," the driver laughed, lighting a cigar. He puffed heavily.

Emmet felt the car rock as if it were a chair slung with wires. "I've always wondered," he said faintly, "about the people who jump. Do you think maybe there's a few seconds on the way down when they feel the air all about them and think, 'Wow, this is great—I want to do it again,' but then they remember what they've done?"

"Dunno," the driver said. "My guess is they're already blobs long before they hit pay dirt. Unless they don't leave themselves enough room to fall. That way, break every bone and they've got a whole life ahead just to sit back and plot how to get a wheelchair through the window the next time."

He spat another pink glob into his handkerchief. "I gotta confess, though, once I had this period when any time I was someplace high, I got an itch to throw myself off. The thing that got me was how it came on so unexpected. I mean, my whole life had gone straight up till that point, and then *wham*, one day I was afraid. I'd been fine before, you know, and then everything changed. Who can figure? I must've been forty or so. About your age."

Emmet stared aghast at his face in the rearview mirror. Even through the scratched partition he could see how his eyes had sunk into the bones of his cheeks. "I'm not that old," he said, tracing a finger along the pucker of fatty tissue pouching from his lower lid.

"You're not? Okay, so whatever. Anybody in jeans looks the same to me. That's not the point."

"I'm twenty-six," Emmet said. "I won't be twenty-seven until next March. At the end of the month."

"Okay, guy. No offense. Twenty. Thirty. Forty. Who gives a shit? You want to hear this or not?"

"Sorry," Emmet said. "It's just it came as a shock. I mean,

how other people perceive you. You know, I see myself one way and then somebody says something like that and it makes you wonder."

The driver puffed several times, filling the front of the car with clouds of smoke. "Okay, okay, so you're twenty-six. We've got that straight. But what I don't get is why that time I was tellin' you about even happened. It was like shootin' drugs or something. I wanted to jump from everything I saw: windows, roofs, bridges. I started searching for higher and higher places; I was drawn to them like a fuckin' magnet, always hangin' off somewhere. But then just as sudden, one day I went outside and I didn't feel it anymore."

"Aren't you worried that talking about it will bring it back?" Emmet asked. "Like bad voodoo or a hex? That you might want to jump when you get home from work tonight? I'm always afraid that thinking anything will make it come true."

"You mean like the guy who says 'Don't think of elephants' and then all you can see is a whole family of 'em shittin' in the woods? I'm clean so far, knock wood." He rapped his knuckles delicately against the grained handle of the knife. "Jesus, nothin' but plastic in these fuckin' cars anymore. From the steering wheel to the seats. Feel how they stick to you?"

The driver pulled himself forward by the wheel and dropped back against the seat. "Hell, what am I sayin'? You could sit on barbed wire and not know with all that padding you got."

Emmet waved his hand dismissively at the driver's back. "Obviously, we feel the heat differently." He shifted in his seat, rocking his spine pleasurably across the upholstery. The bones cracked from his back to his chest.

"You can say that again, brother. Me, I hate to sweat. Maybe you like it. Anyhow, I hope it was just a time in my life, like maybe somethin' was goin' on in my brain that I didn't know about. But I don't want to get too close to it, you know? Keep my distance and hope what's done is done."

"Maybe it was a premonition. You've got to keep track of what your brain is telling you. It might be something you need to know. For later."

"Not me, brother. I ain't got nothin' to learn from bein' weird. I got to admit, though, that I still get the shakes sometimes, especially at night when I wake up sweatin', you know, like maybe it will all come back and one day I'll be stuck on some kind of higher ground and that'll be it. I've got this picture of me, see, where I'm standin' with my fingers grabbin' the suspension wires of a bridge and I don't know how I got there and I'm like—what's the word I'm thinking of?—yeah, I'm like *buffeted* by the wind, with my knees bangin' against the wires and my shirt unbuttoned so that it's flyin' out behind me loud as a sail, but sort of frenzied, you know? Sometimes I just hear the sound and it wakes me up. That *slapslapslap*. And while I'm up there I'm light as a fuckin' baby and all these people come with nets and bibles because they think I'm a goner; they think they're gonna save me, but they don't mean a thing. I'm just hangin' on for dear life. And when I look down it's like there's these strong hands holdin' my head there, not lettin' me turn away, and I've got to give in because I'm no match for it, and then I don't worry anymore, you know? I just unhook my fingers from that wire and let it all go and fall."

When he was a child, often in November, Emmet used to go to Jamaica with his brother. Every afternoon before it grew dark, their father would hurl their bodies from the cliffs outside their hotel.

His father would grasp Emmet's wrists and swing him by his arms until he was almost faint from dizziness. At the last foot before the precipice, Emmet's father would wind him like a lasso and then let him go over the edge of the cliff.

The earth shook as he flew. Every part of the world seemed undone, as if it had been freed from its axis. Everything he saw—the trees, the blue sea, the sky, the rocky sides of the bluffs—became another part of the falling. Below him, men-of-war floated on the surface, thin and white as communion wafers. They scooted over the waves lightly, sometimes drawing together in groups and then dispersing with a start, like split mercury.

The game was for Emmet to gain control while he was still a projectile: his father told him he had to learn to govern that wild space as he plummeted and land between the fish without getting stung.

His brother perfected the dive with ease. Emmet always flew, body parts loose and rubbery, and slammed against the surface. Sometimes the men-of-war were killed by the impact. Sometimes they wrapped their gluey tentacles around his chest and left red puckers for days afterwards. Usually Emmet landed someplace in between and crashed beneath the surface. If he opened his eyes below, he could look up to see the strings of the fish trailing all around him like the wings of an infection.

Once Emmet was airborne, his father would prance in his Bermuda shorts and shout down from the cliff, "Aim, damn it, aim," as if Emmet were some kind of weapon that could point itself at will. From the first, Emmet felt powerless against the drafts, currents, and invisible energy governing the air, pulling him down so that he vanished into the ocean with scarcely a trace: his whole body and even its echoing ripple erased by the swelling of the next wave.

Their father made them jump until it was too dark to dodge the fish. At the end, the sky was black and when the men-of-war slipped over the waves, the ocean glowed as if it had been dumped with lenses.

As Emmet half-listened to the driver's monologue, he wondered how it would be to fall now from the cliffs, how compact and slight his new body would feel as it cut headlong through the surface.

"No heavier than this," he thought as he lifted the sack from the floor and dropped it into his lap.

He shielded it protectively with his hands. Its weight obsessed him. He let his mind wander over what the bag might contain. There might be something he could sell. He would find the address of a pawn shop in the telephone book after he returned home. He might receive enough money in exchange to hold off the bill collectors who besieged his answering machine morning and night.

Cold air blew unrelentingly from the vents. Emmet clutched his jacket under his chin. He saw people on the street walk listlessly in short pants and T-shirts. He tried to concentrate on what he would tell his doctor during their hour together. The driver had distracted him with all the images he put in his mind. He had to plan every word of his session carefully so that he did not betray something he was not ready to have known.

He would not tell the doctor about finding the bag. He would not even refer to it. He would wait until he returned home to unwrap the package, secretly, with no one but the dog as a witness. He might tell the doctor about the jumper. He might pretend that he, too, had stood shocked among the crowd as they watched the woman whizz past. He would describe how her hat came loose in the air from eight stories up: both falling at the same precise speed, as if together they proved the laws of gravity.

The cab driver cleared his throat several times. He looked furtively at Emmet. He sighed. "Sorry 'bout that. Guess I went on a stretch too long."

"No, no," Emmet said. "I was very interested in what you were saying. It's just you've given me a lot to think about and I already have some things on my mind."

"You know, you spend twelve hours a day with strangers, you begin to talk to them like you know 'em. I've been doin' this so long, I forget if there's a difference."

The driver seemed overwhelmed by the pressure of what he had not said. "Was there something else?" Emmet asked. He coddled the bag in his lap. He rattled the plastic guiltlessly as he fingered the hard outlines of the object inside.

"I was wonderin' about one thing. Just for my own information."

"Go ahead. We're almost to my stop. Ask me anything. You don't even know my name. What could be safer?"

The cab pulled up to the awning outside his doctor's office. Emmet counted the fare from the money in his pocket. He unfolded each bill neatly and passed it through the slot in the partition. Often he felt himself to be more like the people he met casually than like the friends he had known for years. But sometimes when he drove in taxis he invented stories about his life. With strangers, he could make himself be anything he wanted. He might pretend he had just been released from jail or he was in town to meet his bride or he was leaving on a world tour with his children. Once, just to see what reaction he would get, he had told a driver he was dying.

The driver stubbed his cigar into the ashtray. "The truth is, I worry a lot about this jumping business, but there's nobody in my life who'd try somethin' like that, so I'm askin' you. Maybe I got too much time to think drivin' all day, but I worry that there's somethin' sleeping in me that I don't understand, that maybe I'm a danger to myself without even knowin' it. And that's what I don't want to happen. If it's gonna be, I wanna know. Don't take this the wrong way, but there's somethin' about you, I was thinkin' maybe you could clue me in."

Emmet paused with the door opened, adjusting to the blast of heat that burst from the outside. He bundled the sack under his arm. He was not sure what the driver wanted to know, but he considered how he might convey his feeling that his whole life consisted of things set in motion that could not be stopped.

"Once you've started falling, there's no way to take it back," he said, leaning his body towards the scratched partition separating the seats, but already in his mind he was miles away from the driver.

He saw himself tumbling from the cliff with a force beyond the possibility of his control. He remembered his amazement as he felt himself vanish within the movement of his first descent, with the sea rushing up from below and his body seeming to burst along with the minuscule particles of light popping all around him, millions and millions of pieces spreading out through space, and he remembered thinking as he plummeted among them, "That's how small I am; that's how small."

CHAPTER

TWO

Emmet's grandmother built a large greenhouse at the end of her property tended by an ancient Japanese gardener. Often when his mother was away, Emmet would sit in the greenhouse watching the gardener lovingly snip the gardenias, roses, and camellias he tended in wooden boxes made from empty cases of wine. The dirt he kneaded around the base of his flowers had an odor like nothing Emmet had ever smelled before, deep and rich, almost like a food.

Gardenias were his mother's favorite flowers. Emmet never saw her wear one, but all her life she kept a photograph of herself as a younger woman on her bureau. A white gardenia sprouted above her left ear. Her lips were painted so she appeared full-mouthed and smiling. Her brows arched as if they had been drawn over her eyes with dark enamel. She seemed caught in a moment of amazement or disbelief. From the way she gazed at the photograph when she sat combing her hair at night, Emmet knew she believed she looked beautiful and pure, but to him her painted features and stiffened hair resembled an undertaker's primping.

In the photograph, a loose strand of hair brushed the largest petal. Beneath it, less distinct, a shadow had formed from where the hair touched the flower. It extended across the surface like a crack.

The photograph sat in a corner of his mother's bureau surrounded by two silver brushes, a hand-carved box her father had bought on a sea trip to China, and three etched glass bottles with wide-rimmed stoppers perched on their ends like tiny silver fedoras.

No matter where she lived, Emmet's mother carried these objects with her. Even in the years she stored their possessions and moved Emmet and his brother, Jonathan, from place to place, she packed them in a leather bag stuffed with tissue paper. She set the photograph, box, brushes, and bottles on the corner of a table even if they stopped in a motel for the night.

Before she ever left the house, Emmet's mother sprayed herself with a gardenia perfume repeatedly, the way some people wash their hands unconsciously, so that the smell never left her. When she entered a room, the scent came on abruptly, like blown-out candles.

Throughout his life, whenever he found himself in a park or a florist's shop or passed a garden on his way down a sidewalk, Emmet would pause to look for her when a scent reminded him of his mother's particular smell. She continued to startle him in this way even during the years when she was nowhere near.

Emmet's mother was called Iris after his grandmother. All they had in common besides their name were the color of their hair and a terror of closed spaces. All their lives, they never lived anywhere but in the mountains or by the sea.

Their hair was the color of sand, not blond, but the palest brown, almost white, that shone when the sun hit it the way a beach sometimes sparkles in the afternoon light.

Whenever Emmet imagined his mother and grandmother together, long after they both were dead, always the same image came to his mind: the three of them together on his grandmother's veranda one summer when he was eight. His mother had just breezed in after months away. She shouted "Surprise!" as Emmet and his grandmother ate their breakfast under the grove of orange trees that had been planted along the back of the house.

Both women were dressed in white: his mother in shorts that flattered the leanness of her tanned legs; his grandmother in a loose cotton dress with large buttons down the front made of the same lacy material. Their hair curled softly behind their ears like stretched ribbons, although by then his grandmother had grown plump and her face was ruddy with broken veins. Up close, she looked like a parody of her daughter, as if she had tried to mimic her style for a costume party.

Emmet's grandmother moved to the edge of the veranda and sat with her back to the sea. His mother began to tell them about the holiday she had just taken with a man neither Emmet nor his grandmother had ever met. As she spoke, she tilted her deck chair as far back as it could go.

Emmet could not take his eyes off her. She seemed almost to float in her chair, balancing her weight on the one hand that rested lightly on the low wall running the length of the veranda. She rocked obliviously, even daring to shift position, while the chair teetered dangerously on the tips of its two back legs.

As his grandmother listened, she collected the soiled dishes and stacked them neatly on a silver tray held under one arm. On her way into the house, she flicked the canvas back of her daughter's chair with her free hand. Emmet's mother lurched once, wildly, but steadied herself without dropping a word by pressing her index finger heavily into the stones of the terrace wall. Emmet saw her fingertip burn red to white as the chair swayed briefly and then resettled its balance. When she had completed her story, she tipped herself forward, rising gracefully out of the chair already in stride, her feet falling faultlessly into step.

To Emmet she seemed like an apparition who had materialized

out of the clouds and had the world around her perfectly in command. She walked a few steps toward the wall and then turned to face them, her hair flying out towards the sea with a wildness that seemed to taunt his grandmother with her youth. She beckoned to Emmet by curling a finger. He trotted across the stones to lean against her legs. She kissed his forehead and mussed his hair with her hand. She glanced up and drawled idly, "Did you want something, Mother?"

Emmet remembered how the wrinkles covering his grandmother's face had dropped lower about her chin, almost touching her neck, like a swatch of unwanted fabric. Finally she had marched backwards into the house with the tray still held under one arm, as if she were afraid to turn her back on them.

After she had gone, Emmet's mother patted his head and sent him to pack his clothes. She told him they were leaving to drive across the country to retrieve his brother. His parents had split the children the first months after their divorce. Emmet's mother left him with his grandmother. Emmet's father took Jonathan to live with him in Philadelphia, where he shared a house with a man who sold cosmetics door to door. But before that first summer had ended, their father had disappeared for good.

Emmet and his mother left immediately and without a word. At that age, he shadowed everything she did, trailing behind her in a kind of trance. They drove all night up the coast of California to collect her luggage. Her new house had only one large room, built on three sides with windows that rose two stories high and were supported by the thinnest steel beams. The other wall consisted entirely of a stone fireplace so large that flames shot up and magnified red and gold against the glass when the fire was lit. From the road below, the house seemed always to be burning.

They loaded seven suitcases into the trunk, and sacks stuffed with food. Once they settled into the car, Emmet forgot his grandmother. His mother told him more about the trip she had just taken, how rocky the coast had been in Sardinia and how she camped in caves dug into the side of an enormous cliff. From the interior, she could only see the darkness, broken by the half-moon shape of the entrance, so that when she moved towards the light, she seemed to walk directly into the sun. She told him that bats slept on the ceiling of the cave and how you could hear their wings beat overhead at dust, loud as a clap of thunder, and then suddenly they would rush out into the night, like a cloud of ash.

His mother seemed like an adventurer to him then. From the moment that he had first been aware of himself in the world, Emmet had sensed that the life he led at home with his grandmother was too small to contain her. He never begrudged her the time she spent away. Something in her manner, a restless arrogance, an uneasy silence no matter who she was with, made people defer to her, as if it were her right by natural inheritance. Whenever he was with her, Emmet used to be amazed at how even the rudest clerk fell silent before her, how planes were held, reservations kept, and general kindnesses were forthcoming from every imaginable source.

That night, settled into the car beside her, Emmet felt as if her presence made him possessed of a similar magic, as if she bestowed upon him the same exemption that made her life seem protected by some invisible sanctuary. He hoped she might take him somewhere that he had never been and from where they might never have to return.

They drove all night up the coast of California, then turned east into Nevada and then further north, out of their way, so that they could pass deep into Wyoming. She wanted Emmet to see the place where she had spent summers as a child. He remembered the names of the towns they left behind on their way there: Thermopolis, and then up to Cody, and across to Greybull at the foot of the Bighorn Mountains. The land before the mountains was flatter and more desolate than anything he had ever seen before.

Emmet feared the isolation as they drew deeper into unsettled country, but his mother flushed with happiness.

As it grew dark in the car, she told him how often at night she had slept outside in a tent made of mosquito netting. From any angle, she had looked out through thousands of crisscrossed panes. She described how the sky at the ranch was blacker than anywhere she had ever been, shot through with an infinite number of stars. In the daylight, it seemed to float higher over the earth and curve at each end, so that no matter where she looked, the earth seemed to become part of its slope. Even, she said, on the most barren stretch of land, far out in the back property where there was nothing but ravines and rock formations scattered for thousands of acres past the edge of the visible horizon, she always had the sense of standing on something round.

The previous day, when they had been more than an hour from Reno, Emmet's mother had shown him the gradations of the sky becoming lighter and lighter as the hour grew later and later.

"See how everything is ruined," she said when they were still miles away.

"That's the city," she said, pointing to a smudge layered over the darkness like a storm cloud.

As they continued to drive, suddenly it was there before them, twinkling out of the desert like Oz. Emmet felt then that the glow of the lighted structures rising up out of the dust was the most beautiful thing he had ever seen.

That day in Wyoming, his mother drove their car into a pasture a mile off the highway. She led Emmet through the foothills along a path beaten into the grass by animals' hooves. Even as he grew tired, she had rushed him forward towards the slope ahead. She remembered from years before that it had been the perfect place to watch the moon rise.

Emmet had never thought of the moon as something that rose

every day like the sun. But with his mother's urging, they reached the last incline and huddled together beside a boulder. She set out their basket of food and laid a cloth on the ground. She pointed to a place in the valley below and Emmet stared dutifully ahead at the line of trees and the hills and the path of a dirt road cut through the land like a spiral. Emmet remembered how a red jeep had moved slowly over the road, pausing occasionally, as if the driver had seen their color from a distance. The moon waited in a corner of the sky, its crust so thin in places that he could see blue pouring through its globe.

Slowly as the sun fell, the moon rose as if it were dragged on a pulley. There was fog in the valley, and as the light failed, the fog lost its puffiness and began to shine, glazed and hard. The moon seemed to float as it climbed, and it was as if you could see each particle of light, as if the atoms within air revealed themselves to the eye. The air swarmed with dots, and then each one of them unraveled to a loose, gray static.

The dusk flipped with life: the moon wavered and then seemed to cut its tethers. As it rose higher, it dragged round shadows after it, and these shadows gleamed and reflected against the hills so that, for an instant, there was a double image of everything. And when the moon reached its highest place, it pulled the shadows to itself and hung there, pulsing with a saucery light.

Emmet saw the sheer face of the cliffs behind them, sweating in the cool air so that the stone appeared polished to glass. Every few minutes the silence was broken by pieces of rock crumbling from the side of the mountain and raining to the ground some-where in the valley below. Crouched at the base of the mountain, Emmet had never felt so exposed. As the wind came up, he dug his fingers into the dirt to grab hold because he feared he was in danger of being swept off into the air. Out there, he felt a vertigo unknown to him before: alone and at the mercy of every element.

In the diminishing light, he felt undone by an insubstantiality that shrunk his body smaller and smaller the more he looked around. When he turned to his mother, she was pelted with gray shadows.

Emmet stood to test his balance. He was aware of the slope and curve of the horizon his mother spoke of, how all around him the stars seemed to tumble off into nowhere from the edge of the earth.

"Look, there's Saturn," his mother said, pointing excitedly to a ragged star charged with light. "And there's Jupiter," she cried, turning his head upward with her hand. She seemed to read the patterns in the planets and swirling galaxies above them as easily as she charted their course through the highways near their home.

Emmet saw a meteor flash against the darkness, tearing a trail of sparks before it fell invisibly behind the mountains. He saw another meteor fall, and then another, until the universe seemed to tremble with explosions. He felt the ground beneath him heave like a ball tossed into the air or shot from a cannon, leaving him to balance on its spheres as it hurled through space. And as the night grew, he felt the world was closing in on them, as if someone were slowly setting a glass bowl over that enormous sky.

They sat for a long time after it became dark, watching the traffic increase on the valley road, the lights from the cars appearing from behind bends and circling the darkness like small bulbs from a flashlight, only to disappear again, as if someone were teasing a child in the dark.

Emmet's mother seemed lost, maybe thinking of a life without him. Emmet imagined the cars, miles away, with windows closed, full of smoke and silence; his body curled next to the driver, sleeping, his feet bunched against the door handle.

Although it was indistinct to him then and became clearer only when he was older and on his own, Emmet had never felt as safe as the times when he dozed in the backseat of a car while his parents drove. He remembered trying to sustain the suspension between waking and sleeping so that he could float in the peace-fulness while he listened to them talk. Sometimes, still, he could hear their murmuring voices, too low to understand, but possessed of an intimacy that promised a stability and faith that were to elude them forever after.

CHAPTER THREE

They moved often as children. Sometimes every few months, sometimes not for a year or more, but frequently enough that they learned even when young to recognize a change come over her. Emmet's mother might turn her head away from the wheel while driving them home from school or come into their room and sit on a corner of the bed and ask, "Have you been happy here?" And then they knew that soon they would be leaving.

Emmet and his brother never admitted any ties to the town where they lived. Maybe they sensed her panic if she was held too fast to one place. Maybe they sensed that in moving on she gave her desperation a form that was easier to bear. Or maybe Emmet only saw this once all of it had passed and he had come to know a similar restlessness in himself.

"Where are we?" she used to ask, laughingly, from the bed of a motel she had chosen, as if they had been kidnapped and moved blindfolded by cover of night.

Emmet remembered her sitting cross-legged with maps spread across the mattress. She traced the lines of the highways with her fingertips, charting the borders of state to state, occasionally stopping when the name of a place reminded her of something she had read or a person she had known. He felt her excitement when she hit upon a new location, as if it were possible to move anywhere as miraculously as her finger traversed the page.

One winter Emmet's mother followed a man to a small mountain town in Colorado. She brought her children with her, stealing them unannounced from her mother's house one afternoon during the last week before the end of the year.

A split-rail fence marked exactly the lease to the property she rented, crisscrossing the hills and streams leading up into the mountains, and then down into the valley that cut along the back of the house to the river miles below.

Emmet and Jonathan learned to ski. The man abandoned their mother weeks after their arrival, leaving her with that huge, unwanted property and no one for a thousand miles—except the teachers in the school, the pharmacist, the postman, and a real estate agent—who even knew her name.

The day before he left, the man shot a deer and bound it upside down to his jeep, so that its head hung against the muffler and leaked a steady stream of blood from its mouth. Before dinner, the man made Emmet and his brother go outside to help him clean it. He cut the deer loose and lay it on its back in the snow. Its legs jutted into the air and its glassy eyes gazed coolly out as if it had been already groomed by the taxidermist. The man slit its stomach with a hunting knife and plunged his fingers into the wound.

"This is the heart," he said as he pulled an organ easily from the body. "Here, hold it."

Emmet cupped his hands and presented them to the man. The heart slipped into them. Through the severed ventricles, Emmet could glimpse the red, fleshy hollow. He remembered his disappointment at how ill formed and insubstantial it seemed, how warm and soft, like a mound of raw meat, only lighter. He somehow expected it to beat as his own heart was pounding, but it was still except for his trembling hands, which shook the last blood from it, splattering the legs of his jeans and the tops of his shoes.

The man rolled up his sleeves and his hands disappeared again, but deeper this time, into the crook beyond his elbows. He brought out a square of shiny pink tissue.

"This is a lung," he said, and smiled at Jonathan. "This one's for you. Here. Take it."

Jonathan clasped the glistening thing. It began to slide from his grip, so he pressed it against his chest, the way he would cradle a small animal.

The man's hands groped inside again. "This is a spleen," he said, and twirled it in front of them for a moment before he tossed it over his shoulder. It made a wet *thwack* as it hit the porch and then slipped silently down the stairs until it settled on the last icy step. Flakes of snow stuck to its surface like translucent white fur.

The man continued to bury his hands in the cavity until his nails were lacquered a deep maroon and the two sides of the deer flapped as thin as a blanket in the breeze. Before they went into the house, Emmet lay the heart on the ground and took the lung from his brother and placed it alongside. For days afterwards, body parts lay in pieces across their lawn and a huge red smear lined their walkway, as if the man had wanted to mark his departure with some kind of sacrifice.

The first evening after the man left, Emmet's mother put dinner on the table and leaned against the refrigerator, her elbows against the door, one foot on top of the other, in a pose she sometimes struck while watching the man eat. She said, as if explaining something, "You know how something gets you and then there's never any going back?"

Emmet and Jonathan rolled their eyes at each other. Jonathan shot peas across the room with his spoon until she grabbed his wrist and tossed his plate in the sink. In the way she cleared the table, in the way she rushed them to bed and flicked off the light, they sensed she hated them for being children and so out of reach of understanding the part of her life that obsessed her more than they did.

After they fell asleep, a wind from the open front door froze Emmet awake. When he rolled, wrapped in blankets, to the window at the foot of his bed, he saw his mother walking swiftly down the drive.

Emmet woke his brother. He pulled ski pants over Jonathan's pajamas and stuffed his arms in his jacket and wound a muffler around his face. His toes were tiny and pink in the cold, so Emmet rubbed them between his hands before he slid a pair of fur-lined boots over them. He dressed himself. Then he took his brother's hand and together they went out after her.

New snow had fallen all week. The road was distinguishable only by the drifts piled higher on either side, but even the flat surface they walked on was several feet above the dirt and gravel that lay beneath it. Emmet felt as if he were balancing in midair no matter where he walked that winter. As they followed the main road out of town, the houses dipped invisibly except for the lights that glowed upward through the drifts.

There was no sign of her. The echo of a few dogs howling and barking collected in the basin at the foothills and multiplied, so that the sound swept across the field as if packs of dogs roamed the hillsides in pursuit of them.

As they began to climb at the edge of the forest, Emmet stopped and looked around. The land below appeared the way he imagined an untouched lunar crescent might be: luminous gray in the moonlight, the snow crusted with scars from the wind, and all around a white dust swirling into their faces. He knew that was why his mother liked living out there, as if they had discovered some uncharted territory known only to themselves.

They followed a path left by skiers that had been pounded into the hillside. They seemed to skate along a precipice, the harder snow bearing them precariously through the softer places that would have buried them had they strayed one foot in the wrong direction. Emmet pulled his brother up the incline that led over an abandoned mine. It had been closed for twenty years, since it collapsed and buried four men from town. Their bodies had never been found, and their ghosts were said to inhabit the forest. Emmet closed his eyes as he dragged Jonathan past it, afraid that even after so long he might still see bones sticking out of the boards that blocked the entrance, or maybe four sets of eyes peering out at them from the darkness.

They both stopped when they heard a thrashing ahead. Jonathan hooked an arm around Emmet's legs. Emmet put a finger to his lips to quiet him and dropped to his knees. They crawled behind the mine to a slope that gave them an unbroken view of the valley. And then they saw her, spinning and hopping in the snow about fifty feet ahead.

"Mom's on fire," Jonathan said, awestruck.

He started to break away to shout for her, but Emmet stuck a gloved hand in his mouth and pulled him closer. They huddled there and watched.

Her arms flapped from side to side and slapped against her chest as if she were fanning flames. She twirled in the snow, each time sinking lower until she was buried to her waist and began to beat the ground with her hands. And then she shouted a man's name as loudly as a human voice could go because she believed she was alone and no one else would ever hear. But even she looked up in surprise as her voice left her and bounced off the crevasses and ledges and ice-covered barks of the trees and rolled off the boulders until every surface seemed to be shouting this name.

Jonathan tried to push Emmet away to call to her again, but Emmet tackled him and lay over his body as they heard the name repeated one hundred times from that one shout. Emmet knew they had stumbled upon a secret and she would never have forgiven them if she learned they had followed her and discovered her need. They stayed there, their faces pressed numbly against the snow, until they heard her feet crunching along the path behind them on her way back into town.

"Never tell," Emmet breathed into his brother's ear as he wriggled to escape. "Never tell. Never tell. Never tell."

CHAPTER
FOUR

Emmet's grandmother on his father's side, Marie, drowned herself in the reservoir outside her home one night after a party. She rowed a dinghy into the middle of the lake. The day before she had collected a pile of stones from her garden and stacked them in the bow of the boat.

"It's for a ballast," she had said when her husband found them. "To keep the boat on course when I am out there alone."

That night when she reached the deepest part of the water, she stuffed her pockets with the stones. Then she climbed over the side.

Emmet never met Marie. He knew her only from two photographs he found in an envelope in the back of a family album. In one, she was surrounded by her husband and two sons. Her husband's arm rested across her shoulders, casually; but it was so long, it hooked back around her neck. He seemed to grip her in a choke hold.

The other was a photograph of Marie and her husband on vacation in Asia: Emmet's grandfather's face set grimly as he stormed several paces ahead of her, dressed in a black suit with thin lapels like that an itinerant minister might wear. Marie seemed to scurry after him to catch up, as if he were setting a pace too fast for her to follow.

Emmet often thought of her spindly body stepping over the side of the boat into the water for the last time and how freely she must have sunk, weighted by those stones. Of all his relatives, Emmet wished he had met Marie, but she died years before he was born. No other person on his father's side had more presence for him than a name inked on a line on a genealogical chart. But he knew his mother's mother's life down to the dimensions of the garden in every house she owned. Everything she had ever done, everything she had ever been, was defined in terms of the places she had lived. She was the last person in his family to have emerged from a past. Everyone since seemed to have been born into an instability that was tied to neither time nor place nor reason.

When he was a child, Emmet's grandmother used to tell him how her husband had drowned off the coast of South Africa in a shipwreck. His body was never found, but for years afterwards parts of the mast lay wedged into the rocks off Cape Town Bay. Sometimes in the clearest weather, when the water sheeted the harbor, you could barely discern the shadow of the ship's bow half-buried in the sand. His family used to walk to the edge of the cliff and peer down in search of it, as a mourner might visit a grave.

On the wall of her living room, Emmet's grandmother hung a death certificate from that time in a gold gilt frame. His grand-father's name was written in black calligraphy under an etching of a boat at full sail racing across the waves. On the bottom were scrolled the words *Lost at Sea*.

Emmet's grandfather went to sea at fifteen and sailed for twenty years until he was drowned. In a photograph taken just before his final voyage, he appeared prematurely aged. He had grown so round that the bottom buttons of his uniform's shirt spread open, revealing a mat of dark, curling hair. Emmet could not imagine how he lumbered across the deck of the ship without stumbling, but his grandmother often remarked on his extraordinary grace: how when they danced, he guided her weightlessly, her swirling feet barely keeping up with his own, her toes barely touching as he led her lightly across the floor.

Emmet's mother was only two years old when the ship was lost. His grandmother moved them first to Ireland and later to America to begin again in California. She carried a letter of introduction from her family to a man she had never met whom she was meant to marry.

When he was a child, Emmet's grandmother used to tell him about crossing the Sierra Nevadas on the way to California for the first time: how the mountains rose forever, range after range, until it seemed they had come to the top of the world. Emmet remembered his grandmother's joy the one time she showed him the low, flat plains beyond the final summit glimmering like a mirage all the way to the ocean. "Look," she exclaimed, gripping the stones of the embankment, as if together they beheld a new world for the first time, although by then she had lived in California for thirty years.

As she grew older, Emmet's grandmother ceased to speak of California or of Ireland before that, but only of her five years in South Africa. When she could no longer remember the names of his cousins, she told Emmet of Queen Esther and her daughter, Australia, the two women who cared for his mother when she was a baby, and how their dresses reeked of starch and bleach. She could describe the exact number of protea bushes that grew wild beyond her garden wall and the red, feathery blooms of the flame trees that seemed to ignite the hills behind her home.

Once in Santa Monica she removed her shoe and tapped her heel against the boardwalk to mimic the sound her feet had made on the wooden sidewalk on her way into town and she recited the name of every street she had passed on their way there. When it was hot, Emmet knew she was feeling the breeze in Cape Town. And when she studied the sky, it was as if she were comparing the degrees of blue and found every other place she had lived paler and wanting.

Emmet's grandmother built her house on a bluff in California where the windows of her bedroom opened directly onto the sea. Twenty feather pillows were arranged in perfect rows on her bed, each one fitted with a white embroidered cover sewn by her aunt who was a missionary in China. A comforter lay across the sheets in all seasons, so thick with down that Emmet imagined he slept in clouds whenever he went to stay there. The bed rested against two glass doors that she closed only when it rained. When he opened his eyes in the middle of the night and looked up at the sky, he could see the North Star.

After they went to bed, Emmet's grandmother would scoop him into the folds of her stomach. Often before he slept, she told him the story of how she went alone to greet her husband's ship as it sailed into the harbor and saw it smash upon the rocks of Cape Town Bay.

She could see no one on deck from the path where she stood, only the lacquered planks glittering in the sun. She remembered that her first thought had been that her life was changing even as she saw the ship shatter like a toy and break beneath the surface. She tried to describe to Emmet how quiet it had been, no louder than the one small cry she gave, and how it passed, even as it was happening, in the silence of a dream. That muffled sound of the sinking, like the sound of air funneling down a drain, was all except for the crack of wood as the mast snapped against the boulders, and then no other sound except for the gulls that flew about her head and the sirens gathering on the dock miles away.

By the next day, what she had witnessed had become unreal to her and she came to wish she had never gone there. The violence she would have imagined—a thunderous crash against rocks, bodies splashing over the sides and calling for help, perhaps a storm, a flotilla of lifeboats, a flare exploding in the sky—she might have felt more keenly than that flash of what she did see: the ship sliding into the current and then nothing but a mast stretched across the rocks, visible there within seconds as if it were already a relic from some earlier voyage.

She lay in bed at night listening to the ocean because she wanted to recapture the sound of the boat being sucked into the water. She wanted to visit Cape Town one last time to look down again at the harbor from the path where she had stood that day, but by then she was too old to travel alone and Emmet's mother would never take her there.

Emmet knew that as a teenager in Dublin, his grandmother had helped to hide two men who took part in the Easter Rebellion. She described their nervous panting as they pounded on the door in the middle of the night and how they stood pleadingly once they were let inside, their hats in their hands, before she led them down the cellar steps. Her family had built a labyrinth of passageways that wound from underneath their home to other houses in the district.

Emmet's grandmother brought the two men food for a week while the police searched the neighborhoods throughout Dublin. Her father snuck them by carriage one night in a storm to the western coast covered in burlap bags. Emmet's grandmother held a black umbrella over her father's head as he guided the horses and wagon along the road. She told him how even over the rattle of the wheels striking the rocks, she could hear the low hum of her cargo's shivering bodies from the back of the wagon. It rained until their bones felt soaked and the air seemed composed of wet straw and horsehair, so strongly did the odor become part of their skin.

When they arrived at the coast, the men were brought to warm themselves by the fire at the safe house. She remembered the pattern of the burlap bags spreading over their faces like a map in the light of the flames.

In Ireland, the tinkers came in luridly painted caravans every season to her village. It was said that they flew like spirits into houses at night and stole babies for their dinner. They cooked them in huge lead pots set boldly by the road. It was said they could crawl into a room invisibly and steal the silver from under your nose. When a wind blew through the house, rattling the glass in the windows, her father used to say, "That's the tinkers come to ruin us."

If he ever complained of the weather, Emmet's grandmother told him of the spring in Ireland when it had rained for seventeen weeks without stopping. Summer passed into winter without any sense of change or release. The earth grew so soggy that even the high ground flooded wet and deep as a marsh. Cattle drowned in their fields. The sodden roofs of cottages crumbled from constant pelting, so that the rooms they covered filled with a heavy mist. Inside or out, the rain oppressed them. By the time it ended, four farmers in the village had hanged themselves, their bodies found swinging like pendulums in the rain.

Emmet knew that after her mother died, his grandmother taught for two years at a girls' school in London. She boarded with a Mrs. Prebble, who let two upstairs bedrooms to strangers. Mrs. Prebble kept a bowl of pickled tomatoes on her kitchen table, wax green and so swollen with liquid that their skins split and spurted when touched. Mrs. Prebble used to eat a tomato with her tea, chopping the pulp with a spoon and sucking its juices as she talked, her teeth freckled with seeds.

Emmet's grandmother met the man who became her husband there one day over tea. He was Mrs. Prebble's nephew, and only three weeks passed before the woman who had been her landlady became her aunt.

After she moved to California, Emmet's grandmother taught

for thirty years at a school for immigrants built on a slip of land off the coast. It was called Terminal Island. From the distance of the city, the school looked like a prison ship, its turrets rising like smokestacks in the heat. "Leave it to her," his mother used to say, "to find herself a place that sounds like a disease and park herself there until she died."

When she was eighty-six, Emmet's grandmother told him she had always wanted to smoke cigarettes. In the nursing home two years later, she began to steal them from the woman in the next room. One night she set the sleeve of a synthetic dress on fire. The fabric melted on her arm, bubbling the skin with a paisley burn.

She never learned to put her car in reverse. She had the gardener remove the back wall to her garage so that she could drive in and out of it, like a tunnel.

Every time she took Emmet to the beach, she carried a canvas umbrella large enough to shade four people. It was orange, with green triangles flying out from the center, like flags.

Emmet knew she counted money every Sunday in the basement of her church for fifty-two years.

He knew she never liked his father.

Emmet's grandmother used to tell him the story of how when she was ten, she was sent to the country from Dublin for one year. She never asked where she was going or if she would ever be coming back. When she did return, her mother met her at the train station. Roll after roll of white bandages still leaked from her freshly amputated arm. Emmet's grandmother changed the gauze every night for months and dabbed at the wound with sponges dipped in green antiseptic. Not once did her mother mention where the arm had gone, and never did his grandmother ask.

She used to tell this story with pride, as if her strange stoicism enabled her to endure anything. When all of it was over, Emmet wondered if his family's carelessness became a kind of dare, as if they wanted to see just how much trouble could remain unspoken.

CHAPTER FIVE

"How the past flies by," Emmet thought with amazement as he lingered on the sidewalk outside his doctor's office.

It had only been an hour since he arrived for his appointment, but already he could hardly remember the cab driver who had brought him there. Had he ever seen his face? A nose, mouth, ears flashed before him. Then the features melted from his sight.

He pretended he needed to describe a culprit to a police artist for a sketch, but all he could summon were the layered fat and buzzed stubble of the driver's neck. If it had not been for the heavy sack twirling in circles at his side, Emmet would not have remembered anything at all.

During his session, he had not mentioned the driver or the jumper. His doctor had moved to a new office that week and Emmet was distracted by the unfamiliar surroundings. The doctor had asked Emmet if he would consent to observation by a class of medical students hidden in another room by a two-way window. The doctor had promised that the students would learn from what Emmet had to say. Emmet had affected unconcern. He had made it a point not to glance once at the mirrored wall after he was told that strangers were watching.

As he conversed with the doctor, Emmet thrilled at the thought of white-suited students scribbling notes on every word he uttered. He surpassed himself by improvising a seven-course meal, complete from soup to dessert, with round scoops of coral-colored melon sherbet served in between. He had effortlessly described his labor down to the size of each pan and utensil he selected and the temperature at which he cooked each dish. He had even defined for his audience the subtlety between "low heat" and "simmer."

Emmet was astounded by his authority. A jambon persillé, a mouclade, a fennel purée, a pissaledière sailed from his lips. He grew giddy as he approached dessert. When he smoothly purred, "Poires, pruneaux, oranges aux vin rouge et aux épices," as if it were one word, chills of delight rumbled up his spine. He had not rehearsed a word.

Emmet congratulated himself once more as he stepped out from under the shade of the awning. "Walk or ride?" he wondered as he felt the city press around him. Despite the heat, he decided he would walk. He felt triumphant after his appointment and fit to conquer the streets.

He needed to detour to buy dog food and carrots. He rummaged in his pocket and counted seven wadded dollar bills. He had enough left for the day. The rest of his cash was buried under a dirty sock in the toe of a black boot in his closet. In case he was mugged, he never carried his entire stash on the street, but eked it out in daily amounts.

For a long time, Emmet had used a cash card. Earlier in the summer, the automatic teller on the street had eaten his card when he had tried to make a withdrawal. A slip of paper clattered out instead that read, "Unable to complete transaction." Emmet did not know if this was a plot by the bank, but he dreaded asking for a new card. Only the day before, he had reported a surly teller to the manager. Perhaps the teller had already worked her revenge late at night and created a deficit in his account so that he would seem to pass rubber checks every time he paid a bill.

Emmet had never saved his statements. He preferred to keep track of his expenses in his head. But without evidence of his balance, he could not prove that he had ever possessed a cent. The teller could prove anything she wanted just by printing his doctored balance from her green computer screen.

To get by, he had sold some of his books for cash. He had carefully hoarded every dollar he received, but it was not enough to pay his rent. His landlord demanded to be paid in cash. Emmet had given him nothing for two months. Lately he had begun to hide whenever he heard his landlord fussing in the hallway outside his door, but Emmet knew he could not stop him for long. The landlord had kept an extra key when Emmet signed the lease.

As he stood in the sun, Emmet fingered the money in his pocket a second time to convince himself he had counted correctly. He turned towards the river, where the streets were less inhabited, so that he might find a deserted market.

As he made his way downtown, Emmet checked the windows of every shop he passed. The huge, well-lighted grocery stores, packed with customers day or night, were beyond his grasp. He found the prying eyes unbearable: the way they searched every item in his basket, appraising him from the food he ate. He could buy nothing if someone watched.

He preferred to shop in the middle of the night, when no one was about except a sleepy cashier. But he had neglected to feed his dog the day before and he could not face her empty-handed a second time.

After he had walked only three blocks, Emmet spied a market with no one inside but three Korean clerks sitting on milk cartons. He waved cheerfully to them as he grabbed a red plastic basket from the column stacked in front. He held out his sack to the clerks, hoping they would offer to check it. Emmet did not want to carry anything inside in case they accused him of stealing once he was deep among the aisles. But even as he shook the bag loudly in their faces, the men sat dumbly on their hands.

Emmet looped the handles of his bag into a knot and tied them tightly four times. He let it bang against the bottom of the basket so that the clerks jumped. He did not want them to have doubts later and demand that he open the bag when even he did not know what it contained.

Emmet went to the rear aisle where cans of dog food were arranged row upon row. The color photographs of hunks of meat sickened him as he searched for his dog's favorite label. He saw horse meat, chicken, kidneys, and fish, but he could not find her brand.

He heard a group of children burst into the store, giggling and screeching so loudly that Emmet felt as if a flock of birds was sweeping through the aisles. He froze under the circular mirror in the ceiling. He saw their faces round and distorted in the glass so that they seemed like one creature, squat and many-headed. He heard the *tap-tap-tap* of their shoes striking against the linoleum. He sensed them pause at the top of the aisle and draw a bead on him.

Their voices dropped to a murmur. Emmet jammed his sunglasses closer against his face. Quickly he rolled five cans of dog food with a plain print label into his basket and covered them with the sack. He moved on.

The children trailed him like a scent. He heard their feet behind him every time he walked and then a rush of silence when they stopped in unison with his steps. To test them, he shuffled left, then right, then left again, and listened to their sound swoosh behind him like gusts of wind.

"You have every right to be here," Emmet assured himself as he tried to concentrate on his shopping. Nervously he selected a bunch of carrots with two-foot stems blooming from their heads. He tried to bend them so that several bunches would fit into the basket. One bunch would only last him the night. He could not face shopping the next day, or even the one after. He gathered more and more carrots into his arms until their stems pushed against his coat like a wild fern.

The fluorescent bulbs burned brighter than the sun on the street. He felt every mole on his face glow red hot as coals. He saw the cashier eye him in the mirror above. The children laughed, boldly this time, pressing nearer and nearer. Emmet backed against the shelf, spilling packages and cans around him, a jumble as loud as if the ceiling had collapsed. Soups, cakes, pies, jars of every size and color smashed to the floor at his feet.

The children hooted. Emmet knelt before his mess. The clerks left their crates and watched him from down the aisle. He picked pieces of broken glass from the tiles and stuck them in his coat pocket like change.

Sticky sauce clung to his fingers like an acid. Unconsciously, he brought them to his lips. "Ugh," he cried as his tongue darted out, licking the substance. He wiped his hands across his chest so that the fabric glistened wetly, like a wound. He scraped his shoe on the floor and rubbed frantically, trying to erase any trace of the accident, but the sauces stained the gray tiles like a blush of diluted blood.

"Calm, calm," he chanted. "You will forget this in an hour. When you are home, it will seem like it never happened."

He stood under the mirror and shook each bunch of carrots so that the clerks could see he had secreted nothing underneath. He scratched his head. He yawned. He stuck a finger into his cheek as if he were thinking hard for something he had forgotten.

The three clerks hesitated halfway down the aisle. The children cheered them on. Emmet set the basket on the floor. He pulled the dollars from his pocket. He dug deep into the other and found a quarter and a dime. He let the lining of his pockets hang out of his pants emptily, like two ears.

"Would this be a dime?" he called in a heavy French accent. He curled his index finger around the quarter. "Please. How much would be a dime?"

All Emmet wanted was to go home. He did not remember if the clerks had heard him speak in a normal voice, but he hoped that if they heard his accent, they might interpret his strangeness as foreignness and permit him to leave.

"Dolar," he said, moving serenely towards them. "Carrotte. Dug fudd."

The children backed away as he inched towards the cashier. "Crazy," one of them spat. Emmet ignored them, as if he were protected by the two-way glass in his doctor's office. "I cannot see them," he told himself. "They are gone."

A clerk guarded either side of him as the cashier rang up his purchases. The bill was three dollars and eighty-nine cents.

"Please, you pick money," Emmet said, spreading the cash on the counter. The man chose seven dollar bills and the quarter and dime. He held out two pennies for Emmet's change.

"Merci, merci," Emmet said. He combined his two bags into one and breezed out the door.

The children followed two steps behind. Emmet quickened his pace. He would have to walk all the way home. He did not even have enough money remaining for the bus. He dipped down a subway staircase where he knew a tunnel wound under the street and exited on the opposite corner. He would lose the children there.

As he slipped into the shadows of the underground station, he grew hot with rage at the clerks in the store. He remembered that the market had rows of fruits and vegetables arranged in wooden boxes under a canvas tent that spilled onto the sidewalk. "Code 604-A," he thought smugly. He was certain those displays were illegal. He might report the store when he returned home. But there were two of those stands on every block throughout the city, even though they were forbidden by the municipal code. The authorities would not be interested in his complaint. Maybe he would return with his camera later and document other violations, enough to make a case.

"I cannot go out anymore," he sighed as he walked. He had spent his triumph after his doctor's appointment. "I cannot."

Years ago a friend had told him that there were cameras in the department stores where he shopped aimed at every person that came through the door. In a control booth, a guard scanned each face on television screens stacked to the ceiling. If he sensed someone corrupt, the guard pushed a button that caught him on film. Emmet knew he acted suspiciously even when he was alone. He imagined that there were rolls and rolls of negatives of him stored in tin canisters in darkrooms throughout the city.

When he was a child, Emmet had become convinced that two characters from a television series had brought cameras into his house to film him. He believed they were recording evidence to decide if he was worthy to be stolen away to live with them. He believed that one day when he was at school, they had broken into his grandmother's house and installed tiny cameras in every room: inside every mirror, under his bed, even in the dark rear shelf of his closet.

He remembered how easily he had adjusted to the certainty that no matter what he did, a stranger always watched. For years he had lived accepting the cameras' presence. For years he had lived anticipating a judgment that had never come. Long after he knew he should no longer believe the fantasy of the cameras, he still behaved as if every step he took were being recorded and observed by someone unseen.

As he neared home, Emmet recalled with amazement how he had never questioned the surveillance. He had not cared that a camera clicked from every recess of his grandmother's house, so that there was no shelter to be found, even in the dark.

He could not remember when it had changed, when the eyes he felt upon him like a sleepless god's no longer watched benevolently. They were with him now not only in the house but everyplace he went: from every car and bus, from every window on every street, from every purse or briefcase slung on the shoulders of the crowd. The sounds of the city came at him from the clatter of millions of tiny shutters clicking shut, as if every light and star refracted a lens, freezing on film every breath he took.

"Look at you now," Emmet thought as he hurried.

On good days, he could still close his ears to the sound. On good days, he knew there were no cameras even when he hid himself from view.

"Look at you now."

The sight of himself rushing mousily down the street repulsed him. He still held out hope that he could outpace the terrors he imagined if he never let down his guard, but his world grew smaller and smaller every day.

"Home," he said as he urged himself forward.

He pictured himself inside his apartment, alone with the dog, out of everyone's reach. He hugged the bag he carried closely, as if it were a body.

"Home," he repeated.

He continued pronouncing the word out loud until his lips grew numb from the vibrations, until to anyone he passed who might have heard him, he seemed to hum jauntily as he made his way there.

CHAPTER
SIX

Emmet made his home in a crumbling blue brownstone on a quiet street in the city. Outside, the limestone facade drooped like a slum. Foot-long cracks separated each step from the front stoop, so that the cement dipped and swayed each time Emmet climbed the stairs.

As he jiggled the front door open after his walk, a spray of sand showered his head from the portico above. Emmet was so used to the house's fragility that he no longer ducked when it shed pieces of itself. In the morning, he often found a trail of blue rubble strewn over the sidewalk. From his bed, he could hear chunks of debris drop off in the night, sometimes so loudly that it sounded as if someone was pounding through a wall in the cellar to break inside.

He had grown accustomed to the building's dilapidation. The faucets dripped in every sink so that a rusted crust ringed the drains. In the quiet, he heard the *ping-ping-ping* of water leaking from every room, so rhythmic and loud that he could not sleep.

Emmet never complained. He never asked that any crack or pipe or fixture be repaired. Even though he knew his landlord hated him, Emmet's silence was what permitted him to stay.

The other houses on the block were uniformly smooth and

brown. Their flat fronts formed a perfect row, set back from the street innocuously, almost deferentially. Emmet sensed that his neighbors were embarrassed by the eyesore he inhabited. If they saw him when he fumbled for his keys at the door, they paused to admonish him silently, as if the shame were his doing.

Emmet was unconcerned by the building's exterior. It was invisible to him except for the few seconds a day he was forced to look on his way through the entrance. Inside, he possessed seven rooms peaked by thirteen-foot ceilings. Each window rose six feet high and was paned with leaded glass. Every piece of molding, every door and cabinet was carved from burnished cherry wood. The closet doors were so heavy that many of them had pulled loose from their hinges; they lay against their frames like boulders blocking a cave.

Emmet had chosen the apartment because of its cavernous space. For years, he had lived with only a picnic table in the dining room, a mattress and a desk in his bedroom, and two folding chairs he had found in a rubbish bin on the street. He had liked the spareness of his life: the confidence of knowing he could pack everything he owned and escape within a half hour of his decision. From the day he moved to the city, he had existed always in this state of readiness. He felt his lightness was the passport that enabled him to live anywhere he chose.

Emmet's mother left no money in her will. She bequeathed her household furnishings to Emmet. To his brother she left her house, a yellow jeep, and a mink coat unworn for twenty years.

His mother's possessions had arrived in two moving vans that blocked traffic on his street for an entire day. Emmet had watched in despair as eight men carried every object his mother had ever owned into his house: tables, sofas, carpets, paintings, chairs, lamps, televisions, stereo equipment, a king-sized brass bed, bookcases, armoires, china, crystal, end tables, lamps, even the blue clay coaster she had set under her coffee cup in the morning to protect the polished wood.

In her desk Emmet discovered the wooden box, the silver brushes, the etched bottles with sterling stoppers, the forty-year-old photograph of her face with the gardenia, wrapped in blue tissue paper and tied with a pink satin bow.

Emmet had not wanted any of it. Her furniture was constructed of ornate mahogany so dark it gleamed almost black. The cushions were covered with double layers of maroon velvet. Figures were carved into the wood of every piece: cat's heads, unicorns, cherubs, frogs, bursts of flowers, suns, moons with faces and eyes, stared from the corner of every room.

Emmet had spent weeks organizing the furniture. He decided to keep one bedroom bare so that he did not entirely forfeit the way he had lived, but it was off a rear corridor, removed from the center of the apartment. He had tried every possible arrangement, but no matter what he did, the furniture usurped him. He slept in her bed. He took notes from her desk. He drank from her cups. His rooms mimicked her own, as if she had bequeathed her possessions purposely to haunt him.

Emmet had considered selling all but a few items. He worried that he would bring a curse upon himself, like a grave digger who sells corpses for profit. In the living room, he covered a sofa that had ten dancing cherubs carved along its rim with a tapestry. He left the rest as it was. Even shrouded in sheets, her legacy would have crowded his rooms.

"I'm home," Emmet called as he sank into an overstuffed chair.

He had walked sixty blocks. He stripped off his jacket and shirt and pulled his T-shirt over his head. He stank like rotten food.

"I'm home," he called again, wiping his body dry with the shirt.

The dog did not rush to greet him. Emmet worried that she was growing distant, often preferring to nap in far corners of the house. Occasionally now he had even heard her howl when he was still blocks away from home, cries loud as those of a woman in pain.

Emmet carried the groceries into the kitchen. He washed the carrots and organized them in the crisper drawer. He arranged the dog food in the cupboard with each label facing out, centering the letters of each word identically over the ones in the can below. He set the package he had found in the cab on the counter. He decided to open it later, as a treat after he had made peace with the dog.

"Please come," he shouted. "I've got food."

He heard the jingle of her collar from somewhere below. "Is that you?" he called anxiously.

He peered down the basement stairs. "Who's there?" he whispered into the darkness. There was no door separating the basement from the kitchen. Emmet knew the boiler, the water heater, and the fuse boxes were down there, but he had never had the nerve to go.

"I'm going to eat without you," he said. He remembered that his mother had said this when he and his brother delayed too long in the yard. Always they had run into the house to find their dinner cold on the table.

The dog climbed guiltily up the stairs. She bared her teeth, revealing the molars behind her black-spotted gums, as if to pacify him with a smile. Her coat was gritty with dirt. Two dust balls clung to the side of her head like a feather boa.

"You mustn't go down there," Emmet reprimanded as she wriggled on the floor. "It isn't safe."

Occasionally he would discover a gigantic water bug crawling slowly across the tiles at the top of the stairs, as if it had climbed to safety to escape a colony of overcrowded nests. The insects were so intimidating that he killed them by tossing a boot from the other side of the room. Sometimes it took every shoe he owned before he scored a direct hit.

Emmet tied the strings of a surgical mask behind his head. "You must be hungry," he said to the dog. She leapt with pleasure as he whirred the electric can opener. "This was very expensive food," he said through the mask. He rambled to her about his journey home to distract himself from the odor of the pressed meat. He had trained himself to empty the can without glancing at the contents, in the way he imagined a blind person learned to cook. He sang loudly the instant he heard the sickening plop of the meat sliding free of the can.

"Won't you try to be more like me?" he pleaded as he placed the bowl on the floor. "Look at you. You're getting fat from the poison." The dog grunted with joy. She gobbled the meat before he had released the dish, slobbering his fingers with her saliva.

Emmet washed his hands and prepared a carrot. He scraped the skin expertly with a knife and sat down at the picnic table to eat it whole. He opened the newspaper to the Metropolitan section to see what had happened in the city the previous day.

Emmet had been transfixed by the newspaper lately, reading accounts of every crime until he began to feel the threat outside personally. It had become his habit to call his brother every afternoon to read the reports of robberies, rapes, and murders he had found in small columns in the back of the newspaper. "Seven robberies and two murders yesterday. Somebody even held up a jewelry store with a machine gun," Emmet had announced to Jonathan the day before.

Even his imperturbable brother was growing exasperated. "Stop reading them," Jonathan had said. "Think of it like a plane crash. When you read about one that crashes, you forget that planes have flown overhead for months without any disaster. Hundreds—thousands maybe. It's just like all the houses we walk by every day. They aren't the scene of a crime."

"Not yet," Emmet had said. "But how do we know the things going on inside them that haven't been reported? Horrors happen secretly in houses all the time. It's only luck that keeps us safe from danger. I'm worried that I'm running out."

"It's not just luck. You can stay out of the way of trouble. Like looking both directions before you cross the street."

Jonathan did not understand that the articles Emmet read in the newspaper seemed more vivid to him than anything that happened in his life. As soon as he returned home from work, Emmet spread the newspaper on the picnic table in the dining room. He would read the reports of the crimes repeatedly. "Facts," he crowed to himself, riveted by every detail.

He had hung a map of the city on the wall in his bedroom. He bought color-coded pins. Red was for murder. Black was for rape. Blue was for muggings. He stuck appropriate pins in the location of every crime. He had seen a similar map once when he visited a police station. There were no pins yet in the streets near his home, but they had begun to crowd every neighborhood around it. Clumps of them pushed closer every week, obscuring the green-and-gray print of the map underneath, marking a trail like the approach of enemy battalions.

Every night as he studied the newspaper to position his pins in the exact spot, he felt as if he were keeping a vigil over the city. For months, he had saved a newspaper a day. He stored them in the empty bedroom. He had now collected so many papers that he had begun to arrange them by weeks of the year in neat piles on the floor. He had thirty-six stacks, each one rising from Monday to Sunday, the corners of each page flush against the others.

Often he walked among the stacks, admiring their order. Before long, he would have a record of everything that had happened in the city during the past year under lock and key, like an enormous calendar. He believed that he was creating a capsule of daily life to which he could return and relive over time.

All Emmet wanted was to buy a little time. He saw his life as it was then and he could not help wondering, "Is this the way I will always be?"

In school Emmet had studied photography. After graduation, he had been too daunted to start a business of his own. He had taken work instead in an office that reproduced slides from works of art.

In his laboratory, Emmet set his camera over the photograph of a painting printed in a textbook, focusing his lens until each detail of the picture was framed by a one-inch square of light. He had to situate the camera perfectly to find the only angle from which he could capture every element. In the evening, he would develop the film, waiting as the images swimming in a bucket of chemicals emerged to life. He had become an expert at guessing the perfect hue under the distortion of the red lamps in the darkroom. When he was satisfied, he hung the film in strips from clothespins strung along a wire attached to the ceiling. After they were dry, Emmet snipped the transparencies until they fit exactly into the white cardboard square with which he framed the border of each slide. In museums now, life-sized paintings seemed unnaturally large and colored, so accustomed had he grown to the negatives he developed from photographs printed on a glossy page.

Except for the Polaroid he kept to document small crimes in the city, Emmet rarely touched his cameras. When he was away from work, he preferred to take notes. At night before bed he copied everything he had done, down to the most minute detail, in his diary. He had started months ago when he first found the events of the day receding, even before he had slept, like the details of a dream.

He recorded every telephone conversation and stored the tapes in garbage bags in a back room. He opened boxes long buried in his closet to reread old letters, yearbooks, and discarded address books that held the names of people from his other lives.

He tacked photographs of everyone he knew on a bulletin board hung next to the map in his bedroom. He tried to acquaint himself with a world beyond his own. From magazines he cut pictures of government officials and pinned them to the wall. He read their captions over and over to memorize the names as he remembered doing with flash cards when he had taught himself French.

"This is the President," he would say as he studied the bulletin board. "This is the secretary of state. And these are the presidents of Poland, Uruguay, and Mauritania." Emmet prided himself that he had collected almost every world leader on his wall, hundreds of photographs from almost every inhabited place.

In his diary he kept track of the route he took to work. He devised a code that he printed on the right-hand side of the page for every person he visited. "Jonathan," he might write, with a circled "6" above his brother's name to indicate the subway route he rode to get there. He jotted down every errand he completed, every item he purchased, and how much money he spent. He recorded the name of every book and magazine he read. Even a shouted insult on the street or the ravings of a lunatic that he sensed were directed at him found their way into its pages.

He recorded his moods with arrows pointing up or down drawn above the date, as if he were a nurse dispassionately charting the rise and fall of a patient. He did not know if it was wise to be aware of every slip and change afflicting him, but he felt it worse to let himself fall away with no effort.

Emmet set his diary on the newspaper spread across the picnic table. His fingers were smudged black from the print. "A gang of twenty thieves robbed six people on 95th Street at 1:35 A.M.," he wrote. "A woman was found floating by the pier at the river."

He noted these two events in his diary. He chose a red and a blue pin from the plastic box he kept in the kitchen drawer. He described everything that had happened to him that day, from the cab driver to the clerks in the grocery store to his long walk home. He checked the thermometer hanging outside his kitchen window and wrote "93 degrees, Fahrenheit" at the top of the page.

Until he had updated his diary, Emmet had forgotten the bag he had stolen from the cab.

"Come see," he said to the dog.

Emmet set the brown paper package on the counter. He averted his eyes as he untied its string, hoping to see a treasure glittering before him when he looked again. But as the paper fell away from the object inside, a stench spoiled the air. Emmet saw half of an egg salad sandwich inside. The cooked yolk had dried dark yellow and hard; the egg whites stood out starkly against it like diseased cells.

A flat, gray stone, the size of a slice of bread, lay under the sandwich. A note was fastened around it with a rubber band.

Emmet unfolded the piece of paper. With a red ribbon someone had typed:

ONE EVENING GRANDPA RACCOON
HURRIED TO ARABELLA AND ALBERT'S
HOUSE. THERE HAS BEEN A HOLD-UP, HE
CALLED. WHERE ARE THE TWINS?

Emmet laughed at the ludicrousness of the message. He read it aloud to the dog. He read it again, silently. Then again.

He juggled the stone absently in his hand. "If it has no meaning," he considered, "why would someone take the trouble to wrap the paper around a stone?"

He studied the sentences: the names, the block letters, the perfect spelling.

"Maybe it was just a child's game," he thought. "To torment a teacher." But a child would have had to hail the cab by himself. Emmet could not believe that a child would wave his arms in the traffic for a ride, then climb into the back of a taxi unattended.

He tried to think logically. Was the stone meant to be thrown through somebody's window in the middle of the night, as a warning? The message could be like the password a kidnapper leaves in the classified section of a newspaper: nonsense to everyone but the person who can unlock the code.

If the culprit had taken the trouble to prepare so complex a scheme, Emmet could not imagine him forgetting his package in a car. For a moment, he considered the possibility that the note was intended for him personally, as a threat. No one could have known that he would hail that particular cab. He had not told a soul where he was going. He varied his route everywhere he went so that he was certain he was never followed.

Emmet paced about the room, dizzy with possibilities. His frustration spiraled unbearably. He did not know what had brought him on that afternoon to discover the note in the cab like a message sent in a bottle. He tried to resign himself to the pure chance of his discovery.

"Crime or accident?" he wondered aloud.

Increasingly, he saw connections in everything that happened, so many that he could not believe they were coincidence. He had pages of them written in his diary: extraordinary events, events that baffled him. Often they appeared to be haphazard, but he worried that they hid other meanings, ones he despaired of ever translating, no matter how hard he tried.

It was impossible to choose among them. As far as he would ever know, as far as he could ever be certain, he would never find a solution to the mystery except one he invented. Long ago, he had ceased to believe in his view of things, no matter how strongly he still hoped for it. He wanted something separate from himself, something removed as far from his brain as it was possible to go. Without it, he feared, he could never hope to change his life.

"It could be anything," Emmet thought desperately. "Anything."

He opened the window and threw the sandwich into the yard. He crumpled the note and held it over the gas flame on the stove. He watched the paper burn blue and orange before it turned to ash. He wanted it out of his sight. He wanted it forgotten. There would never be a reason.

CHAPTER
SEVEN

"Just imagine," Emmet's mother used to preface her good-byes to him before she went away.

"Just imagine where I'll be and what I'm doing. Describe the room I might inhabit down to the smallest detail. Where I sleep. Where I might go for dinner. How I'll get there. Then you'll have a picture of me in your mind. And if at night you worry that I'm never coming back, just imagine me dead and how your life will be with your grandmother. Then you'll learn that you can see your way out of anything."

From the moment she returned to his grandmother's house and embraced them, she would become edgy, even before she had set her bags by the bed in her room. She rarely said to them, "You should have seen where I've been." Instead, she treated them to descriptions of the place she was headed next, as if the purpose of every journey was the promise it held in her mind.

Just imagine.

Emmet could remember her vividly as she was when he was a child: her eyes, the smell of her hair, the way she sat with her legs crossed at the shins. He would have given anything to have spied on her when she was younger, unencumbered by children or a past. When she had aged, he tried to find her wilder self in her impassive, prematurely wrinkled face; but nothing in her expression betrayed anything about what she might have known or feared or felt about her life.

Often he had tried to take her by surprise, to rush into her bedroom unexpectedly, or sneak out the back door to follow her on walks, or to lift the receiver of the telephone and eavesdrop on her conversations. Emmet wished he had owned a tape recorder then, so that he could recapture the sound of her. He had no memory for voices. He thought hers had been languid and sly, but when it came to him in dreams, it was small and unmusical, like a child's whine heard from another room.

She never kept a diary. She never wrote letters, except for thank-you notes to acquaintances for a dinner, a gift, or a small kindness. She always telephoned when she was away. Only once did she send him a postcard: an orange monkey swinging from a bush in the West Indies. On the back she wrote: "More monkeys than people inhabit this island and that's just fine with me."

The only facts Emmet knew about her were those he had witnessed himself, stories his grandmother told him, or the few censored anecdotes his mother offered whenever she slipped briefly back into their lives.

She had given birth to a dead one two years before him. She had carried it for eight months before it was pulled from her womb, like a doll. It was given a name and a plot in a cemetery at the foot of a volcano in Hawaii and a white tombstone with a plump angel cut into the side of the marble. She flew alone to Hawaii to bury it. She wanted to return the body to the place where it had been conceived. She stored the coffin in the basement of a pink hotel while she made arrangements. Or so his grandmother told him.

Once in Colorado he came upon her napping on the floor in front of the stove, face down, her arms stretched flat above her head like a diver's. The man entered from another door at the same time, but he did not notice Emmet. From the corner of the room, Emmet saw the man plant a foot on her neck and rock it back and forth. The motion woke her. Emmet remembered her eyes, a fraction of an inch above the grain in the floor, bugging out, like those of a fish flung upon a pier.

The man held her with his boot, massaging her back and pushing on her spine. Her bones snapped like flames. Her breath came out in gasps, timed to the pressure of his boot, so that he seemed to play her like an instrument, controlling every breath she took. Finally, with his leg rigid, his foot still pinning her to the floor, the man had bent over and softly brushed her neck with his lips, as agile as a wild animal.

When he was young, Emmet's image of her was of someone imprisoned by movement: her thin legs vibrated so violently when she sat that the table hummed with tremors. She seemed always to be bending forward, pushing her hair from her eyes with the back of her hand; the diamond birthstone around her neck swiping her chin as it swung in and out of her blouse; her muscles rippling throughout her body as if charged by a current.

Later her movements became overly cautious, like those of someone who had suffered a stroke and learned to walk again without fully trusting her body.

When she was forty, she returned from a trip and announced to them, "I'm sick of traveling; I don't want to go anywhere anymore." By then Emmet and Jonathan were long away at school. She bought a house, filling it with the possessions she would leave them in her will.

She had grown less beautiful quickly. She stopped wearing stockings, so varicose veins popped from her legs like blue worms. She wore plaid skirts that accentuated her thickening hips. She let her hair revert to its natural gray. She encouraged a primness in her manner that had been lacking before, as if she dared anyone to believe she had once been desirable. She claimed never to read a book with an unhappy ending or to see a film in which anyone died or became unlucky in love. She stated these beliefs with pride, as if her narrowness demonstrated an honorable restraint.

When Emmet and Jonathan were grown and visited her, she studied their faces as if trying to gauge how much they had forgotten, hoping they remembered her only as she had become in middle life: tense and proper with an edge that made them tentative with her. She behaved as if she were living underground and every conversation might disclose clues to their early lives together that could ruin her. Often when he left, Emmet was bewildered by her guilt, wondering for days afterward, "What has she done? What has she done?"

There were frequent thunderstorms in the mountains when they lived with her, attacking unexpectedly in the middle of the day, the cloudless sky turning black and dangerous, the loud bangs rending the stillness of their house like blasts from a gun.

Their mother would gather them in the entry hall, away from all the windows in the house, and distract them with a game. "It's the gods banging on metal strips," she would tell them, shouting and whooping. She would grab pots from the kitchen and give them each a wooden spoon. Together they would bang on the copper bottoms until the sound almost drowned out the thunder. "Louder than heaven," his mother would shout. "Make it louder than heaven."

As lightning cracked the air around them, she would holler, "It's shots from a ray gun; the angels are coming to get us." She would take a flashlight from the drawer in the kitchen and lower the shades, flipping the light on and off in the near-darkness while Emmet and Jonathan banged on their pots.

Once they drove in the car as a thunderstorm approached. Emmet saw his mother stiffen and look desperately for a place to take shelter. In her nervousness, her hands failed on the gear shift and the car stalled, just as the lightning flashed around them, splitting the car with its light. They were miles from home.

"Sing," his mother ordered. She chirped in a pinched soprano the first verse of a hymn she had learned in school: " 'If I should fall from grace with God . . .' " Her voice gathered strength as the storm paused in the sky above them, venting its fury directly over their car. Emmet remembered the rain pounding the canvas roof like bullets as she cried "Sing, sing, sing," over the sound. They mimicked her lead hesitantly, but she returned each time to the beginning until the words of the hymn filled the car in a ritual of protection, round and round them, like a circle of garlic.

"Louder," she urged as they reached the end, refusing to let them stop. "Louder," until the three of them shrieked hysterically in the car.

When the storm passed, they sat mutely, each embarrassed and regretful. "Well," she said primly. "That was something, wasn't it, boys?" Then she laughed, as if it had all been a game.

Emmet remembered that as she started the car and pulled back onto the road, the storm left one of the clearest nights he had ever seen in its wake. The moon was blinding from its place in the sky.

He stood on the floor, his head between the two front seats, so that he could look through the rearview mirror to see the headlights approach from behind. As his mother turned the car and began driving fast towards their home, the moon caught in the mirror like the blue-white flash of a siren. And with each revolution of light, he had felt that nature was with them and was sounding its alarm.

CHAPTER

EIGHT

"**I** dreamed I had a gun," Emmet whispered into the telephone receiver resting in the folds of the pillow by his ear.

He pulled the sleeping dog close to him for warmth. She nuzzled her snout into his neck and snorted happily. Emmet could feel her heart beat peacefully against his own racing chest.

"I dreamed I had a gun and the city was on fire and all around me the night was loud with the sound of sirens and breaking glass. There was a crowd crouched on the sidewalk and each person held a pistol pointed at my head, but nobody fired a shot. Except me. I ran through the bodies shooting in every direction; I was so close that I could put the barrel right up against their ears. I kept going *bam, bam, bam* and every time I hit one of them, you could see the skin split open down to the muscles and bones, but not one of them ever bled or fell. They just kept aiming their guns at me with their jaws set fiercely, and all I could think of was that I had to get away.

"I don't know why they wouldn't return my fire. I don't know why none of them would die. I don't even know why I wanted to kill them, except that they had banded together to stop me from doing something. But they couldn't touch me: I was so light. I jumped their bodies for miles and miles, all the way across town, until I made it to the corner near my house. But somehow hordes of them had beaten me there. A mob blocked the entrance to my street, hooting and cheering as my house burned. I pushed past them to rush inside to rescue the dog, and they let me through, but just as the door shut behind me, the whole house exploded, like it was timed for my arrival, blasting me into a fireball that hurled into the air over the street, burning, burning—just this round thing without any limbs, nothing but heat and flames.

"Pieces of me started to fly off—you know, traces of ash slipping out of the fire—and each time part of me escaped, the crowd snatched it out of the air to smear over their faces like war paint. Finally there was nothing left of me but tiny bits of embers, and as each one floated to the sidewalk, the people stomped them out, merrily, like they were dancing a jig, and just as the last one fell, I woke up. Weird, huh? Sorry to call so late, but I don't know what it means."

"That's something," Jonathan agreed hoarsely. "But forget about it. It was just a dream. It doesn't mean anything."

"But I was shooting them," Emmet said. "They were in danger, not me. I never have dreams where I'm the one who's causing harm. Do you think it means anything?"

"Only that it's summer and it's hot and you need some sleep. I have dreams all the time, but I just put them out of my mind. They don't have anything to do with the way we live."

"But everything is changing," Emmet said. "Don't you feel it, too? Remember how it was when we first came? How we couldn't imagine that we would ever leave?"

"I still don't want to leave," Jonathan mumbled.

"You don't? But can't you remember what it was like in the beginning? How fearless we were? How every place we went seemed to be ours? It isn't like that anymore. Everywhere I go, I feel like I'm trespassing. It doesn't matter if it's day or night, no matter where I am, something follows me."

Emmet heard Jonathan rummaging in his bed as if he were sitting up. His voice was deep with fatigue. "But you forget," he said. "It never was safe. You just didn't care. Remember, I see the same streets as you do whenever I open my door. Nothing's changed. This is where you live. You belong here."

"You don't understand," Emmet said. "I loved having that gun in my dream. "I loved the feel of it, like I'd become invincible or something."

"It's ridiculous to think of you with a gun. Somebody'd grab it away and shoot you. You're too easy a mark."

"You don't know. You're just used to me. That's why people in newspapers always sound so surprised when the person they love commits a crime. They can't believe they missed something so big in someone they lived with day after day. So you don't know. You don't know."

"I know it's late. We need to sleep. Listen, remember that first summer I spent in Philadelphia with Dad? And how I called you in California every night after he went to bed and we would sleep with the telephone lines open? It was the first telephone number I ever memorized. Why don't we do that now? You lay back and shut your eyes. And if the dream returns, all you have to do is shout into the wires and wake me up. It'll be almost like we're in the same room."

"I used to listen to you all night long, the way you breathed into the phone, like your mouth was wrapped around the receiver," Emmet said.

"I used to think you were dead when I'd wake up and not hear anything, like the wires had been cut," Jonathan said.

"You were younger than me, then," Emmet said. "You sure you don't mind? Will you tell me when I've gone too far? I'm sure I need your patience just a little while more." Although he did not believe this himself, Emmet knew it was what his brother wanted to hear.

"If we don't sleep soon, it's going too far. The rest is easy. You sleep. I'll sleep. Everyone will be happy. Good night, Emmet."

"You really wouldn't worry about the gun?"

"Good night, Emmet."

Emmet pushed the dog away and sat with his back against the bed frame, listening intently to the sound of his brother's breath as it grew stronger through the wires. He imagined Jonathan's long body buried under piles of pillows in his bed only seven blocks away.

Through the telephone, Emmet heard Jonathan mutter deep within a dream. He put his hand over his mouth to squelch the sound of his own breath. He leaned heavily into the receiver, as if he were pressing the cool steel of a stethoscope to his brother's body, but he could not discern a word, only grunts punctuated by a long sigh.

With the receiver clutched possessively in one hand, Emmet switched on the bedside lamp. Every object in his room bloomed in the shadows: black at the edges; thin, almost transparent, at the center. The quiet was unearthly, as if Emmet were the only creature on the planet who breathed. He wanted to disturb the silence by barking something into the still air, but he felt the unnatural calm creep upon him, too, as if he were being slowly smothered by ghosts.

"It's like swimming in glass," Emmet thought to himself. "Liquid glass."

The walls, the ceiling, the floor, every surface and plane, rolled in place, soft and puttyish. As he looked about him, Emmet no longer felt as if he inhabited a solid space.

"Jonathan?" he whispered into the telephone. "Are you awake? Jonathan?"

Emmet did not know what he would tell his brother if he answered from the other end. He could not describe to anyone how he felt the past break off entirely from everything he knew and carry his purpose away. Or how he felt expelled from even the places he belonged, even from his own body. The surge of energy hit him pitilessly, when he was at work, when he visited his friends, when he walked the streets, when he was quietly removed, as he was then, huddled motionlessly in his bed.

To orient himself, Emmet imagined the infinite layers grounding the world beneath him: he saw his body as it sat on the mattress which rested squarely on its heavy brass frame. Below it, the solid feet stood flat against the waxed planks of the wooden floor nailed into four feet of cement. He knew rock beams from the basement's ceiling stretched as one piece to the foundation of the house that had been set for one hundred and eleven years in a pit dug deep into the street. Emmet pictured the packed dirt beneath this structure, invisible to the eye upon which the city was built, and the thousands of miles of earth, from the crust to the center and beyond to the hemisphere on the other side. But even with this image planted firmly in his mind, he felt unmoored, as if he flew perilously about, loose in the dark night air.

Some nights his fear was so great, he could think of nothing but to run up and down the streets all night shouting for help, maybe abandoned to that private language of gibberish he had heard men babble on the subway. But Emmet still wanted to live in the world. He knew he could never revoke so dramatic an act. If he lost control in front of witnesses, everything would change.

He was haunted by stories he had heard of a poet who alienated his friends with his insanity. When he died alone in Times Square, his body cooled unclaimed for days in the morgue. No one had noticed he was missing. Maybe his friends had spent days guiltily relieved by the silence of the telephone and the end of his drunken, late-night visits.

If Emmet had been granted a wish, he would have wanted to meet this man's friends and ask them how it was: what the rules were for giving up on someone so completely. He did not know what the limits were to caring. He did not know how far he had gone already or how far he had left to go.

Emmet knew he was losing. His craziness galloped upon him. Every morning he looked back on himself in horror, as if he could document visible signs of his decline accumulating in a mirror. He wanted to know what his chances were before anything else happened. He did not want to believe in a life with no rescue, some net that safely caught the falling body, even if it was beyond trust itself.

The dog whimpered in her sleep. Her legs kicked rapidly, as if she chased, or was chased by, something unseen. "What does she see?" Emmet wondered. "Rabbits and birds? A stampede thundering upon her?"

He looked at her eyes, rotating madly in their sockets. He did not know if she dreamed in pictures or if a faceless fear tormented her, an instinct from somewhere deep inside her brain urging her to flee.

"Good dog," he said, placing a hand on her heart to quiet her.

His touch abruptly stopped her running. She groaned happily and wiggled onto her back, her paws flopping limply towards her chest. Emmet nestled his head into her fur with the telephone balanced on his ear, hoping that his brother would stir. He heard nothing.

He wondered what would happen if he screamed into the receiver. He doubted he could wake him. Dreaming unconsciously, his brother was further away than he had been before, further than if he had hung up and Emmet were able to call him back.

"Save me," he whispered into the telephone, securely, because he knew that Jonathan could not hear. Secretly he hoped his message might take root in Jonathan's sleeping brain, like a foreign language learned from a tape recorder placed under a pillow at night.

Emmet looked about the room, the heavy furniture, the mirrors framed with dark wood, the three etched bottles grouped on the linen cloth that lined his bureau. The bodies of two slender, dancing women were cut into each glass, grooved so that their figures appeared to be frosted with snow. As he studied them, they began to snake around the base, twirling the hems of their skirts about their legs, each one shaking a foot in turn at Emmet, who lay rigid on his bed.

"You are here," he said, gripping the chilly brass posts behind him. He felt the pillowcases crushed against him, soft and white as a skin. Everything in the room quaked with movement, as if nature had reversed itself and he had become the dead one in a house of living things.

He thought of his brother, blocks away, linked only by wires free of even the cackle of static electricity, completely beyond his reach.

"Save me."

CHAPTER NINE

"**Y**ou're dirty," Emmet said to the dog as he wiped muddy paw prints from the bleached sheets of his bed. "Get off."

Emmet bundled her into his arms and carried her to the well underneath his desk. "It's safer for you here," he said as he positioned the chair to block her exit.

He slipped on his jeans and snapped a rubber band tightly around each ankle so that his baggy hems would not trip him as he walked. He donned a T-shirt, many sizes too large, and wound the excess folds behind his back in a bun, as if he were knotting a mane of hair.

He moved about the room, first switching on the overhead light, next the lamp on his desk with the fluted glass shade, then the pen light screwed to the post of his bed. Redeemed from its shadows, his bedroom pulsed with life. Although he tried to ignore them, Emmet could not help seeing the etched figures continue to sashay across the glass bottles on his bureau. Each time he caught them in the corner of his eye, they snaked an inch or two left, then right, as if high-stepping in a chorus line.

Emmet sat in his easy chair and faced his bureau. He locked his arms around his knees. He made himself follow every movement the figures made until he had become familiar, nearly bored, with each of their fancy steps.

"I can grow used to anything if I let it become a regular part of my day," he reminded himself.

As he sat and watched, Emmet tried to recall the biographies he had read of people who learned to take the worst catastrophes in stride. He remembered a story a teacher had told him about a writer who became paralyzed with a disease that crept from his toes to his neck, deliberately, until no part of him moved but the lashes of his eyes. For months the man lay dead on a sofa except for the flutter of his lids while he dictated the last chapter of a book, spelling the letters of each word with blinks.

Emmet imagined himself buried in sand up to his face, tapping a sentence letter by letter, word by word, until he had filled a page. "You are weak," he admonished himself as the women kicked and twirled. "This is nothing. At least you are able to move. You are so alive that the world everywhere you look exists in complete motion."

But even as he sought to console himself, Emmet knew it was hopeless. In every moment of his life, he felt cursed with a miserable alertness. He could not rest his guard. What existed beyond the pirouetting figures? What would happen to him next? Everywhere about him he sensed an unknown presence, like a thief hiding in a room, about to burst forth: from within the objects strewn about his apartment, from within the particles in the very air he breathed. His vigilance tired him. He was no closer to discovering the trigger that made every part of him change, as the world around him changed faster still.

He knew no rules for living as he did now. Time itself had become something tangible, a wind that raced about him, as if his days were measured now by the passage of light years or as if he traveled at the speed of sound. He felt as if he were shooting past and looking down at everyone he knew from an untransversible space, as if he were held prisoner in a foreign world that had no place for him, yet would not let him leave.

Emmet lifted one of the bottles from his bureau. He rolled the glass in the palm of his hand, astonished at how ordinary it looked. The figures ceased to swirl, receding the instant he brought them near his eyes. He pulled a T-shirt from a basket of soiled clothes and wiped the dust ground into the grooves of the glass. He slapped the bottle, then threw it into the air, catching it between two fingers. He shook it over his head, then tossed it between his legs, recklessly, and snatched it blindly behind his back.

"I can smash it to bits if it moves again," Emmet thought confidently, remembering that he held a power over it still.

He replaced the bottle among the others on the bureau. For the moment he had won. He paced about the room, waiting for the next disruption to occur. He knew he was beyond sleep.

He regarded the walls and the shuttered windows. He stood on his toes and peeked through the top panes. All he saw was his own face reflected back at him, dark and blurry in the black glass.

"Outside?" he wondered aloud. The dog crashed out from under the desk and nipped at his shoes. She pranced in circles on the wooden floor and rooted among the shelves with her nose, hunting for her leash.

"Oh no, not you. You'll make us too apparent," Emmet said, edging his way out the door as the dog tried to wriggle through the crack to join him. As he stepped into the hallway, she threw herself against the frame.

"Go lie down," he ordered through the wall as he heard her body rush across the slick floor, butting the door again and again.

She yelped, hammering her paws around the lock. "Good dog," Emmet soothed. "Good dog, good dog," louder and louder until he made his way through the front door and out into the street.

As he reached his stoop, Emmet froze and looked both ways, listening. He saw puffs of smoke cloud the window across the street and then the red tip of a cigarette draw brilliantly and fade.

All summer Emmet believed his neighbors had kept watch, keeping their vigil in shifts. They napped in chairs on their porches or swept the sidewalks in front of their homes until the concrete was smooth as pumice. Whenever they sensed something out of order, an alarm swept through them like a code tapped through prison walls. People he had never met had begun to nod at him knowingly, as if they had read a dossier in a file somewhere and been made to memorize his photograph. Emmet believed he was the subject they spoke about over dinner, and even, as the days wore on, the person they wrote about in letters to friends and relatives he would never meet.

In case someone observed him, Emmet affected a jaunty air and jumped down the steps two at a time, working his lips soundlessly, as if he could whistle. As he scurried along the sidewalk, he tried to block out the thought of his prying neighbors. He concentrated on the way his body moved in the humid night. His T-shirt caught in the air, billowing behind as he passed the corner drugstore, the grocery, the bank, the movie theater complex, all the familiar signposts of his neighborhood, and beat a path to the river. The colors of the streetlights dazzled his eye as he ran, their diamond rays ribboning from his periphery as he dashed along: red yellow and green, red yellow and green, leaving a shower of colored sparks in his wake.

"Wings," he thought incredulously as he gathered his speed.

He flapped his arms at his sides, sprinting along the sidewalk so swiftly that the bones in his ankles cracked like castanets, *click click, click click, click click, click click,* against the cement. The sound riveted him, as if he were nothing but rhythm, pure movement, sweeping through the city.

"Wings," he told himself as his body revolted against his quickening pace.

His heart thudded against the bones in his chest. Air pinched his lungs. He practiced blowing his breath out calmly, as if his ribs did not constrict with each step. The rubber bands caught on the fine hairs at his ankles, cutting an angry red ridge into his skin each time he lifted a leg. His feet grew numb. His shoes flopped along the sidewalk, emptily, as if they were sewn onto his legs.

Emmet widened his stride so that he touched the earth only a yard at a time. "Flick, flack, break your mother's back," he laughed as he jumped over the cracks in the pavement, three, four, five, feet apart, then longer and longer, until he leapt over whole sections of the sidewalk, flying.

"Room to breathe," he panted as he neared the avenue by the river where the apartments ceased and the warehouses began.

"Room to breathe," Emmet's mother used to exclaim when they traveled far into the country. Often as she drove, she would warn him against the meanness of the city. She said that the people who lived there suffocated and fed upon themselves. "Worse than piranhas," she threatened. "You wouldn't last a minute."

Once in Colorado, she had pointed to a group of men making their way along the main street of a mining town. Within minutes, they had walked the length of the street and paused at its end, uncertainly, before they turned and retraced their steps. They paced back and forth countless times as Emmet and his mother watched, always halting abruptly at the border of the town, as if they had stumbled upon a fence.

"Multiply them by a million," his mother had said in disgust. "Then you've got your city. Those four that many times as bad."

Emmet had been secretly thrilled at the idea of streets teeming with all those millions. The bareness of that mining town had frightened him, even though from the distance, the men were nothing but hats and coats passing indistinctly before him. "They are free to do anything they want," Emmet remembered thinking as he imagined a life among them. "There are too few people to see or stop them." The life they promised seemed to mimic the same sanctuary held by a family. Bad behavior could be kept within its folds, secretly, passed from one generation to another, forever.

"They will get me," Emmet thought, as if he were already trapped, a dread that may not have been conscious then but straight from his heart, in the way an animal sniffs danger. An alarm tingled through his body, ringing, "Get out, get out," even as he sat on the hill holding his mother's hand.

From the time he was a child, Emmet had sensed an oddness about himself that made strangers wary. He did not know if they glimpsed some secret of his personality from the way he carried himself or if something less distinct, like a scent, emanated from his pores. A room would fall silent even if he entered meekly and did not speak, scrutinizing him with a fervor that he learned to feel as hate. Everywhere he had lived it had always been the same. But when he had first come alone to the city, an airiness released him, as if for the first time in his life he was visible without being seen: a unacknowledged body that could slip unheralded through the streets.

No matter where he was, no matter how far he strayed from home, he never knew harm, because he believed any street he entered was like an extension of his apartment. The buildings were his walls. Whenever he was out, he looked forward to returning home, to the way he could disappear through the angles of avenues, corridors, and stairs to get there, as if he made his way among secret passageways. Every time he turned a corner, he felt that a door shut behind him as he sped his way forward.

Some nights he would pick an arbitrary landmark miles away and make it his object. Other nights he would have no purpose except to see where his uncharted wanderings took him. It had been his plan to touch every inch of the city with his feet, to memorize every crevasse and shadow like the most scrupulous cartographer, as if every time he walked, he burrowed nearer to the heart of the most unfathomable mystery. He could go forever, inviolably, in any one direction, with only the river to stop him and force him to retrace his steps towards home.

From a park bench, from the street, from the window of his apartment, Emmet would invent the lives of the people he saw from a comment they might make to a companion or from the clothes they wore or from the cut of their hair. He had once believed that he could describe a person's background down to the smallest detail by the shoes he wore and the cut of his jeans, like linguists can pinpoint where a person was born by detecting an almost untraceable accent.

Emmet braked himself with his heels as he raced past a For Sale sign he had not noticed the night before. It was tacked to the entrance of the building where he had lived before moving to his present home. A century ago, it had been a hotel for sailors. His apartment there had been built into the lower floor of a turret that held an unobstructed view of the river. The same fluorescent light he had installed to grow flowers still clouded the front window with a lavender haze.

He stood on his tiptoes to see if he could determine any sign of the people who lived there now. He saw walls lacquered red that had once been white. He saw a tree topped with orange blossoms in the corner of the living room. For a moment, he considered ringing the bell to ask if he could inspect his former rooms, but he doubted the owners would ever let a person un-known to them inside.

In his mind, he counted the people he had befriended when he lived there who had dropped from his life. He counted the strangers he had summoned upstairs on summer nights as he leaned out the windowsill. He remembered every face, even the ones who had not left their names. This was the same apartment where

Jonathan had come to stay when he first moved to the city. This was the same apartment where Emmet had lived when his mother died.

In previous years, Emmet had occupied four other homes scattered throughout the city. Often he lingered in front of them to see if some quality of past attachment returned to him, but the buildings left him as empty as the rooms had been left the moment he moved out. He wondered if it would be different if he stood again in front of his grandmother's house or by one of the places he had lived with his mother, or if they would hold the same remoteness as he felt then, outside on the deserted street.

"There is nothing for me here," Emmet shrugged as he walked to the corner and picked his way through the traffic. He rested on the concrete wall built along the pier. He massaged the knots cramped into his thighs. He pulled off his T-shirt to dry his hair, then draped it over his shoulders, arranging the material carefully so that he hid his wren-thin chest from view.

He hooked his fingers through the chain-link fence and stretched his legs. With his face pressed into the wire, he could see across the river to the city on the other side: the lit buildings, the neon purpling the horizon above the highway, the black water crazy with current.

When he had first come to the city, Emmet had not believed that the river at night could have been more beautiful before there were lights strung along its shore. He had seen paintings in the local museum of the land before it was settled: no roads, no towns, nothing but low buildings and farms. In the daylight, it could have been anywhere. In the dark, it vanished entirely from sight. The adornment had made it beautiful to him, the way the light at night in the city was like nowhere else on earth: the brightest darkness imaginable, so clear that sometimes he held a book before him and read as he walked, even after midnight. In those years, Emmet had believed there was time for everything, because the day was not closed off as it was in other places, but continuous, one hour evolving into the next: as if his whole life were there, waiting, each day ready to begin at any moment he chose.

As he stood dreaming against the fence, Emmet knew that all the same elements were still visible there: the lights, the river, the sound of the traffic behind him, even the building that had once been his home. But now the water looked black and horrible to him, a sea alive with floating sewage and the corpses of nameless people dumped from the streets.

Before, Emmet had never felt a danger. Before, he had not believed that there could be a threat. "Could Jonathan be right?" he wondered. "Has it been the same all along and it is me who changed, so now the place has changed, too?"

"But I have evidence," he thought as he pictured the lists and snapshots of violations hoarded in his desk. "More and more every day." Quickly he surveyed the area around him: the holes in the planks of the pier, the garbage rotting at the top of the dumpster, the cars parked illegally by fire hydrants. "702-A . . . 357-C . . . 509-4 . . . 34-D . . . 857-1," he counted just within his range of sight.

"It is clear to anyone who sees," he assured himself. "The trouble escalates." He had to admit that in the years when he first arrived, he had walked carelessly, obsessed by nothing but the view. But he had not been aware then of all that he had learned since.

He could not believe he could have been blind to so much. He had spent years on the same streets that now rolled and swelled under his feet as if to erase him. He could not believe his brain had become so poisonous that it ruined every inch of ground his body touched. "Then it doesn't matter where I am. Any place I go, it will follow me," he thought, hopelessly.

Emmet stepped into the moon-shaped circle of light shining from the security lamp above him. "Am I to blame?" he wondered.

He stepped back into the shadows of the pier. He ducked deeper into the recesses of the cement wall. Below him, the water lapped at the moorings, licking closer and closer, like tongues.

"Am I to blame?"

CHAPTER
TEN

Maybe the dog was lonely. Maybe all she longed for was another animal by her side when Emmet was away.

He worried that her howling betrayed the secrets of their house, as if the walls themselves sounded messages to the street outside for help. Emmet had begged her to cease. He had sat on the bench by the picnic table day after day before he left the apartment, beseeching her to be silent. He had bribed her with promises of boundless treats. He had stared into her eyes in the manner instruction books had taught him, commanding her to meet his gaze. None of it had worked. Before his feet left the last step of his stoop, the sound of her misery blew through him and out into the neighborhood beyond.

Emmet had tried to save her. He had tried to keep his agitation secret, soothing her with countless examples of her goodness when she trembled, never hinting at the despair he felt for their lives. But with each day her cries reached a new pitch, as if there were no keeping it from her, as if he had tainted her anyway, as if she mirrored everything he sought to keep concealed in his mind.

Emmet heard her howl when he was miles away from the apartment, even walking at rush hour in traffic, even drinking in a basement bar by the river, even riding underground in a crowded subway car.

He did not know if she was beyond rescue. In desperation, he thought of adopting a second animal. He considered a dog but decided he could not risk it. His own might incite another dog with her misery. He imagined the two beasts manning positions in separate rooms, orchestrating their laments to a chorus of wails. If it was companionship she lacked, Emmet believed it would be safer to move in a cat. Cats, at least, could not be heard through the walls of a house, no matter how wretchedly they lived.

Emmet had never owned a cat. Their fur itched his skin, as if a poison seeped from their pores. When he was young, the mother of his best friend kept sixteen cats in her cottage. When the woman napped, the cats spread across her bed, intertwined like pelts in a quilt of fur.

Emmet studied the telephone book for agencies that offered free animals. Most of them were far away, in boroughs of the city to which he had never been. But the one with the smallest ad, only a single line in small print in the directory, was near his home.

He showered. He dressed conservatively. He rubbed an ice cube over his pale cheeks to freeze them pink with health. He rummaged in a drawer for a photograph he remembered from college in which he listened to a concert on the grass with his dog: her face resting on his chest, her eyes winking at the camera. Emmet's hand caressed her ear; the other stroked the curls of her chest. He remembered how she had rolled with delight as the lens snapped: the feathers on her tail wagging so they blurred on the film.

He stuffed the photograph in his back pocket. He massaged the dog's snout. "Just wait till you see the present I'm bringing you. No more worry. Our life will be different now."

*　*　*

Inside the shelter, a miniature dog shivered on a stool alongside a counter in the reception area. No one else was present. A stained bandage wound loose as a kerchief around its neck. Emmet could see hair shaved along the rim of the gauze, the skin underneath gray and inflamed with red boils. From unseen rooms he heard frantic barking, loud as tin cans banged on prison bars.

"It has to be a cat," Emmet said to himself, imagining again what would happen if two dogs roamed inside his apartment unattended. Through a glass window in the opposite wall he saw a room stacked with cages, each containing a cat of every conceivable stripe and color. "Will one of them be mine?" he wondered excitedly, feeling in that instant the promise of a better life.

Emmet faced the dog wriggling on the stool. "Cat," he said, guiltily. The dog trembled more severely.

He moved closer, extending his hand for it to sniff. As he inched nearer and nearer, the dog convulsed with anxiety, vibrating from the tips of its pointed pink ears to its dwarfed beige feet. When Emmet leaned over the counter to pat it, its nails tapped in terror on the high seat of the stool, as if a sadist were holding a gun before a captive and ordering him to dance.

"It's all right," Emmet cooed, resting his chin on the counter. "No one will ever adopt you if you behave like this. Take deep breaths."

The dog gasped for air. Its tongue darted in and out of its mouth. Its eyes oozed gluey tears that collected in clumps on its cheeks. "Someone will love you," Emmet said, doubtfully.

"Don't touch Pigeon," a voice ordered from behind.

Emmet snapped back his hand, spinning guiltily away from the dog. "Sorry," he said to a round woman in a blue uniform such as a mechanic might wear. "Joan" was sewn onto the pocket in bold red script. "I didn't know if anybody worked here," Emmet said. "What's the dog's name? Pigeon?"

"Yeah," Joan said. "What's the matter? You don't like it? I name 'em all myself."

"Oh, I think it's an unusual name. Very distinctive," Emmet said. "How long has it been here?"

"It's a she, not an it," Joan snapped, stroking Pigeon's wound so lovingly that she might have been petting a sable pelt. "Found her runnin' loose by the river nearly starved to death a few weeks ago. She's just had surgery. I have her out front as a treat. Make her feel like a watchdog, maybe build her confidence a little. Take a little time, but you can train anything back to normal if you start slow enough. So what you lookin' for? A nice little dog?"

"Cat, actually. To keep my dog company while I am away."

"Oh, I dunno about that. A dog gets used to keepin' you company and suddenly there's a cat, well, the dog could kill it. Think how you'd feel if your mom had brought home a foster child when you were little and locked you in the same room. Not much, huh? Add to that the fact of the killer instinct, which you don't got, right? But even the cutest dog does. Your cat and your dog, they're natural enemies. I gotta think about it. How long you gone each day? You better fill out this application."

Joan handed Emmet a three-page form. "Have a seat at the counter next to Pigeon," she said as she left for the cat room. The cats snapped to attention when Joan entered. Through the window, Emmet could see their mouths stretch open and shut as they meowed through the bars of their cages.

The form asked more questions than an application for employment. It wanted to know his address, his telephone number, if he owned or rented, how many rooms he lived in, and if his apartment had access to a yard. How many hours a day was he away? Lately Emmet had gone to work only an afternoon or two a week, but counting his walks, he was almost never at home. "Sixteen hours," he thought. "Sometimes more." He printed "three" in the blank. In answer to the question that asked his profession, he wrote, "Private income," as if that might explain all his free time at home.

It wanted to know the number and age of his children. "Nothing but pets," he wrote. It wanted two character references with day and night telephone numbers. It wanted the address of the nearest relative not living with him. It wanted the number of pets he had owned in his life and how they had died. He wrote "old age" in the blank.

In capital letters at the bottom of the form was an agreement he had to sign. If the shelter accepted him, it reserved the right to visit unannounced to ensure the welfare of the animal. Someone might appear at any time. Emmet froze, imagining already how he would become afraid to leave his home as he awaited their inspection.

"I'll just drop a note and say I've moved to another state unexpectedly once a week has passed. To a farm," he decided as he scratched his signature on the dotted line. Between the first and second pages, Emmet pressed the photograph of his dog.

He tapped the window of the cat room with the form in his hand. Three cats wormed over Joan's lap. One was white with brown ears. One was black. The other had muscled legs and striped orange fur. As Joan stood, the cat paused on her stomach, unruffled by gravity, all four feet flat against her uniform, before it glided into the air. It soared, suspended for several beats, until it cleared half the room. The cat landed upright on its haunches, yawning casually; then it licked its paw before swiping hurriedly under its chin.

Joan joined Emmet in the foyer, oblivious to the winged cat. "Private income, huh?" she said as she perused the form. "I knew somebody with one of those once. They're dead. And I don't mean from old age."

As she flipped to the second page, the photograph fell into her lap. She saw the dog stretched across Emmet as if they were lovers. "Nice dog," she said, warming. "I like a big dog. It spayed?"

"At six months," Emmet said. "There's so many unwanted puppies in the world already, I'd hate to be responsible for more."

"Good boy. So how long you had this dog?"

"Years and years. We've done everything together. She even goes on vacation with me. But I thought maybe during the few hours I'm away during each day, she might like company. Now that she's old. You know, it's silly to worry about these things, but I'd hate for her to die alone when I was out seeing my banker. With a cat, at least—"

Joan cut him off. "Why not another dog? Something small and compatible?" She leaned over so that Pigeon kissed her cheeks with her snakey tongue.

"It's part of my lease. Only one dog. I figure nobody would notice a cat. I can sneak the dirty litter out in garbage bags. No one will be the wiser."

"Well, maybe an older cat," Joan sighed. "One that's lived with a dog already. Then maybe you'll see how things go and come back another time. I could check the files on cats. I don't know them as well as the dogs. They kinda blend in together. Have a look around and open the cages while I see what we've got."

"You mean let them all out at once?" Emmet had imagined an orderly bringing him one cat at a time while he waited in a special room. He did not want to be left in the room alone, outnumbered by cats.

"Don't be shy. It takes two to tango. You might like one, but it might not be crazy 'bout your smell or something about the way you move. They've got their own sense, cats. You can't fool 'em. Kinda creepy in a way. You sure you wouldn't rather have another dog?"

Emmet hesitated. "Cat," he said. "Yes. I'm sure. Cat."

Joan busily thumbed through a shoe box of dog-eared file cards while Emmet tiptoed into the cat room. They hissed when they saw him, crinkling their noses as if his smell repulsed them. Emmet held his hand hesitantly before the first cage, as he had done in the past when he steeled himself to smash a spider. Then he flicked the catch of the cage door with his finger.

He moved to the next, gaining confidence as he unfastened lock after lock, each tiny door swinging free with a single metallic squeal. None of the cats showed any interest in stepping out, except for a cage of kittens who peeked their muffed heads through the hole. "Get back," Emmet said, pushing the gate gently closed. He imagined the dog crushing their gummy bones with one paw as she raced howling from room to room.

Emmet backed into the center of the room with the cage doors open before him. Every black oval pupil watched him. Every muscle tensed to strike. Emmet was afraid Joan would enter the room and discover the cowering cats. She would reject him. Emmet kissed the air so that his lips squeaked sharply, a sound he hoped an excited mouse might make if it scampered recklessly across the floor. He clapped merrily at the cages. With each slap of his hands, the cats' ears rumbled unhappily, as if a breeze blew along the wall, striking each head, one by one.

The first cage on the top tier was empty. Emmet had not noticed that the striped orange cat had slipped out the door after gliding from Joan's lap. It sauntered into the room to rub against Emmet's legs. The cat cocked its neck as it swaggered. It lifted each paw before deliberately setting it down, as if encumbered by heavy climbing boots instead of the pink, hairless pads that coasted over the floor.

Emmet was relieved that one of them did not shun him. He told himself that it was meant to be his. He squatted to stroke its brow. It shut its eyes contentedly and raised its sturdy head against Emmet's fingers, purring from deep inside, so that its vibrations seemed to emanate from every strand of hair. The cat's lips dripped wetly with joy.

"Are you mine?" Emmet asked, dropping lower to pick it up. He cradled it upside down, exposing the soft pouches under its arms and the traces of nipples dotting its belly. The cat moaned ecstatically. It opened its mouth to mew. The sound it made was cracked like a squeak: not a meow at all, but like a shoe striking polished wood. Its high, pinched voice was so unsuited to its manly stride that Emmet felt swept with love for the cat, as if together they had come to share the secret of its freakishness.

"Made a friend, huh?" Joan called from the doorway. Emmet felt oddly embarrassed, as if surprised in a sexual act. He shielded the cat modestly from view as he hugged it, turning his head to greet Joan.

"It's happy, I think," Emmet said. "It chose me out of all of them. Like it wanted me instead of the other way around."

"That's the way it's supposed to be. Let the animal decide. I don't know much about this one. I'd guess it's about four years old. Strolled in off the streets a few months ago and made itself to home. Must have lived somewhere before here, though, 'cause it's already been neutered. Notice the way it walks? Weird, huh? Like a meat packer or something. Makes you think about reincarnation and things like that, doesn't it? Like where we were before—or worse, where we're gonna end up. You know, if it's true, whatdya think the direction is? I mean, do cats and dogs come after humans? Or vice versa? I mean, does a bad dog become a human or a bad man become a dog? And then you add your bugs, your fish. Birds. The whole idea of a ranking somewhere screws me up."

"The cat could have an easy time in this life," Emmet said, rocking the animal in his arms. It slept as deeply as someone who first relaxes after a shock, a sleep of stubborn unconsciousness.

"Looks sort of innocent that way, don't it?" Joan said, moving closer. "But I imagine so do baby snakes, seen from the right angle."

"Can I have it?" Emmet whispered, careful not to awaken the cat.

"You seem okay," Joan said. "And the cat likes you. Whatdya do? Slip it a mickey or somethin' to get it to sleep like that?"

"No," Emmet said indignantly, raising his voice so that the cat stirred. "How could you think such a thing? Why, this cat—"

"Okay, okay. Calm down. I was only joking. Jeez, some of you guys are so sensitive. You can have the cat, but you've got to sign the form. Every once in a while on my days off I pay a surprise visit. Don't stay long, mind you. I just like to see the animals in their natural habitat. Make sure it's adjusting. There's some tricks you can do in anybody's living room, you know, like raisin' your hand suddenly over a dog's head to see if it ducks. That way you can tell if they've been beaten. Or else kick your leg out suddenly to see if they run for cover. You gotta do it with quick movements.

"Dogs don't talk. Dogs don't bruise, or not the way we do. Lot of 'em have black skin. So you've gotta sense their fear, kinda feel the abuse in the atmosphere, if you know what I mean. A dog will let you know when it's miserable in all sorts of ways, sort of like sign language. Now your cat can't. Or won't. They keep their problems to themselves. To tell you the truth, I'd be hard pressed to swear to the sufferings of a cat. You can make sure all the outer signs of a nice home are there—your bed, your bowl, your toys, your litter box. But outside of overt maiming, well, as I say, I couldn't swear; I couldn't swear."

"You needn't worry. Since I live alone, my animals get more attention than most people. It will have a nice life." Emmet kissed the slumbering cat on its nose. Its motor began to rumble warmly deep within its throat.

"Kinda like they're machines, don'tcha think?" Joan asked.

"It feels alive," Emmet said, stroking the cat. "To me, it's like a lie-detector test built into their bodies. They're happy or they're not, but they can't hide it, not even from themselves. They're helpless before their own bodies."

"Says you," Joan harrumphed. "Half the time they're turning it on because they want somethin'. Cats. People always think they've got the edge on animals, but I wouldn't bet on it. I'm telling you, a cat knows. I haven't figured it out, but they're on to somethin'. Anyway, sign here and you can have it. On a trial basis till we've checked things out. Not that I don't trust you, but we'd doubt the Pope if he tried to adopt a pet. It's my one hard and fast rule—don't trust nobody till you take 'em by surprise. I'll go get you a box."

Emmet shifted the cat to his shoulder as he leaned over to sign the form. The cat's purr intensified as it awakened. It snuggled against Emmet's neck. "That can't be fake," he thought as the cat dampened his skin with its bony mouth. With his free hand, Emmet signed the form awkwardly. Already his face itched from the fur wafting onto his skin.

Joan returned with a box lined with newspaper. "This will get you home. Can't carry a cat free on the streets. Somethin' scares it and next thing you know, its nails dig into your skin and it's off in a flash. Never see 'em again."

She checked Emmet's signature, then initialed under it with her pen. "That's it, I guess," she said. She seemed eager for Emmet to stay, but at a loss for reasons to delay him. He could not tell if she had doubts about releasing the cat or if she was lonely day after day in the shelter.

Emmet hooked the box under one arm. The cat slid to one side in a heap, unbalancing the center. "Keep in touch," he said confidently as he righted the box, hoping Joan might forgo her visit if she saw he was unconcerned.

Joan carried Pigeon to the door. "You know where to find me if you change your mind about a dog. Fix you up good," she called, shaking one of Pigeon's paws in her hand as if the dog were waving good-bye.

Emmet thanked her. He sighed with relief as he stepped out of sight. Everything he did lately, even the simplest act, seemed as complex and intricate as a carefully considered crime.

"There is no reason I cannot adopt a cat," he assured himself as he walked home. "I haven't done anything." But he worried as if he had.

As he hurried, he gripped the box closer to his side. "I have tried to fix it, I have tried to fix it," he thought, hoping the cat would silence the dog. He reassured himself that for once he had acted early to prevent more trouble from ruining their lives. He imagined all the good that this first step would breed. He hoped, at least, that the dog's silence would cut his fear in half.

When Emmet reached the corner near his home, he heard his dog wail with loneliness. "This has got to work," he thought as he raced up the stairs. The cat squeaked as he set the box down roughly while he unlatched the door. Its claws scratched futilely on the slick cardboard as it grabbed for a hold. He calmed himself as he went inside, praying that night would be the last time he would ever hear the dog howl.

"Yes. Yes. Yes. I'm home," Emmet said as the dog snorted with delight.

"You howled," he admonished her, but in her joy at seeing him, she was impervious to any reprimand. Her teeth gleamed rapturously from her lips.

"Guess what's in here?" he asked proudly, tapping the box. He set it on the floor, ordering the dog to sit. She trembled with anticipation, barking softly as she often did when tempted with a treat. "Stay," Emmet ordered, holding her at bay with one hand held over her eyes while he flipped open the lid of the box.

The cat stuck its head out sleepily. It surveyed the room until it saw the dog, quaking with excitement a few feet away. Aghast, the cat spit meanly. It leapt from the box: moaning in circles, swiping its tail menacingly, like a provoked tiger.

"Woof," the dog whispered once, almost teasingly. The cat shot into the air, flying across the room as it had done in the shelter, traversing so much space that it landed in the hallway, beyond Emmet's reach.

Emmet went in search of the cat, certain he would find it waiting angrily in the next room. It was not in the hallway, nor in the dining room, nor in the kitchen beyond. He pursed his lips and squeaked with that mousy kiss as he hunted. As he realized the cat was gone, the sound became insistent, even pleading. "It must be here," he cried as he looked under every piece of furniture, in every closet, in every cupboard, in every room.

The cat had vanished.

Emmet felt a breeze from a window in the dining room opened just wide enough for a cat to slip through. The window had no screen. "It couldn't have . . ." he thought as checked the pavement below for the cat's corpse.

The phone rang loudly. "It's the shelter," he thought, stilled with terror. "Joan forgot to tell me something." He knew that if he answered the phone, he could not disguise the guilt in his voice. She would suspect Emmet of harming the cat, as if he were so perverted he was not able to contain himself for even an hour after he brought it home. If he did not answer, Joan might believe he had abandoned the cat to the dog already. She would know how irresponsible he was. She might wait outside on her next day off, clocking the time Emmet left and counting the hours until he returned.

"I've made it worse already," he cried to himself as he tore through the apartment. "Now Joan will also be after me," he thought, seeing his signature scrawled upon the form, as incriminating as if he had affixed his name to a confession.

"CAT. . . . CAT. . . . PLEASE. . . . CAT. . . . COME," Emmet shrieked hysterically at the walls. He locked the dog in the house and ran into the street, calling softly into the shrubbery bordering his yard in case the cat had jumped from the window unharmed.

He could hear the dog howl madly from inside the apartment. He had never realized how sustained her wails were, how they rose to a crescendo, then dropped to a whimper so that it seemed for an instant as if they might cease. But they gathered force again, each wave sounding more completely unhinged.

"I will kill the dog," he thought for a moment as he listened. He would hold her down on the living room floor, and crush her throat with his hands.

"Her eyes would haunt me always," he thought, imagining the betrayal and fright in her face when she learned the person she loved most wanted her dead. The memory would plague his life.

A rat dashed from behind a bush, exciting Emmet for a moment that he had found the cat. Nothing else moved. He worried that his rustling in the bushes would summon his neighbors.

"It is worse to have the dog howl this late," he decided, "than to lie to Joan about the cat." He would tell her he was mugged for the box on the way home. He would make himself cry. He would convince her to escort him safely home with another cat. "I will make her believe me, I will make her believe me," he chanted as he returned to the apartment.

The dog was so undone by his leaving that she did not hear him enter. Inside the apartment, her howls were unbearably loud, like screams of torture. "Come here, come here," Emmet cried, running into the living room to embrace her.

The cat sat poised to strike on the sofa. It no longer hissed.

"It must have hidden in a closet," he thought as he quieted the dog. She ran in circles from Emmet to the cat, nudging each with her snout while she danced.

The cat did not wince when she approached. It stared territorially. "I am home," it seemed to announce from the couch.

Now the three of them would live there.

The dog leapt into Emmet's lap. He heard the cat's motor warming from the floor below. Its eyes squinted shut. It grinned at him as it moved closer. Individual strands of hair came unloose as the cat brushed Emmet's jeans, swimming in the air, alight, as if they burned with radioactivity.

CHAPTER
ELEVEN

Emmet left the light burning in his bedroom when he stole outside at midnight with his dog. He still could not risk leaving her alone. The cat had made no difference. Even when the dog curled peacefully on the corner of the sofa, her eyes remained vigilant through closed lids. If Emmet reached for his coat or even tucked in the tail of his shirt, she raced for the door, scratching so eagerly that wood chips zinged around their ankles. Then she would cough, as if clearing her throat to unloose a torrent of screams.

Emmet wound the dog's leash around his fingers as he checked his window from the street. He considered entering the house to switch off the light. He could not decide if darkness would make his apartment seem more inhabited. Lately he had learned new things about his neighborhood, things that made him certain he had to increase his guard.

The week before, Emmet had opened his door to find his neighbor Mrs. Dew handing out fliers on the street. From ten feet away, he could read the headline, EXTERMINATE VERMIN, printed in block letters at the top of the form.

Emmet had been considering ways to upgrade his image on the block. He had decided to beguile his neighbors with friendliness, but they had proved elusive, rushing past whenever they saw him on the street. But occupied with her fliers, Mrs. Dew was a stationary object, so he approached her cheerfully.

"Cockroaches?" he asked, indicating the paper in her hand.

"You could say that," Mrs. Dew replied dismissively. She passed a flier to an elderly couple who greeted her by name.

Emmet hovered by her side, even as she turned her back to him. "They're indestructible," he said in her ear. "As ancient as dinosaurs. They're so old, part of me thinks we should treat them with reverence. After all, they've been on the earth longer than we have. You'd think that would entitle them at least to squatters' rights." He choked back a little laugh.

"Marjorie!" Mrs. Dew called, hailing a woman in a flowered blue housecoat. As the women conversed, Emmet tried to place himself at the perfect distance so that he would not appear to eavesdrop, but not so far that Mrs. Dew could elude him. Every few words, one of the women raised her head, as if they hoped that Emmet would be gone when they looked up.

"This is my chance to win them over," he thought as he held his ground. "If I give in now, I'll never find the nerve to try again." He bent over and picked two weeds that grew from a crack in the sidewalk. In case Mrs. Dew noticed, he dusted the dirt from the cement with his hand and wiped it carefully on the inside of his shirt.

When Marjorie moved away, Emmet tugged at Mrs. Dew's sleeve. "I've read they'll be the only living beings to survive a nuclear attack. I mean, we'll fry in the heat, but cockroaches have internal organs that can withstand anything, even an atomic blast. But don't despair. I know the perfect way to kill them. Radiation might fail us, but dust your counters with boric acid and bingo— their bodies burst from the inside out. It doesn't even leave a mess. I mean, they don't explode or anything. They just rot away."

"What are you talking about?" Mrs. Dew asked.

"I couldn't help but see the headline of your flier. About vermin." Emmet peered nearer to Mrs. Dew's hand, but she flapped the papers against her bosom. He grinned into her eyes, hopefully. "If I can persuade her to give me a flier, then I know my life will change," he wagered, as if he were plucking the leaves from a four-leaf clover.

"It's people I'm worried about, not bugs. I don't have insects in my house."

"Oh, neither do I," Emmet lied, picturing the colonies of cockroaches nesting in the stacks of newspapers in his empty room. "It's something I've read about in magazines. I keep a file of solutions so that I will have something to refer to if I encounter trouble at any point. I believe it is important to be prepared, don't you?"

"That's why I'm sweating out here in the sun," Mrs. Dew said, studying the sheets in her hand. She sized Emmet up for the tenth time, her eyes lingering on the gray T-shirt that covered his body like a sleeping gown. "I guess we can tell you, too," she said, reluctantly, as she passed him a flier. "There's a meeting next week. To get the people in 202 out before it's too late. They're up to no good." She mimed injecting a hypodermic needle into her arm. She even tied off her veins with an invisible piece of rubber. Then she rubbed her fingers together as if to say "money."

"But how do we know for certain what those people are up to?" Emmet asked eagerly.

"Some of us know everything that passes in front of our windows." She paused meaningfully, as if she addressed a secret known only between them.

Emmet blushed brightly. He felt guilty whenever someone was blamed for a misdeed, even a stranger accused in his proximity. When a police car drove past him with its siren blaring, he held his breath until it was gone. Long ago he had memorized the address of every house on his block, but in case Mrs. Dew associated him with the trouble, he asked innocently, "Which house is 202?"

"The gray one catty-cornered to yours. I'd say you walk past it ten times a day. With your big dog. At all hours, I might add, when decent people are sleeping."

"I'm cursed with insomnia," Emmet said. "Those who suffer from it believe it to be as bad as any disease." Then he added more boldly, "If you know my schedule, I imagine you must suffer from it, too."

"Sometimes," Mrs. Dew said, regarding the ground. "But people talk. You learn things."

"But sometimes those things might not be true," Emmet said, pleadingly. "Sometimes those things are mistakes."

"Yeah," Mrs. Dew grunted. "Maybe."

"Well, I'll see you at the meeting," Emmet said. "With bells on, as my mother used to say."

Mrs. Dew snorted and turned her back, passing a flier to a woman who pushed a baby stroller tied with pink balloons.

Emmet rushed back into the house, elated that Mrs. Dew had included him. "I've won," he rejoiced. He imagined dinner parties with all of his neighbors. He imagined them soliciting his advice about their wayward children. He considered offering his services for baby-sitting to earn extra money.

For days afterwards, he had read the flier until he could recite it from memory. He kept the building across the street under obsessive scrutiny, as if it were his job. He wanted to be able to document everything that happened in the house so that he could impress his neighbors at the meeting. Then they might welcome him into their community.

Every morning, the blinds in 202 were drawn. The house seemed asleep. But late at night, groups of people Emmet had never seen before gathered on the stoop. The woman who lived there let them inside one by one and ushered them out minutes later with a smile. She always appeared perfectly composed. The only suspicious thing about her were the long sleeves she wore even on the most humid days. Emmet imagined her arms scarred and bruised from needle marks. He had never spoken to her, but waved amiably from a distance, hoping that if Mrs. Dew succeeded in evicting her, the woman would not believe that Emmet had been part of the plan.

But that evening just as he prepared to leave the house with his dog, the woman from 202 had knocked on his door.

"Hello," she said when he stuck his head out. "I'm Anita from across the street. I was wondering if you could loan me a hammer?"

Emmet hesitated. It seemed so bold of her to borrow a hammer from a stranger. She must have known someone else on the block of whom she could ask a favor, unless all of them shunned her.

The dog pushed through the door to welcome her. When Emmet reached out to grab her collar, the woman sidestepped him into the living room. She turned a full circle. "Such a large apartment," she said appreciatively.

"I need plenty of space for my children's visits," Emmet told her. If she was dangerous, he hoped that she would believe his house was often full of innocent children. She regarded his ringless hands.

"I'm divorced," Emmet said. "But I see the children as much as possible. I have three."

The woman moved closer to Emmet's face, as if searching the skin under his eyes for signs of age. He stepped back. "You must have been very young," she said.

"Too young . . ." Emmet said meaningfully. Then he added, "But when you're in love . . ."

He pointed to a photograph of his godchildren, as if to introduce her.

"Handsome boys. So blond," she said.

Emmet touched his brown hair self-consciously. "I guess I don't have dominant genes," he said, faking a laugh.

The woman walked around the room, running a finger over the shelf by his stereo equipment as if checking for dust. "How many rooms?" she asked.

"Only three," Emmet said. The doors to the rest of the apartment were closed. "Those are mostly closets. So good for hiding toys. Let me get you a hammer."

When he returned, he found Anita examining the photographs on his walls. She pointed to a picture of Susan, his friend from college. "Is this your wife?" she asked.

"My wife is dead," Emmet said. As the woman opened her mouth to speak, he added, "Oh, I mean she is dead to me. There aren't any pictures of her. There's never a point in dredging up the past. What's dead is dead, I always say."

"Quite," Anita said vaguely as she read the labels of his record collection.

Emmet held out the hammer. "Here, keep it. I have several."

"How kind," she said. "Sorry to have bothered you, but I thought it made a good excuse to introduce myself. I mean, once I realized our hammer was missing."

"See it as a present," Emmet said. "A kind of reverse housewarming. Maybe I'll borrow something from you someday."

"Maybe," she said. "It doesn't look like you need very much."

Emmet hovered close behind as she surveyed his belongings. She had an attitude as if she were perusing objects in a store. Every time Emmet stepped in front to block her view, she tilted her head a few degrees in another direction. They performed this halting dance for several beats until he said, "Shall we go out together? It's time to walk my dog."

"I've seen you out very late at night," Anita said. "Often I can't sleep so I sit in front of the window. You're gone for hours at a time."

Emmet blanched that yet another person had followed his movements. "Are you sure it's me?" he asked. "I'm really always home. I like to be available when my children call, so that they worry less about their broken home."

"Maybe not, but your dog is so huge. Could I be mistaken?" She seemed genuinely confused.

"Oh, everyone makes that mistake," Emmet said. "She has a brother. He lives around the corner. A student at the university owns him." He came to a full stop after each sentence. Before he continued, he studied the woman's face for signs of belief. Her expression did not change as he piled lie upon lie.

She patted the dog's nose with the distinctive white patch that spread under her eyes like a half-mask. It gave his dog a slightly malevolent look when she was in repose. "They're twins, actually," Emmet said.

"Twins?" Anita sat down comfortably in an overstuffed chair, crossing her legs. The cat wandered into the room after a nap. It leapt into the woman's lap, purring, as if they were acquainted. Anita stroked it absently.

Emmet winced. The longer she stayed, the more engaged she became. He struggled to continue speaking while other thoughts barraged his brain. "Yes," he said, as if hearing himself from a distance. "What do you call them? Fraternal? Paternal? I can't ever remember."

As he spoke, he tried to remember the lies he had told since she arrived. He felt dizzy from the pressure of sustaining his story. "Did I tell her how many rooms I had? Did I tell her what I did for a living? Have I said my name? Did I say how many children I had? Did I tell her where they lived?"

"California," he muttered. For a moment, he wasn't sure if he had spoken the word aloud.

"What?" she asked, clearly startled.

"California," Emmet said. "It's her brother's name. Funny thing to call a dog, don't you think? But then my dog's name is Pigeon, so who am I to talk? The boy treats her well—I m-m-mean *him*. The other dog, that is. Gives him plenty of exercise, as you've seen."

Anita tapped the hammer against her palm. "Funny indeed," she said.

Emmet tried to divert attention from himself. "What kind of work do you do?"

"What does it matter?" she asked passionately. "Everyone these days wants to know what you do for a living. They don't care what kind of person you are. It's like they need to see your bank balance before they'll even speak to you. Like all the old crones on this block. Always trying to get the scoop. They disgust me."

"Sorry," Emmet said, ashamed. "I don't like people prying into my life, either."

"No, I'm sorry. I'm the one who barged into your house. We're in exports, actually. We've built the business up from nothing. Would you like to meet my husband? Are you free for dinner Tuesday?"

Emmet sat on the arm of the sofa, only to rise a second later to walk to the window. He perched on the edge of the shelf by his stereo, his legs knocking tremulously against the cabinet. He stood again. He sat. Anita remained immobile, except for her left hand, which stroked the cat. "Maybe Mrs. Dew is mistaken," he thought. "Maybe Anita is nothing but the victim of strangers' obsessions." He tried to read something in her eyes, some sign that would give her secrets away.

"Tuesday?" Emmet asked uncertainly. He wondered what it would be like to become friends with Anita. He no longer saw anyone but his brother. But even if he knew her better, he would never relax his lies and confess to what his life had become. "I cannot risk it," he decided.

Anita rose from the chair, holding the cat in her arms. "Or Wednesday. Any day next week, actually. We're almost always free. With a little warning."

"My children are visiting Tuesday. We spend so little time together, I hate to go out."

"You could bring them along."

"Oh, I couldn't. They're very picky eaters. They could drive a hostess crazy."

"I'll stop over again, then," Anita said. "Once your children leave."

When Emmet reached for her hand to say good-bye, his fingers closed around the steel head of the hammer. He shook it like a claw.

He peeked through the curtains as Anita crossed the street. It took her several minutes to unfasten all the locks on her front door. A man in a motorcycle jacket accosted her on the steps. He whispered something into her ear. Emmet saw her respond. The man shook his head. She spoke again. The man nodded, then followed her into the house. Emmet waited until the door shut behind them before he hooked the dog's leash.

"Quick," he said. "Before she has time to look."

As he scurried down the steps, the bare light burning in his bedroom froze him. He wished he had bought one of those switches that turned lights on and off automatically so that it seemed like a family moved happily from room to room even inside a deserted house. But it was too late. The dog tugged at his hand, eager to leave. Emmet gazed hopelessly at the house. "Light or dark?" he thought. He could not decide. He left it as it was.

As they headed for the river, Emmet passed his neighbors idling on their stoops to breathe some air in the heat. His and the dog's shadows stretched gigantically, yards ahead, as if they chased two thin figures no matter where they moved. Whenever someone approached in back of them, their shadows overtook Emmet's own. Exposed on the sidewalk, he felt as if he were being pursued both in front and from behind. He urged the dog to go faster. She leapt gleefully in the air, snatching her leash with her mouth as if they played a game.

"Hurry," Emmet hissed, no longer stopping at traffic lights, but dashing into the streets so that cars squealed to a stop. They headed for the pier, flying so fast past the prostitutes and drug dealers working by the river that his shirt grew heavy with sweat.

When they reached the water, Emmet grasped the chain-link fence with his fingers. He dropped the leash. The dog threw herself upon the fence, barking, then darted between the cars, pouncing onto their doors, panting against their windows. Each time Emmet called to her, she crouched on the ground until he came within a foot; then she tore off into the darkness. All around him, he could hear chunks of floating debris plunk against the foundation. There was laughter somewhere in the shadows, sometimes a splash.

Emmet chased the dog onto the pier. "Come back," he called. She barreled away until she vanished from sight. Emmet made himself walk out after her. As he gingerly took each step, planks were missing in so many places that water splashed lazily upward at his feet. Even halfway across, he felt as if he were coming dangerously close to its edge. A fog blew in from the river. Figures appeared in and out of the clouds like people engulfed by a fire. Some called out to him with a gesture or a word, beckoning him into the mist. The dog jumped in and out of the fog, her collar tinkling gently as wind chimes.

Emmet heard a yelp; then the dog shot out of the clouds, her tail curved under her hind legs.

"Sorry now?" he asked as he hugged her, shivering, against his chest. He ran with his eyes closed, dragging her behind, holding his breath as he leapt between the rotted planks, praying that they did not stumble blindly into the water below.

Emmet rested on the cement wall at the entrance to the pier. Sirens flashed along the highway. Car after car drove into the parking area, cruising the fence slowly, so that Emmet was illuminated, as if police searchlights held him pinned against the fence.

"Where do we go? Home?" he wondered for the hundredth

time, dreading being exposed back on the street; dreading even more the silence awaiting him at home.

How dead he felt from the tug and split and blindness that made him heave with fear. As he patted the dog, Emmet saw himself a decade before, during the years he took drugs, sneaking down the hallways of his grandmother's house to hide in his room. He remembered the creeping feeling as the chemicals tickling his body began to consume him. As each minute ticked slower than an hour, he would become convinced that he had swallowed the wrong quantity of drugs, that his muscles would forever after be beset by the rubbery paralysis that held him fast against the chair.

He would grow afraid that his grandmother would discover him. He would pace his bedroom, repeating that he would live that way forever. As dawn came, he could try to assure himself that he could learn to make it tolerable. Until he passed out, he would practice speaking normally even as his voice reverberated in his head like a conversation heard under water. But always he had finally slept; always the drug had finally left him. Now it was different. He lived as if he had awoken in the middle of those nights and neither sleep nor time could save him.

Emmet dialed Jonathan's number from the pay telephone on the pier. He listened to his easy voice on the answering machine. He considered leaving a message that told his brother the truth of how he lived. In his head, he wrote a list of words that might express the exhaustion he felt: *Desolate. Disembodied. Scared to death.* As he recited them, each word sounded vacant and flat. He could imagine no way to describe to someone who felt his own presence vividly how his body emptied and faded even as he stood there.

"I cannot explain, no matter what I say," he thought as he pronounced the words again. They sounded like phrases from an untranslatable language. Anything he knew was useless to describe a life that went on as his did, unceasing.

"I have to learn to live with this," he decided, just as he had those evenings when the drugs promised to fix him forever. He hung up the telephone. He flicked the dog's leash. He headed home. It was only four hours until dawn. He would wait it out.

As he walked, he remembered how he had lain awake after his grandmother had told him the story of the shipwreck in South Africa. In his mind, he had watched the boat break apart until there was nothing left but the ocean and the unreachable shore. Emmet wondered how long his grandfather had forced himself to swim after realizing no hope would come.

How tempting it must have been to slip under the water's surface and let go when every muscle fought the command. But he imagined some instinct beyond desire, some insurmountable buoyancy pushing the body back, refusing to let it sink. In his mind, Emmet saw a head break the surface, desperate to rest, before it sunk down again, only to bob up and down and up, interminably, until it was freed at last to float dead upon the waves.

"I am him, run aground," Emmet thought as he imagined his grandfather lost alone in that blue sea, willing it all to be over.

CHAPTER
TWELVE

When Emmet reached his block, he paused at the hedge on the corner to see if the street was clear. Every house was dark, except for an upstairs light in 202. Ducking his head forward as if pelted by a driving rain, he hurried to his stoop.

As he turned the key in the lock, Emmet heard the comforting purr of the air conditioner. Through the glass panels he saw the door from the hall closet lying flat against the floor, as if a wind had ripped it free.

"Could I have missed a storm from only blocks away?" he wondered. He unlatched the door. He heard every click of the bolt revolve in the lock. He kept thinking, "Storm. There must have been a storm," as he made his way inside.

Emmet unleashed the dog. He patted her snout as he always did when they returned. "So, did you like your walk?" he asked, which was part of their ritual, as if it were for her benefit that they spent all those hours each night outside.

Emmet stepped over the fallen door on his way into the living room, blithely, as if it had always been there. As he entered the darkened hallway, the dog's paws went *tick tick tick* against the wood. She ran ahead into the kitchen for water, skidding across the floor until she thumped against the door frame.

Emmet moved calmly. He switched on the overhead light. Its starkness dazed him, so accustomed had he grown to the glassy light of the streets. For an instant, he beheld the white walls, starkly illuminated, stripped of every decoration but the nails upon which his photographs and paintings had hung.

He shut his eyes. He counted a series of numbers in his head. He followed his breath as it entered his lungs from his diaphragm, then blew it out from his mouth, as if it were smoke.

He thought, "I will keep counting no matter what I do; I will not stop for anything," as if it might keep his brain focused apart from the faintness that overtook him. "One . . . two . . ." he said. He opened his eyes on "three" but did not stop. "Four . . . five . . ." he continued as he squinted closed. In his mind he saw a coat of dust forming a perfect rectangle where the couch had been, like a chalk mark outlining a body.

He turned himself around blindly a few degrees, spinning higher and higher numbers, until he knew he faced the shelves by the front windows. "Thirty-six . . . thirty seven . . ." he continued deliberately. He peeked through slit lids. "Forty-one . . . forty-two . . ." he counted as he saw the shelves where his stereo and books had been, empty now except for extension cords and wires.

"What was over there? . . . What was there?" he tried to remember as he spun on his heels to take in every corner. The light dazed him like a strobe. He swayed with guilt. "I must have left the door unlocked; I must have left the door unlocked," he thought in a frenzy. "I have to break a window. It has to look like they forced their way in so that no one blames me," until he remembered he lived alone and everything stolen was his own.

The dog brushed against him. "Police," Emmet said to her. She wagged her tail.

She accompanied him throughout the apartment as he took stock. The mattress was the only piece of furniture left in his bedroom. The headboard, even the sheets were gone. Black, blue, and red pins were scattered on the floor underneath where his maps had hung. The bulletin board had been torn from the wall. Chunks of cork dotted the plaster, brown as meat.

When they reached the kitchen, the dog looked hopefully from Emmet to the sink. Every counter was bare. Even the freshly washed dishes set out to dry had been taken from the sideboard. In the corner where the animals' bowls had been, only a few clumps of dried food were caked to the floor. Emmet opened the refrigerator. A box of baking soda sat under the light, swollen with moisture, a cluster of ice dusting its sides.

There was no sign of the cat. Emmet searched every room, throwing open closet doors and cupboards. He found a postcard of the town in California where his grandmother had lived jammed in a crack in a drawer. One old running shoe, missing its laces, lay in a corner of his bedroom closet. All his other clothes, including the boots where he stashed his money, were gone. The mattress was in his bedroom. The refrigerator was in the kitchen. The picnic table was in the dining room. In the empty bedroom, the stacks of newspapers remained undisturbed, except for the sports section from the previous day, spread open as if someone had paused to check a score. Everything else was gone.

Emmet stopped at the head of the basement stairs. "I'm home," he called, hoping the cat would slink up to rub against his legs. His voice echoed at him emptily, as if it were bouncing off the walls of a cave.

Emmet was afraid to descend to the basement alone. What if the robbers had fled down the stairs when he returned home? What if they lurked there still? Maybe they held the cat prisoner, its neck gripped in their hands.

"Police," Emmet said again. He walked to the kitchen wall to reach for the telephone, but only the metal plate remained screwed to the plaster. He had no way to call them. The metal cord to the pay telephone on the corner had been cleanly snipped off by vandals months before and never replaced.

"What do we do?" he said to the dog. They stood together on the porch. Until he was certain what had happened, he did not want his brother to know. He saw a lamp burning in the bedroom of the house next door. An elderly woman lived there who was dying of cancer. Emmet could not bring himself to disturb her in case he woke her from a painless sleep.

He looked up the block. Every other house was dark except for the top floor of 202. Anita must be working late inside. Emmet grew weak when he considered the millions of possible suspects everywhere in the city. He knew strangers could have robbed him or his landlord might have taken his revenge or Mrs. Dew's vigilantes could have organized a sneak attack or Anita could have conspired against him. But he also knew he needed help, and Anita was the nearest person he could ask. If he rang the bell of strangers, they might think he was a criminal tricking his way inside. He locked the dog in the house and made his way across the street.

Anita answered the door so quickly that she must have waited just inside.

Emmet's shirt was stained with sweat. He covered it with his hands self-consciously.

"Oh, hullo," she said, surprised, but not unkindly. She wore the same dress Emmet had seen earlier.

"I need a phone," he said.

"Phone?" Anita asked. "Like the hammer?"

"Yes. No," Emmet said. "Everything is gone."

"You mean . . . But how is that possible? Why, I was there only hours ago."

"Everything," Emmet said again.

She ushered him into the living room. All the other doors were shut. A huge red Japanese screen blocked an entire wall. Mists and waterfalls fell from the mountains. Emmet could see boxes stacked behind it in disarray.

"We'll never have the room to unpack everything," she said. "It's one of the drawbacks of living in the city. Never enough space. But I guess it's tactless of me to say that now."

"All I have is space," Emmet said as he reached for the telephone to dial 911.

"I've been robbed," he said to the woman who answered from the other end.

Maybe because of an uncertain quake in his voice, she trusted immediately that he was not a crank. "Where do you live, honey?" she asked. "What's your name?"

Emmet told her everything she needed to know.

"Some city isn't it, sugar?" she clucked affectionately. "Well, better days are ahead," she said before she hung up.

"Is there anything I can do?" Anita asked.

"I have to meet the police," Emmet said.

"I'm coming with you," Anita said, grabbing her coat from atop a tightly taped box.

Emmet hesitated, weighing his suspicions. "Could she be guilty?" he wondered again, trying to discern some unease in her manner. He saw nothing. For the moment, maybe forever, he knew he could never prove who robbed him. He did not want to return to his ruined home alone. "Thanks," he told her.

Anita and Emmet waited on his steps for the police. The car cruised soundlessly up the block; even its headlights were extinguished. Emmet flagged them down. "It's me," he called from the stairs. "I'm the one."

Two officers met him, each one tapping a huge yellow flashlight against his pants. "I left the door unlocked," Emmet confessed before they could speak. "I must have. It's my fault. Everything is gone."

He escorted them from room to room. "Phew," one of the officers said from time to time.

"That room's always empty," Emmet said as they stopped outside the newspaper room. "No need to look inside. I've saved some papers to cover the floor when I paint."

"Are you an artist?" an officer asked.

"Of a sort," Emmet replied.

The policemen peered down the basement stairs. When they shone their flashlights into the darkness, cobwebs fluttered in the light.

"My cat is gone," Emmet said.

"What's its name?" one of them asked.

"It didn't have one. I couldn't decide. I haven't had it very long. It really was here just to keep my dog company. She howls. Well, not enough to be a public nuisance. Just to say she's lonely. I don't like the cat, even. But don't get me wrong, it gets a loving home."

"Take it easy, buddy," the policeman said. "So what else besides the cat?"

Emmet tried to picture the things that had been in his living room. "Stereo," he said. "Television. Clock. Telephone. Carpets. A maroon velvet sofa. Three glass bottles with silver tops. Three hundred record albums. Two paintings in gold frames on that wall. Photographs. Chairs. Tables. A desk. Magazine rack."

"Don't forget that figurine," Anita said. "The brass one of the beetle."

"Right. My brother gave it to me. And a crystal vase. With flowers."

"And the coffee table," Anita said. "And that silver lamp. There was a silver lamp, wasn't there? In that corner?"

"Yes," Emmet said. "By the bookcase. Cameras. Dishes." He looked up. "Why would anybody steal dishes?"

"A dollar is a dollar on the street," the policeman said.

"All my clothes," Emmet continued. "Thirteen pairs of sneakers. The dog's dish. The cat's dish. The rubber mat underneath them."

"Can I borrow some paper?" the policeman asked sheepishly. "The call came over the air as a domestic and we thought we wouldn't need anything."

"Sorry," Emmet said. He pointed to the wall where the desk had been. "I haven't got any."

"Use this," Anita said, pulling a crumpled receipt from her pocket.

"Computer," Emmet said, moving his attention to his bedroom. "Map. Printer. Table. Desk. Chair. Alarm clock. Chest of drawers. Cabinet. Tape recorder."

"There was a calculator," Anita said. "I mean, everyone has one for their checkbook, don't they?"

"Yes," Emmet said. "And a mirror in a wooden frame. And paper. Pencils. Stamps. Envelopes. Erasers. Paper clips. Socks."

"Look, there's no hurry," the policeman said. "Take some time. Relax. You can mail a list in later."

"But I might not remember later," Emmet said. Already the rooms were beginning to seem established. The whiteness of the walls was settling in.

"Yes you will," the policeman said. "Just hypnotize yourself. Everyone remembers better once the shock has worn off. Believe me, guy, you're in shock. That's why you're acting sort of weird. Nothing personal, but I see these things all the time. Hell, we're all human. For now we've got to get the print man over here. Have you touched anything?"

"Yes," Emmet said. "For the cat. I opened all the doors."

"Does that basement have a light?"

"There's a switch on the wall," Emmet said. "But I've never been down there. There could be almost anything living in those rooms. I think my landlord stores his tools in there somewhere."

Emmet followed the policemen to the basement. As they made their way through the cement rooms, Emmet crouched on the last step. He clapped his hands for the cat.

The policemen flashed their lights on the door to the alley. A hole splintered through the panels as if someone had whacked it with an axe.

"Maybe you left the door unlocked," the policeman said. "But they made their own entrance."

Emmet probed the hole with his hand. The panel was only a fraction of an inch thick. He could not believe its flimsiness. The thieves could have pressed a finger through it.

"Is this the place?" someone called from upstairs. A stocky man in a dark suit waited in the hallway. "Fingerprints," he said, indicating a black leather bag.

The man dipped a brush in a bottle of pale gray dust. He walked to the sill near the front window and dabbed the bristles against the wood. The ridged outlines of prints materialized behind every stroke. As he painted the apartment, fingerprints climbed up the bookcases, over the blue enamel counter on the kitchen, on the doors, on the light switches. Everywhere, on every surface, thumb prints, tips, whole palms of everyone who had ever been in the apartment were revealed to them.

"Well, I'd better be off," Anita said. "If you don't need me anymore."

"You don't live here, lady?" the policeman said.

"Heavens no. I'm a neighbor. I was here earlier this afternoon, visiting," she said eyeing the shelf where the stereo had been. The man dusted along its edge. A line of prints of an index finger traveled along the shelf like track marks. He pressed a piece of tape over them, then held it up to the light. "Some good ones here," he said.

"Come over and sleep if you want, later," Anita said to Emmet.

"You can have the living room sofa. Until you get settled, what's mine is yours. Just knock."

"That about does it," the fingerprint man said, snapping shut his case. He wiped his hands on his suit, leaving smudges of dust on his pants.

"Don't worry about your cat," the policeman said. "Maybe it ran out the door. It'll turn up. It's hard to get rid of a cat. Shit, once my son's cat jumped out of the car on vacation. It turned up three weeks later at our apartment. Pissed as hell, but alive. They don't ever give up. I hate the fuckin' things personally. Cats."

Emmet followed the policemen outside. Their uniforms smelled of tobacco and cleaning fluids. He did not want them to abandon him. "Will I get anything back?" he asked.

"No way, buddy. Safe bet it's already on the other side of the river. By tomorrow night, your dishes will be serving somebody else's dinner, good as new. You got receipts? You can claim it on your taxes."

"Nothing," Emmet said. "Even the drawers are gone. I can't prove I ever owned anything."

"You better not lie, either. You could get audited," the policeman said. "Well, tough break, kid. Think of it this way—if you were asleep, you might be dead. Somebody comes through your door with an axe, they don't leave any witnesses."

After the police had gone, Emmet stood in the living room with the dog at his feet. She shadowed every move. He wiped one of the dusted prints with his shirttail. It remained indelibly on the wood. "Will they be there always?" he wondered. "To remind me?"

He imagined the thieves fingering his belongings. They knew everything about him, but he might never learn their identity. They knew his name. They had his bank statements, notebooks, scrapbooks, letters, the tapes of his telephone conversations. From his missing photographs, they even knew what he looked like. A stranger might pass him on the street one day and wink, having read each scrap of paper, having listened to his tapes.

"Oh my God, just think what they know!" he thought, growing cold with shame. He assured himself that somewhere on a government computer, a typist probably knew as much about him. But the thieves knew other things, the things that never left his house. It was like living inside of his mind.

He made a list of the things in his drawers that embarrassed him. Had they laughed as they rifled through them, calling out to one another, "Hey, look at this!" when they discovered something buried? Were they afraid? Did they have a plan? Emmet admired their nerve, how a thief could break so boldly through a door on a public street. Did one of them wait by the entrance to club him if he returned home before they were finished? Had they stolen the cat, or had they left it dead somewhere inside the house?

"Cat," Emmet called.

He tore from room to room, ripping open drawers, throwing open closets one last time. Graphite rubbed off on his palm from every smooth surface he touched, staining his skin. Every line stood out on his hand, as if he had been booked for a crime.

"Cat," he called.

In the kitchen, he flung open the refrigerator again, this time pulling out the crisper drawers. He even flipped open the small door that said Butter.

With his head inside the refrigerator, Emmet reached above him and opened the freezer. He heard a hiss, loud as pressurized steam, as claws dug into the skin of his back. He stumbled from the pain. He saw an orange flash as the cat soared through the air, landing on its front feet in the dining room. It backed into a corner, rising on its rear legs, its paws striking the air, as if it were boxing. Saliva dripped from its fangs; its tiny pink tongue was thick with white bubbles.

Emmet moved towards it. "Sorry," he said. He bent to stroke its head. The cat screamed, as if it had been kicked, catching Emmet's nose with its left paw, then striking against his eye with the other. It flailed against him, tearing deeply with its claws; left, then right, then left again, even as Emmet buried his face in his hands.

"Stop, please stop," he said. The dog barked from the other side of the room, hunching forward, but keeping her distance.

With one last thrust against Emmet's knuckle, the cat thumped to the other side of the room, rumbling with loathing.

Emmet wiped his face with his shirt. Thin lines of blood, as long as each scratch, dotted the material. He saw the walls, empty except for the nails. The extension cord lay on the shelf. The police had taken the list. "Concentrate," he said aloud, angrily, as he tried to reconstruct how the apartment had been earlier in the day and all those years before, perfect with his possessions. In his mind he retraced the information he had given the police, but he could remember only a few items. "Stereo," he thought. "Books." He went blank. "Stereo," he began again. He felt unsure, as when he had recited the newspaper reports to Jonathan on the telephone from memory, faltering as the details grew too fantastic to be believed.

To ground himself, he wrote an imaginary list of the essential things he required. "Clothes," he traced with his finger on his skin. "Telephone. A plate. A spoon. A bowl. A pillow for my bed. A cat's dish. A dog's dish." He promised himself that he would buy the items the next day. He would make himself go to the bank, since now all the money in his shoes was gone.

Emmet lay across his mattress with his eyes closed. Even with the light on, when he shut his eyes, he felt as if he were hurling through space, as far as if he were dropping from another planet. "I must get out of here," he said.

The cat shot between his legs as he entered the hallway. It

hissed hatefully at him. "It will never forgive me," Emmet thought. He took the dog outside with him because he feared the cat might kill her if he left them alone.

He made his way unconsciously towards the pay telephone by the river. It was almost dawn. He dialed Jonathan's number. It rang seven times before he sleepily answered.

As Emmet listened to his brother shout "Hello," a numbness stunned him for a moment with such force that it transfixed him even as he grabbed for support.

"That's me," he thought as he saw how he huddled at the telephone, pale and frantic, the dog chewing on her leash, trying to pull him away.

Emmet cupped his hands over the receiver. "I'm gone," he thought with amazement, because he had never expected to see it all so clearly.

"I'm gone," he said again, wilder this time, almost exhilarated, as if he witnessed from afar another person who was beyond saving.

"Hello? Is someone there? Emmet?" Jonathan asked, his alarm apparent.

"What can I tell him?" Emmet wondered as he heard his brother's bewildered voice shout through the wires.

How he wanted her back: he let the idea float upon him as a glancing thought, but he cringed to admit it even to himself. Or maybe it wasn't she that he longed for, but only the thrill of expectation that freed him whenever his mother returned to steal him away.

She had no way of knowing that in his heart he begged her to take him with her. But how he welcomed her each time as a dream of escape, even when he knew she came only to test the waters, even when he knew she came only to play at the life she was supposed to live. Each time, how quickly she learned she couldn't; how quickly she vanished and was gone, and gone again, until she returned the last time and then was gone entirely from life.

Once she took him skiing.

As the lift pulled them through space, Emmet tried to settle his back into his mother's arm. His breath was smoky with cold. Their nylon coats had grown so hard with frost that they threatened to break into blue and purple chips if he pressed too firmly against her.

She took Emmet's hand from the railing. "Go ahead," she said. "Lean back."

He lay his head tentatively on her shoulder. Her scarf was damp with sweat and melting ice. He closed his eyes and pushed his head downward to force it into warmth and comfort. His mother raised his goggles and ran her finger over one eye. Out there, they felt as if they had turned to cheap green glass. She poked her finger into a tear duct and pinched a droplet of snow.

"Having fun?" She put her mouth so close to his ear that her words disturbed its numbness.

She stretched an arm around him. Emmet opened an eye and grinned. When their jackets brushed together, they made the sound of two tarpaulins dragged on cement.

His mother pointed to a swirl of colored dots. "It's getting crowded," she said. They watched the specks reach a peak of hill simultaneously and collide in the air.

Their chairs rocked for a moment as the lift slowed and they came to a stop. They were at the highest point above where the slopes met at the bottom of the mountain.

When she pressed against Emmet's arm, her bones stuck through his coat. They felt fused together, as if someone had slipped stainless-steel straws through her joints. She kicked her feet in and out. Each tip brought them closer to the railing and then she pulled them back, so that the chair rocked like a swing. She turned to him and smiled. "Do you think we'd die if we jumped from here?"

The sky was so pale with clouds that it seemed part of the snow. The whiteness hooked and closed around them.

His mother raised the bar that protected them. She grabbed Emmet's side in a tickle and pushed him forward, only to grab him back, and held him there, laughing, their knees stuck to their chests, their skis flapping like broken propellers.

It seemed for a moment, as he pressed against her, that he could fall into that space, substanceless, and not a bone would break. His mother pointed to the mounds of snow, the wind breezing their tops to a fine dust, like a Sahara, and she leaned closer to him and said, "Look how soft it looks." She pulled a glove from her hand and waved it before Emmet's eyes with two fingers and winked, as if to say, "Just like magic."

Then she let it go over the edge of the chair. They watched the black hand swoop and tumble in huge, lifeless hoops, as if it owned the air, but then its circles became choked and it lost control and ripped dangerously through space. It shivered and rattled and seemed to leave a spray of black cells in its wake. If it had been given more room to fall, it might have come apart entirely, its molecules unhinged, but it struck the surface of the snow and vanished completely, like a fist through clouds.

CHAPTER
THIRTEEN

The cat was on to him.

Ever since the robbery, it would not be still. It spit whenever Emmet or the dog entered a room, hunched in the corners of the empty apartment with its side pressed tightly against the wall.

The cat was the only one who knew for certain what had happened. Emmet had tried to appease it. He had bought a new, ceramic dish for its meals. He had bought a flannel pillow for its bed. None of it had mattered. The cat would not forgive him.

All night it patrolled his bed, eavesdropping. It listened to his conversations in the dark. It even tapped the sounds from his dreams that Emmet would never hear. He could only guess what he surrendered to once he was asleep. The cat knew for certain. Emmet dreaded this advantage. One night he borrowed a tape recorder from Jonathan and set it near his bed to chronicle everything that happened. He slept five hours. The tape betrayed only the cat's smooth purr, as if it snuggled over the machine to keep it warm, like an egg.

The cat had found out everything. And with each new thing it discovered, it paced more furtively. Its back slunk against plaster and its eyes never shut, even when it was night.

Emmet pretended to sleep. For weeks he had practiced the

slow, effortless breath and the careless toss of the body known to guiltless sleepers. He even called out sometimes: a name, an idea, a fear, to feed the cat disinformation and play on its mercy. It had made no difference. The cat peered over Emmet and batted at his lids with its paws, as if it were extracting a spider from a web without disturbing a single strand.

When Emmet wanted to sleep, the cat napped on his face. When Emmet blinked, fur tickled his eyes. But he had trained himself to freeze. He had read of people in Africa who felt a snake wriggle into their sleeping bag to settle against a leg for warmth. They would wait there paralyzed, praying the snake would rest and move on quickly. Those people were versed in the rules of panic; they knew that even breathing was dangerous.

Emmet had revealed too much about himself. He felt secrets rise from his skin, as if each pore slid open to signal his alarm. Sometimes he believed he could hear those invisible hatches shake open and shut, like the sound of cheap wooden bracelets rattling against one another. He rubbed his arms with his hands constantly now and said he was always cold.

After the robbery, Emmet had his mail diverted. He asked the secretary where he worked to pick up a change-of-address form from the post office near her home. He confided to her that his great aunt was being forced to change nursing homes and was too ill to obtain a form for herself. He believed he had once told the secretary that his mother and grandmother were dead, but he knew he had never lied about a great aunt. He might have many great aunts. She could not know that all of them were nuns and died years ago in convents in France.

Carefully he printed his address on the form. For his new home he wrote "c/o General Delivery, Casper, Wyoming." He read the atlas for a long time before he remembered becoming lost in a blizzard there as a child. He hoped that Casper was still desolate enough for no one to think of stalking him, but not so small that he would be conspicuous as a stranger, as he was now in his neighborhood in the city. He telephoned for the correct zip code at the post office information number. He wrote it in block letters on the form. 82601. In two weeks, his mail dried up. He had begun to send postcards to people he knew slightly, announcing his move. People who knew him well were less easy to get rid of. He would get away from everyone, eventually. But first the cat had to go. The cat was trying to drive him out before he was ready.

His landlord had stopped sending letters to his apartment demanding rent. Now he nailed printed notices to the front door of the building, signed by officials in the city government, so that all the neighbors could see. Bill collectors telephoned his office to dun him for payment. Emmet told them the person they sought was dead. "In a robbery," he added. "I'm surprised you didn't read about it. It was in all the newspapers. We're still in a state of shock here. He was a harmless guy."

Sometimes when the collectors called, he would shout heartily towards the shut door of his darkroom, "Does anybody know what happened to that Emmet character?" as if directing his question to a room full of secretaries. He would hold his hand over the receiver while he counted to thirty. "I hear he moved to France," he would say. "To live with his aunts. They are nuns."

Emmet did not know how long it would be before the collection agencies called the director of his company. He did not know how long it would be before his landlord got him out. He barely moved now when he was home. He had filed the dog's nails to nubs so that they tapped more silently against the hardwood floors. He had changed the locks one day when he knew the landlord was out. Some nights Emmet believed he heard the landlord tinkering with the lock, his tools striking the latch so silently that he had to strain to hear, as if he were listening to a mouse scampering across glass.

Ever since the robbery, the cat had brought in fleas. Now that the furniture was gone, they sprang from the floorboards and collected on Emmet's socks like maggots. They itched the dog mercilessly. Emmet sat for hours on the mattress and picked fleas off his legs and the dog's belly one at a time. He trapped them between his fingers and drowned them one by one in bowls of hot ammonia, where they swam at the bottom like tea leaves. His legs were lousy with bites. The cat held back, amused, as Emmet battled the fleas. When it scratched its neck with its hind feet, Emmet saw fleas fall to the floor in sprays of dust as the cat leveled him with a smile.

Emmet wanted more than anything for the cat to run away. He left the back door open, but the cat was suspicious. It sat on the stoop sniffing the air. Whenever Emmet approached the door, the cat ducked back inside. The week before, he had lured the cat with the head of a fish he had bought from the butcher, and flung it into the yard. The cat dove after it. Emmet slammed the door. The cat never opened its mouth to protest, but stood staring at the window all day and night, refusing to sleep, so that Emmet felt as if he were under house arrest. The next morning he had relented, afraid a neighbor might see the exhausted cat and warn the shelter.

The cat was making friends. The previous day when Emmet returned home, he had found four other cats loitering near his building. He worried what would happen if the cats jumped him when he left the house. The cats understood his language, but what passed among their heads was impenetrable to him. He had observed their movements all summer and listened to their sighs and spits and sounds, but he was no closer to infiltrating any part of it as a sign.

So far he could distinguish only one word. When the cat was hungry, it roamed the kitchen, dropping its squeak an octave and repeating *"Mair, mair, mair"* as it clawed its bowl and flipped it to Emmet. One day the cat purposely timed each wobble of the bowl to a groan of *"mair."* The bowl tipped on the floor to the sound until Emmet could stand it no longer. He kicked the cat like a pillow. It hurled in loops into the dining room. The cat hid from him for days, spitting from under the picnic table and from deep inside its throat.

The cat refused to let Emmet forget. It was the beginning of their trouble. Today all four cats shouted *"Mair, mair, mair"* when they saw Emmet. He hit at them to shut up because everyone could hear, but they ran to the bushes and kept calling. Now everyone in the neighborhood believed he had harmed them. He could tell by the way the clerk in the grocery store gave him change. He always placed it in the hands of the local women and inquired after their families or their health. But when it was Emmet's turn, the clerk left his money in a pile near his shopping bag. Then he leaned on the foot petal so that the rubber counter began to move. Emmet was forced to grapple for coins. He picked at them frantically one by one and tried to behave as if it were a natural act.

The woman who managed the Laundromat was married to the clerk. They were in cahoots. Emmet believed they led the neighborhood in some way, headquartered in one of the clubs on side streets that had windows painted black. The woman said she was out of change whenever Emmet asked for more. He was made to take home damp clothes and hang them like mobiles from the light in his kitchen. The cat stood on its hind legs and batted at them as if they had been placed there for its pleasure.

Earlier in the summer, Emmet had come upon the woman from the Laundromat speaking to the cat through the front window, her face too near the glass, her lips moving and grinning. She had held her ground when Emmet surprised her. "Your cat looks thin," she scolded him, as if he meant to starve it.

He had bought many cans of cat food since then, more than he needed. Each time he shopped he loaded his cart with the most expensive brand. He hoped the clerk would tell his wife that the cat was well fed. He always said, "My cat eats well, even if I do not." He added a laugh that he hoped was charming and self-effacing. The clerk ignored him. Sometimes they watched the counter together as his change slid onto the floor.

Emmet had begun to shop secretly for himself in another part of town. He bought only small amounts of carrots at a time and packed them carefully in his briefcase. No one ever saw a bag. He stacked the cans of cat food on the radiator by his front window so that the neighbors would see them when they peeked through the curtains to find clues to what his life was like.

Emmet had tried to court the cat's favor. He reminded it often of its rescue from the shelter. Without him, he said, the cat would still be living in a dormitory crowded with cages and would lack protection at night. "How could you have screamed for help with your voice?" Emmet reminded it. "No one could hear you." Emmet wondered what Joan would think of him, plotting against the cat, and she too preoccupied with new animals to mount a guerrilla visit to save it.

Emmet attempted one last time to trick the cat outside. It snarled against the door frame. Outside the back door, Emmet saw two pairs of eyes catch the light from the alley and flash once in the dark. He felt you could not underestimate the power of a sneak attack. He had seen photographs of an actress in Hollywood who was eaten by her dachshund. He believed the cat's friends had banded together in the yard. He imagined opening the door to a glitter of green, fluorescent eyes fixed only on him and the warning of a communal hiss, louder than the sea at night.

So far the dog still loved him, but Emmet believed it was only a matter of time before the cats corrupted her. He did not know where her loyalties would lie if she were forced to choose. He did not know if she would throw her lot with the animals. Then there would be two of them in the house hating him.

Emmet lowered the shade over the door. He searched the telephone directory for an animal shelter in another borough of the city, one far enough away so that its employees might never have heard of Joan. He wondered if a network existed among them, if maybe they transmitted photographs of blacklisted customers from shelter to shelter to tape over their desks. Joan had kept the photograph of Emmet and his dog. Copies of it could be pinned to bulletin boards all over the city.

A woman answered the telephone at the shelter. She sounded nothing like Joan, her voice drunken and deep. Emmet told her that a cat had been abandoned near his apartment and he was afraid it might starve. He let the frenzy in his voice appear to be feline concern. There was silence at the other end of the phone. He added that he thought the neighborhood children were tormenting it. "You know how cruel children can be," he said, hoping she was a mother. "Could you send a car to save the cat?"

She laughed. She told Emmet they might accept the cat if he brought it to the shelter. "All things considered," she said at the end.

Emmet did not know what that meant. "Can't you do anything for something so helpless?" he asked, appealing to her heart.

The woman laughed again. "Why not give it a dollar and put it on the subway?" she said as she hung up.

Emmet could not take the cat on the subway. He knew the number of the city code that prohibited it. If he covered the cat with a blanket, he could not trust it to keep quiet. If he were one of those people who smoked blithely in the cars even at rush hour and had a lunatic stare, he would go. But his guilt was a beacon. Emmet knew the transit police would see the shivering cat and he would begin to confess before they were close enough to hear his whisper.

Emmet locked the dog in the bedroom so she could not see. He took five sleeping pills from their bottle and pounded them to powder with the spine of a book. He stirred them into a bowl of milk. He said, "Here, kitty." He had never said this to the cat before. It looked to Emmet and back at the bowl. Its tongue lapped the milk once and then snapped back.

He left the kitchen followed by the cat's eyes. When he was out of sight, the cat relaxed its haunches and drew the milk in quickly. It strolled to its pillow in the corner and turned its face to the wall.

The cat rolled onto its back in a natural sleep. The pills would not kill it. Emmet crushed the three remaining pills from the bottle and sopped them in a bowl of milk. He wet his finger and pressed it against the cat's mouth. It would not open. The cat was almost smiling, dreaming of something.

Someone knocked. The dog barked and clawed against the bedroom door. For a moment, Emmet worried that the woman from the shelter had traced his call. He expected to see Joan with a police officer outside, ordering his arrest. But it was only the boy from next door.

"I'm redecorating," Emmet crowed heartily before the boy had uttered a word. "That's why the apartment is so bare. Start from scratch, I always say. Throw the old away."

"Do you have a minute?" the boy asked.

They had never had a conversation. Emmet wondered if the boy had sensed his murderous intent through the walls of the building and had come to spy.

Emmet barred the entrance, planting his feet on either side of the door so the boy could not slip through as Anita had done. He looked nervously behind, hoping the cat did not stumble into the foyer to escape. "It isn't a good time," Emmet told him. Cups of cold ammonia and dead fleas were scattered on the picnic table, as if a circle of friends had sat talking long after dinner.

"Please," the boy pleaded.

From his tone, Emmet thought he sounded as if his distress were real. Some nights when he had lain sleepless and afraid, Emmet had imagined knocking on the door of a stranger's house. Sometimes he imagined the person taking him in and brewing a pot of tea. Sometimes he saw a nose peek behind the chain before the door slammed in his face. In case the boy had taken hours summoning his courage to approach a stranger, Emmet could not turn him away.

"Sit here," Emmet said, leading the boy to the picnic table. "It's all I've got until my decorator finishes."

"I've seen you come in and out of the building with your dog," the boy said. "I hoped you wouldn't mind my barging in. I wondered if you knew anything about cameras? I've seen you with a couple around your neck when you go out at night. I wondered what you thought about it. Photography, that is. As a career."

The boy, too, had been watching. He might be the relative of the woman in the Laundromat. He might have Emmet's possessions hidden in his own apartment. "I'm sorry," Emmet said, "but I cannot concentrate on what you are saying. I think my cat is ill."

The cat entered the dining room; its eyes rolled upward as it leaned against the wall for support. It headed straight for the boy, but Emmet swept it into his lap. The cat bit the wedge of flesh near his thumb. "See, it's so disoriented it doesn't even know me." He gripped the cat's throat and wiped blood into its fur.

"Something is happening that I don't understand," Emmet said.

The boy nodded.

Particles of light drifted above Emmet's head. He could not move except to sigh. The dog's cries from the bedroom had grown so despairing that Emmet could barely hear above the din. "I'm devoted to this cat, you know. My dog, too. They become like children after a while." He remembered his mother having said this.

The boy reached over to pat the cat's head with two fingers. The cat flicked its neck three times before it collapsed to the floor. "I'm sorry," Emmet said, "but I must get this cat to a vet." He realized it was nearly midnight. "Our vet has emergency hours for favored clients. I don't know what I'd do without him. We've been through so much together."

"Maybe another time would be better," the boy said, still sitting. "Maybe you could think about it and let me know. We could have dinner or something."

"Anytime," Emmet said. "Once my cat has recovered."

He looked the boy in the eye and beamed with friendliness. Emmet was happy now he'd come. He could subpoena the boy as a witness to his love for the cat.

"Come back whenever you feel like talking. I'll ask some of my friends and see what they think. About which camera would be the best."

"Thank you," the boy said.

"Anytime," Emmet said again.

The boy stood to leave. As Emmet opened the door, it dragged roughly against the floor, swollen with the humidity. The sound jarred the cat. It tried to scoot from under the bench to the open corridor, but it was no match for the two of them. The boy reached down slowly and passed the cat to Emmet with one hand.

"I hope your cat is better," the boy said.

"Here's to your future," Emmet said, and tipped the cat slightly, as he might tip a champagne flute.

Once the boy was gone, Emmet cradled the cat in his arm as he carried it into the kitchen. Softly he recounted his love. "Remember how I saved you?" he whispered. He animated his voice as he told the cat that they might move to another apartment. He promised to adopt a second cat for company. "It must get lonely for you when I'm not around," Emmet said, as if he were admitting to a fault days after an accusation. "Leaving you here with no one but the dog is no life." He put his mouth close to the cat's ear as he said this so that the dog could not hear.

Emmet planted the cat in front of the bowl. It did not hesitate; it sucked the milk tainted with the three remaining pills. Emmet waited for the pauses between breaths to become labored. As it sprawled on the floor, the cat looked haunted and numb.

Emmet wondered if the cat would suffocate if he stuffed it into a garbage bag. But he worried that it might awaken and feel itself swallowed by the bag as the seams closed around it. He wanted to sense what the cat would know. He took a bag from under the sink, yanked it over his head, and gathered it tightly at the neck. He stood there for several minutes, sniffing the plastic. He was not afraid. It would be almost peaceful for the cat. If it awakened inside the bag, the cat might believe it was dead already and settle into the darkness and thin air. Emmet wrapped the cat in a towel and placed it gently in the bag.

The phone rang twice and then stopped. Then it rang again. It was a code known only to his brother. Jonathan loved cats. He kept three of them in his apartment. Emmet told him that the cat had run away. His voice became hoarse as he said this. He seemed to be distraught at the loss. Jonathan believed him; it would not occur to him to accuse Emmet of such deceit.

They talked for twenty minutes. Emmet could not take his eyes off the bag. The plastic rattled outwards and drew itself back in steady beats. The cat was not going anywhere. It breathed like it was sleeping off a binge. Emmet had gone too far to stop now. He knew the cat would walk up and down his bed every night, never letting him sleep. The cat would pursue him. It was only four. This could continue for another twenty years.

Emmet looked outside. The street was clear. He grabbed the bag with the drugged cat inside and rushed out the door toward the bridge that straddled the expressway three blocks away. He lifted the bag to his chest to toss the cat over, but there was too much traffic even at that hour. Emmet imagined the noise of the brakes as the cars swerved to avoid the thing tumbling out of the sky.

If there was an accident, the police would hunt throughout the neighborhood to find him. He wondered if fingerprints could leave their trace on slick, cheap plastic. Gray dust still shone on the wood in his apartment, weeks after the robbery. When the police had come, they had neglected to take his prints. But he worried that they might exist in a file somewhere. He believed that someone had snuck up on him in the incubator where he slept as an infant and quietly pressed black ink to his fingers and toes.

The bag rested on the sidewalk near his leg. The cat slept, round and lumpy, at the bottom. Each time the cat breathed, the bag crinkled like weeds. It was not yet dead. If it lived, the cat would be there always, a threat like a past.

A gang of teenagers drifted towards him. If they saw the bag, moving with its puffs of air, they were likely to think Emmet was molesting a child. They might lynch him. He gathered the bag to his chest and ran to his apartment. The street in front of his door was empty, and he had a moment to slip inside with the cat unnoticed.

From the bedroom, the dog panted with screams. Emmet lay the cat across the picnic table and freed the dog from the bedroom. She seemed so mad from her isolation that she did not recognize him at first, cowering when he came upon her. "I've lost her, too," Emmet thought as he crawled towards her on his knees.

"It's me," Emmet said, begging to be acknowledged. "Look, I'm back. Everything is fine." The dog dropped to her haunches, shaking with fright. "She heard me," he panicked as he crept closer. "She knows what I've done."

Emmet could not bear that the dog distrusted him. He thought tenderly of how she had loved him the past months, even as he ruined her. "I need you," he said softly. "The cat is ill and you must help me save it. Please, please, please." As he moved closer, his hand groped through the space in front of them as if he walked blindly in the dark. When he lay his hand on the dog's head, her shivering ceased. "Come help me," he said, leading her by the collar into the dining room.

The dog put her paws on the table to sniff the bag. She whined as she rooted against the plastic with her snout. The cat was waking up. If the cat was conscious, Emmet could not allow the dog to see it. He did not know what messages would pass secretly between them, some language so mysterious to the human ear that he would not be able to tell even the moment at which they communicated.

"We must keep the cat in the dark," Emmet told the dog. "We must be careful not to disturb it."

He grabbed the bag and stashed it behind the toilet. He shut the door. With no light, no one could ever find the cat, hidden by rolls of paper towels and rags. Emmet sat on the bathtub. He could hear the bag pause and move, one, two; one, two. If he took the cat to the shelter now, they would see its limp body and know he had poisoned it. He was sure to be punished.

Emmet telephoned the animal shelter again. A tired male voice answered instead of the woman's. Emmet said he rang earlier about an abandoned cat. He did not wait for the man to respond. He did not plan what he would say. He just opened his mind and talked and talked until he felt he had been saved.

"My neighbors moved away two weeks ago and forgot their cat. Or else they abandoned it. I don't know for sure. I heard he accepted a teaching job in Iowa. They were tired of the city and wanted a place to raise their children. I don't know what town they've gone to, but if I did, I'd call and demand they return to get their cat. I've always thought those are the ones to watch, the people who speak of family and then leave a cat, nearly a kitten, actually, in the street to fend for itself.

"I would take the cat in, but I suffer from allergies. I've been feeding it all week, and now it won't leave my yard. It moans all night and I can't sleep. It's been a nightmare, listening to this defenseless animal crying outside my door. My doctor absolutely won't allow it inside. I'm allergic to antihistamines and they make my heart pound so fast I'm unable to move.

"I would be happy to feed the cat indefinitely. I mean, affording the food isn't the problem. But winter is coming and I think it might freeze. When I called earlier tonight the woman who answered your phone had something of an attitude. I swore I would never call you people again, except just now I saw teenagers from the neighborhood feeding the cat drugs. It has been lurching along the wall in my backyard and falling down. I have tried to shut it out; I even pulled the blinds, but you can't drown out the sound. I mean, it's practically the death rattle, the sound this thing makes. What sort of person would torment an animal? If I weren't afraid of the repercussions, I would notify the authorities, but I have to live here. People forget that. There's no telling what those boys might do to me, if they would take revenge on something so helpless as a cat.

"I don't mind telling you, things like this make me afraid of living in the city. I mean, there's no one to help you. I have a dog, but they aren't much protection, not against bands of roving thugs. One grows helpless here to stop these things from happening. It's gotten so it's hard to look at a newspaper with the chronicle of horrors listed every day. But I feel that one must. I feel that one must keep track of things. I'm sure in your job you've seen unspeakable acts done to animals. Horrors I cannot even imagine. But you must prepare yourself before I bring the cat in. I think what has happened will shock even you.

"I can't do anything myself. That's why I'm calling on you as a stranger for help. I cannot save it. Forgive me for speaking as I do, but I'm at my wit's end watching these boys. You should see how they laugh. I've heard about things like this before, but I've never seen direct evidence. Something you can prove. I wouldn't be surprised if they were the ones who robbed me. Did I mention that? Yes. They stole everything I owned while I was away. There's nothing here but a few things for me and my dog, so what kind of home would it be for a cat? I've never been to a shelter before, but I imagine they're rather well run. And anything would be better than living so exposed and unprotected on the streets. I've often thought that I wouldn't mind living in a cage. I know it sounds mad, but with the door locked, knowing nothing could get at you, I imagine one could sleep like a child. As long as you could get out. As long as you hadn't signed yourself away forever.

"I'm not rich, but I'll take a cab to your shelter if you absolutely promise to meet me at the door. Can I have your name? I don't want to have to explain any of this again, and I don't want to fill out any forms or sign anything. I just want to give you the cat and come back home and get some sleep. Can I have your name? What time does your shift end? Will you be there in an hour? You know, I really don't want any publicity. My family is rather well known and I'd like to keep this out of the papers. Just between us. Drop the cat off, forget it, and get some sleep. I'm afraid what might happen to it by tomorrow if I don't do something. Can I come now? I know the car service will get me there in an hour. Will you still be on duty? I don't want to sound like a lunatic, but I've been awake all night and sleeplessness unnerves me. I'm sure you've found this to be true, working midnight shifts as you do. I know we've never met, but I really must ask for your help. Please. We must do something quickly before it gets worse. As citizens. You must trust me. Can I have your name? Will you still be there in an hour?"

The man at the shelter was named Nate. He said he worked until 9:00 A.M.

Emmet telephoned the car service and told the dispatcher the address where he needed to go. While he waited, he carefully lined the bottom of the box Joan had given him with newspaper, as if he were protecting a breakable object. "The cat is ill and we are saving it," he told the dog as he lifted the body into the box. The cat's hair was missing in spots where it had scratched and bitten too hard against the fleas.

Emmet led the dog into the bedroom. He tied a T-shirt around her mouth to bind back her howls. He trussed her feet with a belt and lay her upon the mattress, like a hostage. "You must be quiet while I'm gone. It's for your own good," he said as he kissed her lightly on the nose. "If the cat is ill, I cannot risk the same thing happening to you. I'll take care of everything. We'll be back like we were before. Remember?"

The driver arrived in a station wagon. He smoked a cigar. Between puffs, he hummed. He ignored Emmet. "Car service" was all he said. Emmet grew afraid that the car might be owned by the neighborhood cabal. They might kidnap him to save the cat and bury his body in a marsh somewhere deep in the woods.

As they left his neighborhood, Emmet tried to win the driver to his side. He could not keep himself from talking. He told the driver the horror he had been living. He spoke for miles, fabricating detail after detail of the cat's torture. He began to feel righteous. He snuggled against the box, blocking the lid shut with one arm.

They had driven so far that they passed through sections of the city never covered by the news. The few people who lived there collected on the street in packs. They stood on corners watching everything that moved. The driver turned and turned so many times that Emmet felt as if he had entered the heart of a landscaped maze and was burrowing towards its center. Against his seat, he felt pinned by darkness.

The car slowed and entered a driveway. The driver had known just where he was going. The shelter was five times the size of Joan's, with a parking lot large enough for a department store. It was ringed by a band of official vehicles. "Here you go," the driver said tonelessly.

Emmet pulled out his wallet. "Will you wait?" he asked. The driver shrugged as he glanced at his watch. Emmet tried not to panic. He handed the driver the money. He thanked him. The driver looked at the box for the first time. "What you got in there?" he asked. "A raccoon?"

Inside, the shelter glared with bare bulbs. Emmet approached the person sitting behind the desk. "Are you Nate?" he asked. The clerk nodded. Every time the metal door behind the desk swung open, the echo of braying animals bounded from the walls. Emmet imagined unspeakable abuses and experiments.

"Cat," Emmet said, wanting everything to be known. He motioned to the box for emphasis.

Nate summoned another man dressed in veterinarian's clothes. The two of them surrounded Emmet like border guards. He wanted to confess everything that had happened, but he felt the story break apart from him.

"Cat," he said again. His smile gave off tiny tremors.

The vet unpacked the cat from the box and lifted it towards the ceiling. Emmet lowered his eyes, certain that when he looked up, the vet would dangle a corpse. But the vet raised the cat above him and examined it in the light. Then he curled it back to his chest. The cat yawned and rested its head against his palm. Emmet caught the red of the exit sign with his eye in case someone moved to nab him. He could not tell for sure if the shelter was a trap, but the cat behaved as if it were in the company of friends.

Nate said something to him, but Emmet could not concentrate. He needed to know if the cat had duped him to make its escape.

But he could not remember how any of it had begun or how he had come so far.

The vet kicked the box to a corner of the room. He tucked the cat under his arm and headed for the swinging door without saying a word.

Nate held out a form. He seemed to be asking for money. Emmet backed away from the desk. He threw the money in his wallet to Nate to keep him at a distance. Emmet did not know what was expected of him, but Nate snapped the tip of his pen as if he were reeling a fish pole to lure his body to the desk.

A man entered the shelter leading a dog. The dog was large and brown like Emmet's. Now he was certain she had betrayed him. They must have picked her up just after he left. He looked from the stranger to Nate and then towards the open door. The stranger had brought a breeze in with him. Emmet felt it sweep through the room and come at them, circling their necks like scarfs. He could not think of anything to break the silence.

"Cat," he said once more.

It no longer sounded like a word at all, but like a spasm caught in the throat and flung between them.

PART TWO

HOSPITAL

When considering the hopes I had formed for life, the one which appeared the most important was the desire to acquire a way of seeing . . . in which life would keep its heavy moments of rise and fall, but would at the same time be recognized, and with no less admirable clarity, as a nothing, a dream, a drifting state.
   —Franz Kafka, in his journals

CHAPTER ONE

When Emmet was in kindergarten, the most solid substance he could imagine was the green ceramic tiles that lined the corridors of his school. Once every few weeks, a siren would sound out in the asphalt yard where the children played at recess. The moment she heard it, his teacher would grasp the wooden pointer that hung on a magnet near the chalkboard and tap it against her open fist. The class would stand obediently beside their desks until she announced, "We are going to walk quietly down the hall and pretend as if the Russians are dropping bombs."

The children would file into the corridor and face the ceramic tiles, bowing in front of them as if they formed some kind of holy wall. Emmet remembered pressing his forehead against the cool surface and cupping his arms protectively over his stomach. Up so closely before them, he could see the brown flecks in the grout that linked each tile together, but their construction seemed so pure that not a single pore marred their glazed, green finish.

As he bent before the wall, Emmet would imagine how the building would shatter when the bombs fell. He knew its timber frame would splinter and the plaster ceilings would crumble to dust, but he believed the tiles would somehow make him inviolate:

as if the heat from the bomb could be no hotter than the kiln's fire that had cooked them.

During these drills, Emmet would remember what his grandmother had told him about blackouts during the war in London: how she pulled thick, black shades over the windows at night and huddled around a single candle at the table in Mrs. Prebble's dining room. She told him how the flame wavered as the bombs dropped in the street outside, its light puffing to smoke as the vibrations shook with the force of a wind. Sometimes they extinguished the candle purposely and sat in the darkness holding hands around the table, as if in a seance. From time to time one of them would rise and peek through the corner of the shade to see the city illuminated by sparks.

Once Emmet and his grandmother watched on television a film of a volcanic eruption in Hawaii. They saw the orange fire burst out of the crater into fragments of flame. His grandmother told him that this was how London had looked through the sliver of window visible from the side of the black shade, as if a volcano had come to life within the city, shooting fire from the tunnels under the street and burning up the sky.

When Emmet was in kindergarten, his family lived in a neighborhood with four houses built along a cul-de-sac. When the families came to believe the reports that their lives were in danger, they pooled their resources and built a bomb shelter in Emmet's backyard, digging deep into the earth, nearly deep as a well. The entrance was a steel door laid flat against the ground that was opened by pulling a chain. Emmet's father nailed a patch of plastic sod over it and painted the chain a glossy green, so that the shelter was camouflaged by the grass.

The door lifted outward to reveal a flight of metal stairs leading down to the main room. The walls were made of packed mud coated with rough plaster. The floor was covered with straw mats. Twelve cots were placed in rows in the center of the room the way they would be in a hospital ward. Each had a plastic tray set next to it with a white wick in a small, glass jar, like a votive candle. There was a smaller room to the left, with three lumpy sofas and a long table built of planks from a barn. Emmet's mother bought shelves and filled an entire wall with books about garden design, histories of the French Revolution, and novels about the Nazis living underground in South America after the war.

The children were given a small treasure trove of presents that were meant to entertain them after the atomic blast. They were forbidden to open the boxes before then. When he was bored, Emmet became so eager to unwrap the toys that he began to look forward to the day the bomb would fall as if it were Christmas.

The man in the house next door was an astronomer. He installed a telescope in a side wall of the shelter that rose above ground like a periscope. When he pressed his eye against the lens, Emmet felt as if he were submerged in a submarine. Another neighbor built a ventilator that was connected by pipes to the outside. It was meant to purify the air of radioactive dust before they breathed it. Emmet helped his father and brother carry gallons of water in plastic jugs sealed with airtight lids to stack against the wall in the main room. They piled cans of food in pyramids against the other wall. His father wanted enough provisions so that they could survive down there for six months without need. No one thought of what would happen if their exile stretched beyond that time.

Once every few months in the middle of the night, Emmet's father would sound a bell in the street outside their homes. He believed they should practice living together so that there would be no surprises once the real emergency came. All of the families would rush into the dark and form a line at the entrance to the bunker. The twelve of them wore pajamas and terry cloth robes and clutched blankets and pillows. Each kept a suitcase of extra clothes already packed under his cot.

During the nights they spent together, everyone whispered, as if soldiers were patrolling in the yard above and might hear them. They sat politely on the couch like strangers brought together at a party. Emmet's mother made tea. Every once in a while, his father climbed the stairs to look outside. When he returned, he reminded them that it would be impossible to open the hatch once the bombs fell. The telescope would be their only eye.

The idea of bombs falling in the night never frightened him. Emmet came to expect that it was only a matter of time before he was awakened for real. His father was so confident that the rooms they built underground would protect them that Emmet always believed they would survive. The world outside the bunker seemed dangerous to him.

Long after his parents stopped conducting drills or worrying about the Russians, Emmet used to climb down to the shelter in the middle of the night. He would take a blanket from the closet and lay on his cot, listening to the whirr of the generator as it circulated the stale air. When he swung the telescope on its pivot and looked around the yard, everything he saw was broken by the thin black lines stenciled over the lens, a three-dimensional rec-tangle with a circle smack in the center, like the eye of a target.

Emmet had not visited the shelter for twenty years, but some-times when he walked in the city, he noticed the yellow sign with black triangles that used to denote a bomb shelter posted on the stairwell of a skyscraper. Sometimes when he walked down a corridor lined with cool, green tiles, he ran his hand along them and remembered how it had been to gather before the wall with the other children in his school during the drills.

A buzzer sounded. Two glass doors swung open and Emmet stepped into the hospital ward. The doors clicked shut behind him so soundly that he jumped forward into the lounge. When he looked back, he saw that the inside of the glass was mirrored so that the corridor outside vanished to a double image of him clutching a shopping bag in each hand. The room was arranged with orange Naugahyde couches and plastic tables littered with ashtrays and paper cups. Emmet slipped a piece of tissue paper from one of his bags onto a cushion and sat uncertainly on its edge as he waited for someone to greet him.

Nurses tiptoed in and out of the ward. Every time the bell rang hoarsely, the door to the corridor swung open, as if controlled by a wizard hidden behind a screen. Dizzy with anxiety, Emmet gripped the sacks close to his knees. All around him, he heard the repeated growl of the buzzer heralding each entrance and exit. If he closed his eyes, the bell rang so clearly that it could have been his father standing in the street outside their home, ready to lead Emmet and his neighbors to safety through the fake-grass door of the bunker.

CHAPTER
TWO

A man so short he could have been a dwarf limped towards Emmet with an outstretched hand. Emmet could not tell from his appearance if he was a patient or a staff member. But as the dwarf approached, Emmet saw a small plastic name tag pinned to his shirt pocket and a beeper hooked to his belt.

The man's head barely reached Emmet's waist. He walked on little bowlegs crammed into gray snakeskin cowboy boots that made his toes seem incongruously pointy and large. Curls of loose frizz escaped from the rubber band knotting his ponytail, fluttering over his head like a net. A handlebar moustache climbed elaborately down the rims of his lips. A crucifix jangled in a hoop from his left ear and a thick silver band of turquoise stones encircled his neck. The nurse seemed to want to draw attention to his huge head so that his size would be less apparent. But he looked to Emmet like an aging cowboy whose face had been sewn onto an unhealthy child's body.

"I'm Chris," the nurse said. "Christian, in fact. Let me take you to your room."

Emmet was silent. He did not know what he expected from a hospital ward, but this greeting seemed as casual as if he had arrived at his college dormitory for the first time.

Chris led him through the recreational area, where two Ping-Pong tables were set with paddles balanced on top of tiny white balls. In the center of the room was a pool table with a rack of cue sticks locked in a movable wooden case. Without any people present, the room could have existed in an elementary school or a church basement in a small town. Primitive paintings in bright colors were tacked to the walls with the artists' names printed in crayon at the top. Emmet had seen a similar display in his god-children's schoolroom, except many of the images in these drawings were violent: of religious figures with their mouths opened in screams, or of couples rutting on the ground.

In a vestibule outside the recreation area, Emmet noticed the nursing station walled off in glass with a locked door. No other light burned in the ward. Four people sat on stools inside, drinking from mugs and laughing, behind the soundproof window.

The patients' rooms were built off a separate wing with wash basins and mirrors spaced at intervals down its corridor. To the left of the hallway, Emmet saw a thick, white steel door, like the entrance to a vault, with a porthole in its center crisscrossed with wire mesh. He regarded it questioningly. He had noticed nothing else besides the paintings that belied the benign character of the ward.

"It's the isolation area," Chris said. "For patients who get agitated. I doubt you're in that class, but I'll take you in if you like. There's no one locked in there at the moment. It's been a quiet week."

Emmet was struck by how naturally the nurse accepted him, almost as a compatriot. On his tour, Emmet felt as if he were inspecting an apartment as a new place to live.

From a ring hooked to his belt, Chris pulled a fat brass key with grooves cut into each side. As he turned it in the lock, he pushed a button in the wall and signaled to a nurse in the station. A bell rang and he pulled the door open.

There were four rooms in the isolation unit, two on either side of a small vestibule. Chris led Emmet into one of the cells. From books he had read about hospitals, Emmet expected padded cushions to be nailed to the walls, but this space was like a room anywhere, painted white. A monk might live there happily.

When Chris flipped on the light, Emmet noticed smudges and handprints climbing one of the walls, as if someone had tried to scale it. The cell was so small that Chris had to close the door for both of them to stand comfortably inside. When the door shut, it fit perfectly into the frame. The wall stretched seamlessly behind them, except for an oval plastic window in the center through which the patient could be observed.

The only furnishings were a small metal cot with a thin mattress covered with a white sheet. A square, flat pillow lay atop a white cotton blanket folded neatly at the foot of the bed. The cement floor was painted white.

"We try to keep things simple in here," Chris said, "so that there's nothing controversial for anyone to get upset about."

Emmet walked to the wall and placed his hands over two of the black prints above his head.

"I guess we need to paint over those lest somebody think there's a way to get out," Chris said, pulling Emmet away. "Let me show you to your room."

Back in the corridor, Chris whispered so as not to wake the other patients. "You'll be in there," he said. "Your roommate is named Winston. He's no trouble, if you don't leave anything around for him to steal."

In the darkness of the room, Emmet saw a body sleeping in the bed at the far side. In the middle of the mattress, the blankets rose steeply to a peak.

"Winston isn't thin," Chris said. "But he won't hurt you. I'll be on duty all day tomorrow. A double shift. Come and find me if there's anything you need."

Emmet patted Chris's arm in gratitude and sat on the bed with his shopping bags at his knees. Since the episode with the cat, his nerves had become so alive that he was unable to speak without stuttering. When he had returned home from the shelter, the dog had been asleep, trussed to the mattress. When he had approached the bed to untie her, she had opened one eye and turned, sighing, her snout to the wall.

Emmet had wanted to forget. He had called Jonathan as a diversion from the horror of his evening. He had wanted to speak to him casually, about the weather or a book he had been reading, but when he said "Hello," the letters shuddered from his mouth, repeating themselves over and over until Emmet seemed to be sputtering "hell" endlessly into the telephone, as if it were the only word he knew.

In his apartment later, he had practiced speaking alone. He recited poems he had memorized. He read aloud from the newspaper. But no matter what he uttered, he was seized by an electrical charge that slammed the words back into his throat.

He had never told his doctor about the bubbling water he drank or the food that repelled him. He had never told his brother most of the secrets of the way he lived. But he could not disguise the tremors that tripped his speech from anyone. Jonathan had consulted with Emmet's doctor. Together they had coaxed Emmet into the hospital.

"You cannot last long like this," they told him. Emmet had conceded. He had sent his dog to live with Jonathan. He had packed his few belongings.

As he sat on his strange new bed in the ward, Emmet could discern only the outline of the room's sparse furnishings. Against one wall were two small dressers such as a child might own. A night table with a lamp was set by each bed.

Emmet reclined against the pillows as he had done in unfamiliar hotels while on vacation, absorbing the space, trying to make it his own.

"Room," he whispered into the air.

"Room," he repeated, savouring the sound. For the first time in weeks, his voice did not stumble over the letters, but floated forth, the word warm and buttery on his tongue. As he paced by his bed, he hummed with pleasure.

"Murmur," he purred. "Marmalade. Junta. Peloponnesian. Pottery. Terra-cotta. Maccabee."

Suddenly he felt invincible. He attempted a sentence, raising his voice a decibel, but not so loud as to awaken Winston.

"She sold sea shells by the seashore," he tossed off with a shrug, pronouncing each *s* smoothly. "What next? What next?" he thought, rippling with joy.

He remembered a twister his speech therapist had used to trip him when he was a child. "One smart fellow, he felt smart. Two smart fellows, they both felt smart. Three smart fellows, they all felt smart."

"I'm free of it," he crowed. For a moment, he considered running to the telephone to call Jonathan. But as he reached into his pocket for a coin, he stopped himself. "Without it, I can never explain the last year. Nothing will have changed, but they will all believe I have been cured."

Emmet was afraid to be discharged before he had spent one night in the hospital. He did not want to be thrown back into his life with no respite. His brother and doctor had seized upon his stutter almost eagerly, as if before they had been blind to his wasted flesh and bunkered isolation.

Emmet, too, had been relieved. He no longer had to explain his behavior to anyone. When he had spit his mangled words, it was as if for the first time his mind released the weight of all that had been hidden in his heart. Without the stutter, he was afraid he might live again at the mercy of everything inside of him.

Emmet ran his fingers over the Formica desk. He positioned the chair flush with the wall. He picked a piece of lint from the cushion. He did not want to leave. He put his hands to his throat and concentrated so that he might hex himself back to stuttering.

"C-c-cat," he said, practicing the snarled *c* until the word seemed wrenched from him. "C-c-cat."

He wished he had brought a photograph of the cat with him. He possessed nothing to assure himself that he had not invented its fury. "Could I really have believed the dog would turn against me?" he blushed as he remembered how he had fled the animal shelter. With the dog and the cat gone, Emmet felt bereft, as he had when a love affair ended, unbelieving that the person had ever existed. All that remained was a longing that seemed to have no source.

He pulled the spread from the bed and lay across the sheets. The pillow was hard and flat, nothing like the downy mounds piled on his bed at home. He crossed to the dresser and slid open its drawer. It rattled on its track so that Winston stirred under his blankets. Emmet was afraid to unpack his shopping bags because the crinkling paper would disturb him. He did not want to be introduced to his roommate on bad terms.

He tiptoed into the hallway as if he were entering a forbidden zone. He crept towards the nursing station. He had no idea what he would ask when he arrived, but he knew he had to see another person before he slept so that he would believe he existed in an inhabited place.

Out in the hallway, Emmet heard a woman snarl. "Yeah, yeah, save your sob stories for the Laundromat, sister. I'm not budging till I smoke this cigarette, so gimme a match."

Emmet froze at the corner. He had never heard so insolent a voice. It was taunting and deep, with an edge that seemed beyond compromise. Emmet heard murmuring and the flick of a lighter.

The voice barked "Thanks"; then footsteps stalked towards the lounge.

When Emmet returned to his room, Winston shouted in his sleep. He did not want to learn the particular demons that obsessed his roommate. He walked to the end of the corridor, where he planned to stand invisibly against the wall. But as he passed the last room, he heard voices and paused outside. Two women and a man sat together on a bed with an ashtray between them, talking.

Before Emmet could retreat into the shadows and disappear, one of the women caught his eye from the bed. She waved him into the room with an arm stacked to the elbow with bracelets. When she lowered her hand, the bracelets rattled together into one piece, encasing her arm in solid gold. "You're the new one," she smiled. "We heard you were coming."

Emmet sat shyly on the opposite bed, pretending to lace his shoes.

"I'm Daphne," the woman said. "This is Bruce. And this is Emily."

Emmet raised his head from his feet. As she waved hello, Emily's neck shook as if her nerve endings were choking her. She appeared to be about forty-five years old, with frosted hair styled in a bubble cut over her head. Her skin was pockmarked and pasty, as if she had been inside for years. Buckteeth pushed her lips outward from her face in a permanent pucker. Each finger was capped with a nail that stretched perfectly to a point a full inch from its tip. As she smiled at Emmet, she scratched her face so that flakes of skin snowed over her wrist. The trails she left on her cheeks were her only color, like a faint rouge.

By instinct, Emmet felt wary of Bruce. His eyes vibrated with recklessness. His skin clung to his face, hot and red, as if seared by a fever. His hair stuck about his head in clumps. As he walked towards the bed to shake Emmet's hand, his blue jeans slipped down around his cheeks so that the elastic strap of his boxer shorts protruded two inches above his belt. Emmet could see green dinosaurs against a pale blue material, their heads turned backwards in a toothy grin.

"I know you," Bruce said slyly as he shook Emmet's hand roughly by the wrist.

Emmet smiled appeasingly. He told them his name.

Bruce winked and said, "Okay, I've got your game."

Emmet did not know what he meant. He started to ask, but Daphne interrupted: "Shut up, Bruce." Turning to Emmet, she said, "Bruce thinks everyone has a secret and he knows them all. You'll have to learn to ignore him and take him for what he is."

"Crazy," Emily said, and they all laughed.

Bruce laughed too, but leaned close until his lips kissed Emmet's ear. "I'll talk to you later," he whispered. Then he added "John," meaningfully, and tweaked Emmet's cheek.

Emmet moved a body's length away. Already he did not want to spend a moment alone with Bruce. He tried desperately to think of a reply, but he was afraid to antagonize him. He faced the women across the room hopelessly, his breath heaving from his lungs.

"What brings you here?" Emily asked kindly.

Emmet shrugged and pointed to his mouth. "N-n-nerves," he said, committing himself. He would have to keep the stutter part of himself, as if he were affecting a foreign accent.

Emily nodded assent. "You should meet Michael. He can't move an inch, much less talk. We call him the Quad. When his parents come to visit him or one of the doctors asks a question he doesn't like, he pees. It's his way of saying hello."

"He talks to me," Bruce said. "At night when the rest of you are sleeping."

"Sure," said Daphne, "and if you don't watch it, soon Jesus

and his mama are gonna be talking to you like they do to Margaret."

Bruce smirked as if she were incapable of understanding the mysteries that were the foundation of his life. "People seek me out," he said. *"Comprenez?"*

"You a first-timer?" Emily asked, turning to Emmet. He nodded, looking across the room unbelievingly. Before, he had not noticed the padlocks drilled into each window frame and the glass formed with wires melted into its center, a pattern so intricate he doubted bullets could pierce its armor.

"My whole family is locked up," Emily said matter-of-factly, as she might say that her family had attended the same university. "I don't mean there's millions of us. There's just three, aside from some cousins I don't know. My brother is the only one who tried to make a life. He got married. It worked for a few years, but then he got tired. One night he killed his wife, her mother, and their child while they took naps on the living room floor. Then he walked into the street and sat down, hugging his axe."

Emily shrugged, running her hands through her hair. Her cigarette singed the curls on top, shriveling several strands, like lit fuses. "It's a relief in a way. I mean, nothing else could ever be as bad. Think about it: imagine the worst thing that could happen. And then it does. Where does that leave you? Here, I guess," she said, waving smoke in the air. "But I have to admit that by the time he killed them I was already in and out pretty regularly. The doctors say the whole lot of us are missing a chromosome and without it, there's this fuzziness that unsettles our brain."

Emmet's eyes flickered in disbelief.

"I know it sounds like I made it up to justify things," Emily said. "Like somebody who's fat and says they have a hormone problem, but it's true. Some people do have hormone problems, right? It's genetic and there's nothing we can do. I don't mean to say that life would have been normal if it weren't for this chromosome. Not with my mother. But this way there was never a chance of escape because we're always carrying ourselves around with us. That missing gene, right? You can't see it, but there's no bigger part of me."

Bruce spun in circles in the middle of the floor, whirring like an engine. He opened his arms like wings and began to dive-bomb each person in the room.

"Bruce can't stand it when somebody talks more than a sentence at a time. Except himself," Emily said. "My mother's as loony as he is. How about yours? What's she like?"

Emmet had never met people who spoke so guardlessly about their lives. They seemed not to care who knew everything about them. Before he had time to censor himself, he said, "My m-m-mother's dead. She killed herself. But I don't like to talk about her. I hate people who complain about their p-p-parents."

"Why?" Emily asked. "Everybody's got two. Like eyes and feet."

"Not everybody's got two eyes; not everybody's got two feet," Bruce said, pausing in mid-flight. "Not everybody's got a father, either, if you count artificial insemination. I wish I had been born in a test tube. Then I wouldn't have a mother. She's worse than anyone's. She stole my sofa. I mean it. I had nowhere to sit, so I came here."

"C-c-can't you get it back?" Emmet fumbled.

Bruce blushed scarlet and jumped towards Emmet. "No!" he screamed. "But I stuck it with invisible pins. Every time she sits in it, they stab her right through. I know they're still there. She limps. She says she had a car accident, but she hasn't. She's too stupid to see the pins."

"Mothers get a bad rap here," Daphne said. "Everyone blames them, but nobody mentions fathers, unless they're rapists. You'll see at family therapy meetings—all the mothers sit and cry while their children scream at them. It never changes. The mothers always get it. Bad."

"I swear she stole it," Bruce said. "It's not like that shitty orange sofa in the lounge. Mine's a proper one. Gray silk with water stains where I drooled as a child. My mother thinks it's me, but it isn't me. It's mine."

Bruce swirled about the room, flapping his arms. Emily shook and smoked. Daphne stared.

Emmet was entranced by her reserve. She might have been a visitor who came one day to the hospital and never left. He wanted to win her confidence so that she might teach him something about the way she had learned to live in the ward. But he felt constrained by his stutter and was not ready to trade an ease in speaking for her trust.

"I'm t-t-tired," he said, rising to leave. The women smiled at him benignly.

"Dead," Bruce said out of the blue.

"What?" All three looked up.

"I said *dead*. He's never getting out."

"Stop," Daphne said.

"I would if I could," Bruce said. "But there's no stopping it. You can't change what's real." He pinched Emmet's cheek with his hand and pulled his face close to his own. "Sorry, buddy, but you picked the wrong door and stepped off into nothing."

"Don't give him a hard time," Daphne said.

"I'm not. I only want him to know what he's got himself in for. I want him to realize I know who he is." Bruce released his grip on Emmet's face. "Here," he said. "Let me tell your fortune."

Emmet tried to hide his hand. He was born without a life line. Those who believed in palms had panicked in the past when they had read his future, as if they had seen a ghost. Emmet had never decided if he believed in prophecies, but he comforted himself with hoping that if his hand did contain a message, he would not have lived even that long.

Bruce grabbed his hand, forcing Emmet's fingers open. Immediately he saw the unbroken space in the middle, like a washed-out map.

"I knew it." Bruce jumped up and down. "He's dead. He's dead. He's dead. I knew the second you walked in what you were. Now who's crazy?" he said to Daphne, turning in triumph.

"It's always been like that," Emmet said quickly. He closed his fist and crammed it into his jeans. "Always."

"Sure it has," Bruce sneered. He pulled a coin from his pocket. He flipped it into the air and slapped it down on the back of his hand.

"See this?" he said. "It's from a corpse. Somebody I know took it right off a skull, dumped in the sockets where the eyes had been. My friend stole it in Egypt or somewhere. I think he broke into a pyramid. They used to believe you could bribe your way to Paradise. I figure it will bring me luck."

Bruce tossed the coin to Emmet. It was brown and ragged, almost a nugget. Emmet turned it over in his palm. He saw the image of a wing etched into the metal.

"I've got a cloth, too," Bruce said, taking the coin from Emmet. "The same friend found it in the Middle East, wrapped around the face of a skeleton. You know, a blindfold, like they were executed. The cloth lasted a lot longer than that guy's skin. Well, it could have been a girl. They shoot them there, too, don't they? He wanted to take the whole skull, but he was afraid that customs would find it when they searched for bombs. I'll show it to you sometime—that is, if you ever get out." He laughed. "Maybe in your next life."

Emmet backed towards the door. "Ignore him," Daphne said. "He's the only person I know who was thrown out of the Quakers.

Even they couldn't stand him running on at their meetings. Think about it next time he goes off: they kept Nixon and they threw Bruce out."

"The truth of what I was telling them was too much," Bruce said. "So fuck 'em. Fuck all of you. I'm going to bed." He threw the coin over his head and snatched it behind his back with one hand. Then he flicked it with his thumb and caught it in his mouth. He stuck out his tongue with the coin balanced at its tip, like a bug.

"Catch you later," he said to Emmet. "I bet when you thought about eternity, you never imagined it would be me."

Bruce strummed an imaginary guitar and bowed once. Emmet heard him singing, "I'm so tired, I don't know what to do I'm so tired, my mind is set on you," as he walked down the corridor to his room. From far away he shouted "La la la," before he was convulsed with giggles.

"Is everybody else like that?" Emmet asked in the unsettled quiet Bruce left in his wake.

Emily blew rings with her cigarette. Four circles of smoke wobbled in the air towards Emmet, roping his face. "He's nothin'. At least he's smart. Wait till you meet some of the others. They'll curl your hair."

Daphne pulled Emily's hand to her mouth and puffed on her cigarette. "For some of us," she said, "a place like this unravels everything. You begin to worry that you're worse than you thought you were because you're surrounded by all these fucked-up people. Everyone begins to see you differently."

She fell back onto the mattress, flipping a pillow over her stomach, her arms encircling it in an embrace. "It's up to you to decide how unreachable you want to be. You can pull yourself back or go all the way forward. It's a clean slate, really. You can paper the walls of your room with shit if you want to. Ernest does that all the time and nobody throws him out. The rest of your life doesn't matter. It's not like anywhere else you've ever been."

Daphne and Emily yawned. In one movement, they kicked off their shoes and slipped their feet under the sheets.

" 'Night," Emmet said, and shuffled towards the door.

"Don't worry," Daphne called after him. She pulled her bracelets off one by one and stacked them on the table by the bed. "You've already got us. As for the rest, you'll figure out how to play it."

"Thanks," Emmet said, unsurely. But he could not imagine the next day: how the strangers sleeping in their rooms would arise and come to change his life. Already he felt he would know Daphne and Emily forever. The day before they had not existed. Often he thought of the events that brought him from one circumstance to another, the way his life might have changed had he moved to a different place. He wondered if all his mother's years of roaming had simply been a way to put herself in line of the right accident. Maybe she hoped she could make her life the way she wanted it to be if she never rested, always changing course, like a moving target.

Sometimes at night Emmet traced the whole long line of his relationships backwards until he returned to the original source. If he displaced one person at any point, the entire order collapsed. His life seemed to form an unbroken line moving forward, but without a single decision he could ever remember having made. He had let himself be pulled along aimlessly for so long that he was brought up short by this new place, as if he knew he was on the verge of something from which nothing else would ever be the same. But what it would be escaped him utterly.

He forced himself to step into the darkened hallway. He ran his hands against the wall as he placed one foot in front of the other, as gingerly as if he were guiding himself along a ledge perched impossibly high on the sheer face of a building.

CHAPTER
THREE

W hen Emmet awoke in the morning, the fattest man he had ever seen stood over him, a hand crooked at his hip.

"Oh, you're a cute little thing," he said. "I could eat you for breakfast."

Winston dangled a hand limply for Emmet to shake. When Emmet raised his arm from the bed, Winston brought his fingers to his lips and sucked their tips.

"Oh, sweet meat. Baby, we're gonna be friends," Winston said. "Want to lend me five dollars?"

Emmet blinked at him sleepily. For a moment he believed he was still in his apartment. He had been dreaming his cat held him pinned to the bed, a paw placed over each shut eye.

Winston threw back the sheets. Emmet spun over, as if he had been stripped. "Shy, aren't you?" he said. "Come on, baby. You're making me hungry. Sundays they make pancakes and I need to get my fill." He lifted his T-shirt and rubbed his belly. Crease after crease of black flesh spilled over his pants, jiggling before Emmet's face like thick, dark glue. Stretch marks rippled at his sides like badly sewn stitches. So many veins broke through the tight curls of hair on Winston's stomach that his skin seemed nearly blue, a field of bruises.

"I'm a big boy," Winston said, slapping his stomach. "With big appetites. And I love my pancakes."

Emmet imagined the buttermilk patties winding their way through fold upon fold of intestine stuffed inside Winston's rolls of fat. Emmet did not want to follow him into a room crowded with hungry, slobbering strangers.

"Maybe later," he said as he rose and pulled a shirt from his shopping bag. He busied himself with unpacking his clothes until he heard Winston shut the door behind him. Then he breathed a long sigh and sat at the small chair by his desk.

The chipped institutional furniture was made of plastic wood, with flat rubber cushions tied to the seat of each chair. The paint peeled from the ceiling, and water stains showed brownly through the walls. Emmet set four books on his desk, and an empty notebook. On the wall he tacked a postcard of the ocean near his grandmother's house in California. In the daylight, his few possessions looked paltry and out of place.

The orange-and-brown-checked carpet was littered with black cigarette burns. When Emmet looked down, the colored squares vibrated, the burns moving across it in a caravan. When he looked up, every mark and chip, every surface not a plane of solid color, vibrated with life.

From the ward he heard carts roll across the linoleum floor. People walked purposefully outside his room, their voices raised in unison, a din as loud as a train station at rush hour. Emmet wondered how long he could remain in his room. He remembered what Daphne had said about any behavior being acceptable. He wondered if no one would disturb him if he affected a catatonic stare and lay numbly on his bed.

"Got a minute?" Bruce said, startling him from the doorway.

He appeared rumpled and exhausted, as if he had been awake all night. He surveyed the corridor shiftily before he blocked his body against the door.

"You can trust me," Bruce asked. "I just wanted you to know I know who you are. But I won't tell anyone, I promise."

Emmet did not turn around. He continued to pull clothes from his bags and organize them in his drawers.

He sensed Bruce approach a few steps nearer. "Look, I've waited my whole life for this, and now finally I understand why I was sent here. But I need to know the truth. You've got to trust me." He sounded as if he were begging for his life to be spared. "I've played it and played it but I can't figure it out. I promise I won't tell a soul. I just need to know. I'm sorry I came on so strong last night, but let's start over. We can be friends. Here, have a cigarette."

As he fumbled in his pocket, Bruce spilled cigarettes over the floor. He dropped to his knees and crawled toward Emmet, offering a fistful in his outstretched hand. "Here. Take them. Take anything you want." He rested his head on Emmet's lap like a child.

He seemed so distraught that Emmet lowered his hand to rest against Bruce's ear. He stopped himself from stroking his hair soothingly.

"I-I-I don't smoke," Emmet said, finally. "I d-d-don't know what you want. This is crazy."

"Of course it's crazy. That's the beauty of it. Nobody normal could figure it out. You've duped the whole world, except for me. It's better than Houdini. You've bought yourself a second life and didn't even have to die for it. I sort of feel sorry for the guy who's doing time, but I guess you paid him plenty to take the fall. Hey, what's a few trust funds to you? I hear you've got cows worth a quarter of a million apiece."

"I d-d-don't understand," Emmet said.

"Yes you do," Bruce said, leaping to his feet. "Please, John, admit it. No one can hear. They don't bug the rooms. I checked them out."

"I'm n-n-not John," Emmet said.

"Okay, so you're not now, but you know what I mean. You were. Or you are and you've become this other person for now. That's fine. I can understand it. Everybody gets trapped. Everybody goes stale. But you can tell me; I can help you. We could collaborate even. McGrath and Lennon. No. What am I saying? Forgive me. Lennon and McGrath. It's got the same sort of ring, don't you think?"

"Lennon?" Emmet asked. He was too startled to remember to stutter.

"Yeah, I know that's who you are. Okay, so you've cut your hair and got contact lenses, but I knew the second I saw you. Believe me, you were sent here for me. It's like I've been trapped inside this burning house all my life and suddenly you appeared in the doorway to show me the way out. I couldn't sleep a wink last night I was so excited. I know everything by heart. You name the song, I can sing it. And I've got the codes all cracked except for the White Album. It's like you've given me the map to a buried treasure, but the last direction is missing. I see this big X in the middle right where the treasure lies, but there's some turn somewhere that I don't get and I could wander around forever trying to find it. You're the only one who can let me in. Please. I'll do anything."

Emmet bent down over Bruce's ear. "I can't help you," he said. "I would if I could, but you've got the wrong guy."

"Look," Bruce said, pushing his face so close that Emmet could see the fine line of blood vessels broken along the ridge of his nose. "That Manson character had it all wrong. You never wanted to kill anybody. I know the score: 'Give peace a chance' and all that. When they said Paul was dead they didn't mean Paul. They meant you. You wanted to throw people off the track. I can understand that. Hey, what does an artist need more than a little peace and quiet? And you just bided your time till you could get away. Am I right? You planted the seeds years before, but you didn't want anyone to know, not even Yoko. Hey, if it's any consolation, I think she's an artist in her own right. I'll bet she's a really good mother, too." Bruce clawed at Emmet's knees. "But tell me now, please. I know the game. No one else can hear."

"Lennon is dead," Emmet said. "I c-c-can't be him. I'm Emmet."

"I know you're dead," Bruce screamed. "But not dead. You've only changed. Come on." He flailed his arms about, like a dervish, not caring if he struck something.

"I've got an appointment," Emmet said, walking cautiously towards the bed. He sat down to avoid Bruce's thrashing body. He glanced at his watch and widened his eyes in surprise, as if he were already late.

Bruce grabbed the cigarettes from Emmet's desk and crushed them. "This could be you," he said, sifting the tobacco through his fingers like sand. "This morning I heard the doctors laughing about you. They said you were too crazy even for this place. Do you know how bad that is? Do you know how low that makes you? They're going to transfer you to the state hospital if you don't watch it. I'll tell them you tried to attack me. I'll tell them I heard you planning a rape. Then they'll ship you out to Thorazine heaven faster than you can say 'Strawberry Fields.' Believe me. One of the nurses is in love with me. I know everything. The same rules don't apply."

Bruce moved menacingly towards Emmet. He seemed possessed by the rage of a person with nothing left to lose. Bruce pushed Emmet onto the bed and straddled his chest. He brought his hands to his throat and teased his flesh. "You ever lose consciousness?" he asked. "It's somewhere between falling asleep and passing out in a gas chamber. I used to do it to myself. Everything goes dark and you can't breathe. I know just when to stop. Or not."

Emmet brought his hands to rest over Bruce's. He rubbed them gently to persuade him to lessen the pressure. He did not want to seem afraid.

"Come on, Bruce," Emmet said.

Bruce squeezed hard, once, and then relaxed his grip. "Just think about it. Remember, I can get anything I want done. This place is like a Mexican prison, and you're easy meat if I say so." He sprayed Emmet's face with saliva.

Emmet tried to think of ways to calm him. Bruce was already in the hospital. He could do anything he wanted. If he killed Emmet, the doctors would only extend his stay.

As if he read his mind, Bruce said, "I like it here. I've got everything I need. *Comprenez?*"

Emmet clasped Bruce's hands and held them in his lap. He gazed into his eyes as if he were his friend.

"I like you, Bruce," he said. "There's no reason to hide anything. Look, I'll tell you a secret. It's the only one I know. I really can talk. This stutter is a scam. I can't explain how it happened, but it's too late to go back now. I'm not ready. Can I trust you not to tell anyone?"

"Nice try," Bruce said. "But I'm not buying it. I don't give a fuck if you only speak Esperanto. You know what I want."

"I can't say any more about it," Emmet said. He rose and inched his way towards the door, as if his back faced a gun.

"So I'm right. There is more. Come back." Bruce lunged towards him. He brought him down on the bed and tumbled on top of him, shaking him by the hair so fiercely that Emmet believed his eyes would come loose from their sockets. "Tell me," Bruce hissed.

"Oh, baby, I see you like it rough," Winston said from the doorway. Bruce bolted upright, smoothing his knotted hair. He cast down his eyes, smiling demurely. "Hi, Winston," he mumbled.

"What's doin' behind this closed door?" he asked. Winston wiggled his girth into the inches separating Bruce and Emmet. The flesh on his hips spread onto Emmet's lap. His body smelled of sweat and syrup.

"I saw him first, so don't go gettin' any ideas," Winston said. He socked Bruce's shoulder playfully. "This boy's mine."

"We were just talking," Bruce said. "I was interested in something he said last night. About music."

"You've got a funny way of showin' it, brother. Why don't you go do your singin' someplace else?"

Bruce stood. Emmet avoided his gaze, but Bruce squeezed his hand. "Catch you later, John," he said.

Emmet remained mute. Once Bruce left, he moved away from Winston. The seams of his jeans were damp from Winston's sweat.

"John?" Winston said. "Is that your name? I thought it was something weirder."

"It's Emmet. With one t-t-t."

"In my neighborhood, they call me Arson. Nobody calls me Winston. I've got this thing about fires."

"Me too," Emmet said. "I've had n-n-nightmares all my life that I was trapped in one. It's what I dread most about dying."

"Not me, baby. I love 'em. You ever see a house burn?"

"Once our neighbor's house burned down, but I slept through most of it. When I woke up, there was nothing left but smoke and a few w-w-wet walls."

"I used to set them all the time," Winston said dreamily. "Where did you live then? Maybe I did it."

"California."

"Nah. Wasn't me. Never been there. The first time it happened it was only a few blocks from here. It was an accident. I was playin' in the backyard with some matches and a jar of kerosene and the grass caught fire. Burned straight towards my neighbor's house as if I'd laid a fuse all the way to his back door.

"Baby, you should've seen it. The fire ate everything on the ground and then started makin' its way up the ivy that hung on these white trellises by the kitchen door. At first the flames just licked the wood, like they were teasing it, but then the paint blackened a bit and the fire started gettin' up its nerve. It kissed the back of that house board by board before it really started bubblin', growing stronger every second.

"The door to the basement was the first to go. It cracked and split and blew off into the yard with only the hinges hangin' there like they'd come unscrewed, and then it was only another minute before the windows exploded, just like bombs thrown from inside. *Bang!* It was the greatest sight I'd ever seen. I didn't give a shit about the owners. They could get another house. Maybe they'd miss some photographs or something, but, baby, it's all transitory, right?"

Emmet nodded dumbly, as if he were watching a television screen.

"Well, then I heard a siren, and then another, and then the roof shot off that mother, shingles flying everywhere, and the front started to let go, floor by floor, until you could see every piece of furniture burnin' by itself. Flames on the floors and flames on the bed and flames on the tables and chairs. Every fuckin' thing, like each bit was dyin' on its own. I loved the chairs with stuffing best, because the cloth went first and left the frame, which burned slower, makin' these hoops of fire. But then the whole building crashed down and there was nothin' but a heap, so I went home.

But I couldn't hide it. My mama knew what I did from the smell of my clothes and the gleam burnin' in my eye."

"Did you go to prison?" Emmet asked.

Winston had been standing against the window as he spoke. He turned to Emmet, laughing in loud whoops that made his stomach heave. "Prison? What suburb you from, baby? They don't do nothin' to eight-year-olds. They sent me to a special school and made me see doctors who tried to figure out my trouble. Only I didn't have any. But I got this reputation. The kids started calling me Arson. It stuck. They'd bring the newspapers into school in the morning and when there'd be a fire somewhere, they'd read the paper out loud, like I wasn't there, and say, 'Oh, damn. I got this friend named Arson and he's done it again. Look here, the paper says there was a fire and Arson is suspected.' They thought it was funny, that one person was startin' fires all over the world.

"They were always watching after that. The hard part was gettin' away from them. The fire was easy. I practiced and practiced until my fires were so big they were three, four, five stories high, burnin' right in my face, but even with the flames up there and me so far down below, every time I felt like I was on top of the world, you know, because I'd made somethin' so beautiful with nothin' but a pack of matches and then I'd brought it down. *Poof.* You know what I mean?"

Winston looked at him eagerly, as if he were waiting for Emmet to applaud his ingeniousness. Emmet nodded inanely. He had never known anyone who had taken so much pleasure in anything he had accomplished, and with so little regret. Winston seemed to be one of the happiest people he had ever met. If he had been at home, Emmet would have tricked him to leave his apartment. But the hospital had brought them together; they might live there indefinitely. Emmet did the only thing he could think of: he surrendered to Winston's enthusiasm.

"That must have been s-s-something," Emmet said. "How many times did you get caught?"

"Oh, I stopped countin'. Every time I could slip out, I set another one. But I still haven't got it exactly right. There's always some smoke, somethin' to ruin the purity of it. And I've been thinkin' lately how much better it would be at night. Picture this: those fire trucks coming with their pretty red lights flashin' against the darkness and the orange of the flames. You can't get color like that in a painting. But you know what else I want?"

Emmet wished the door were open so that someone might visit. Not one doctor or nurse had checked on him yet that morning. He wondered if they remembered he was there. "No, what?" he replied, weakly.

"I want it to get bigger. I've got this house in the suburbs in mind. It's got millions of windows spread over three wings and a circular drive that could fit ten trucks. I'm working it out to have all those windows explode at once. That's my dream, anyway, once I get out of here. Do you think houses like that have alarms hooked up to the fire department? I know that some of them have a line right to the police, but I don't think rich people expect fires as much as they do to get robbed. You agree?"

"I don't think people in houses like that ever expect anything is going to h-h-happen, from the outside, anyway."

"Well, baby, we're both here, so things are happenin' all over, right? Jesus. What time is it?" Winston picked up Emmet's hand and looked at his watch. "Pretty watch," he said. "I bet it cost a lot. Can I wear it?"

Emmet draped his hand protectively over his wrist. "Oh, well, some other time," Winston said. "Baby, stop draggin' your ass. It's time for our community meeting. Everybody brings their gripes, but you'd better be careful. These doctors are always watchin' and watchin', and they take more notes than a stenographer."

Winston threw open the door. The noise from the hallway hit

the room like a blast of air. "Hi, sugar," Winston screeched when he saw someone he recognized. "Wait till you see what I've got." He raised one leg and pointed it like a finger at Emmet. "Come on, baby. Let's go. No more hiding. It's time you met your new friends."

CHAPTER
FOUR

When Emmet stepped outside, a teenaged boy was being pushed in a wheelchair down the corridor. Winston slid past Emmet, traipsing ahead as if he had already forgotten they had just spent an hour talking. A nurse slowly guided the chair, swinging it in circles, rocking it backwards by jiggling the handles, as if she were entertaining a child in a stroller. As they approached, Emmet heard her describe everything they saw.

"Oh, look, Michael, there's the wash basins. And there's the door to the isolation unit. Look, there's the nursing station. We're almost there, Michael. Who would you most like to sit next to once we arrive at our meeting? Do you have a special friend?"

She paused when she saw Emmet. A blue plastic sunflower etched with the name "Ruth" was pinned to her turtleneck.

"Oh, look, Michael, here's a new friend. What's your name?"

Emmet told her. The boy sprawled in his seat, his arms strapped tightly to the metal rail. His feet were encased in steel slippers attached to the wheels of the chair so that he sat spread-eagled and exposed. A thick rubber belt looped around his waist. His eyes lolled upwards through drugged lids. Emmet saw his eyeballs sway back and forth lazily under the skin, as if he were in the throes of a dream. A steady stream of drool dripped from his mouth. It traced a line down the buttons of his pajamas before settling in a pucker of cloth near his crotch.

"This is Michael. He's getting better every day. Aren't you?" She prodded the slumped boy.

"Hi," Emmet said as he thought, "He must be the Quad."

The cascade of drool was Michael's only sign of life. The nurse took Emmet's hand and brought it down around the lifeless fingers. She squeezed them together. Michael's hand felt boneless against the metal rail. He did not move or change or give any response.

Emmet snapped back his hand, rubbing his palm against his jeans to erase the sensation of the boy's doughy flesh.

"That was nice," the nurse said. "See how easy it is to make friends?" Michael's head rolled to his chest. The nurse pushed him upright with her hand, then waved to Emmet. "Say good-bye, Michael," she said airily as they moved away.

Emmet turned around. Patients suddenly filed into the hallway from their rooms as if summoned by a silent bell. A spastic girl with yellow hair rounded the corner. Her head rolled on her neck as if it were a separate body part, unattached by tendons, muscles, or blood vessels. Her arms flailed against her sides as she stumbled, as if they propelled each step like flapping wings.

Emmet tensed the muscles in his arms so that he could feel them stiffen and contract at will. "Does everyone here lose motor control after a while?" he wondered.

A nurse followed the girl, clapping his hands for encouragement. As they lurched along, they reminded Emmet of a mechanical rabbit he had bought for his godson. With each slap of his palms, the rabbit ran erratically across the floor, driven by the sound of the hands. It seemed to Emmet that if the nurse stopped clapping, the girl would collapse into a heap.

As they made their way, the nurse boomed cheerfully, "Jesus walked on water, Edith—the least you can do is walk across this rug." Edith paid him no notice. She made her way determinedly towards some invisible point she held fixed with her eyes, the only part of her body not afflicted by her ungovernable movements.

Many of the other patients chattered to themselves, their heads pointed up or down or behind them, but rarely in the direction they walked. They moved aimlessly, as if the space they inhabited were irrelevant to anything that occupied their minds.

Emmet fell in line next to a middle-aged man dressed in a maroon suit. "Hello," the man said.

Emmet nodded.

"I hate your hat," the man said, brushing the top of Emmet's head. "Hate it."

"But I'm not . . ." Emmet said.

"Shut up. You look like a fool," the man said. "Take it off." He locked his fingers around Emmet's hair. " 'Willie,' my wife always says, 'you've got to go to a topless bar in Texas to see the titties,' " the man said, dragging Emmet along. Other patients crowded in behind, as if on cue, blocking Emmet from anyone who might have come to his aid.

"I said," the man repeated, "have you ever been to Texas to see the titties?" He tugged harder on Emmet's hair.

"No," Emmet said.

"Huh?" The man yanked so savagely that Emmet gasped for air, as if the hands clutched his throat instead of his scalp.

"No," Emmet panted. "I'm a p-p-priest."

"I don't see why that should stop you," the man said, but he released his grip. Emmet dropped to his knees. A heavy woman in a housecoat walked into him, sending him sprawling. "Help. He's trying to trip me," she screamed.

The other patients began to stampede, knocking Emmet flat against the carpet. As they scrambled over him, he shielded his head with hands. Some sidestepped his body; some planted their feet directly on his back. The procession seemed interminable, as if one of them had opened a trap door in the back of the ward, inviting every person in the city to enter and file purposely over his body. He did not turn or look or lift his head as the shoes hammered down upon him, for fear someone would kick his face. He cowered there until the last foot made its way past his head.

He lay stunned for a moment until he was sure no one else lurked behind. When he raised himself to his knees, a prim young woman in a daffodil-gold sweatshirt and a matching cap glowered down at him. A silver crucifix nestled in her bosom.

"You're late for the community meeting," she said, aggrieved. "Come with me." She offered her hand, but Emmet steadied himself without it. He followed her sullenly towards the recreation room.

The area was unrecognizable from the night before. The game tables had been moved to one side to make room for twenty folding chairs set in a circle. Patients were everywhere, their jabbering voices mixed in the murmurings of a mob. In the daylight, the drawings he remembered appeared more menacing, as if they documented a series of crimes.

The patients passed a cigarette in a chain around the room, each one sucking a light before handing it to the next. They shared the fire among themselves, gently protecting the smoking butt, as if it were a substance in danger of extinction.

Emmet saw Winston gesturing wildly with his hands to a group of patients convulsed with laughter. They stole glances at Emmet as Winston spoke. Winston put his nose in the air and walked stiffly a few paces back and forth. The patients laughed harder. Emmet saw Emily and Bruce together in a corner and shuffled over to join them.

"Where's Daphne?" he asked.

"She needed to stay in bed this morning," Emily said. The rawness of her voice made her message sound ominous.

Bruce winked at him. "What's happening, John?" he asked.

He snapped his gum. " 'Will you won't you want me to make you,' " he sang in a low voice.

"What's this John shit?" Emily asked.

"Nothing." Emmet cringed with guilt. "Private joke."

"Yeah," Bruce said. "We got better acquainted in his room after you girls went to bed." He snapped his gum again.

"Remember your wife just had a baby," Emily said.

Bruce blushed. "Baby," he said, as if the word were unfamiliar. "It isn't mine. It's my father's. They put me in here so they could be together. I dreamed it. Then I knew." He rubbed his face with his palms. "Baby," he repeated.

Emmet looked at Bruce's skin, moist and inflamed, his body quaking with miserable energy. He could not imagine Bruce ever having lived a life outside the ward. He felt sympathy for him for the first time, a sense that maybe he had fallen from another life more suddenly and dangerously than Emmet had imagined.

"Is it a b-b-boy or a girl?" Emmet asked.

"I said it's my father's," Bruce shouted. "It's a bastard. It doesn't have a sex. I hope the baby dies."

A black woman walking in circles by the door stopped and turned to them.

"My baby's father is the devil, but I know he's gonna be born with wings," she said. "Richard Nixon knocked me up, but my baby don't need no helicopter to fly. Barry Goldwater knocked me up too. Maybe I got twins. They're gonna be my wings."

She spit once on the floor and continued pacing, walking faster and faster in circles until she whirled about the room, twirling her arms, chanting, "Ee-o, ee-o, ee-o." A bath towel was wrapped around her head like a turban. The folds were held together with a wooden spoon. She had drawn two pink suns on her cheek with lipstick, their rays spreading to her ears. She had painted her lips electric blue with a frosty eye shadow. A sheer stocking hung around one ankle with a spiked patent-leather shoe on her foot. The other leg was bare. As she spun, the stocking coiled and recoiled around her ankle. She blithely stepped over it, as if this were part of a choreographed dance.

"That's Juanita," Emily said. "She wants to be a mass murderer when she grows up. All she's missing is somebody to sell her the rifle. She claims she's pregnant, but none of us believe her. The doctors won't tell us either way, but look at her stomach. That can't be real."

Juanita's stomach was perfectly round, as if she'd slipped a globe of the world inside her shift.

As Emily spoke, Juanita danced up to an elderly woman kneeling on the carpet in prayer and kicked her. "Barren hag," she said. "My name's Immaculate. Santa Immaculata. Santa Claus. Mrs. Claus von Bülow. I've got an angel right in here." She rubbed her stomach with both hands, as if rotating the hemispheres of the globe.

"Cunt," the old woman said. "Nigger—Polynesian cunt."

"Sister," Juanita said. "Tokyo Rose. Betsy Ross. I know you sewed those stars on that flag. All thirteen of them. You're the victim of a smear campaign." Juanita hugged the old woman, then tumbled on top of her.

"Juanita's got a political bent," Emily whispered. "When she isn't wearing a hole in the carpet, she reads newspapers. She doesn't know what year it is, but something connects."

"She kissed me. She kissed me. She licked my ear," the old woman screamed. She ran the words together until the sound lost all meaning.

Juanita jumped up, cutting the air with a banshee's shriek. "Ya, ya, ya," she yelled, each time jabbing closer and closer to the old woman's face with a kick of her leg.

The other patients ignored them. Emmet turned to Emily. "Where are the doctors? They're going to kill each other."

"No they're not," Emily said. "Anyway, who cares? It would be a lot quieter around here if they did. The staff always ignores us before community meeting so we can relate to each other unsupervised. It's supposed to breed independence, but I'm sure they've got a camera somewhere."

"It's unbearable here," Emmet said. "Nothing on the outside was as b-b-bad as this, was it?" He tried to list the things he used to do all day, but the shrieking women blotted everything from his mind. The patterns in the carpet pulsed with life.

"Probably," Emily said cheerfully. "This might even be better. But either way, you'd be spooked by those two. Look at 'em. It cheers me up to know that bad as I get, I'm nothing compared to them."

Juanita and the old woman tussled on the floor, knocking into chairs, squealing at each other in a language known only to themselves. "Don't they sort of fascinate you? I mean they'd have to have been a little different before to know anything about the world, wouldn't they?" Emily asked.

Juanita and the old woman wrapped their arms around each other. The old woman cooed into Juanita's ears. Juanita pulled a lipstick from her bra and drew a pink sun on the old woman's cheek.

"But what about us?" Emmet said. "How do we know we aren't just like them? Don't you notice p-p-people staring at you on the street, and you wonder what's wrong? Juanita and that old woman are on the same wavelength. How do we know we're not as b-b-bad as they are and we're just too crazy to notice? It scares me not to be certain how far gone I am. I feel these people's eyes and I don't know what they want."

"People stare because they know who you are," Bruce whispered. "It's the price of being famous. You'd think you'd be used to it after thirty years."

"No, that's not it," Emmet rounded on him. "Stop saying that.

What I mean is that when I'm anywhere but home, I feel the people I meet want to k-k-kill me. Like when you go into a truck stop in a small town and everyone's attention gravitates to you? Sometimes driving on the highway I close my eyes when a car passes because I think that if I look up, I'm going to see a rifle p-p-pointed at my head."

"Yeah," Emily said. "One day it might be Juanita."

"People do want to kill you," Bruce said, aloud this time. "That should come as no surprise. It's already happened once. You're right to be paranoid."

"What are you talking about, Bruce?" Emily said. "Shut up." She turned to Emmet. "Maybe you *are* crazy, but that's not the point. Think what it's like to have you walk into a truck stop. 'Married with children' isn't the first thing to strike their mind. They see you and they think, 'This freak is living freely—what does that mean for me?' They do want you dead; they don't want to have to look at you. They think they've got it all figured out and you aren't part of the picture."

She chuckled. "My doctors tell me I have to examine my rage, but it isn't rage to me—it's sense. When I see those other people, I think, 'I'd like to blow you all away.' They're scum; most people are scum. It's stupid to believe anything else. I would do it, too. Kill them. And I wouldn't feel guilty later."

"Nice, Emily," Bruce said. "Good to know you're upholding the family tradition. Forgive me if I don't rush to you for advice about how to live on the outside."

"Maybe you should. Maybe you'd like to find out how long you'd last on Highway 101. One look at your whirling eyeballs and they'd drown you in the toilet. We like to think everybody's the same underneath, but that's shit. People are afraid of each other. People hate each other. And when you're where you're not supposed to be, they want to get you. Your being alive undercuts everything they believe."

Emmet could not explain to Emily how he believed there was something about him that made the hatred he sensed from strangers personal. Other people who dressed more oddly than he did went anywhere they wanted freely. Other people could pass invisibly on the street. Whenever he went outside, Emmet felt the fear that gripped him was visible to anyone who looked, as if the black marks streaked on his soul radiated from his clothing brighter than the pink rays on Juanita's cheeks.

Once Emmet read in the newspaper about a bus accident in which the driver, realizing the gas tank had exploded, gazed rapturously at the sky and shouted, "Lord, I'm coming home!" as a ball of flame rolled down upon him. There were days when Emmet dreamed of finding a serenity like the bus driver's. But there were other days when the driver's confidence seemed more deluded than the maddest ravings he had heard. Emmet did not know if his life had dimmed because he had seen through to the real heart of the world, or if some defect, like Emily's missing chromosome, blinded him to the peace that other people seemed to embrace faithfully and with ease.

"Praise Jesus," the old woman exclaimed, kneeling. Juanita straddled her, locking her torso between her legs. "Praise His name. I have seen Him through the portholes. I have seen Him through the Virgin's vagina." She threw back her head, jabbering "Cunt-cuntcunt." She clapped her hands, babbling in a frenzy, as if she were speaking in tongues.

Juanita squatted, crushing the old woman to the floor. She raised herself a few inches, her legs akimbo. "Tongue this, Rose Kennedy," she said.

The woman flapped her arms against the carpet in surrender. "Take me," she sighed. "I bless the body of Christ." Juanita sat down solidly on the woman's face, crowing with pleasure.

Chris ran into the room. He dug the heels of his cowboy boots into the rug and tugged Juanita's arms. She slipped through his stubby legs. "Touch my baby and I'll cut your fuckin' heart out, shorty," she taunted. Juanita towered over Chris. He squared his chest to face her. She flicked his shoulder with two fingers as she walked past. "Out of my way, bug," she said.

Juanita strode up to Emmet. "Gimme a cigarette," she ordered. She held out her palm as if it were a weapon.

Emmet reached into the pocket of Emily's sweater and snatched her pack. "Keep them," he said, as if they had been his own.

Emily cocked an eyebrow. "Generous of you. Maybe you'd like to lend her some of my clothes to replace the lovely turban she's wearing?"

"S-s-sorry," Emmet said. "I wasn't thinking. I just wanted her to go away."

"It's a submarine, baby," Emily said. "Nobody's got any room. You'd better get used to it."

As they spoke, Juanita unbuttoned the top of her shift and stuffed the pack between her breasts. The skin on her hands glistened over her bones. When she closed the buttons, her fingers climbed up her body elegantly, as if they were scaling piano keys. She stormed from the room.

The old woman rocked on her knees, keening.

"Who is she?" Emmet asked, desperate for her to stop.

"That's Margaret," Emily said. "She's been locked up for twenty years. Her husband comes to visit every night but she hasn't said a sane word in all that time. She sees the Virgin Mary every day at lunch. Only the body parts differ. Sometimes it happens at dinner, too, if it's been a bad day."

A man Emmet had not seen before entered the room. He averted his eyes as he walked, even as he passed Margaret. He was small, with a shiny baby's face. His hairline receded all the way to the back of his head, with a few wisps plastered across the dome. As he walked, a tuft of hair bobbed like an antenna. He licked his finger and repeatedly wiped his hand across his head to flatten it. He peered over glasses with red frames and blue-tinted lenses set halfway down his nose. The cracked edge of his toenail stuck out from one of the brown socks he wore with his sandals. Around his neck hung a wide paisley tie.

"Almost chic as Juanita, no?" Emily said. "He's called Dr. Franklin. He writes poetry in his spare time." The doctor fussed with a clipboard of papers as the patients drifted towards their seats.

Suddenly from the hallway, Emmet heard the terrifying voice that had resounded from the nursing station the night before.

"I hate these fucking meetings," she snarled from the other room. "You're going to be sorry you made me come."

"Oh no," said Emily. "It's Louise."

As Emily spoke, a woman flung herself into the room as if she had been pushed. She battered her way forward as if she believed the air itself to be an impediment to her progress.

Emmet was transfixed by her. Louise was tall, with a fine, thin nose. Her dark blue pupils were offset by white triangles on either side. They were so geometrically perfect that they seemed to have been constructed by a machine, like a doll's eyes inserted into her sockets. They gave her face a fierce and alien look.

Louise trounced to a chair in the center of the room. As she sat, she pulled a brush from her purse. She threw her light-brown mane over her face, swiping it roughly, then flung it back over her head. Her hair stood out wildly, charged with static. She possessed a narrow waist that spread on a widening plane to thick thighs. She wore brief shorts and a matching halter top cut from a square of plaid material. Her thighs fought against the seams so that a quarter-inch of flesh pinched over the cloth. Her breasts hung almost to her waist, long as arms.

She stroked her chest idly as she surveyed the room. She stopped when she saw Emmet. "Hi," she mouthed.

Emmet looked at Bruce and Emily to see if Louise meant them.

He did not understand how she could know him after one morning on the ward. Louise saw him hesitate and shook her head. "No, you," she mouthed again, wiggling her finger right at him.

"Looks like somebody's taken a fancy to you already," Emily said. "Just don't bring her to my room at night. I've never figured her out, and she makes me nervous."

Emmet slumped in his seat. "Maybe she's just being friendly," he said.

"Maybe she knows, too," Bruce whispered. "Maybe she wants an autograph. Just remember: I was there first. Anything you have to say, you say to me. No three-way information, *comprenez?*"

"Stop it, Bruce," Emmet pleaded.

"No. You stop it. Stop stalling. Remember what I told you. We can be friends or I can take care of you. Either way it's up to you." Bruce had a way of keeping his voice threatening but low enough so no one else could listen, the way Emmet had heard kidnappers speak in movies.

Emmet was afraid that if someone knew of Bruce's obsession, it would be used against him. He could not imagine explaining Bruce's delusions to his doctors without sounding like an accomplice. People in the ward saw meaning everywhere, especially in accidents. He did not trust even Emily or Daphne to know.

Louise rose from her chair to loosen the hem of her shorts from her flesh. Round clumps of cellulite jiggled in her legs like scooped balls of melon. The underside of each nipple popped out of the bottom of her halter, thick and purple, like two lips. When she beamed at Emmet for the second time, she seemed to be smiling from three mouths.

The other patients waited in their chairs. Their deafening chatter lowered to a soft hum, like the pulse of a loose energy coursing through the room. Even Margaret knelt quietly on the floor, raising her arms to heaven.

"Let's get this charade rolling," Louise scowled.

Dr. Franklin peered over the rim of his glasses. "Somewhere to go, Louise?"

"Out of your sight, doc, just as soon as you'll let me."

"We're free to do anything we want here," the doctor said. "As long as we follow certain rules."

"You make 'em, you follow 'em," Louise said. "No matter what face you want to put on it, we're still your prisoners. What if I told everyone in the room to get up and follow me? You'd have your meeting by yourself? Want to try it?"

The doctor nervously checked the faces in the room to see who listened. A few of the patients watched them intently; the rest sat blankly. "Sit down, Louise," he said.

"Fine. I just wanted to make it clear that you're as full of shit as I thought you were." The triangles in Louise's eyes pinched shut, leaving the dark blue pupils dead still.

It had not occurred to Emmet that a person could be held in the hospital against his will. He had been told he could sign himself out any time he wanted, even against medical advice. What if his doctor had lied and would not let him leave?

Across the room he saw a large window looped with padlocks. He could discern nothing beyond its wire mesh screen but the shadow of another tower of the hospital. He turned to Emily to seek assurance that she had seen people leave of their own free will, but she shushed him with a wink, clearly amused by what was happening.

"You certainly have an inflated sense of your own power, Louise, if you believe you can make everyone follow your bidding. What makes you think the other patients don't want to stay?" the doctor said.

"Want to give it a test?" Louise sneered.

"You're free to go, Louise," the doctor said. He flipped through his papers intently, as if Louise were already the farthest thing from his mind.

"Fine. Have a fruitful session." Louise marched across the room to stand before Emmet's chair. She lifted his hand. "Emmet, are you coming?" she ordered.

Emmet blanched. He could not conceive how Louise knew his name. When he raised his head, her strange eyes bore upon him, pleading with him not to humiliate her in front of the others. Emmet knew the doctor was studying him, as if he were imprinting Emmet's face on his mind forever, as if from that moment on he would remember everything Emmet said or did.

Emmet stood. For a moment he hesitated, wondering if he would ruin himself forever by leaving. Louise tugged at his arm beseechingly while she tossed a contemptuous look at the doctor. Emmet lowered his head as if he could make himself less noticeable, hugging his arms to his chest.

"Good boy," Louise breathed into his ear. Silently, he allowed her to lead him from the room.

CHAPTER FIVE

Except for her manner of dress, there was nothing flamboyant about Louise's illness. She had been admitted to the hospital weeks before Emmet. One Thursday evening she had eaten the fluorescent light bulb that hung from the ceiling in her college dormitory. After her roommate summoned the security forces, Louise was found reclining in bed with a small piece of the bulb's stem held in her hand, like a heel of bread.

Louise had always believed herself to be more intelligent than any doctor or nurse she had met in her years in and out of the hospital. She grew impatient explaining to them the reasons for her despair. After the guards had brought her to the ward, she matter-of-factly told the doctor who examined her that she ate glass because she wanted to feel a physical pain that matched the agony she suffered in her mind. She had nothing else to say about it. When they X-rayed her stomach, they found no pieces of glass left inside her body, so finely had she chewed each bite. Only her lips and gums were encrusted with chunks of the bulb, stuck between her teeth like pale jewels.

Louise viewed her incarceration in the hospital as a personal affront. She defined herself as a kind of political prisoner, victimized by social workers and relatives who sought to brainwash her against the things she knew to be most true about the world.

"Go ahead, sign me in," Louise had taunted her mother when she committed her. "You can't keep me here forever. One day I'll get out and finish the job." Louise threatened violence against herself the way some people vow to settle a score with an enemy. She plotted her own murder like the perfect crime.

"I've seen what life has to offer and it isn't anything I want," Louise said to anyone who would listen.

Louise's rage unnerved her doctors and nurses. She could out-last them in any conversation. She could quote sources that affirmed her despair from writers they had never read. Her relentless fury made any response they made to her sound paltry and hollow. Often the staff discussed her case at meetings: especially the way Louise scoffed at any solution they offered. She made them sound like idiots even to themselves. A few tried to reach her. Most despised her and hoped she would go away.

The doctors who cared believed they could appeal to Louise's reason, but she had none. Instead, she possessed a wild panic, a fearless intelligence, and a confidence that she was blessed with deadly insight.

"Thanks for not showing me up," Louise said to Emmet when they stood in the hallway after leaving the meeting.

Emmet regretted having left. He was afraid that he would be branded as a troublemaker. He wanted to return to the meeting, but the idea of making an enemy of Louise disturbed him more than any punishment the staff might devise. He hoped he could explain to them later that he felt more ambivalent than Louise did, that he did not entirely reject their help. But for the moment he had thrown his lot with Louise, so he said only, "It was n-n-nothing," trying to sound convincing.

"Let's go to my room," Louise said. She led Emmet into a

corridor he had not noticed before, identical to the one outside his own room. On the way, they passed another hall, and then another. The ward was larger than he had imagined. He wondered if those hallways were inhabited by people who never saw the light of day. He wondered if a secret rating system existed in which the staff punished disobedient patients by leaving them at the mercy of inmates who were worse than anything Emmet had yet dreamed.

In Louise's room clothes were heaped upon the unmade bed. Several suitcases hung open, draped with stockings and underwear, as if she had rushed home from a trip. The other bed was stripped.

"They don't give me a roommate," she said. "I'm too difficult. Something to keep in mind if you're planning on staying awhile. Being easy doesn't get you very far. 'Take 'em for everything you can get' is my motto."

"How did you know my n-n-name?" Emmet asked.

"It was a cinch. You know that basket of charts outside the nursing station? I sneak over there at night sometimes when I'm bored and read them. I'd never seen your name before last night. And I'd never seen you before today. I put two and two together and came up with Emmet. Interesting chart, by the way."

Emmet had never read it. Always in their session, his psychiatrist scribbled notes as rapidly as Emmet spoke. Emmet wondered if his doctor simply transcribed what he heard or if he interpreted at the same pace as Emmet talked. Once he had asked to read his chart, but his doctor had refused. "It doesn't have anything to do with you, really," the doctor had said. "It's my view of things. What matters is how you see things, not how I do."

Often Emmet tried to sneak a look at the doctor's notes. Sometimes Emmet paced about the room, pretending to be lost in his subconscious, but actually positioning himself at the perfect angle to peer over his doctor's shoulder. Whenever Emmet moved behind him, the doctor covered the page with his hand. The only words

Emmet had ever seen were "soft-pedaled." He did not know what they referred to or what the moment had been when his doctor decided he had lied.

"What does it say?" Emmet asked Louise.

"Oh, lots of things. I know where you live. Nice area, by the way. I know what you do, such as it is. I know what drugs you take. You've got to watch the drugs. They dope you silly and after a while you can't tell what's a symptom and what's a drug. The staff believes everything is a symptom, so you can't talk to them about it. Hold the pills under your tongue and spit them out once you're alone, if you want my advice."

Emmet still believed that he needed the drugs to rid himself of his sickening anxieties. He feared that without medication his sight would become even more distorted. But the more he took the pills, the more every object vibrated with life, as if he had swallowed hallucinogens. When he complained to his doctors, they claimed his distress had only grown more acute. They increased his dosage. His vision grew worse. He had begun to suspect they were poisoning him, but he was more afraid to throw the drugs away and allow his mind to function unchecked.

"D-d-does the chart say anything else?"

"Oh, a few things. I didn't have much time to look. But there's a lot about your mother being a jumper. That why you're here?"

Emmet had never known which of his secrets his doctors had chosen to explain his behavior. Always in his sessions they seemed determined for him to fix blame like a fault line running directly through his past. But he never could. He knew he had existed as he was long before his mother died, so long before that he remembered his nerves stun him like a sickness even as he lay surrounded by pillows in his grandmother's bed; so long before that it might have crept upon him in the womb, like a murmur of the heart or like a limb badly shapen.

"I don't know," he said to Louise after a moment. "Maybe somewhere, b-b-but I didn't know her very well."

"I wish my mother would jump," she said. "Maybe then I could get out of here."

As they overcame their awkwardness, Emmet and Louise regarded each other openly. Emmet noticed for the first time how pale her flesh was, as if she had never lived in the sun. Up close, he saw that rings of dirt caked her fingernails and small scabs ridged her lips.

"You don't say much, do you?" Louise said.

"No. I never know what to say. My s-s-stutter embarrasses me." Emmet reddened with shame as he lied to Louise.

"Ah, forget it. Just send up a flare, you know?"

He looked at her questioningly.

"Send up a flare. You know, give a sign. Hang a white cloth out the window. Nod. Blink your eyes. Spit. I don't care. Just let me know you're there from time to time. It's all I need."

All his life, Emmet had never known what to say to strangers. Often he stared at people so intently when they approached him that they grew unnerved. His mind always went blank, as if he had never had an idea or thought in his life. Already he felt drawn to Louise, but he did not know how to express it. He pulled a red handkerchief from his pocket, flapping it in the air between them. "Okay?"

"It's a start," she said. "So tell me, did you go to school around here? The chart doesn't say."

"Yes."

"Me too, but I think I've had it. They probably won't take me back after having bloodied myself twice. Not good for the dorm's morale. You ever tried it?"

"I think everybody expected me to, so I haven't." He thought for a moment. "It isn't that I want to be dead, it's just that I get so worried about what will happen next I can't m-m-move. But I keep hoping it won't be like this forever."

"You never know. I've given up on it. I see life with oneself as a kind of marriage, and what I've got is irreconcilable differences. I'm getting a divorce. They don't believe I'm serious—but you will, won't you, when I say I want out?"

Emmet had always dreaded that one of his friends would call in the middle of the night to say he planned to commit suicide. Emmet worried that he would betray him if he did not try to describe the pleasures of a life he did not feel. But he did not know if he would betray him equally by persuading him to last a while longer.

Louise seemed determined, so he said only, "Well, I'm not there yet." He thought of his mother. "When you tried it, did you think of anyone else? I mean, did you w-w-wonder how your family would react, or did you just block everything out?"

"I didn't think of anything but wanting it to be over. It sounds stupid, but it really was like a dream. You know, I pulled the light bulb from the ceiling and stroked it. And there I was, alive on the bed, thinking, 'Louise, after you chomp on this baby, you're gonna be dead.' I wanted it to be slow. I figured this was the most important moment in my life and I wanted to savor it, you know, feel it creep up on me, to make my body pay or something—really feel it like I did in my brain. But you can't help but think—I mean, anybody would—what's gonna happen next? You know, white lights, fields of flowers, somebody with a beard holding out a hand in a narrow passageway? Or one big black sleep? Frankly, I vote for sleep."

"You really mean to do it," Emmet said. "The m-m-minute you get out?"

"The way things stand now. But I keep my options open. One day at a time, like they tell us." She chuckled. "You know that weird nurse with the curly hair? Ruth, I think her name is. The night they brought me here, I was sitting in the lounge smoking a cigarette. And the red stuff on the butt wasn't lipstick, it was blood from my fluorescent meal. And this broad comes up to me and says, 'Mind if I share the couch?' Well, I did mind, but she sat down anyway. She gave me this long rap about life. She told me that I had to stop feeling sorry for myself. Well, I didn't feel sorry for myself. I felt like I wanted to be dead. There's a difference, you know? She made a list for me of the things I could do to feel better. Take a trip to Hawaii. Get more exercise. Write my favorite movie star a letter. She made sure to tell me to enclose a self-addressed stamped envelope so that they could send me back an autographed picture. Can you beat it?"

"I'd h-h-hate to make a list," Emmet laughed. "I like to walk my dog and do my laundry. When you start adding up the reasons you're alive, they all sound pretty stupid."

"They *are* stupid—that's the point. I've got nothing against old Ruth, but if I were her, I'd have gotten it over with quick, under the first available truck."

She paused. "Once my mother's preacher took me aside and told me I'd fallen from grace with God. I wasn't sure how he knew, but he said there was still time to save my soul. Well, I thought about it and I realized I didn't want to be saved. There was nothing I felt drawn to, and I'd lost the trick or whatever it is to dupe myself again."

"My doctor would say you're depressed," Emmet said. "All you need is the right mix of drugs to set you straight. Once I was totally obsessed with somebody. I used to drive around his house all night. I'd telephone twenty times a day just to listen to him say 'Hello,' before I hung up. I didn't sleep for weeks. I've never been so miserable in my life. My doctor said it was because I was manic depressive and needed lithium. The lithium made me throw up. The doctor said it was anxiety because I was in love, but I hadn't thrown up before. He increased the dose. Then I blacked out. He said it was because I didn't want to face reality. He was driving me crazier than I ever could have managed by myself."

Emmet forgot himself as he spoke, rambling as easily as he had in his other life.

"So what's with the stutter?" she asked, eyeing him.

"Sometimes I don't," Emmet said. "If I'm relaxed."

"Relaxed with me?" Louise laughed. "Boy, you are crazy. Usually I can make anybody miserable. I can't ever relax. Even when I'm sleeping I feel this unease, you know what I mean? My problem as I see it is I've got an artistic temperament but no talent. I've got no eye. I'm too smart to do something badly and be content, like those guys who sing in motel lounges on the highway. All I do is read more and more until I can't get out of bed. I'm what everybody writes about, but I can't do it myself. Maybe I should open a salon for artists who want to meet someone more depressed than they are. I've got a genius for despair, but I've got no way to tell it, you know what I mean? I've become a kind of performance artist. What I do to myself is my work."

"The doctors never believe us when we admit these things," Emmet said. "They don't have any trouble getting up in the morning, so they think you can't mean it since it isn't part of their lives. So why did I come here? I'm beginning to worry that it might be worse than living outside because I feel stranger every minute. Not with you, here, but like I'm sinking, that maybe it is all over."

"Come on," Louise said. "I don't want any disciples to follow me out. What works or doesn't work for me isn't for anybody else. Look, let me tell you a story if you promise not to laugh. Promise?"

"Sure," Emmet said.

"When I was younger, I wanted to be a ballerina. I took classes for years. I stayed thin. I wasn't terrible, either. I got taken by a company in the West, in the corps. But one day somebody got sick an hour before the performance and the director came to our dressing room and said he wanted me to replace her. It wasn't a big part, just a duet with another girl. We had to do the same steps from opposite sides of the stage. I'd seen the ballet a million times, but I'd never taken it all in—you know, like you can drive the same route ten times a day and still not be able to give somebody directions? I was nervous as shit and I told him so. He said all I had to do was watch Alicia, the other girl, out of the corner of my eye. He said to empty my mind of everything else. And the last thing he said was, 'Louise, whatever you do, keep moving. Don't stop for anything.'

"I blew it, of course. I was all over the fucking stage, like some kind of thudding elephant. The funny thing was, I had no memory for steps when I wasn't in the corps and could mimic the person next to or in front of me. All I could see was Alicia spinning perfectly in her corner of the stage. I knew I looked spastic by comparison, but there was nothing I could do about it. I had to play it out until it was over. I quit pretty soon after. I mean, who wants to dance in the boondocks and be stuck behind the scenery when you know you're never gonna go any further? It was a ticket to nowhere. That's when I came here. But I used to see it as a metaphor, that 'keep moving' stuff. I did it as long as I could. It hasn't worked out for me, but you're smart. It could for you."

"Sitting here," Emmet said, "it's hard to remember what was wrong, like we're just on a date in a restaurant or something."

"It always comes back," Louise said. "Always. You know how it is when you first wake up in the morning? There's that moment when you blink your eyes and take everything in and for a second or two you think, 'Oh, thank God, I feel good; it's over.' But then you start to move and you realize it isn't over at all.

"I used to think that those few seconds of bliss meant it was possible to be happy, that there had to be a way of multiplying them a little bit each day until you had learned to stretch them into a couple of hours at least, to give yourself a break. But I don't believe that anymore. I think all it means is that your brain is slower to wake up. Those seconds are just a dead zone before it all comes back to life, and it never gets any better and we never learn to forget."

"I can't imagine forgetting anything, especially something horrible," Emmet said. "I've read about people who've had some trauma in their past and claim no memory of it, but I don't believe it. It's like when you've got insomnia and the more you think about sleep, the more you're awake. I think if you try to make yourself forget, you only imprint it deeper on your mind. But I don't know. Everything seems unreal to me the minute it happens, so I'm never sure what I've remembered. I worry that's what's most wrong with me—that I never know the difference because there's part of my brain that doesn't connect to anything."

"Well, who can blame you?" Louise said. "With all the stuff that's in our heads, the world seems pretty tame by comparison."

"My mother did jump," Emmet said. "And I was there. I saw it. She did it in front of me."

"Wow," Louise said. "While you watched? That's amazing."

"But I feel like I made it up. I've never known what she meant."

"Hell, maybe she didn't mean anything. You can't figure something like that out. Nobody ever knows what another person's thinking or why they do anything. Once I read in the newspaper about somebody's mother who crawled into a dishwasher and shut the door behind her. She waited in there for hours. She'd left a note for her son that said, 'Please wash the dishes when you come home from school.' So he did. Locked the door and flipped the switch. She drowned in all those suds."

Emmet laughed in spite of himself. "That can't be true."

"I swear it is. It was only a one-column item. I showed it to a friend of mine because it was so weird I felt I was hallucinating. But I wasn't. So you see, no matter what you come up with, there's always something stranger out there that's happened to somebody else."

For months Emmet had not thought of anything beyond the panic that beset his days. But suddenly, there with Louise, an image of his mother tumbling through space struck him, her hat zinging past her body in the air. He felt breathless at how vividly he saw her, almost as if the force of her falling body ruffled the room around him. Louise looked at him eagerly, coaxing him with her eyes to tell every detail he remembered.

Emmet had met his mother in Philadelphia for Jonathan's graduation from high school. They stayed in a hotel in the center of town, near the museum. She said there were some paintings by Eakins she wanted to see in the hours when she was alone.

Emmet's mother took photographs throughout the ceremony. She hired a man with a video camera to film every moment. At the party afterwards, she held her camera in front of her eyes as the guests gathered in a circle around a vast chocolate cake decorated with birds spun from sugar. Each phrase anyone uttered was punctuated by the click of the shutter: everything she saw was narrowed and distorted by the lens. When Emmet cleared his throat to propose a toast, she pointed the camera directly at the glass he raised in salute.

After dinner, they returned to their rooms. Emmet's mother's adjoined his, the door locked. Emmet swallowed a pill and fell easily asleep. In the middle of the night, he awoke to what he thought was a tapping outside his window. But he remembered later that he had been dreaming he watched his mother's boyfriend in Colorado build an extension to the shed, driving nail after nail with a hammer into the soft wood, each time selecting one from a box Emmet cupped in his palm.

When Emmet awoke in the blur without his glasses, he could see only a field of white against the window outside his room, as indistinct as snow on a television screen. When he put on his glasses, he saw a figure perched on the ledge outside. As he took everything in, the city beyond his room was slowly extinguished. The lights went out, then the grayness of the sky, then the noise of the air conditioner, leaving only the white form of a woman teetering on the ledge.

The figure was his mother. She was still dressed in the clothes she had worn to the ceremony. Even her flowered hat remained pinned neatly to her hair. Emmet did not move. His mother turned around to look inside the room, steadying herself on the bricks lining the window frame as if she were afraid of falling. Emmet believed she looked at him in surprise when she saw him staring back at her, glasses set against his eyes; but he later thought that it had not been surprise at all, but delight or triumph in realizing he had awakened.

Emmet did not remember if he reached for the telephone or if he threw off the covers, preparing to rise. He remembered almost a giddiness of anticipation at what would happen next. He remembered thinking, "What will my life be like without her?" just as his grandmother had done the day she watched her husband's ship sink in the harbor; but then he thought, "How much will I care?"

He must have made some movement, for his mother shook her head "no" and froze him to the pillows with her gaze. She pressed her finger to her lips as if to say "Sshh." He noticed how her finger, bent with arthritis, curled over her mouth. Then she stepped back to let herself go, but gently, as if her body dipped into a river to float easily downstream, leaving nothing but the night and the lights of the city blinking back at him from the window.

Then Emmet did something he had never confessed to anyone. He became afraid he could never explain to the authorities why he did not rise to stop her. Even as he heard the sirens, minutes after she jumped, he rolled over and fell again to sleep. He wanted to delay the last moment, to suspend time as long as possible before he lived the change her death would make. She carried no purse or identification with her. It was hours before the manager from the hotel, accompanied by a police officer, knocked on his door.

In later years, Emmet would come to mistrust all he had remembered, even the rapping on the window he had heard. He did not know if his mother had truly awakened him or if her tapping was a trick of memory and guilt. He did not know if years of minute planning had led her there, or if she had found herself seized by an ungovernable impulse to jump, unknown to her before, while she rested on her bed after the ceremony.

Sometimes when Emmet looked out of a window, even on the calmest day, his mind shouted *Jump*. Sometimes when the subway pulled into the station, he pressed himself against the tile walls so that he did not leap, drawn by the rushing headlight visible from blocks down the tunnel, urging him to fling his body onto the tracks. He did not know if that night a similar rapture had befallen her: her brain screaming *Now* when she had not intended it, her body following a summons from the dark, such as a sleepwalker hears.

Often, still, in dreams, an image of her rapping, her face pressed against the glass, disturbed him. Over the years, the sound he dreamed grew more insistent, sometimes louder than the pounding of someone trapped inside a room: her face close against the glass, grotesquely, so that her lips swelled open and thick. Once he dreamed her mouth left a series of imprints ridged with the flesh of her lips, like kisses blown upon the pane.

But when Emmet was awake, he remembered how lightly he believed she had rapped that night, almost tentatively, yet twice, and how she had held her face back, so that except for her hair and hat, she could have been anyone. He did not know if the knocking he heard had been an afterthought when she realized she would fall alone and unseen. He did not know if she had wanted him to bear witness to what she could not express in words, to tell him that it had all added up to nothing for her; and if in the last minute, when she knew he watched her from the bed, he had set her free to finish what she had desired from the first moment she had been awakened by terror and wanted a way out, all those years before.

Emmet thought of telling Louise that one thing: how he had returned to sleep after watching his mother fall. In the past he had often felt compelled to confess, as if he would live more freely if he eased the weight of what preoccupied him. But he had come to believe his last control was to parcel out the view of himself, as if his secrets made a kind of skin that wrapped him. He had begun to fear that he might lose his substance entirely if they leaked from him.

"Hey, hey," Louise said, waving his red handkerchief madly in the air. "Where are you? We had a deal, right? Send up a flare. Come back."

CHAPTER
SIX

Emmet shook himself. Louise smiled as she dropped the handkerchief into his lap, her hand lingering palm-up against his jeans.

Emmet inched away. "Sorry," he said. "I forgot myself."

"No kidding. You gave me a fright. I thought you'd gone off to visit Margaret's planet right in front of my eyes."

"I'm back. I'm tired," Emmet said, rubbing his eyes. "What happens next? How long does that meeting go on? No one's told me what I'm supposed to do here. Is this it? Sitting around a room?"

"Thanks a lot. Don't worry, they're only gearing up. They'll give you tests. You'll see a shrink every few days. On Monday nights they make you go to family therapy. It's really a nightmare. Everybody's family comes to slug it out."

"I've only got a brother," Emmet said. "But he couldn't take it. He's very reserved."

"Even if you lie and say you're an orphan, they'll make you bring a friend. There's no escaping it. They love this one. So call somebody up and go wild with a story. Invent really outrageous things to keep yourself interested. Like your mother kept you locked in a closet and made you wear dresses to first grade, or maybe she auctioned you for dates with businessmen. Anything to get the sympathy on your side."

"When I was little," Emmet said, "I used to lie in bed—maybe it was a crib, I don't remember—and I liked to pull the hems loose from the curtains that hung over my pillow and suck on the threads. It drove my mother crazy. Nothing she said would make me stop. I remember her coming into my room and stabbing the air with an opened safety pin, her eyes wild like an old woman's. She'd jab the point inches from my eyes and snarl, 'Next time I'm going to pin you to the curtains.' She never did, but I remember the tip so near my pupils that it split into triple images. Even that young, I believed she would kill me, although I didn't know what 'dead' meant yet. But I could feel the fear, you know, that she wasn't kidding."

"That's pretty good," Louise said. "But for a really successful meeting you've got to elaborate. You've gotta lie and say she did it; describe how it felt when the pins pricked your skin and you were hemmed to the material."

"It was green polyester."

"Now you're getting it. Maybe green with little flecks of blood, huh? And maybe she kept you there a whole day, without a bottle or a change of diapers? They eat this stuff up, believe me."

"Do you ever tell them the truth?"

"Never. It's a point of honor with me. They think they know everything, and so I like to see 'em grab on to something I've invented and try to make me face it, you know? 'Confront your past,' like they always say. Only it isn't my past at all. It's just a story, and it gets written down on my chart and passed from doctor to doctor and hospital to hospital, like they know the secrets of me. But they don't. Only now I've jinxed myself. They won't give me passes to get out of here for the day. They don't even let me go on field trips to the bowling alley and stuff, so maybe I'd better ease up a little. They're afraid I'll run straight for a light bulb meal if they let me out of their sight."

Louise stretched, then rubbed her stomach. "Speaking of which—you hungry? It's probably time for lunch. You haven't lived till you've seen this crowd eat."

Emmet had not eaten since he arrived. He did not know how it would be to have a plate of food set before him after so long. To test himself, he pictured the most disgusting meal he could imagine: raw hamburger swimming in a curdled sauce with a rainbow of grease. He leaned his face close to the plate and inhaled the odor. He licked the food with his tongue. He felt some of his revulsion easing. He believed the cream might taste like paste.

"I haven't eaten much lately," he said.

Well, I'm not one to talk," Louise said, unsticking the seams of her shorts from her thighs, "but you could use a few more layers. I've never seen anyone so thin—that wasn't dead, anyway. The skin on your face is almost translucent. It's sort of neat. It looks like flesh does in a painting or something, but it isn't normal."

Emmet touched his face. His skin stretched as tautly as the blindfold Bruce had described dried around the bones of the skull. "It feels beautiful," he thought, in spite of himself. "I mustn't weigh more than a hundred pounds."

"I don't want to pressure you," Louise said, "but if you don't eat they'll hook you up to a machine and force fluids into you. There's no point in bullshitting, though. The food here sucks. It's the reason we get so fat. The only thing anybody can stomach is the potatoes, and they come straight from a box."

"Will you come?" Emmet asked.

"Me miss a meal? Are you serious? I don't want to die hungry."

Louise chose a bottle imprinted with lilacs from her bureau and spritzed herself behind the ears. She flipped her hair over her face and attacked the knots with a brush, parting the strands until she peeked at Emmet through one eye. "You can tell me anything, you know. I mean, I just spilled my guts, so you can see talking to me as if it's just your thoughts—even the craziest ones—racing through your mind, just like we're one brain."

Emmet smiled so that again he felt his skin drag heavy as a plaster mask. "Yes," he said, smoothing the lines on either side of his mouth to erase their crease.

"I'll never tell," Louise said, dropping the strand of hair, like a curtain.

As they stepped from the room, a woman in a pink housecoat and brown loafers raced up and down the hallway, chirping with a birdy squeak. She clutched her purse to her breast with one hand. The other patted springy pink curlers that shook on her head like electrodes.

"Excuse me," she repeated as she dashed in circles, bumping Louise and Emmet every few steps. "Excuse me."

"That's Isabel," Louise said. "She's harmless. She used to be a scientist. I kinda like her, except no matter where she is, she dashes around like a rat. But if you ignore her, she'll go away."

Emmet could hear a racket of dishes around the corner, as if plates and spoons were being slammed against a table. He heard music piped through the loudspeaker for the first time: soft, stringed instruments, with no beat.

The bird woman butted him again. "Excuse me," she said, but no matter where he moved, she returned. A nurse rounded the corner carrying a long wire hooked to two test tubes. A yellow liquid jiggled in the glass as she whistled. She grinned at Emmet as she passed, holding the tubes tightly between two fingers and shaking them before his eyes so that a layer of froth foamed at the top.

The green tiles of the walls nauseated him. He imagined the nurse throwing the bottles against them, the yellow liquid splashing across the carpet and onto his shoes. The bird woman knocked against his waist. Two patients came out of their room in examination gowns, their fingers hooked through each other's plastic identification bracelets, as if they were cuffed in place. Emmet could see the stretched, puffy skin of their buttocks bounce as they moved away.

"Excuse me," the woman said, bumping so closely that she backed Emmet against the wall. "Excuse me." Even though she peered directly into his eyes, almost sweetly, she seemed to believe she traveled in another place, like through a crowded street, laden with packages.

Emmet slipped down the tiles so that he slumped at the woman's knees. She pecked at his shins with her tiny feet. "Where is Louise?" he thought as he tried to take stock. "This is a hospital," he told himself. "You must expect trouble. This woman doesn't mean anything. She is gone." But even as he tried to absent himself, her purse flapped against his face like the slap of a hand.

"Louise!" Emmet yelled as he grabbed the woman's ankle and yanked so that she flipped onto her back. Her purse spilled open at his feet. A lipstick, a pair of eyeglasses, a barrette, and a thick wad of lint tied with a ribbon scattered across the carpet. Emmet jumped away.

"Purse snatcher," the woman screeched. "Bully." She put two fingers into her mouth and whistled louder than a scream.

"L-L-Louise!" Emmet called again, his voice truly slipping from him, the words lost like those of someone shouting through a mask.

Louise raced down the hallway as the woman whistled again. "Back off," she said, squeezing Isabel's wrinkled throat until her eyes bugged open. Her tongue, bubbly and white, popped through her teeth.

"Back off," Louise panted, drops of sweat swimming on her lips. She forced Isabel's head to the carpet and locked her eyes above the litter of things. "Pick them up," she ordered.

Isabel sniveled but began to stuff the objects into her purse. The bundle of lint disintegrated into a pouf of dust when she touched it. The ribbon slipped into her hand. "He broke it," she whimpered.

"Time for a nap, Isabel," Louise said. She planted both hands on the woman's back and shoved. Isabel raced away. At the end of the corridor she stopped and blew her siren whistle one last time. Then she waved her arms, as if she were hailing a group of bodyguards to surround her.

Louise slapped her palms together. "See, no problem," she said jauntily. "Hey, where were you? I thought you were behind me while I was jabbering away, really saying something, you know, more secrets, but when I looked around, there was just me and the air." She winked. "You really missed something. Things I've never told a soul."

Emmet pointed a finger where Isabel had stood. "She's c-c-crazy," he said.

"Of course she's crazy. This is a hospital, remember?"

"Yes," Emmet said, almost inaudibly.

"You gotta do better than that. Come on, let's go eat" Louise tugged at his arm.

A rush of nerves boiled his stomach. He held fast to the carpet. "Move your arm," he told himself, as he had seen doctors order accident victims in movies. He imagined the command forming in his brain and shooting through every nerve ending, until it settled in the tips of his fingers.

"Move," he repeated, soft as a sigh. He remained rigid because he believed that if he looked down at the carpet, the ground would rush upon him, as it does upon a body falling with its eyes open.

He felt Louise grasp his hand and guide him. He heard her mutter, "Jesus, this is going to be tougher than I thought," as she led him into the dining room, his steps halting and timid as if he were walking with bound feet. Emmet reeled so stiffly that he believed he must seem to be the maddest person in the dining room. He felt his eyes dry and crack in their sockets. "Remember to blink," he told himself as he floated past the tables. "Remember to blink."

Louise seated Emmet in a chair across from a middle-aged man in circular black glasses. His head seemed unnaturally bald, as if he had undergone chemotherapy. Small patches of fuzz covered his pate like lichen. "Is this mine?" his eyes seemed to ask each time he raised his fork to eat. A nurse sat at his arm, gently touching the underside of his hand to guide the fork towards his mouth. When she tapped his chin with her fingers, his mouth snapped open, like a puppet's. Then she mouthed huge, exaggerated bites, and the man would mimic her and begin to chew.

An orderly in a white uniform slapped a plate of meat in front of Emmet. In the center, a blue-gray artichoke rose out of a mound of mashed potatoes. Its leaves were swollen and wrinkled, like fingers left too long under water.

"Told you," Louise grimaced. "Maybe they'll have cake."

Emily and Daphne sauntered over with plates in their hands. Silverware gleamed from their pockets. Daphne touched the back of Emmet's head and eyed Louise coldly. "May we join you?" she asked.

"It's a free country," Louise said, dropping her fork to rest her arm across Emmet's shoulders.

"We've been looking for you," Emily said. "You made quite an impression leaving the meeting. But then Juanita gave a speech about leadership and everybody forgot. She claims she's about to give birth. Her stomach was really jumping."

"Hi, John," Bruce winked as he sat backwards in the chair beside Emmet. He dipped his fork into Emmet's mashed potatoes and slurped a bite.

"Do you want to stay?" Louise whispered into his ear. Emmet leaned against her, letting himself go limp until she supported all his weight. "Eat," she said, indicating the congealing mass of food.

Emmet licked a spoonful of potatoes and let it melt on his tongue. The lump felt cold and hard, like a tumor.

Louise tapped his lips with a spoon heaped with food. Obediently, he stuck out his tongue. He saw Emily and Daphne eye one another, but he ignored them. As he smelled Louise's lavender scent, he breathed deeply, like in a meadow of flowers. "She will protect me," he thought dreamily. He imagined them walking the dog through the streets, arm in arm. He imagined her outwitting the cat. If she had lived with him, none of this might have happened.

Emmet bit a piece of meat and chewed it twenty times as he imagined life with Louise. Strings of beef caught in his crowns. He beamed at her with his mouth full. She stroked the soft hair at the nape of his neck. Already he wanted to give himself over to her, as if he could love anyone.

A nurse entered the room pushing a middle-aged man in a wheelchair. His hands were tied to the handles with strips of white gauze. She parked the chair at the table and began to feed him.

"Jesus, there's Henry," Daphne said. "We haven't seen him in weeks." Emmet noticed a bright bruise rimming the lids of his eyes, purple as tulips.

"Henry's really gross," Emily said. "He's got this thing about popping out his eyes. He pokes his index finger into the socket and out they come. He can't stop himself. The second they free his hands, he does it." She made a wet, clicking sound with her tongue.

Emmet felt Louise tense with excitement. "I've never seen him before. I thought I knew everybody. You mean he really pulls them out? Like they're plastic or something?"

"That's the story," Emily said. "But I've never seen it. My doctor told me. He shouldn't have, but he did."

"Gross," Bruce said. "You girls are disgusting. I'm trying to eat." He stuck a finger into Emmet's potatoes and sucked it clean.

"I wonder if he can still see," Louise said. "I mean, wouldn't it be amazing to have eyes that still work at the end of a membrane? That's always been my dream—but even I figured it was too sick to tell anybody. Just imagine—you could point them back at yourself and see everything straight on, just like everybody else sees you, not like in a mirror but like it really is. God, I'd love to see my face that way, with my own eyes. God. Do you think we can ask him if it works?"

"Henry doesn't talk," Emily said. "He does math problems on a chalkboard, but that's it. So I guess you'll never know, unless you try it yourself."

"I'm too chicken," Louise said. "It took me four years to practice getting my contact lenses in right. Despite my reputation, you know, as a saboteur, most of the time I'm afraid of pain." Emily, Emmet, and Daphne eyed the fluorescent light bulbs in the ceiling above them. "I'd hate to go blind," Louise continued. "I mean, dead is one thing, but no seeing-eye dogs for me. No thank you."

"I thought you were a bitch," Bruce said. "Everybody said you were. But maybe you're not so bad." He turned to Emmet. "Or maybe she's just a star fucker, eh, John?"

Emmet opened his mouth to speak, but Juanita paused at the back of his chair. "Star?" she said. "My baby's gonna be a star. My baby's gonna twinkle with lights."

"My mother was of the sky, my father was of the earth, but I am of the universe," Bruce sang, snapping his fingers. "Come on, John, what's next? What's the next verse?"

"Satan," Juanita said. "Flower fag. I know it's time. This morning when I awoke I felt like I was being stuffed with puppies, a whole litter wriggling and giggling inside me, but they weren't no dogs. It was my baby comin' to life." She grabbed a cube of ice from Emmet's cup. She crunched it close to his ear. "See how strong my jaws are? I'm in training. I can open them wide in case my baby comes from here."

She pranced to the center of the room, swinging her stomach from side to side. "Diners," she bellowed. "Fellow diners. May I have your attention? Never trust a leader who doesn't wear the finest lederhosen. That is my word for the day." Several of the tables applauded.

The nurse feeding Henry rose and approached Juanita. "Sit down or go to your room," she said evenly.

"Get back, Eva Braun," Juanita ordered. "This baby's mine. You only want to wash me in your showers." She kicked her legs high. Emmet was amazed at how limber she was, loose as a dancer.

A second nurse circled behind Juanita so that she was surrounded. Juanita laughed. "Nazi bitches," she taunted. "Feel the heat of your shower. Feel it." She blew air through her teeth like sizzling bacon. "Ee-o, ee-o, ee-o," she sang, shaking her head with abandon.

Emmet noticed an orderly hovering in the doorway, the corner of a wet sheet held in each hand, like a net. Droplets of water dripped from its hem onto the floor.

"So eat," Louise said, turning his head to his plate. "If we were someplace else, I'd say 'Finish your vegetables,' but these look like poison."

Emmet pulled leaf after leaf from his artichoke. Each one slipped easily from the core until only the center remained, spongy and gray. He bit into one of the leaves piled on his plate and spat it out. "Yuck," he said. "It tastes like w-w-weeds." He turned to Louise. "Do you want my heart?"

"We'll see about that," Louise said, stabbing the soggy mass with her knife. "For now it's potatoes. Two bites."

"2,531.87, 2,531.86, 2,531.85, 2,531.84," the man with hair like moss counted, rising from the table. "The Dow Jones averages are down. They are falling, falling." He twitched with itches, swatting himself as if swarms of insects were nibbling at his skin, as if he did not know it was his own body that attacked him.

"Full moon?" Daphne asked, bemused.

"If he plans to go to zero, I'm gonna kill myself," Emily said.

She and Emily blew smoke rings into the air. When two circles linked above them, they laughed and slapped their hands together, exclaiming, "Sister!"

"Your sister's broke and living in a hovel in England," Bruce said to Emmet. "I read about it. You should be ashamed."

"Sister," Daphne said.

"Falling, falling," the man said.

"We're here to help you," the nurse said.

"Ee-o, ee-o, ee-o," Juanita sang.

"Ashamed," Bruce said. "You should be ashamed."

"Eat," Louise whispered. "Eat."

Emmet saw light particles fly through the air like dust, exploding in front of his eyes.

"Nigger bitch," Margaret screamed. "Whore." She darted from the table, quick as a hummingbird, and lunged at Juanita with her fork. She moved so agilely that even the nurses stared in shock for a moment. Their hesitation gave Margaret just enough time to snatch Juanita's raised leg as it kicked the air. Emmet saw the old woman's bicep, brown and lean, flex from her sleeveless dress as she flipped Juanita onto the ground.

Margaret jabbed the fork upwards into Juanita's stomach. Emmet heard a gasp of breath, then a pop, like a tire exploding, as Juanita's stomach deflated. She cried so mournfully, patting her hands against her dress, that for a moment Emmet shared her longing, as if he too witnessed the air escape like a life expiring.

"Satan is dead," Margaret crowed, raising the fork above her head like a warrior's sword. "I have slain the devil child."

A rumble went through the room, like a signal, as the patients arose from the table: some crying, some shouting, some banging their chairs against the table, until the room rocked with violence.

The orderly netted Margaret from behind with the wet sheet, mummifying her body with the fork still clutched in her hand.

"You can't touch me," she exclaimed as the sodden cloth enveloped her. "I'm pure as a baby. Pure."

"Baby," Juanita wailed from the carpet. "Baby, baby, baby," as a blue and orange beach ball dropped from her dress. It plopped between her legs, one hemisphere flat and airless. She crawled forward as if in supplication, rocking it in her arms like a deformed head.

The patients encircled Juanita, gawking, shoving closer and closer until they seemed to trample her. The staff flooded into the room, but the patients pushed ahead, emboldened by the energy crackling among them.

"Let's beat it," Louise said, pulling Emmet to his feet.

"It's time for the Zine sisters," Bruce laughed. "Stella! Thora! Come out, come out. We need you."

"I knew that was no baby," Emily said smugly. "I knew it."

The patients clapped their hands as Juanita thrashed at their feet, clutching the ball to her heart so tightly that nothing remained but bright, limp plastic.

"Baby," she cried as the nurses held back, powerless, pretending to occupy themselves with Margaret's trussed, wriggling form.

"Baby," she cried as the patients stomped their feet, whirling round and round her, hand in hand.

Emmet wanted to storm into their midst to stop them, but he held his distance, awestruck, as if he had stumbled upon a clearing at the edge of a forest on an uncharted island and witnessed from afar a ceremony for the dead or a sacrificial murder, as if Juanita were lost beyond his power to save her, like a mother anywhere, blinded by sorrow.

CHAPTER
SEVEN

"**T**ooth fairy left somethin' under your pillow," Winston said, snapping his thumb over the edge of a fat wad of bills. "I couldn't help but notice. I was cleanin' up." He pulled the waist of his pants loose and slipped the money into his underwear. "I was just countin' my stash. It'll be safe in here, unless somebody wants to go fishin'," he added with a smile.

Emmet walked to the bureau and searched among his socks where he had hidden the money Jonathan had given him the night he left for the hospital. Each toe was flat and empty. Winston reclined on his bed, his hands crossed demurely at the bulge in his zipper. Emmet regarded it despairingly. "How could I prove the money was mine when there is no name on it?" he thought, defeated. He berated himself for not recording in his diary the serial number of every dollar he possessed.

Winston watched as Emmet casually went to his closet, pretending to organize his clothes on their hangers. Emmet had pinned half his money to an interior seam of his black jeans. He ran his hand along the leg until felt the bump of bills. He yawned to hide his relief. Quickly he moved to the next pair and fluffed the legs.

"Nice pants," Winston drawled. "So what you waitin' for? Don't you wanna read the tooth fairy's letter?"

Emmet kept his back to Winston as he lifted the pillow. A dollar bill was taped to a piece of paper and weighted to the sheet with a chocolate kiss.

"I will give you something every day, if only you'll tell me," the note read. It was signed with a *B*, drawn at an angle so that the letter looked like a heart.

"I'll give you somethin' every day and you don't have to tell me nothin'," Winston leered from the bed.

"S-s-stay away from my things," Emmet said as he crumpled the note into the wastebasket.

"I g-g-got what I need," Winston mimicked as he drummed his fingers along his crotch.

"I smell trash burning. Do you think it could be Arson?" Emmet snapped. Immediately he flushed with panic. Always he feared the consequences if he did not pacify the person who threatened him. If he antagonized Winston, he could forever take revenge while Emmet slept. He could root among his possessions whenever he was out of the room. Emmet turned, prepared to grovel to regain his sympathy, but Winston chortled from the bed.

"Touché," he said.

"Please don't take my money. I really haven't got any. My h-h-house was just robbed."

"The thing about fires," Winston said, "is there aren't any fingerprints. How can you leave a trace if there's nothin' left?" He snapped his fingers. "All gone. Presto. Get it?"

"I h-h-hoped we could be friends," Emmet said. "Especially after all the things you told me."

"Oh, baby, you take life too seriously. I was just jerkin' myself off, talkin' and talkin'. Anyway, I'm goin' home. I'm just waitin' for the papers to be signed. They're sending me to a halfway house. But I reckon, halfway out is halfway to another blaze of glory."

Emmet was stunned to see a suitcase and a knapsack dumped

at the foot of Winston's bed. "But how can you be leaving? Don't they kn-kn-know you still want to set fires?"

"Hell no, sugar. You think I'm crazy? I just batted my pretty eyes and told them I didn't know what came over me. What can they do? There's nothin' else crazy about me that they can see. I'm just the victim of a misguided youth." Winston cackled gaily.

"I will be left here alone," Emmet thought, feeling trapped. For a moment, madly, he was overcome with sadness at Winston's departure. Already he had come to define Winston as part of his new life. He hated anything to change, even something horrible.

The door swung open and Bruce stepped into the room, a suitcase in each hand. A record album was tucked under his left arm. "I'm home," he cried as he threw himself upon Winston's bed.

"Look familiar?" Bruce laughed as he tossed the album to Emmet. He saw no image on the outside, only blank white paper. Two black discs flew out of the slots and flopped onto the rug. The cardboard jacket sailed towards Emmet. He batted it to the floor.

"But I didn't know," Emmet said, as if it would have made a difference.

"How could you?" Bruce said. "It happened in a flash. I fixed it as soon as I heard. I told the charge nurse you and me wanted to spend more time together. She fell for it hook, line, and sinker. She's so proud I'm making friends."

Bruce retrieved the records from the floor and replaced them in their jackets. "So, buddy—'Tell me tell me tell me the answer/ You may be a lover but you ain't no dancer,'" he sang. "What does that mean? 'You're a lover but not a dancer'? Does it have something to do with death?"

"I don't know," Emmet said. "Please leave me alone. Those aren't my words."

"You mean Paul wrote them? Okay, but didn't he ever tell you? He must have said something."

"I don't know. Sometimes things are just words," Emmet said. "They don't have to mean anything."

"Is it sex, the 'lover' part? I always thought somehow it must be death, or maybe a resurrection or something." Bruce began filling the drawers with his clothes. He opened the bottom drawer of Emmet's bureau. "You mind? You don't have much stuff and I brought my whole collection here in case my mother tried to sell it." In his hands, he held two pairs of boxer shorts. One was imprinted with berries, the other with beetles sleeping on little straw beds. "These are very rare," he said. "I know people who'd kill to own a pair."

Emmet could not imagine living with Bruce day and night. He would never have any peace. "How do you convince someone they are caught by a demon?" he wondered as he watched him fill his drawers with underwear. Bruce was serene in his delusions. Even if he summoned all of his wiles, nothing Emmet could say would convince him that he was wrong. It would be like trying to persuade a believer that there was no God.

"What are you boys talkin' about?" Winston asked.

"Shall I tell him?" Bruce asked. His tone was threatening, as if he had the power to reveal something Emmet would kill to keep unknown.

Emmet met Bruce's eyes. They were bright with triumph. "No," Emmet said, looking down. He turned to Winston. "It's just he thinks he knew me in another life, before the hospital."

"I woulda remembered. But this life, that life, who can keep up?" Winston said. "I'm burnin' to get back to my other one." He lifted his suitcase and flung the knapsack over his shoulder. "I'll leave you boys to whatever it is you're doin'."

Winston went to the desk and examined Emmet's pen. "Pretty," he said as he stuffed it into his pocket. "Well, I'm gone. You boys be good."

"Keep the home fires burning," Bruce said. He sat on Emmet's bed, his shoes flat against the sheets.

Emmet looked from Bruce to Winston. He felt as if he were being held prisoner and his guards were changing shifts. He saw Winston's belly billowing under the blue lightning bolts printed on his shirt. The silver tip of Emmet's pen poked from his pocket. "This is what I will see, forever," Emmet thought as the image locked in his mind. Even though he had no feeling for him, he wanted to call out to beg Winston to wait, to freeze time just a moment longer; but before he could speak, Winston flounced past with his bags and was out the door and gone.

"Well, he's history," Bruce said. "Now, where were we? You were telling me about the song you wrote, or didn't write, as the case may be."

"Can't we do this later?" Emmet asked. He needed time to think. Bruce seemed insatiable. If Emmet acceded to his delusion, he would want to write songs. He would question Emmet ceaselessly about things he had never known.

"As I've said, we've got all the time in the world. But I want to hear you say it. I want to hear you say your name."

"Emmet?"

"Nah. Come on, guy, the real one. You've already told me about your stutter. You've already admitted you're a liar. We've got that straight. I wanna hear something true out of your mouth. I want to hear your name."

"Bruce," Emmet sighed.

"No, that's me. Come on, man, say it. Say your name."

"Why am I resisting?" Emmet thought. "What could be worse than this?" He saw the letters of the name Bruce wanted to hear form clearly in his brain, but they faltered on the edge of his tongue. He felt unbodied, as he had when he stood on the cliffs in Jamaica and heard Jonathan treading in the water below, calling

"Jump, jump, jump," as Emmet tried to force his legs to walk into the air.

"Say it."

"J-J-John," Emmet said.

Bruce leaned closer. He did not seem remotely surprised or grateful that Emmet had admitted who he was not. "I can't hear you," he said.

"John. My name's John." The room quaked with movement. Emmet steeled himself by gripping the sheets in his hands like a rope.

"Emmet?" someone called from the door.

"John," Bruce whispered.

"Emmet?"

"John. Remember it's John."

"Emmet?"

Chris walked to the bed. Even with Emmet sitting, they met eye to eye. "Emmet?" As Chris repeated his name, it grew more urgent, like a plea.

"No one here called that," Bruce laughed. "Tell him."

"What's going on?"

"Tell him," Bruce whispered in his ear. "Tell him you're John."

"Emmet?"

"John, John, John," Bruce whispered, in a tone someone might use when he spoke of love.

"I'm coming." Emmet rose shakily. He did not know where Chris intended to take him, but he would have followed him anywhere.

"You've got an appointment with Dr. Franklin," Chris said. He looked quizzically from Bruce to Emmet, as if waiting for them to explain.

Emmet locked his fingers around Chris's hand. "Get me out of here," he whispered. "Please."

"Tell him," Bruce hissed as they left. "Tell him how you lie."

CHAPTER

EIGHT

"**W**hat was that about?" Chris asked as he led Emmet towards the electrified door at the entrance to the ward.
"N-n-nothing."

"It didn't sound like nothing to me. You sure?"

"Winston stole my m-m-money."

"I hope not very much. You should have told me before. Now that he's gone, there's not much I can do. So who's John?"

Emmet shrugged. He shuddered as the buzzer sounded and they stepped through the violet electric eye. The door locked behind them.

"I am out," he thought, instantly nostalgic, as he looked back through the meshed glass into the ward.

They waited for the elevator. There was barely room to squeeze inside past the nurses, visitors, and delivery men holding spiky bunches of flowers. The strangers with their packages and faces clouded with private concern reminded Emmet that a whole life existed outside the ward, even within the same building. Among them, he felt conspicuous with the plastic identification bracelet branding his wrist. He stuffed his hand into his pocket to conceal it, but the more he dug into his pants, the further the bracelet pushed up his arm. It grew slippery with sweat. "They know what it means," he fretted, counting the lighted floors drop down the elevator panel: seven, six, five, four.

Chris punched him lightly on the arm and spoke easily about the weather so that it would appear to the others that Emmet knew it was hot. "A real scorcher, huh?"

Emmet nodded gratefully. As they overheard Chris, Emmet sensed a sigh pass through the other occupants, as if they believed he too shared a knowledge of the outside.

At the door to Dr. Franklin's office, Chris took his leave. "I'll be back to get you in an hour," he called over his shoulder as Emmet watched his stumpy body clomp away.

Emmet hesitated in the vestibule. "I am free," he thought. He checked behind him to be certain the corridor was clear. Because it was possible in that instant, he entertained the idea of fleeing, but there was nowhere he wanted to go. Even standing in the unlocked corridors of the hospital he felt woozy, as if he were too soon too free.

Dr. Franklin strode from his desk to greet Emmet by the door. "Welcome, welcome," he said.

Emmet stared at him dumbly. In his mind, he began to fabricate apologies for having stalked from the meeting with Louise. But he could not think of a reason to explain how he felt naturally bound to the other patients. He did not know how to explain why he had followed someone so easily whom he did not know.

"Sit down, sit down," Dr. Franklin said, indicating a gleaming mahogany chair. "I'm curious to know how you feel you're adjusting."

"What can I tell him?" Emmet thought in a flurry. He could not conceive how he might convey the tumult of the past months, even the past hour, to someone who had not lived it. In a jumble, he saw himself trampled by patients in the hallway. He saw Isabel slap his head with her purse. He saw Winston illuminated by a burning house. He saw Juanita moan with the beach ball clutched in her arms. He saw Louise in her dormitory bed, crunching the stem of a light bulb like a pretzel. He heard Bruce calling him by that other name.

Before him, he saw the doctor who listened from across the table. "How can I tell him my life?" Emmet wondered as he studied the doctor's wide maroon tie with a dollop of egg at its center. With the other patients, he felt more at ease than he would ever be with the doctor. With Emily, Daphne, and Louise, even Bruce and Winston, there was nothing of his past he had to explain. They assumed he was one of them. Emmet did not understand why there were impossible distances between people that were bridged or not, no matter the desire, or what quality of trust drew him naturally to some rather than others and made them part of his life. All he knew was that Dr. Franklin had never been anywhere that he had been, so he despaired of ever describing the things he had seen.

The doctor smiled at him patiently, waiting for his answer.

"Fine," Emmet mumbled blandly. "It's fine," as if they sat together in a room, anywhere.

"I'm glad. Life will get even better once we change your medication. We want to get you on an even keel."

"My eyes," Emmet said. "Sometimes things still m-m-move that shouldn't."

"But nothing that isn't there?"

"I don't think so, but how would I know? I mean, if I see it, then it's there. For m-m-me, anyway."

"But you have to learn to distinguish, wouldn't you agree? I'd like to run a series of tests to gauge how you view yourself in the world. Nothing complicated, just nice and easy, as if we're having a conversation about life. Okay?"

Emmet nodded assent. He was so tired, he hoped that he could divine the answers the doctor wanted to hear and then be allowed to return to his room.

"Can you give me three states that begin with the letter *A*?" the doctor asked.

Emmet imagined a map spread on the table before them, the coastlines and peninsulas painted yellow against the blue of a paper sea. He imagined driving in the car with Jonathan and his mother. Over the summers when they traveled, they had made it their object to touch the border of every state, as if it gave their mother's wanderings a purpose. They had made it to every one except two. "Alaska, Alabama, and Arkansas," Emmet said, thinking of how it had been his dream to drive across glaciers to the heart of the Alaskan wilderness.

"Good." The doctor glowed as if Emmet had said something brilliant. "Now can you tell me the name of the President?"

"A child could answer that," Emmet balked. "I-I-I know where I am. That isn't my problem."

"But we have to be certain. Sometimes the most disturbed patients can cloak their delusions with charm."

Emmet had an image of Winston sneaking from the halfway house that very evening, greedily pouring kerosene from a glass bottle and striking the tip of a long wooden match. "I know," was all he said.

"So let's move on to something else, shall we? What's twenty-seven times nine?" the doctor asked. "Come on, quickly. Don't stop to think."

In his mind, Emmet drew the numbers on a blackboard. "Nine by twenty-seven," he thought. "So that leaves a three at the bottom and then the six goes to the other side and then nine by two is eighteen and you add the six to that and so then you get eighteen plus six with a three at the end."

He could not come up with a number. Math problems had always muddled him, even when he had the clearest mind. No one in his family could do them. But now his dumbness was being used to test his sanity.

"It ends in a three," he said, sweating.

"Good. And what does it begin with?"

"Eighteen plus six?" he ventured, unsure now that he could succeed at even the simplest addition. "Look, I c-c-could never do them. I think it's genetic. I don't have a spatial m-m-mind. Once they gave me a test in school with pictures of flat boxes and I had to imagine what they would look like when they were built. I got the lowest score in the history of the state. The teacher called my grandmother to say I was r-r-retarded."

The doctor removed his glasses and peered at Emmet earnestly. "Did that experience shape you?"

"No. We thought it was f-f-funny. All my grandmother said was, 'Don't let him know he's r-r-retarded and maybe he won't notice.' " Emmet chuckled.

Dr. Franklin scribbled grimly in his notebook. "Hmmm," he said. "Shall we try something else? Take this sheet of five incomplete sentences. I'll remove the tabs one by one and reveal the question. Don't think. Jot down the first idea that comes to mind."

The first sentence read, "My mother is _____ ."

"What do I write?" Emmet thought frantically. He remembered what Louise had told him: that he should elaborate every detail to divert them. He considered writing "a killer" or "an abuser," but even as a joke, he did not want something inscribed on paper that would taint her.

"Hurry. Don't stop to think," Dr. Franklin urged.

"Dead," Emmet printed in the blank.

The doctor pulled free the next piece of white tape. The second sentence read, "My father is _____ ."

"Dead," he scrawled quickly, without even thinking.

"Now you're getting it," Dr. Franklin barked. "Next." He pulled the cover from the third sentence. "My brother is _____ ," it read.

"Dead?" Emmet considered, to give the page symmetry. But

then the doctor might believe he wanted Jonathan dead, or, worse, that he harbored a wish to kill.

"Don't think, don't think," Dr. Franklin said.

"Beautiful?" Emmet wondered, but then they might believe he was envious. He never had been. Emmet liked the way he looked, as if he had been given the body that suited his personality. "A lover of cats," he wrote, finally.

"One-word answers are the best," Dr. Franklin admonished. "We don't want a narrative here, just a short association."

"But it's sort of one w-w-word," Emmet said. "It's a thing, isn't it?"

"Well, yes, but try. Here, we're almost done," he said, revealing the fourth sentence.

"I am not a _____ ," it read.

"Lover of cats?" Emmet thought, chuckling.

Dr. Franklin swooped upon him. "Something funny? Tell me. Write it down."

"No. No," Emmet stammered. "A private joke, but it doesn't m-m-mean anything. Really."

"Try me," Dr. Franklin said.

"No. I just thought of something f-f-funny somebody said. Yesterday."

"You won't share?"

"It was nothing. Now what was that sentence? 'I am not . . .'" Emmet read aloud.

"French?" he wondered. "Forty? Crazy? A gourmet? A troublemaker?" There were so many things he was not, he could think of nothing to write.

"Hurry, hurry," Dr. Franklin said. "You're cheating."

"A nurse," Emmet wrote at last.

"Here we go," Dr. Franklin said, pulling away the final tab with a flourish.

"I want to be _____ ," it read.

What was the truth? What did Emmet want to be if he could have anything in the world? "Unnervous," he wrote, because it was what he desired most in his heart.

"Okay," Dr. Franklin said, snatching the paper away. "We'll look at these later. Now I want you to read these images for me and tell me what you see."

He selected a folded piece of cardboard from his briefcase and opened it like a greeting card. The only mark was a puddle of purple ink dried in the crease.

"It d-d-doesn't look like anything," Emmet said. "It looks like a smudge of ink."

"You're not trying," Dr. Franklin said. "Use your imagination. Think in pictures. Didn't you ever see forms in the clouds when you were a child, like cows flying overhead in the sky?"

"No, I-I-I never did. I just thought of them as clouds."

"Come on. Empty your mind. What do you see here?" Dr. Franklin offered the paper on outstretched hands.

"Sorry," Emmet said after a minute. "It still looks like ink."

"You're resisting." Dr. Franklin's eyes flashed. "You've got to let yourself go." He opened a second card. There was a purple circle of ink to one side with several thin strands curling out from its center.

"It could be a s-s-sun," Emmet said. "With rays. Only it's purple."

"And what does the sun mean to you?"

"Heat? And getting tanned. I love to get tanned, but now I've got these b-b-blotches on my shoulders and I'm getting wrinkles. So I sort of regret it, but I can't seem to stop." Emmet sat back in his chair, exhausted.

"There's nothing special about the beach you'd like to tell me?"

"I don't think so," Emmet said. "Should there be?"

Dr. Franklin slapped the card on the table a little too hard. "I just don't believe you're trying. How can you be so literal minded about your life? People see all sorts of things in these blots, things more vivid than dreams."

"Sorry," Emmet said meekly. "Maybe we could try another?"

Dr. Franklin perused several cards before he passed one to Emmet triumphantly. The ink spread down the crack in the page, thin and elongated, a purple oval swinging at its end.

"A b-b-balloon falling. A wrecking ball. A head swinging on a noose," Emmet offered.

"Well, which is it?"

"Do I have to pick? It could be anything." He studied the picture again. "Okay, it's a h-h-head in a noose."

"Do you feel like your head's in a noose?"

"Of course," Emmet said. "But not because of p-p-pictures. It's something I feel. I only said I saw a head because, you know, Juanita had her baby yesterday and, well, maybe you heard about it? But it wasn't a baby, not really; it was a beach ball. It still upset me because she believed it was real and now she has this grief."

"Yes, I heard. And maybe you should think more about the way you're avoiding things. It takes work to become healthy. I can't do it for you."

"I'll try," Emmet mumbled, abashed. "Maybe one last card? Maybe this one will be different."

He shut his eyes and concentrated on emptying his mind so that the purple ink would rush upon him. He counted to three and looked at the page. To his horror, there was nothing but spots of dripping, faded color.

"There is nothing in my mind," he panicked as he tried to read the image. He was not pretending. He wanted to say something to Dr. Franklin, something true that would amaze them both, but he saw nothing before him but a smudge shimmering with nerves. It moved on the page, just as the patterns raced across the carpet in his room, the marks faceless as cells. He remembered how often his mother had tried to show him the patterns in the stars. She could read the figures in the galaxies as clearly as if they were the faces of people she loved; but no matter how often she had tried, no matter how often Emmet had faked his enthusiasm as she pointed out the constellations, he had never seen anything but separate points of light.

"I'm sorry," Emmet said. "I think there's something wrong with me. Maybe it's like those b-b-boxes I could never see as anything but flat squares. Maybe I am retarded."

He spoke so earnestly that Dr. Franklin reached across the table and patted his arm. "Maybe next time," he said, "when you're more relaxed."

"Yes," Emmet said, standing to leave. "When I'm more used to it here."

"Are you in a hurry?" Dr. Franklin asked, pulling out the sheet of answers Emmet had written to the sentences. "I'd like to discuss what you wrote."

Emmet tried to recall his responses to prepare himself, but all he could remember was the word "dead." As if he had read Emmet's mind, Dr. Franklin said, "Your parents are dead." He spoke as if he were bracing him for bad news.

Emmet squirmed in his seat.

"And so?" The doctor waved his hand to draw Emmet in.

"I have a brother."

"And?"

"He's alive."

"I gathered that," Dr. Franklin snapped. "Is there anything else you feel about him?"

"No," Emmet said. "I mean, well, of-of-of course." He slumped in his seat, struck dumb. He knew the staff would decide his future from anything he said. He could not be like Louise and fabricate things that had never happened. He did not want anything held against him by the doctors, not even lies.

"Why do you say you're not a nurse?" Dr. Franklin barked, changing course.

"It's from a poem. I just thought of it because this is a h-h-hospital and there's lots of nurses and I'm not one, you know?"

"Yes," Dr. Franklin said, weakly.

Emmet felt as if he were failing. He could not imagine what the doctor would write on his chart after he had left: that he was a malingerer, that he had no interest in ever getting well?

To appease him, Emmet remembered the final question on the sheet of sentences. He rose from his chair excitedly. "I know 'unnervous' isn't a word, but you said to try for one-word answers and I wanted to be cooperative. But once I saw this really b-b-bad movie about Vietnam, and the only good thing in it was that all these soldiers were in the jungle and the enemy had set trip wires among the foliage. They couldn't walk anywhere without worrying that land mines were buried in every inch of mud. You got the feeling that they would still feel them even after they returned h-h-home, and that they would be forever walking on tenterhooks even in a field a million miles from battle. That's me—that's how I f-f-feel. I've got this nervousness, like there's wires everywhere."

Dr. Franklin licked his finger and pressed a curl flat against his scalp. He kept his face impassive, but Emmet saw his pupils dilate, in and out, as if he were censoring the response forming in his mind. He snapped the locks of his briefcase closed and pressed his fingertips against the edge of the table. He set his face in a smile that announced the end of their session. Emmet panicked that the doctor seemed prepared to leave without saying another word. Despite the elaborate evasions he had devised to keep part of himself private, Emmet still hoped his doctors possessed a kind of magic: that whenever he was ready to hear, they would share a word that would explain the reasons he lived as he did. He wanted to believe that at some time in their training, they had learned a language that would set him free.

Emmet beamed hopefully at Dr. Franklin, ashamed that his face glowed with the expectancy of a child who still believed his parents to be invincible. "Can you help me?" he asked. "I don't want to l-l-live this way any longer."

Even as he spoke the words, Emmet felt his optimism drain. He pictured the patients on the ward. He heard them moan and rage. He saw them stumble and drool. He believed they had been created as they were and could never be undone. "How could I expect to be different?" he wondered as he thought of how he tensed and swooned every moment of his life. It seemed impossible to unlearn everything he had become.

"Have you ever s-s-seen anyone change? I mean, do people get better?" Emmet asked, embarrassed that he was reduced to pleading his soul to someone he would never have trusted in his life on the outside. He wondered if somewhere in the doctor's heart, part of what he heard every day afflicted him, and secretly he shared fears that his life had become something other than what he had wanted it to be.

The doctor sucked on his lower lip, musing, as if he were dragging on the stem of a pipe. From across the table, Emmet sent him messages, begging him to tell the truth.

"I don't know," Dr. Franklin said. "Sometimes people surprise you, but I've stopped guessing who wins and who doesn't. A lot depends on luck. And what you can forget."

"But it isn't any one thing," Emmet said. "It's just this sense I've got, you know, even when there's n-n-nothing there, like in that movie I was telling you about. But once there *was* something, you know what I mean? Once the wire existed. They just couldn't get it out of their minds later because of what they remembered from the jungle. And so it became something else, something that came alive again every day, so how could they forget? It was really a bad m-m-movie, don't get me wrong, but that part, how something can be everywhere and nowhere at all, that's what I liked—

that's what I'm afraid of. All the unseen things that can get you. It's something that l-l-lives with you, like a dread. How can you forget something when it's always there?"

"I don't know," Dr. Franklin said. "But maybe you can lose it. I'm not sure it's the same thing, but those feelings, sometimes they can be lost."

"But have you ever seen it? Have you ever known anybody who did it? I mean, really, how do you forget a dread?"

"I don't know," Dr. Franklin mumbled. "You can learn to build fences. That much I've seen. . . ."

"Give me an example," Emmet demanded. "What are their names? How did they do it? How do you forget a dread?"

CHAPTER
NINE

"**D**id you forget to tell us someone was coming?" the nurse
asked. "Your brother is here to see you."

Emmet had been ducking Jonathan's phone calls for two weeks.
He had insisted that a notation be put on his chart that said, "No
visitors." He had wanted no reminders from his other life. But
doctors would let family members in at any time. It was impossible
to keep them away.

"I guess you couldn't tell him I've gone out?" Emmet asked.

"Where would you go?" she said grimly as she left the room.

Emmet followed the nurse into the lounge. Jonathan waited
on the orange sofa, sockless, the bone of his ankle chiseled against
the cuff of his jeans.

Each time he dragged on his cigarette, Jonathan shook the hair
from his eyes with a flick of his neck. Isabel huddled next to him,
inspecting the contents of her purse. She held up a satin bow, a
magenta lipstick, a soup spoon, and the nub of an eyebrow pencil
for his approval. "See?" she said as she fingered her things. "See?"

From across the room, Emmet watched his brother examine
each object gamely, as if he were prepared to be dazzled by a
quality not immediately apparent to his eye. But as Isabel paraded
the pieces of junk, exclaiming, "See? See? See?" in her own private

thrall, Jonathan's expression grew dimmer. Then he ceased to raise his eyes from his lap at all.

"Jonathan? Are you here?" Emmet called from ten feet away. He screwed his face rapturously in greeting to disguise the fact that he had not wanted his brother to come.

"Oh, oh, oh," Isabel whimpered when she heard Emmet's voice. She clutched her treasures to her breast. "My things," she trilled to Jonathan. "My things. Come, come, we must take cover. He's a bully." She nestled against Jonathan's side. "Help me, help," she cried.

Instinctively, Jonathan stretched an arm around her reedy shoulders. Emmet saw him blanch as he turned from the terrified woman to see his brother striding towards them, his black clothes flapping over his bones. "He believes I have tortured her," Emmet thought. "He is imagining the cruelty I can do."

Isabel sucked two fingers into her mouth and blew her siren's whistle. Jonathan clapped his hands to his ears. A rivulet of spit gushed down her arm. She blew again, wetly.

"Is it really you?" Emmet called incredulously over the sound, as if they had been separated for decades. He stood before the couch. Jonathan gently detached himself from Isabel and rose politely.

"Then you're one too," she cried as she watched them reach out to lightly touch each other's hands. The brothers dropped them abruptly when she whistled yet again, as if they were caught passing secret documents.

"Oh, oh, oh," she whined to the other patients who clustered around the couch, peering curiously into Jonathan's face, stroking the sheen and quality of his clothes, invading him unashamedly, as they did with every new specimen who came to the ward.

"She th-th-thinks everyone's out to get her," Emmet said as Isabel scuttled into the robes of the crowd.

"Yes, yes, I could tell."

"She's one of the c-c-crazy ones," Emmet explained as the patients inched closer. He felt their sour breath and a humid air, almost a sweat, misting from their flesh and matted hair onto his skin. When he touched his brother's pressed linen coat, he noticed for the first time an odor thick about the room, as if it poured in gusts from the vents in the ceiling and floors, a smell he imagined would steam from rotted bodies. He flattened the square tuft of hair jutting over his brow. He straightened the edge of the T-shirt tucked into his waist. He checked to make sure Louise or Emily or some other friend who might address him by name was not present.

A woman in strawberry lace bloomers and black pumps cruised up to Jonathan. She wore a polka-dot blouse with white threads curled where each button had been sewn. The folds of cloth were hooked in the center with a paper clip bent through a hole. Emmet did not know her name. Patients came and went so quickly on the ward that already he felt like a veteran. He kept his distance from the ones who were more dramatically crazy, as if they were members of an untouchable class.

"You wanna call my mother and tell her to walk the dog?" she asked. She slipped a finger into Jonathan's snug pants pocket. "You got a quarter in here, honey? You gotta roll of dimes?"

Jonathan flinched and shook free from the woman's hand. He gave her a coin. "That's a dime," she snorted. "I can't make a call with that. You don't know the difference between a quarter and a dime, you chintzy bastard? You wanna be stingy? You call my mother and tell her to walk the dog. Sweet-talk her. Maybe she'll fuck you."

Jonathan smiled patiently. He dug his hands into his blazer pockets. He turned his attention to two patients playing pool. Each time one of them cracked a shot, he dug a groove deep into the green felt, so that the stick screeched as it scraped through to the slate beneath.

"Call her, call her, call her," the woman rasped. She tapped her heels on the linoleum. She swung her mane of hair. She dug her fingernails into the flesh over her heart. She abandoned herself to her words as if she were growling a blues lyric. "Call her, call her, call her. All I want is a quarter. Wait until you're starving on the street. You won't be pretty then. Not even a quarter? Pretty, pretty, pretty please?"

"Is there somewhere we can go?" Jonathan asked. He stared over the woman's head as if she were invisible. He arched an eyebrow at Emmet conspiratorially.

"Call her, call her, call her," the woman brayed. "Call my mother." She reached for Jonathan's arms, as if to dance. He spun away in one movement, ushering Emmet in the opposite direction with a brush of his hand.

"So," he said, guiding them forward, their backs to the other patients.

"So," Emmet replied. In the distance, he could hear Juanita laughing hysterically behind the walls of the white isolation room. Her fists beat against the wood. Soon the nurses would enter to quiet her. With the outer door open, her volume would increase. He wanted to get Jonathan out of there before he could make sense of her words.

He was afraid to bring him to his room. Bruce was napping. If he awoke, he might tell Jonathan unimaginable lies. Emmet was ashamed to be tainted by the delusions of the others, as if even in the hospital ward, he might keep his brother from believing he was mad.

"Keep talking," he told himself, hoping he could drown out the sound. Emmet imagined the floor plan of the ward in his head as he decided on a place for them to go. He flung his arm towards two chairs set in a corner of the recreation room.

"Here is . . . ," he said with a flourish. The moment he spoke, he saw a series of new finger paintings pinned to the wall over the chairs, each one dripping with swirls the color of blood.

"Here is . . . ," he said, spinning Jonathan towards the nursing station. He saw an orderly wheeling Henry around the corner, coming right towards them. Henry's hands were bound with miles of gauze to the rails of the chair. Black skin, like handfuls of thrown mud, stained his eyes.

Every inch of the room revealed another horror. "How can I explain that I eat dinner with a man who pops out his eyes?" Emmet thought. Before Jonathan came, Henry had not seemed so grotesque; he simply had seemed as if he were afflicted with a habit that could not be broken. Now he seemed monstrous and sick, maybe a danger to know.

"This way," Emmet said, distracted by his own guilt. "What would he think if I told him how I tried to murder the cat?" he wondered. Even now, Jonathan probably did not believe that Emmet was very different from him. But Emmet had no clue to the life that passed beneath his brother's placid exterior. Maybe he committed all sorts of crimes when he was alone, but did not worry about them, as Emmet did.

Emmet opened the door to the crafts room and switched on the light. The narrow folding tables were littered with animals molded from clay. Thumbprints lined the trunks of their bodies like saddles. There were horses and dogs, ducks and rabbits; and a snake stomped in the center, its two ends wound within the feet of a stout, pottery bird. The menagerie was glazed in lurid colors: hot pink, burnt sienna, lavender, and aqua.

"Quite a zoo," Jonathan said, indicating a cow coated a rich chartreuse.

"How's the dog?" Emmet asked.

"She won't eat. She misses you. I brought you a picture." Jonathan presented Emmet with a photograph of the dog sprawled across the floor, her eyes lidded with despair.

"She mopes as if her heart were broken," Jonathan said. "She wants you to come home."

"How c-c-can she miss me when our life was so bad? It's better with you. Sh-sh-she can have a normal life."

"It's you she loves. It's you she's used to."

Their life seemed so far away. From her photograph, the dog appeared to have lost ten pounds in the time Emmet had been gone, until her flesh had thinned as finely as his own. He could not help warming to her devotion. "She is getting small," he thought proudly. But to his brother he said, "There's no going back."

"Sometime you have to. It can't be like this forever."

"No," Emmet said, but he hugged himself cozily, as if he could wrap the walls of the room around him, like a blanket. He would not admit it to anyone, not even to his brother, but in his heart the hospital had become the favorite place he had ever been. He could imagine living there forever, surrendering his life to the routine until he had spent decades within those walls. He felt as he had during the nights he snuggled in the bomb shelter and surveyed his house through the telescope. Sometimes when he looked out the window in the ward from the exact angle, the bars made the same pattern as the lens had through the boxed eye of the bunker.

"You got evicted," Jonathan said. "I tried to stop them, but I couldn't. Your landlord hates you, I guess."

"Fine," Emmet said. He fought to keep an inadvertent smile from marring his expressionless face. "Then there is nowhere but here," he thought happily. He tried to mist his eyes so that his brother would believe he suffered the loss keenly, but he felt himself grow lighter with the image of his apartment, deserted now, or maybe filled with the possessions of a new family. "Finally it is a dead place," he sighed privately, hoping all the trouble was gone from him.

"Don't worry," Jonathan said. "You and the dog can live with me until you find a new place." He lit a cigarette and held the smoking match uncertainly between two fingers.

Emmet chose a red clay bowl from the shelf by the door. One side wobbled three inches high, the other only two, such as a child might make. "Here," he said.

"Quite an artisan, this one," Jonathan said, flicking an ash.

"He's my friend," Emmet snapped as he thought of the boy who had labored at the pottery wheel.

"Sorry."

Emmet knew which patient had fashioned each of the clumsy animals on the table. He would not tell Jonathan, but the glossy orange dog was his own creation. Even Louise and Emily did not know that the past weeks he had snuck to art class in the mornings while they slept.

"Why did he come?" Emmet wondered as he watched his brother cross and recross his legs. Jonathan chose animals from the table and feigned interest in their design. He sucked long breaths from his cigarette, forcing the smoke into the deepest recesses of his lungs. Then he let it escape in slow bursts. Each puff popped from his lips, as if he wanted to fill the silence with its sound.

Throughout their life, Emmet had learned to interpret his brother's gestures and silences for signals of his mood. He knew Jonathan's support was predicated on never prying into his life or in forcing him to speak of events he had closed within his life. Often Emmet grew bewildered at the significance of their bond, because it seemed based entirely on things that could never be said. Yet when they were present in the same place, he felt as if he had crossed into a different field of energy, drawn naturally the way two magnets snap together, erasing the space in between. Since they were young, Emmet had demanded of his brother things he would never request of a friend. Never once had Jonathan complained. And although he believed Jonathan would have flown to deepest Africa to rescue him, every time they met, Emmet left dissatisfied.

"Two of us were there," Jonathan's presence had often assured him. All their lives they kept returning to each other, as if they could make the past something tangible, like a body. But always Emmet found that past eluding him, like smoke caught within a net. He had learned too early to be intimidated by his brother's silence, as if by speaking he might drag him unconsenting towards some catastrophe that would unravel everything each had become.

"But I am nothing now," Emmet thought. "There is nothing less that I can be."

He wanted to ask what Jonathan remembered, not for any resolution of the past but because he needed to know for certain how it was. First four, then three, now only two: soon there would be no witnesses. His family's amnesia had made him believe he had invented everything he recalled, so he found himself without a shape, as if he had leapt miraculously into midair and been held there, suspended by nothing, ever since.

Alone in the crafts room with no one else to hear, Emmet could ask his brother anything. Jonathan seemed to sense this: his skin tensed tighter against his cheekbones; his eyes flitted to every object in the room as if he sought a subject they might discuss. Locked in the ward, seven stories above the ground, Emmet had him cornered. Out in the world, secure on his own turf, Jonathan would be able to slip away. Emmet felt the uselessness of their bond press upon him unless the rules were changed, that beyond all planning the one moment had come where he might say all that was in his heart. If he let it pass, it might never return again.

"But what do I pick?" Emmet wondered. He tried to replay their life as the seconds ticked past as he had heard drowning people see during their last seconds in the water.

He saw a red sports car. A highway buried in drifts of snow. A bed piled high with pillows, its whiteness broken only by the starburst pattern of the lace. He saw the moon, dimmed by fog, out the windshield of the car and heard the clang of metal striking the pavement as his father changed a tire near dawn. He saw his grandmother, her robe wrinkled with mauve flowers, sneak into his room when he was ill, alighting on the edge of his bed as he dozed, watching to be certain he still breathed. He saw his mother's hat hovering in the air outside the hotel room window, its brim glassy and transparent as an insect's wing. Moment after moment clicked by, each one bleeding into the next, unceasing, like wraiths returning from the dead.

Emmet rifled through the animals on the table until he found a green creature with a gangling neck and four stubby legs. "What do you think of this?" he asked, handling its body so roughly that the tail snapped in his hand.

Jonathan studied the creature almost reverently. He seemed eager not to repeat the mistake he had made by mocking the ashtray. "I don't know. What is it? A snake with feet?"

"It's a dinosaur," Emmet said. "My roommate made it. He's obsessed by them. He's even got them on his underwear."

"It's very lifelike."

"Do you remember how afraid you were of dinosaurs?"

"No . . . but I remember loving cows. For some reason, I loved cows."

"You don't remember when you were two and Mom came home from a trip and brought you that plastic dinosaur?"

"No," Jonathan said. "I don't remember anything from when I was two."

"I do," Emmet said, resolutely. He closed his eyes and meditated on the creature in his hand until he had memorized the curve and slope of its body. He rubbed the broken piece of tail against his palm as he spoke, letting it travel over the joints of his fingers, like a worry bead. He wanted to steel himself from any resistance he might read in his brother's face.

"We were staying with Grandma for the summer, but Mom returned home unexpectedly, in June. She brought presents. I got a model of a bomber, but she forgot to buy the glue, so pieces of wings and engines were strewn all over the rug. She handed you a paper sack with a bow taped to the handle. Your hands were so small, especially the fingernails, almost microscopic over the moons of your fingertips, a real baby's hands. They scratched at the paper to tear the bag open, but you couldn't manage the staples, so I helped rip it. I saw what it was at the same moment as you. The dinosaur had bumpy green scales and sharp white teeth with traces of blood painted on their tips, like it had just eaten someone. I tried to stuff it back in the bag, but Mom came over and shook it in your face, saying, 'Here, darling, take it. It's yours.' You screamed, like it was real and would bite you, but she wouldn't stop, insisting, 'Here, darling, take it, it's yours,' until you ran upstairs to your room."

"You've told me this before," Jonathan said. He walked to the sink to sip from the faucet, but the water dribbled over his face and into his eyes, dislodging a contact lens. "Shit," he said as he rubbed under his lid, rolling his eye back and forth, forcing it open wide, until he stared at Emmet with the entire oval bared: its rims netted with angry red veins.

Emmet blinked back serenely. He felt his own eyes swim, loose and greased, in their sockets. He rolled the fragment of clay between his palms. "How can you forget," he whispered, "the way she glowered at Grandma, as if to say, 'What have you done to them while I was away?,' wanting to believe she had left perfect children. Then suddenly you came into the room, lugging this really prehistoric camera. Nobody knew where you'd gotten it from. I don't know how you even knew what a camera was, but you dragged it over to me and pointed to the dinosaur and said, 'Take a picture.' I tried, but the camera was too heavy. I couldn't aim it properly. You screamed 'Take a picture, take a picture,' as if you were begging me to kill it. Mom stormed off to dinner, like we'd spoiled her homecoming, and left us with Grandma, who did take a picture, later, and it was one of those instant cameras, so we got it right then, and you took the photograph to bed with you and carried it around for days until it was crumpled into bits. But it got washed in the laundry, and when you pulled the soggy lump from your shorts, you cried, like you were at the mercy of the creature all over again without it."

Jonathan cringed with embarrassment that Emmet recalled a moment so vividly from a time when he had been defenseless. "Yes, yes, you've said all this before, but I don't remember it."

"I do," Emmet said again. "But it happened to you, not me. I almost feel like I've stolen it."

"Well, it's our life, I guess—the same thing, more or less." Jonathan opened the cabinet where the art supplies were kept. He jiggled the drawers filled with paintbrushes, crayons, and jars stained with brightly colored liquid. "So what do you do here all day?"

"Meetings," Emmet said, defeated. "Mostly lots of meetings."

"Your voice is much better. I'm happy. You must be getting well."

"No, I'm not. N-n-no. It was just remembering that story. I got carried away."

"Well, it's a start. You should be happy."

"N-n-no," Emmet said. "That's not what I want."

His life was such a jumble of things that he could not explain, despite everything that had happened, how many times he had been happy. Once on vacation with his grandmother in Nevis he had slept in an enormous bed swaddled with mosquito netting and had lain awake all night buzzing with pleasure as the insects whirred outside, unable to get at him. He could still feel the air rattling the window and the touch of the breeze cooling his skin. But that was just one night. There had been thousands of them since, each falling into another, and then another, without any rhythm or relation to the next. The more he lived, the more he was buried among them, until they piled into his mind, useless as collected stamps.

He wanted to be rid of them; yet dead, they bewitched him, as if no matter where he lived, his houses were crowded with ghosts. They could find him anywhere, their whiteness palpable, as if he saw them pour from under transoms, through keyholes, disquietly, like a milky air. He saw them hardened to fog on windows whenever he looked outside in the dark, or rise before his eyes whenever he breathed frostily in the cold.

He did not remember what it had been like before. He did not know if the legacy his mother left him was to cloud everything he saw forever after, as if his life were witnessed from afar, from behind the glass of a shut window on a ledge. He did not know if his compulsion to document everything—his keeping of notes and the photographs that had lined the walls of his bedroom at home, his recording telephone conversations until his closet had overflowed with garbage bags of tapes—stemmed from that one event: to verify independently things that had existed. He needed to apprehend them from outside of himself to believe them, to prove everything he knew lived elsewhere than inside of his mind.

"How else can I know when I lie?" Emmet thought. "How else can I ever be sure?"

He looked at Jonathan, stiff as the animals grouped on the table. He thought of how he might convey the urgency he felt, how he hoped that together they might become the vessel through which the dead might speak again, and how alone, he found himself too meager for the task. Emmet summoned all his courage to ask his brother one last thing, the only question he had ever wanted him to answer:

"So, sometimes—I mean, ever—don't you wonder what it was like to fall?"

By that question he meant everything: their mother tumbling through the air, her eyes opened wide or gripped shut, either by unconsciousness or by fear, and how her body snapped or crushed or maybe rolled like cloth on the ground below. But by it he also meant: how could she have jumped without hating us?

Jonathan paused. From his face, Emmet could not tell if he was carefully weighing his response or if he was merely plotting his escape. Emmet wanted to say to him, "No one else can hear." He wanted to tell him to pretend they sat strapped in a plane plummeting towards the earth and that in their last few seconds they had nothing left to lose. But already he felt himself undone by embarrassment.

Jonathan leaned forward in his chair until he was inches from Emmet's face. "I can't worry about the things that obsess you," he said, not unkindly. "I'm sorry, but it's not my way. You have to stop believing any of it means anything. That's what I learned long ago. That's what you don't know."

An image of his brother crushed beneath him in the snow rose so vividly in Emmet's mind that they might have been on that mountain again, as if they had never left. He could not believe that when Jonathan looked in the mirror, he did not see it too. But what if he had said yes? What if he had admitted that he could bury none of it, that the past blinded his days so that he could not see his way forward? Would anything have changed?

Emmet did not know what it meant to remember. His past held him like a trap, but he also believed it to be the ground that gave him whatever weight he had. For years he had coveted his brother's nerveless, almost soldierly calm; but now as they sat there, he had never felt more estranged from anyone, the distance between them so vast they might have been separated by acres of fields crowded with cattle instead of those two feet of table cluttered with clay.

"But I want it to mean something," he said. "It isn't enough for me, the way you live your life."

Jonathan shrugged as he ran his hand along the table. Orange dust from one of the animals sprinkled his palm. He stared at it aghast, stopping himself from brushing the residue on his pants. He went to the sink and ran his fingers daintily under the spout. He reached for a paper towel, but the dispenser was empty.

"My hand," he said.

"Here," Emmet said, untucking the faded black shirt from his pants. He held out the hem.

Jonathan hesitated before he wiped his fingers on the cloth. "Thanks," he said, sheepishly.

Emmet nodded once, politely. "Save me," he muttered under his breath as he thought of their midnight telephone call, all those months before.

"What?" Jonathan started.

"Nothing. I just said it was safe here."

"Ah, yes . . . well . . ." Jonathan glanced at his watch. He adjusted the shoulder pads of his blazer, as if he prepared to go outside to meet another part of his life. He opened the door with one hand. With the other, he patted Emmet's shirt. He grimaced as his flesh met the brittle bones of his brother's chest, his damp palm leaving a shadow at its center, perfectly formed, like an appliqué or a brand.

As he followed Jonathan out into the ward, Emmet placed his own hand over the mark. His fingers were dwarfed by its size:

smaller than a child's hand, not human at all, but papery and clawed, like a mummy's. As Emmet stood there, mesmerized by its thinness, Jonathan loped through the corridor ahead of him, maneuvering the turns so expertly that Emmet had to quicken his pace to catch up, yet not seem to be running after him.

PART THREE
CARNIVAL

The human soul never ceases to be modified by its encounter with force, swept on, blinded by that which it believes itself able to handle, bowed beneath the power of that which it suffers. . . . Force is that which makes a thing of anybody who comes under its sway. When exercised to the full, it makes a thing of man in the most literal sense, for it makes him a corpse. . . . The force which kills outright is an elementary and coarse form of force. How much more varied in its devices, how much more astonishing in its effects is that other which does not kill; or which delays killing. It must surely kill, or it will perhaps kill, or else it is only suspended above him whom it may at any moment destroy. This of all procedures turns a man to stone.
—Simone Weil
   "The Iliad, Poem of Force"

CHAPTER
ONE

"**P**sst."
Emmet was dreaming: he was a racehorse, tearing down a track, close upon three other thoroughbreds blanketed in red, yellow, and blue silks. The sun struck the gleaming cloths like beams reflected on metal. He could not look away. He felt a body upon the hard, leathered edge of his saddle, straddling his back, and a breath moist upon his ear, whispering "Psst" as his hooves snapped across the dirt, his legs a clatter of bones. And with the dust flying in clouds around his face and the urgent "Psst" bugging his ear, he ran as if steam were gushing from the center of the earth and would scald him with its heat.

"Psst."

Emmet felt someone shake his toe through the sheets. He snapped open his eyes. A hand stroked his bare feet, then nestled against him, skin to skin. "Am I dreaming still?" he wondered as he tried to discern the shapes in the room. He saw the window, grimy with dirt in the afternoon light. He saw the outline of the desk. He saw the dresser drawer partially opened, with handfuls of Bruce's underwear bunched against the rim, like gags.

"Psst," he heard again from the bottom of the bed. Then, more tentatively, "John? Am I bothering you?"

Emmet moaned loudly and flipped onto his side, as if he were seized by sleep, but Bruce tickled the unhardened flesh under his feet so that he squirmed helplessly. "Psst. Wake up, John. It's time."

Emmet raised his head from the pillow. Up close, Bruce smelled fruity and ripe. Emmet had lived with him for three months, longer than he had ever shared a room with anyone except for members of his family; long enough to learn his secrets and to see him change. Lately, Bruce had ceased to wash. He wore the same clothes week after week. Even his prized underwear lay dark and stiff on the floor. His speech had grown toneless and insistent, as in the rhythms Emmet had heard in people who speak Chinese. He spent his leisure hours blissfully naked, buffing the hairs on the back of his thighs contemplatively as he paced about the room, the way some people stroke their foreheads when deep in thought.

The first time he undressed before Emmet, Bruce had bared his chest proudly, displaying two porpoises tattooed over each nipple, their rain-gray bodies frozen in a leap over the purplish dots. "My fish," Bruce had proclaimed lovingly, pointing out their fins, their white underbellies, their multicolored eyes. Bruce's stomach drooped over his belt, slack and hairy, but the skin under the tattoos was firm and shaved, so that every detail of their design showed. "You can't imagine the pain it cost to make my body a living fresco," he had added as he petted their snouts.

Every day at lunch Bruce besieged his mother with collect, person-to-person telephone calls, each placed in the name of a different mass murderer. In the evenings, he wrote the governor letters on speckled oatmeal parchment, offering advice, soliciting opinions, requesting pardons for criminals he felt had languished too long. He read the letters aloud to Emmet. They were thoughtful and eloquent, nothing like Bruce's manner in private. If he had not known Bruce, Emmet might have been swayed by them. Only their frequency gave him away.

Some weeks, Bruce seemed contented with his many projects. Entire days would pass quietly. But as soon as Emmet was lulled into believing that Bruce had begun to see him as he was, not as who he wanted him to be, Bruce would be at him again, menacing him with questions.

Bruce pounced upon him like a beggar whenever he stepped into the hallway. He sat close to Emmet at every meeting, whispering in his ear. He stood next to him at the urinal, jiggling his penis in his pocket like a handful of loose pennies. He begged for Emmet's autograph, loudly, at dinner, so that now some of the patients applauded whenever Emmet tried to eat. He fashioned ashtrays, bowls, cups, vases, saucers, in arts and crafts and presented them to Emmet with crudely tied crepe-paper bows. He lay upon the bed with his legs opened suggestively, a come-hither look burned into his eyes as he whispered, "Is it sex you want? Come here."

Bruce watched him when he was asleep, so Emmet kept guard at night to protect himself, lying so stiffly and watchfully that he could hear the flutter of Bruce's lashes as he blinked from the other bed. Emmet's vigilance so tired him that he snuck naps in the afternoons when Bruce met with his doctors and was forced to go alone.

Emmet had no life anymore. When he visited his doctor, he could speak only of Bruce, Bruce, Bruce, as if he had known him all his life, as if he were responsible for all his torment. Every moment Emmet lived, even when he hid in the most obscure place, scrunched in an armchair facing the wall so that no body part was visible, he could not think except to fret, "Is he coming now? Is he near?" He felt Bruce's power like a hex, until his doctors turned the pursuit against him, demanding of Emmet, "Why does he bother you so much? Why do you care?"

When the nurses found him alone, hiding from Bruce, they admonished him, as if he were regressing. They asked him why his brother no longer visited. They asked why he shied from meals as if he meant to starve himself, when he no longer did. They asked him why he walked more nervously than ever, like a snitch, always watching his back. "What have you done to him?" they asked, sensing his guilt. Bruce was solicitous of Emmet when anyone else was near, as if he were the only person Bruce trusted, until Emmet seemed to be the miser for denying him. Even when Bruce was overheard singing in his ear, repeating verses to the songs until Emmet could recite them when he never could before, Bruce only seemed to be entertaining him, with a sort of serenade.

Emmet had grown surly and scared. "Is it the same as with the cat?" he worried when he grew faint with hatred and doubt. Around him the other patients bloomed. Even Juanita had become more reasonable. Her dresses fit her body snugly. She smoothed the glossy lipstick suns into her cheeks artfully, shading the color, so that her skin glowed pinkly: not a symptom anymore, but part of a personal style.

The other patients worshiped Bruce. His friendship was the treasure they dreamed to possess. When the nurses were busy with the final minutes of their shifts, Bruce held court in the lounge, unchaperoned, his disciples grouped at his feet.

"Everything is magic," he cried as he told them how he meditated until he could press his body through concrete walls as if it were air, only to materialize on the other side.

"Everything is magic," he cried as he told them stories of the places he visited at night while they lazily slept, as if he could fly beyond the planets, even to heaven and hell.

"Everything is magic," he cried as he promised to train them to follow him outside, like an invisible army.

Sometimes when Emmet stumbled upon the group in the middle of the night, he even found Louise rapt among the patients. If Bruce could dupe her, Emmet despaired of ever winning.

The past month he had tried to take tentative steps. He had

ceased to stutter and did not argue when his doctors praised his progress. The world outside had begun to tempt him bit by bit, not clearly enough that he had a plan, but enough to encourage a fantasy or two. He had begun to dream of painting a new apartment, spackling the cracks on every surface and sanding them smooth. He would capture every particle of dust with strips of tape. Then he would paint the walls white with multiple thick coats, rubbing in between with balls of steel wool so that no brush strokes showed. He dreamed of the gleaming, perfect walls until his hands itched. But Bruce was dragging him back, unbalancing his resolve before he had taken one step out.

"I must get away," Emmet thought in a frenzy as he felt the cinder block wall cold and hard behind him. He still reeled from the speed at which he had moved in his dream. He felt a disappointment upon awaking and tried to readjust to being himself. In the light of his dream, he had thrilled at being the horse, at the way its flanks had felt pounding heavily over the track. In the dark of their room, he could see Bruce's eyes spin before him: white-green, nearly fluorescent.

Bruce squatted in the lotus position. He took three studied breaths as if preparing to meditate. He smiled blissfully.

"What do you want from me?" Emmet asked for the hundredth time. Despite all his doubts, despite everyone who lived around him, he still believed in reason.

"I want everything," Bruce replied solemnly. "Everything." Then he reached over to touch Emmet's forehead, as if to anoint him.

"On the outside, I would kill him," Emmet thought. He would have lured him like the cat, only more heartlessly. He would not have weakened. But the ward offered no escape. Even if Bruce were forbidden to approach him, Emmet could imagine him mouthing "Psst" from across a room so that only he could see, buzzing him silently, like a sickness of the inner ear.

"I must get him," Emmet thought murderously. He tried to remember the song that had been his torment all week. Bruce sang it like a theme to trumpet Emmet's entrance into a room.

"Let's play," Emmet called, rising up on one arm excitedly, as the chorus floated through his mind. Bruce cocked his head, his eyes darting with blinks.

" 'The deeper you go, the higher you fly,' " Emmet croaked, almost a whisper. "Come on, Bruce. Help me. Sing. 'The deeper you go,' " he began again. " 'The higher you fly. The higher you fly, the deeper you go. So come on. Come on.' "

"So you *do* know it," Bruce gasped, reverently, as if in the presence of an apparition.

Emmet did not look at him in case he faltered. He remembered how it had been that time in the thunder when his mother made them sing. Emmet wanted to close Bruce in, as if they were locked in a space smaller than the car, as if his mind wrapped over Bruce's like a hood. To infect him with his fervor, Emmet freed his arms from the sheets and snapped his fingers. He began the verse again, more confidently, dropping his voice an octave, in a baritone.

" 'The deeper you go, the higher you fly,' " he sang, his voice warming to the lyrics, louder and louder, as he repeated the verse. It was the only one he knew. He jumped onto the floor and clapped his hands. " 'So come on, come on,' " he crooned gaily.

"Sshh, someone might hear," Bruce said primly.

"Who cares?" Emmet exclaimed. He danced with all the abandon he could muster, prancing in circles as he had watched Juanita do, more freely than he had ever danced in public, willing himself not to be embarrassed. He swayed to his toneless voice. He swiveled his hips. He prayed that no one would come upon them as he enticed Bruce to rise up and sing, as if a band played in their room and he was helpless before the rhythm.

"I want more, I want more," Emmet laughed, as if his song

were a drug. He turned eagerly to Bruce, "Do you have the record?"

"Yes," Bruce said warily.

"Well, get it. It's nothing without the music. You wanted to know. Well, tonight's the night."

Bruce went to the bed and slipped the album from between the box spring and the mattress. He propped it before his chest like a shield.

"Don't let up, don't let up," Emmet told himself as he led Bruce to the music room. He knew a record player was stored in its closet. On holidays, the nurses made the patients sing along to carols, like children around a campfire.

Emmet felt his determination flag, but he knew that if he did not cripple Bruce, he could never lure him again. He placed the stereo on a high chair in the middle of the rug. It was similar to one he had owned as a child that opened like a box with one tinny speaker screwed into its top.

"Side four has a secret code only a few can understand," Emmet said, conspiratorially.

"I know, I know. You have to play it backwards. I learned that from reading about Charles Manson."

"So what are you waiting for?" Emmet asked. Bruce regarded him shyly, but placed a thumb tentatively on the record. He moved it squeakily in the wrong direction.

"You have to do better than that," Emmet said. "Get into it. Turn it as fast as if it were propelled by the motor."

"Can't we talk about it first? I mean, there's so many things I want to know. I need the overview."

"Everything is there," Emmet said, indicating the record sitting motionlessly on the phonograph.

Bruce arched his arm gracefully over the record, as a ballet dancer might bend. Then he began to trot around the pedestal as he gathered his speed, his thumb never veering from the slick green paper label. The needle grated and squealed. He got nothing that sounded like a word, only syllables and grunts.

"Baa aaah aaah," the record croaked.

"Faster, faster," Emmet ordered, pushing him to string the sounds together. He shouted encouragement as Bruce circled the high chair. His sneakers slipped on the carpet. His belt buckle jangled loosely, loud as chains. He tried to clutch his waist with his free hand, but he surrendered as his balance faltered. His pants dropped lower and lower, bunching at his knees before creeping thickly down to his ankles. Bruce's favorite pair of underwear, with beetles slumbering on tiny straw mats, appeared from under his jeans. They slid low enough that Emmet saw the crack between Bruce's cheeks, rosy as a moustached grin.

"Baa aah aah roi baa aah aah," the record sang.

"Help me . . . help," Bruce cried, but his panic jammed the words back into his throat.

"Faster, faster," Emmet shouted, pushing him relentlessly. "What am I doing?" he panicked. "Do I have to destroy him to be free?" He left it to chance. If a nurse entered the room, he would cease and Bruce would win. If no one came, he would press on, because otherwise he would never be rid of him.

No one came. It was the hour before dinner when the patients were left to mingle independently while the nurses washed the helpless. Bruce sweated and panted, as if he were racing for miles along a track. Although his body stumbled and fell, he was so desperate to know the secrets buried in the plastic disc that his thumb never slipped as he tried to run fast enough to turn all that gibberish into a word.

"Can't you hear it?" Emmet asked, astonished.

"It doesn't make sense," Bruce cried. His face dripped with tears and sweat. "I can't run fast enough. I cannot make it work."

Emmet had to struggle to understand him. His words were broken in the middle by gasps.

"Bahaa roi bahaa baah baah dwa," the record crooned, almost lovely and deep, like an opera singer, maybe dying.

Emmet trained his eyes on the carpet. He made his voice solemn with disappointment. A breeze from Bruce's racing body ruffled his hair.

"Can't you hear it?" he repeated, as if it were the easiest thing in the world. "Listen: everything is there. Listen: everything is magic."

The room pounded with pants.

"Baaha roi baa ha roi baah baah baah rah," the record sang, over and over, like a mantra, or a moan, or maybe a hymn of peace.

CHAPTER
TWO

Screams blew from somewhere out in the ward, howling through the hallways towards Emmet's room, unstoppably, as if swept across an open field. Screams like those of someone being murdered. Then a thunder of feet.

"Someone is dying," Emmet thought as he rose from his desk.

He peeked around the corner of the door. The charged air buffeted his face. He grabbed the molding to steady his balance. "What is it?" he wondered as the pitch climbed higher and higher, wilder than he had ever heard before, wilder even than the cries of patients dragged to the isolation room. The building shook with the rage until the walls crackled with static.

Along the hallway, patients huddled within their door frames as if to protect themselves from falling debris. Two beefy orderlies patrolled outside with damp towels draped over their arms, murmuring soothingly to calm the anxious faces. They appeared friendly, but they carried their towels pointedly, as if the cloth concealed knives.

"Aaaaaah . . ."

The screams rolled over them, like thunder.

"Aaaaaaah . . ."

Emmet tried to identify its source, but it had no character, only fear. There was no modulation or timbre, as with a voice. In his months in the ward, he had learned that all screams sounded anonymous, high or low, one for each sex. This one was a man's.

"Aaaaaaaah . . ."

Emmet nipped into his room and grabbed a sheaf of papers from the bureau. He tucked the roll under his arm. If the orderlies detained him, he would claim the papers were his journal. The doctors required the patients to keep a record of their thoughts covering the time they were not in therapy. Some detailed every minute of their day; some drew pictures on the pages, misshapen, like figures traced in the dark; some wrote sonnets in complicated rhyme; some, like Emmet, did nothing. He was sick of keeping records.

Emmet walked purposefully towards the nursing station. As he passed, the patients twitched guiltily in their doorways, as people do in the city when they hear a victim cry but do not move to help. He waved the papers importantly at the orderlies. They did not attempt to detain him. The journals were sacred to the doctors, almost like religious texts.

"Aaaaaaaaah . . ."

Up close, the scream was ungodly. A cluster of patients sat transfixed on the couch. One strained to get a better look. One covered his ears with his hands. One pulsed with the energy, her knees quaking, quicker and quicker, as if a rhythm possessed her, inaudible to the ear. Then she began to scream in a lower register, complementing the anguished cries, almost like a background melody.

Another patient stood at a distance from the couch, burning with excitement. He was tall and muscled, with long, fluffy slippers. His hair was shaved on the side so that only the barest bristle poked from his scalp, like a pig's skin. He wore a purple bandanna, loosely tied, around his neck. His glasses swung against his chest, hooked to a sparkling blue chain. He snapped his fingers and tapped his heel soundlessly on the linoleum. "Get smart, get scared, get lost," he intoned, over and over. His chain shimmered with blue lights.

Five nurses ringed the pool table. Two bent towards the carpet, struggling with a body. Emmet saw a pair of dirty white sneakers flailing in the air, each one tipped with strawberry socks. He saw an ill-fitting pair of blue jeans, ragged with holes along the seams. As the legs thrashed, loosening the pants, he saw the flash of fuchsia-colored underwear spotted with blue otters.

"Bruce," Emmet thought, stiff with guilt. He had not seen him all day. Since the afternoon in the music room, Bruce had kept his distance. Emmet had been so relieved to be rid of him that he even pretended not to hear when Bruce whispered "Good night" from the opposite bed. But as the screams cut through him, he could not help thinking, "Have I done this to him? Could it be a delayed reaction?"

Emmet had struck blindly to save himself. Frequently in the past he had let himself be rendered nearly substanceless by the person he loved, but never before had he been the one to ruin. As Bruce writhed on the floor inhumanly, his mind transfigured to a scream, Emmet was aghast at his power to change.

"You must relax and come with us," a nurse cooed soothingly. Bruce kicked upward, catching her in the face. Emmet heard her nose crack like a nut, then saw a thick stream of blood drool from her nostril.

"Get smart, get scared," the muscled patient shouted.

"Get the restraints," a doctor called softly, almost embarrassed, as if he believed that by whispering the other patients might not notice the leather straps with shiny buckles clanking in the orderlies' arms.

"Aaaaaaaaaah . . ."

The screams were no longer separate but one long, furious breath. Bruce seemed to gain new energy as his shrieks increased.

He thrashed and kicked at everything that moved. Emmet heard the thud of soft shoes striking muscle and bone. A nurse rushed towards the circle with reams of white sheets clutched to her breast.

He heard the slap of cloth and the sound of flesh pummeled and trussed. He heard Bruce howl like an animal caught in a trap in the middle of a wintry forest, gnashing as it tried to eat its leg free. The nurse passed one sheet after another as the orderlies wrapped Bruce roughly into them, his body disappearing into fold after fold of damp cloth, as if they layered a form with papier-mâché. First his legs, then his torso, then above his neck, almost to his mouth, so that he strained his head as if trying to stay afloat above water.

"Aaaaaaaaaaaaaah . . ."

He would not let up, even as they spread one last sheet on the ground and rolled his sacked body onto it, enveloping every part.

"Sweet dreams, little white asshole," an orderly snarled as he tied a swatch of cloth over Bruce's head and tucked it neatly under his chin.

Months ago, Emmet had fantasized that this very event would come to be. Now that it had, he reeled with regret, but he did not move to offer support. As he stood there wishing only to be safe in his room, he felt as he imagined a person did watching a neighbor carted away by soldiers in the dead of night. If he approached Bruce, the staff might turn their energy against him. Emmet hoped he would act less cowardly if he saw someone he loved being manhandled so unceremoniously. He hoped he would fling his body upon his friend however fruitlessly, to prove his loyalty.

"Aaaaaaaaaaah . . ."

Bruce screamed louder than ever, a sound that pierced Emmet's heart and jolted his nerve endings so that he shuddered from the force.

Emmet inched towards the entrance. He noticed a woman in a cream-colored business suit by the door. Her hands gripped the handles of a black metallic purse built like a lunch box. She studied every face in the room until her eyes met Emmet's.

He moved closer until he could see the verdigris crust caked to the post of her copper earrings. She nodded at him distractedly. "Are you his friend?" she asked. "He mentioned he was friends with someone named John. Are you John?"

"I'm Emmet. John was discharged. I'm his roommate now."

"They're forcing him to leave. His insurance ran out. There's nothing else to do. I can't leave him alone and his wife won't have him. She's afraid for the baby. The state hospital is the only place." She said it defensively, as if Emmet might accuse her of neglect.

The woman gnawed the skin around her cuticles. Her fingertips were raw and cracked, but her nails were artfully manicured, stretching to a sharp, scarlet tip. She bounced from one well-soled foot to another as she talked. Her eyes were round and hollow like her son's, but disguised with blue shadows and soft, blond lashes, bleached and thick, like hairs on an expensive brush.

"I hear the grounds are nice there," Emmet lied. "I believe their gardeners have won awards." He had seen photographs in magazines of its buildings yellowed with disrepute. Its sadistic staff and zombied patients were legends in the ward. Patients who had never been there spoke of the state hospital with fearful reverence, as they would the last circle of hell. The threat of it was the only leverage their families held to keep them in check. Emmet had seen many patients mysteriously improve when the state hospital loomed closer and closer, like a death sentence.

The orderlies snapped the leather tethers over the sheets. The metal buckles clicked shut.

"I don't know," the woman said worriedly. "I can't keep him here unless I sell my house. People expect mothers to be willing

to do anything, but I can't. Imagine twenty years of this already."
She hooked Emmet's wrist with two fingers. "How long have you
lived with him? A few months? Imagine twenty years." She spoke
with amazement, like someone would at a funeral after everything
was over.

"Two months," Emmet said blandly as the orderlies carried
Bruce up to them. The sheets capping Bruce's head cut straight
across his eyes, cloaking him like a woman in purdah. The cloth
bunched so tightly against his mouth that it locked his jaw in
place, but he continued to struggle. The "aaaah" sounded disembodied, pinched and flat, as if a ventriloquist were throwing a
scream.

Emmet remembered the first moment he had met Bruce in
Emily and Daphne's room. In the bonded form, he tried to see
Bruce as he had been, flapping his arms like an airplane, tossing
the coin behind his head, squeezing Emmet's throat with his hands.
How had they gotten from there to here?

Bruce's mother blinked disbelievingly at her son. She seemed
dazed in a way Emmet imagined parents looked when they were
made to identify a corpse, trying to find their child in the lifeless
thing. "He was strange even as a baby," she said, indicating the
wet, white bundle. "But this . . . I mean, I'm not a stupid woman,
but how could I have known it would come to this?"

Emmet wanted to assure her that it would have been impossible, that often he felt swept away by life, the way one can be
swept along by the power of a mob, and that in those instances,
nothing could redeem him. But the woman looked beyond him
in a private grief that he could not pierce. "You couldn't have,"
was all he mumbled. He touched her arm.

"Maybe. Who knows? I'm not a monster, you know," she
added sadly. "Everyone thinks I must be to have a son like him,
but I've got three normal children."

Emmet heard the buzzer as the orderlies maneuvered Bruce

through the door. In the tiled corridor, Bruce's cries echoed, tone-less as footsteps.

"Twenty years," his mother muttered, fearfully, as if she re-alized that when she left the ward a new life was only beginning, one more horrible than the first.

"Twenty years," Emmet thought as he tried to imagine Bruce as a baby, swaddled in soft blankets instead of sheets, asleep in his mother's arms. When spoken, "twenty years" seemed to mark a specific block of time within which one could chart one's course, like on a sea journey. But lived, it passed in fits and starts: vaguely, ungovernably. Twenty years before, he had been practicing drills in the bomb shelter. Twenty years from now he could not imagine where he would be. He saw the way he was then and all he saw was time spreading out before him, a whole life's worth, leaving him without a clue as to how he might sustain it. "Day by day by day," his doctors told him, but twenty years was 7,300 days, 175,200 hours, 10,512,000 minutes, and still he would only be in midlife, if the law of averages prevailed.

His mother had been twenty when she married his father. Emmet had been twenty when she died. When his mother was twenty, she must have believed she had escaped. She must have expected she would live long into her grandchildren's lives. When Emmet was twenty, he had believed time would carry him along, the way a breeze carries perfume or the scent of flowers on its air. But now it rushed upon him, wild as white water, sweeping his purpose away.

To rein it in, he counted every breath, timed to the ticks of his watch. Twenty years meant 630,720,000 times, one by one by one: year after year, week after week, day after day. And around him he felt a danger everywhere, one for every second he was alive.

He had tried to keep his guard, but his vigilance had poisoned him. He had wanted his own life to be a haven. He had wanted to protect himself from the calamity, disillusionment, and fear he felt as the ground beneath him and so learn to maneuver through the threat of the world outside. He had learned that nothing he could think of doing or that could happen to him was without a name. At first he had been exhilarated to find that a word for who he was existed somewhere in a book. He had relaxed knowing that his behavior, even his dreams, were mysteriously tied to a language connecting him to everyone who had ever lived. The world became larger than he had ever imagined, but then it began to crowd him in. It was not possible to feel protected, no matter what he knew: not by study nor by stealth nor by preparedness, nor even by love. What he could not reconcile was that in trying to live happily, he found himself in constant flight from life itself.

Every day he read of people who survived impossible odds: poverty, disease, inconceivable heartbreak, catastrophes that made him ashamed of the smaller troubles afflicting him. He knew he had been lucky. His family was rich. He was white. He was handsome. He was a man. He had wanted for nothing, but nothing had come upon him as a dead energy, seeking only to extinguish what lived inside of him, like a person rushing blindly towards water, his clothes aflame. He longed to beat it back, to lose himself in the passage of day after day, the way the world did, as if there would never be an end.

He thought of how his mother had lived in her isolated houses, the cliffs and mountains and deserted beaches that had been her home. In each place she had planted her stakes and hoped her life might change. It never had, but for years she had moved, hopefully, as if the next house or city or state would become her refuge, until one night she found herself facing out the window of a hotel with nothing holding her back but a millimeter of glass: the world outside like a mirage, beckoning, such as a person might see who has wandered too long in the desert, praying for rain.

What she did, Emmet could never do. He was too frightened of what might be waiting, after. The world, at least, he knew. But what was left to him? To keep on going until he could not stand it anymore. But what would happen after that? And next? And then?

CHAPTER THREE

"It's late," Louise said, curling her legs against her seat cushion. Emmet did not stir himself to speak. He hung his head off the arm of his chair so Louise yawned at him, upside down. His body felt so weak and spongy that he fantasized he had overdosed on drugs. As the light in the recreation room grew darker and darker, he pretended that unconsciousness, not night, slowly blackened his eyes.

The windows were shut. It was winter now. Without the horns, shouts, and sirens to ground its place in the city outside, the hospital seemed built on a soundless tundra. It was so quiet in the ward that Emmet believed the globe must share its stillness. If the windows had not been locked, he might have felt the chill of an early-November wind. He remembered how he had loved the first blasts of serious winter, before the months slumped damp and gray, and how the frost seemed to purge the air of every poison.

The ward, too, seemed purged in Bruce's wake. People spoke in hushed voices, as after a death. They drifted from hour to hour, disconnected, by either shock or fear or wariness that they would be threatened with expulsion next. All around him, Emmet saw patients grow compliant, like children seeking to seduce angry parents. When they had come to the ward, many believed they had found a safe place and had let themselves regress in that comfort. But Bruce had taught them something else: that there was no end to their falling. Those who had believed they knew the bottom had found it layered with crust, like dust on a moon's surface or warm ice on a pond.

Emmet had known the state hospital existed, but Bruce was the first to be forced there. He had heard rumors of other patients being locked forever in its cells, but he had listened in the way people are able to hear of death, even see others around them dying, and still believe themselves to be exempt. Suddenly Emmet felt his body grow heavier, as if even with his caution and care, he had trudged too clumsily.

Louise's reflection bobbed in the window. Mirrored beyond her, a white-hatted nurse carried a tray piled high with syringes and strips of muffy gauze. "Who for?" he wondered, imagining a patient strapped to a bed and doped against his will. In the past Emmet would not have noticed her. The staff had never seemed relevant; he had not guessed their power. Now the doctors strutted through their rounds, cocky with secrets.

Until he came to the ward, it had been Emmet's habit to fall in love with his doctors. He had searched directories for their addresses and stalked their apartments after dark, reading the shadows flickering past windows, waiting to catch them entering or leaving. He had rung their telephones in the middle of the night to hear if a woman or a man answered, to discover clues as to what their lives were like.

Once he had followed his doctor to the grocery store and watched as he expertly tapped melons with his knuckles, as he thumbed the soft underside of the tomatoes, as he stroked the stiffness of the carrots and beans. Emmet had been mesmerized by the sureness with which he had handled the vegetables, deft as a surgeon. Emmet had followed him home. Hours later, the doctor walked to the movies with a man. Emmet chose a seat in the row behind, leaning forward so closely to listen that the doctor shook off his breath like the tickle of a roach's foot. When they left the theater, the doctor's pace quickened to a trot, but if he had noticed Emmet lurking behind, he gave no acknowledgement. That night when Emmet called the doctor's number, no one answered, not even at dawn.

Emmet had never confessed to his doctors that he shadowed them like a detective. He had believed he loved them and did not want to be convinced otherwise. He had assumed he could behave any way he wanted. He had believed their hours together offered an unlimited freedom not permitted on the street. He had not foreseen that here, barricaded in their offices, the staff plotted against the patients, orchestrating their futures, and leaving them unequipped to fight back, even with all the desire and lawlessness they could summon.

"Hey, come see," Louise said. She reached blindly behind for Emmet's hand. They saw couples stroll across the grass in the quadrangle below, with books stacked on their arms, chatting easily. Emmet followed a girl as she cut a path from the library to the dormitory, whipping her braid behind her with every step. They saw clouds above her, even in the dark, whitening the sky.

"Looks like a storm, maybe a blizzard," Louise said.

"Hmm," Emmet murmured. He wanted to respond more warmly, but in his mind he replayed every word Dr. Franklin had uttered since his first day on the ward. He searched for a hint or sign of the plans the doctor withheld when he coaxed Emmet to talk about his life. Suddenly, when he was not in session, Emmet worried like someone left unattended by his captors, the door unlocked, uncertain if he had been abandoned to freedom or if they toyed with him, laying a trap at the hearth of his room.

"I don't know snow," Louise said. "In Florida you hardly ever get frost." She spoke wistfully, pressing her face so closely against the pane that her cheeks pinkened from the pressure, as they would in a cold wind. She bunched her collar higher, almost to her ears.

Emily hailed them from the corner by the nursing station. Her voice rolled through the quiet, echo upon echo. She kissed Emmet's cheek and nodded to Louise. The women stood together shyly, the wool of their blue sweaters mingling hairily, so that they seemed attached at the arm. Emmet felt a small satisfaction knowing that through him they had made their peace the past weeks. Emily's cigarette slipped in her fingers. She shifted it to her other hand, absently, so that its tip singed Louise's sweater. The wool hissed.

"Weird around here, huh?" she said, brushing away the smoldering hairs. Her palm was speckled with black cinders.

Emmet and Louise sighed in unison. Emily smiled expectantly, but neither spoke. She coughed as she joined them at the window, their three heads pinched into the same two feet of glass. Emmet wanted to hear the women speak excitedly of the day's events, as was their habit, of the squabbles and shifting alliances that characterized their life on the ward. The first night in Emily's room, he had hoped that life might continue indefinitely, as he often had in the past when he stepped into a rhythm that enveloped him so completely he could never imagine his contentment ending, no matter how many times it had before.

But in the awkwardness of the women's smiles, he saw a disaffection pass between them, like a chill, as if they were meeting for the first time. He felt the spell of the last months break around him as they stood there, confounding each at precisely the same moment.

To dispel it, Emmet filled his mind with images of his friends talking late into the night, of shared dinners, of glances exchanged over the heads of doctors that had linked them in ways he had dreamed of possessing all his life. He tensed his body so that the images grew stronger, but Louise and Emily turned away from him, towards the window.

They watched a car race around a corner several blocks away, its lights beaming crazily in the dark. It skidded onto the curb, tilting a mailbox, smashing a newspaper stand, sending a garbage can sailing over its hood. Emmet imagined the squealing breaks, the clang of metal bouncing on the pavement, the sound of the newspapers skirting over the tar like tumbleweeds. But from where he stood, the violence passed noiselessly, like a film with no sound track.

"I love to drive fast," Louise said. "Really race along the highway."

"Even I'd like to have a car again," Emmet said. "I used to pay cabbies just to cruise on the outer drive. I became so addicted I even budgeted for it. You could see things you never saw walking, almost like from an airplane, but you didn't have to leave the ground."

"No, no—I mean to really let loose," Louise snapped. "I like to go so fast that everything out the window melts to a blur. I like to see the headlights behind me grow pinched as match heads. I like . . . ah, forget it." The ridges of her knuckles blanched from red to white.

Emily cocked an eyebrow as she perched on the arm of Emmet's chair. They had grown accustomed to waiting until Louise's small furies broke like fevers. At the window, they sat like people transfixed on a long car journey, silently driving mile after mile.

"Funny how all these days go by and we forget we haven't seen the sun," Emily said finally. "But I don't mind. I like artificial air or whatever it is they've got here. With lots of smoke," she laughed, blowing rings that fluttered above them like webs.

"I used to bake in the sun," Louise said, forgiving them. She tilted her face upward towards the lights. "I couldn't get enough. I don't even tan. I burn up, but I didn't care. I used to love the way the wind blew in from the sea when it was hot and how my skin would get all fired by the end of the day. I could do that forever."

"Who remembers?" Emily asked. "Funny, I get more patient the longer I stay. I'm not even sure if I still believe a miracle might happen if I wait around long enough. I'm not even sure that's what I want. Weird that it could soon be ten years from now, time just floating along, and before we know it, we might have waited forever."

"You may have to," Louise said. "This place is nowhere."

"Maybe," Emily said petulantly. "But you forget. I pay cash. I asked to be here."

"Well, I didn't," Louise said. "And now I've wasted all this time. For what? I never wanted to be protected. I gotta go, do you understand? I want to stay out all night. I want to get mail in a mailbox with my own little key and read the letters in bed. I want to cook dinner. I want to forget about myself and just have a day, you know what I mean? A regular boring day where I go to the store, take my clothes to the cleaners, maybe watch a little TV, nothing special. Eat cake. Whatever it is these people do. I wanna kiss somebody good-bye in the morning. I wanna job, you know; I want to go to work and have somebody say, 'You look tired, Louise' or 'Nice dress, Louise,' and if I like 'em, I'll invite them to lunch and if I don't, I'll walk right on by. But not this— not this. I mean, a vacation's one thing, but this . . ." She sneered at Emmet and Emily with as much distaste as she did the orange Naugahyde sofas and the plaid plastic tablecloths in the lounge. "Shit. If I'm gonna be locked up, I'd rather kill the President or something and rot in a regular jail. I wanna be someplace real again. Come on, guys, don't you ever think about it, especially now? We could all go, like on a prison break or something?"

Emmet and Emily edged towards each other. They exchanged a look that people get when they know they're about to be asked for money.

"Outside?" Emily said. "No, not me. I don't want to go outside anymore."

"How about you?" Louise asked, turning to Emmet.

In his plans, he had never imagined further than seeing his body step outside and into a new apartment with hardly a breath in between. It was trouble enough to imagine pushing his legs through the brass revolving door at the entrance to the hospital. He could not conceive how it would be if someone followed a few paces behind.

When Emmet lived with his grandmother, once she took him down to the harbor in San Francisco, where they could look upon Alcatraz rising from the island a mile offshore. From where they stood, he could separate the bars on every window, so close did they seem. Late that afternoon they rode the ferry across, and as evening fell, the lights of the city seemed almost to illuminate the stone walls of the prison. Emmet imagined the prisoners on their cots, the city wafting into their cells, tormenting them with another life so near at hand, yet unreachably far. He used to think how it must have been for them to dream of escape and know that when they cut the bars they were nowhere still until they had swum for hours over the dark, shark-ridden waves. Only a few attempted; the rest let the routine close upon them, like a life.

On the tour of the prison, the guide had told them how some prisoners grew so accustomed to living behind bars that they panicked when they were discharged. At the gate, a strangeness undid them. So desperate were they to return, they committed any small crime—smashing a window, stealing a purse, kicking a passerby— to send themselves back inside. The guide had shared this information as if to describe the criminals' intractability, but even then, Emmet understood their dread. When he imagined leaving, he thought only of the ways he had forgotten how to live. In his other life, the simplest details had stumped him. He could not imagine how he might shop, work, do his banking, unconsciously, as others did. He did not know how to free himself from what he had become.

Emmet had not told Emily or Louise, but the past week he had tested the outdoors. He had requested passes to the cafeteria in the basement. He had sipped coffee in public. He had wandered along the corridors and peered into offices. He had stood at the revolving door and watched people come and go. But he had not yet ventured even to the stone steps of the path.

"I would like to read a paper and watch the news every day," he said finally, hedging Louise's question. He ran his fingers through the curls that sprouted newly from his head. "And I would like to get my hair cut," he added, dreaming of how it had been to shave his fingers along the coarse bristle of his scalp.

"There you go," Louise said.

"I would like to take a scented bath filled with bubbles in a deep marble tub and have nobody sitting on the rim to make sure I don't drown myself," Emily said.

"See," Louise said, appeased.

"But I don't want it enough to leave."

"Jesus," Louise said. "What's with you guys? What's the worst that can happen? You leave. You return. You're back where you started."

"Not exactly," Emmet said. In his months in the ward, he had seen people come and go and come again, each time more quickly and easily than the time before. If he left too soon, he could see returning become part of him, like a second nature.

"If you hate it, you miss a week, tops," Louise said.

"I already know I hate it," Emily said.

"But you could go," Emmet said, unsurely.

"Not alone, I can't. You can get passes, remember? You can get the door opened. You can get me out."

"Well, on that note, I'm off to bed," Emily said, tapping her cigarette pack against her palm. She slipped her matchbook neatly into the cellophane wrapper. "Will I see you in the morning or are you taking the night flight?"

"In the morning," Emmet said, yawning.

"You never know," Louise smiled.

Emily switched off the light in the lounge behind her as she left. Across the room, the nursing station glowed orange, like a fireball at the end of a tunnel.

"Can't see you anymore," Louise said.

"Me neither."

Emmet heard her pick at the meshed wire screen with her nails. "Please, I need air," she said. "I want to feel it. I want to go out on my own two legs. I want it to be over one way or another. You with me? I don't have anybody else I can ask."

"But we're too crazy to help each other," Emmet said, his panic rising. "It's like two junkies sharing a needle. We need someone else as a buffer. It can't just be us."

"There is no one else anymore," Louise said. "Think about it."

Emmet listed the people he still knew. His brother was out of reach. He was done with doctors. Bruce, Winston, and Daphne were gone. Even Margaret had been discharged to her husband's care. Their world grew smaller and smaller. The ward was empty of any purpose except to drag out his days, longer and longer.

Louise moved close behind him, fluffing the hair at the nape of his neck. She massaged his back with her fingertips, thumbing the muscles bolted with tension, reading the bumps over his skin like braille.

"In the dark I'm just the same as you," she said, propping her chin on his shoulder. Her perfume was so heavy that the scent became part of him. When he breathed, it was impossible to tell where she ended and the air began.

He leaned into her. He tried to imagine the life waiting for them on the outside. What he saw were two bodies tripping through fog and the smoke of burning buildings: everywhere around them the charred foundations of a city. He pictured them as the last two people on earth, who neither by choice nor by planning had become each other's only chance, drawn together by a hopelessness they could not name, and so they lied and called it love.

"So, you with me?" she whispered. "Say yes."

Emmet saw the lights on the highway below swing in the breeze like party lanterns on a cruise ship. "I will try," he said.

"In the morning," Louise said, moving away. "I don't want to give you time to think about it. You'll come up with all sorts of excuses to stay. If we're gonna do it, we've just gotta fly. There's nothing to prepare for. If you wait, they'll smell the guilt. You'll end up confessing to your doctor. Anybody can read you. They'll know something's up."

"But we will have no provisions," Emmet said, patting the empty pockets of his jeans.

"I've already packed my purse. I've got a few dollars. I know a fast route to the bus station. What else do we need?"

In his room, Emmet inventoried his possessions, piece by piece. He did not sleep. At first light, he dressed in multiple layers of clothes. He pulled on triple underwear, triple socks. He buttoned three shirts under a sweater. He was so thin, the layers of his clothes made him appear to be a person of normal weight. No one would notice him. He stole the liner from the trash can in his room and padded it around his waist. He could pack his surplus clothes in the bag once they got outside.

He went to his closet and unpinned the money he had hidden in his jeans. He spread the bills like playing cards on the sheet. He could barely form seven perfect rows. "Twenty, forty, sixty, eighty," Emmet counted as his eyes raced across the dollars. He turned away before he finished, but already he knew there was not enough money left to begin a life. "This is a mistake," his alarms sounded in his head. He wanted to ask Louise to postpone their escape, but he knew he was no match for her. She was determined to leave.

He felt his clothes thick about him. He stuck a bar of soap in his back pocket like a wallet stuffed with bills. He folded the real money between his sock and his shoe. It lumped under his foot, rough as a callus. He dreaded leaving so lightly. He would own nothing but the things packed about his body. Every time he changed places, he seemed to go with fewer and fewer possessions. Now there was almost nothing. He pressed the photograph of the dog Jonathan had left him under his shirt. It was slick and cold against his skin. He wanted to sneak into Jonathan's apartment to kidnap her, but unless he pretended he was blind she would never be allowed on the bus. The dog could wait, until he sent for her, like a bride.

He waited until he heard the shifts change. He scattered papers messily on his desk and threw his favorite pair of jeans carelessly over the bed. He placed his toothbrush on the chair by the door with a slathering of clear blue paste swirled on its bristles. He dropped a small towel next to it. He spilled his prescriptions among his socks inside the top drawer. He left the lights on.

As he walked to the nursing station, he saw Louise reading a magazine in an easy chair parked by the door. She wore a red, plasticine car coat so stiff that its epaulets stuck from her shoulders like splints. Her hair was teased wildly over her head, jutting in long, rigid tufts. Her face was a palette of bright colors: a citrus yellow shadow for her eyes, a deep rose for her cheeks, a pure orange for her lips. He saw the shiny toes of black patent-leather pumps and a sheer glimpse of sparkled nylons under her wool pants. Her purse bulged at her feet.

Emmet calmed himself by concentrating on the pale skin of the charge nurse and the starched creases of her uniform. "I'm going to the cafeteria for coffee," he announced.

"Okay," she said.

He lifted the clipboard from the hook by the wall and signed his name. He noted the correct time. It was 7:03 A.M. "I'll be back in the blink of an eye."

She nodded, checking names off a roster of patients.

"Only a quickie," he said.

"Have fun."

"Can I bring you something back? A nice hot tea?"

"Nothing, no."

Emmet patted his chest. "Cold this morning. I needed an extra shirt."

"Bundle up," she said, still looking down.

Emmet saw an orderly pushing a large metal cart stacked with cartons of milk and thermoses of coffee. He saw a nurse kneeling before an elderly patient, pushing a red pill between her lips. She dangled a paper cup in her free hand, like a bribe.

"Coffee smells good," he called to the orderly.

"Fine morning," he called to the nurse.

"Pretty robe," he called to the patient. The pill stuck out from her lips like a tongue.

He heard Louise mutter "Jesus" as he passed her chair on the way to the door. He did not acknowledge her. He centered his finger over the round white button and pressed. He waited for a hand to snatch him from behind, but in an instant he heard the buzzer as the door swung free. He was stunned by a rush of heat and a dazzle of lights. He heard Louise fling her magazine to the floor as she rushed to his side.

"Let's go," she hissed as she stepped into the hallway. It was empty except for a janitor mopping the floor. Louise ripped the plastic identification bracelet off her arm with her teeth. She tossed it into the janitor's cart as she raced past, shouting, "Run, Emmet, run."

Emmet paused, like a bird gathering its wings before flight.

He tied his laces into knots until his shoes bit his flesh. He counted to three. He saw the long stretch of green corridor, the glistening tile walls, the stairwell lit with a red exit sign. He saw the janitor study him, mop in hand.

"Am I going to do this?" he wondered as he watched Louise turn the first corner. He considered returning to his room, but her departing pulled him forward like a magnet.

"Wings, wings," Emmet thought as he sprinted after her. He kept his head low. His sneakers made no sound on the floor as he ran, but Louise's high heels clattered so loudly that he followed without having to look up, hearing her voice sailing ahead, "Run, Emmet, run," as if she needed to feel the staff chased upon their heels, desperate to bring them back.

CHAPTER FOUR

They raced down the stairs, one landing per leap. At the ground, Emmet stopped dead at the fire-exit door blocked with an Emergency Only sign. He hesitated before it, imagining a siren echoing throughout the building if he touched the wood.

"Fuck it," Louise said, pushing through.

No bell rang. They slipped into the bustle of the main hospital corridor, among the doctors and nurses, among the patients wheeled on beds, among the messengers carrying arrangements of flowers and helium balloons. Louise held Emmet's hand, swinging it easily between their bodies, as with any couple on a date. She chattered easily as they passed the gift shop, stopping to admire the cards and tin toys displayed in the window and the stuffed animals swinging on plastic-branched trees by the cash register. She smiled at the guard posted by the front desk as they made their way towards the revolving door. At the threshold, she tightened her grip so that she dragged Emmet by his wrist.

"Almost there," she whispered soothingly. "Almost there."

She motioned him into the first compartment. He moved within as if walled inside a glass coffin, but Louise forced him forward with her hands. Emmet swung with the door and stumbled free out onto the flagstone slabs.

She followed quickly behind, tapping her heels, laughing gaily as she sucked the air. "We're out, we're out, we're out," she sang. Then she turned towards the sun. She blinked rapidly, like a lizard chased from its shade. "Oh," she said, looking around. "Oh." She swallowed hard. "Kinda makes you dizzy, doesn't it?"

Never in his life had Emmet been outside with no place to return to. He had always had a home. Even in foreign countries or in unfamiliar towns he had rented a hotel room the moment he arrived. As he unpacked, he folded his clothes in drawers exactly as he did in his apartment and set his photographs on the windowsill. He hid his suitcases from view. When he was out mastering the streets, the image of his possessions trailed after him, keeping him secure, like a leash. With Louise, he was free to travel anywhere in the world, rootlessly; they were free as skydivers leaping blindly from a plane.

"We must have a destination," Emmet thought as he saw the streets stretching for blocks to the highway and the river beyond. He felt the hospital's shadow upon his back, palpable as a whisper, summoning him to return. He imagined his clothing hanging in the closet, his postcard pinned to the wall, his shoes neatly set in rows on the floor. No guards, not even a nurse, patrolled the area in search of them. Except for the janitor, no one had noticed them leave. Their exit had been so effortless, he felt it had been out of their control. He had expected to force his way through locked doors and bars, hiding for hours in stairwells or under desks in empty offices until the coast had cleared. Instead they had slipped out, like genies disappearing through clouds of colored smoke.

On the street, dust flew through the air like bullets. People rushed by on errands; trucks braked for deliveries: newspapers, cases of boxed food, medical supplies piled up on the sidewalk in front of the hospital. Boys whizzed past on bicycles; men, sometimes children, begged for change. The din rose higher and higher, but never so high as the pitch of Louise's voice. Outside, it seemed amplified in a way Emmet had never noticed in the ward, as if the hospital ceiling had muted it like soundproofing. Now it pierced through the roofless city like a shout.

"Where are we going?" she screeched. "Where next?" She did not loosen her grip on Emmet's hand.

"Left or right?" Emmet thought, trying to feel the old rhythm of the streets form under his feet. Instinctively he led her west towards his former apartment, but he stopped dead at the corner. There was nothing for them there. "We must leave the area," he ordered quietly, hoping to lower her volume by his example.

"What?" she shouted. "Where?"

Emmet felt like a guide. She tottered after him on her laddered shoes, her purse cracking heavily with the bottles and treasures zippered inside. She stopped at a sidewalk stand and bought a frankfurter slathered with mustard. Her hands oozed yellow. She licked at her fingers, messing her face, so that her skin grew jaundiced under the pink haze of her rouge.

Emmet moved away, distracted by the newspaper headlines visible through the plastic window of the stand. He itched to stick money in the slot and feel again the crisp ears of the metropolitan section, even feel the print numb his fingertips with smudges of black ink; but he worried they would squander their resources too early. The news could wait until they were settled.

As they walked past buildings worn with disrepute, past dumpsters piled high with trash, past fire hydrants leaking water into gutters, Emmet calmed himself by reciting, "702-A . . . 357-C, . . . 509-4," warming as the codes returned to him like speech. He had not forgotten.

In the subway, they sat on a deserted row of orange seats. As the car paused at each station, commuters poured through the doors, filling every bench except the spaces to the side of Emmet and Louise. Emmet scrunched his arms to his side and crossed his ankles tightly on the floor so that he filled only a portion of his own seat. But no matter how small he shrunk his body, no strangers sat near. They stayed on their feet, grasping metal straps that rocked and swayed with the motion of the car. Their bodies pushed close, then backed away, back and forth, back and forth, until Emmet could not see through their legs. He felt a mark upon him, as when he had avoided someone sleeping spread out along a row, their skin popping with lice.

"I'm hungry," Louise announced to anyone. "Got any food?" She smacked her lips.

Emmet's plastic identification bracelet slipped from his sleeve. Every eye judged his infirmity. To appear guiltless and healthy, Emmet twirled the band like a jewel and placed it perfectly in view over his cuff. He licked his finger and rubbed at a yellowed spot on Louise's cheek. She pounded her heels impatiently against the bottom of the seat so that the car echoed with blows.

"Let's move," she said impatiently as the train lurched between stations. "I want to ride in front so we can follow the light." She led them through the interior doors, past the signs forbidding transit, as the train rumbled darkly underground. Each time they entered a car, the passengers started from their seats, expecting to see a gang of thieves descend upon them with clubs.

In the front car, Louise stood mesmerized by the gray shadows of the tunnel as the conductor lit their way. Emmet had read of men, even alligators, who lived for years unbothered under the city, but all he saw were families of rats scurrying carelessly along the edge of the electrified rail.

"Wear your sunglasses," he snapped as the train pulled into the bus station. He lifted them from the studded chain that swung on Louise's chest and set the lenses over her eyes.

"Got any gum?" she asked a woman waiting to exit. "Hey, lady, you got any gum?"

Emmet pulled her after him, sidestepping a bum slumbering

on a bed of newspapers. The veins in his ankles were so rotted and dark that they swam like tentacles under his skin.

"I gotta do my makeup," Louise announced when they entered the cavernous waiting lounge. Emmet went inside the men's room. Before the rows of mirrors, one man brushed his teeth. Another shaved slowly and deliberately, patting the cream over his beard, as if he were at home. An old man stood in his underwear against the far wall, toying with a stiff brown sock. From a distance, Emmet arranged his hair in the mirror. He felt the soap bulge in his pocket. He would have to purchase a new toothbrush. He was humiliated to become part of the people who performed their toilets in public. He dashed into a stall and fastened the lock. He unbuttoned his outer layers of clothes. He saw two worn black shoes tiptoe outside his door and a pair of eyes peer through the crack, watching Emmet's clothes drop article by article, as if he performed a striptease.

"The police will suspect I'm a pervert," Emmet worried as he quickly bundled the clothes into his plastic sack. The black-shoed man followed him outside. Emmet saw Louise brilliant with fresh makeup licking a vermilion Italian ice. As the man shadowed his steps, Emmet greeted her with a husbandly kiss. The man veered away.

"You're in a good mood suddenly," Louise said. "Want a lick?" She held the sticky paper cup to his lips. The syrup dribbled onto his tongue.

In the waiting room, Emmet searched for a map or a schedule posted on the wall. "Where do we go?" he wondered as he imagined an atlas spidered with the thousands of cities, villages, and towns in every state. He could not conceive how he might arrive somewhere unannounced and make it his home. Always in the past there had been a specific reason or person to draw him to a place. With no guide to help him, he could not choose.

On the wall by the ticket counter, he saw the blue departure screen. "Why don't we pick the town written on the first line and call it home?" he asked.

"Okay by me," Louise said, burying her nose in the bottom of the paper cup.

They stood with their eyes downcast before the screen, as if blindfolded, and then together they looked up and read the white letters spelling "C-A-N-A-N-D-A-I-G-U-A" on the first line. He hoped it was a distant place, far off in another state. He pronounced the word phonetically. Then he said it again, more quickly, then again, and again, until it tripped from his tongue. He turned to Louise and repeated it in her ear, softly, as if whispering an endearment.

"How can I live in a town I can't pronounce?" Louise whined. But Emmet believed those letters spelled their destiny and that if they cheated by selecting another place, like the towns written on the second or third line, they would jinx any chance they had.

"We promised," he said as he went to the window to purchase tickets. They cost twenty-seven dollars, one way. Canandaigua could not be far.

Their bus did not leave until evening. Emmet grew frantic as they waited, watching Louise slurp soda after soda from a jumbo cup. She was drinking their money. He followed every sip as she tipped the cup to her lips and let the liquid dribble down her throat, rippling the skin like fingers under a glove. To set an example, he returned to the restroom and sipped water from the faucet. He made certain his chin glistened wetly when he returned so that Louise could not mistake his parsimony. She dabbed at his face with her sleeve. "You'll get germs from those sinks. I'd watch it. So, you got a dollar for candy?"

At the gate, Louise pushed to the front of the line. The bus riders let her pass, instinctively, as people do in a city when they encounter someone wilder and more hostile than them. Emmet held back at the rear, but Louise shouted down to him from the steps, refusing to let another traveler by until he had joined her. Murmuring apologies, he shuffled past their hate.

She trounced into the front seat, arranging the contents of her purse over her lap. She pulled out fashion magazines and books of crossword puzzles, packages of chewing gum, a powder compact, two kinds of lipstick, and a yogurt with a plastic spoon taped to its side. Emmet set his sack of clothes at his feet.

He tried to relax as the bus driver guided them down the ramp and out onto the web of unpopulated side streets at the edge of the city. They roared through the tunnel and under the river, over bridges, through tollbooths, until the motor kicked into high gear and they were loose on the highway. Emmet imagined the tires spinning along the pavement, driving them further and further away. He had not left the city for years. He did not know if it was possible to leave his past behind; but as he settled into his cushioned seat, the skyline grew tinier and tinier out the window until it seemed constructed of plastic boxes and glue, and then smaller still, smaller than a photograph shot from the sky: and then it was gone.

Louise nudged his side. "So what's another word for 'shrivel'?" she asked, sucking the tip of a red pencil.

"I don't know. 'Dry'? 'Shrink'? 'Age'?"

"No, it's got a *z*, unless I've made a mistake somewhere. Is 'ozera' a word?" Louise climbed onto the back of the seat and pushed the crossword puzzle book into the face of the woman behind her.

"You ever heard of 'ozera'? How about 'anachorism'? It sounds like something, doesn't it? But you know, it doesn't have that second *n*."

The woman bundled her child to her breast and shook her head. Emmet tugged Louise's sleeve. "Please sit down."

It grew dark. The trees alongside the highway disappeared

until the road was lit by fluorescent markers. The oncoming cars vanished to their headlights.

Louise looked up from her book alarmed. "Why isn't he driving with the blue light on the dashboard? I don't feel safe unless he drives with the blue light. You tell him."

"What?"

"Tell the driver what we want," she ordered. "We want the blue light."

The cars rushed at them ceaselessly from the opposite direction. "But he can't use the blue light. Then he'll blind the other drivers with his brights," Emmet whispered.

"But I can't see," she whined. "The light makes the bus go. I always drive with it, day or night. It's like a religion." She looked around, disgusted. "I hate buses anyway. If we had any money, we could have rented a car."

Emmet tried to think of something to distract her. He looked at the partially filled boxes of her crossword. "What's another word for 'hijack'?" he asked.

"Tell him about the blue light," she screeched. "I want it!"

Emmet felt the pressure on the accelerator lessen as the bus coasted along the road. In the mirror, he saw the driver's eyes grow luminous and threatening, fixed directly on their seat.

"Please keep it down," Emmet muttered. He did not want to be dumped on the highway. Although he had never been to Canandaigua, already he was desperate to arrive, as if it were the place he had been born.

"Keep *what* down?" Louise screamed. "What are you talking about? I only want to see the blue light."

As if by magic, the bus climbed the crest of a hill. Below them, the valley stretched blackly with no cars in sight. Emmet heard a click, and suddenly the road was illuminated by the brights of the bus. The blue light shone brilliantly from the dashboard.

"See," Louise said. "He didn't mind. All you had to do is ask. Jeez, what's the matter with you?"

As they drove, Emmet chattered excitedly every time a car came from the opposite direction, so that Louise might not notice the *click click click* as the bus driver flicked the blue light off and on. He peered, fascinated, at her fashion magazines. "You'd look nice in this," he said, pointing to a sleek silk sheath. He pored over her crossword answers, trying to form new words out of ones she had misspelled, thinking quickly to vault over her errors.

Finally she slept. The bus pulled off the highway and took to the country roads, stopping in village after village. In the smallest towns there was no station, only a sign posted on the main street where people stood in line with their luggage and sacks filled with food. Each time they slowed to a stop, the driver called out the name of the town softly. The places were all unfamiliar. Emmet did not know where he was or how close they had come to their destination. He worried that he would fall asleep and be driven beyond their stop. He held himself riveted awake, listening intently for the driver to announce "Canandaigua" and send them on their way.

Louise snored beside him in little snorts, like a puppy, her ear pressed against the metal rail of the window. Asleep, her face lost the creases of energy that had made her appear unknown to him all day. To distract himself from worry, he counted the mile markers staked along the road; but as the bus shot into the dark he could not refrain from listing the things they would need to live a normal life—not just a home, but the objects to furnish it: beds, blankets, pillows, sheets, tables, chairs, lamps. Not simply food three times a day, but a fire to cook it and utensils to prepare it: pots, pans, plates, cups, saucers, spoons, forks, knives, glasses. They needed references, identification papers, promises of employment to open a bank account even before they had the means to purchase heat, a telephone, a method of transportation. They needed clothes for work. They needed skills. If they were to be accepted by the community, they needed a respectability Emmet had never won and could not imagine winning with Louise.

At each stop, a reflex told him to rise up and abandon her there, to lose himself in the handful of disembarking passengers and disappear into the night. At each new town, Emmet gathered his bag to his lap and prepared to leave, checking to make certain his movement did not disturb her. It was possible to slip away. But each time he delayed until the door swung shut.

Emmet rested his hand against her thigh, wanting to feel some impulse pass between them. He felt bound to her, but by nothing he could define. He wanted something more to hold him there, some vast feeling of protectiveness or love, but it was only the image of her face when she awoke to find herself alone that kept him sitting by her side.

After six hours, they pulled into the parking lot of a gas station. Clearly and distinctly, the driver called "Canandaigua." Emmet watched row after row of passengers rise from their seats and file down the aisle. He waited as long as possible, wishing madly that someone he knew would appear from the back of the bus or that a distant relative might be waiting outside the door to take them home. Halfheartedly he hoped to see a white-uniformed orderly ready on the ramp to tell him everything was over.

The last passenger stepped off the bus. Emmet heard the driver rev the engine. "Louise . . . Louise," he called, shaking her. She stirred sleepily. "We're home."

Her voice was puffy with sleep. "Home?"

"We're there." Emmet helped gather her things into her purse. He held his sack of clothes. He held his breath. He placed his hand at the base of her neck and then together they walked down the steps and out into the night air.

CHAPTER

FIVE

The other passengers vanished quickly, leaving Emmet and Louise stranded in the parking lot with no company but a taxi idling in the driveway. The driver snoozed in the front seat with his cap pulled down over his nose. Emmet considered waking him to take them somewhere inexpensive for the night, but he believed they would look suspicious if they asked for lodging before dawn. He checked his watch. It was 12:07 A.M. The bus had carried them into the next day. He breathed a sigh of relief. Already they could look back on their escape and say, "That was yesterday."

They staked out the town in widening spirals, branching out from the center until they had covered every back alley and side residential street. They peered into the windows of the post office, the pharmacy, the butcher's, the stationery store, the rows and rows of antique shops and clothing boutiques. They imagined each darkened office crowded with townspeople, months from then, greeting Emmet and Louise by name. When they saw an article of clothing buttoned on a mannequin in a shop window, they imagined themselves wearing it out to dinner at a friend's. When they saw a piece of furniture arranged in a display, they placed it in a room of their new house. They added pictures to their walls, knickknacks to their shelves, and a set of hand-blown blue glasses to the sideboard in their dining room. They rejected some neighborhoods as too noisy; they longed after others. On a landscaped cul-de-sac, they found a single-story house sheltered by oaks that they agreed would be their dream.

Through the kitchen curtains of that house they saw a couple dressed in bathrobes talking across a table: two empty cups, a teapot, and plates littered with crumbs between them. It was 3:00 A.M. From her chair, the woman reached across and stroked the man's head. He pressed her hand into the crook of his neck and held it there in a small embrace.

"That's us, not long from now," Louise whispered confidently as they stepped back through the bushes. She clasped his hand.

Emmet did not reply. But as they wandered down the driveway and into the neighborhood beyond, he thought of how he had often sought an intimacy such as they had just witnessed. He had kept the idea in his mind as a hope to be achieved once his life was settled. On holidays with his relatives, he had often wondered if he would be different if he had made a family of his own. But always he grew restless as he listened to his cousins speak of their children's accomplishments, of sports events they had attended, of vacations they had enjoyed, of movies they had seen or books they had read, of their work, their Sundays at church, how they had fallen in love or become divorced. In his own life, he could never see daily tasks as more than barricades built against chaos. He could not accept them naturally, as others seemed to, as the most one could ever hope to find.

For a long time, Emmet had not been involved in another person's life. He had forgotten how to distinguish one emotion from another when all he knew everywhere was fear. He did not know if he had ever been capable of more, but after a certain point he could no longer trace, he had lost track of what he was supposed to feel. As Louise bounded ahead of him, he tried to recall how it had come to pass that she alone was his world companion. He wondered if there had been a moment when he had chosen the slips and falls and detours that had changed him. Although he dreamed of calm, he did not know the degree to which his heart courted drama, as if worry were the only fuel that kept his life in motion.

But as the night slipped away on his journey with Louise, he tried to immerse himself in their fantasy of a new life. He did not allow himself to remark that everything they saw existed beyond their reach. He told himself that there was no reason that night could not carry them through the months ahead and make their wishes real.

In the morning, they found a campground that rented tents on the outskirts of town. "We are on our honeymoon," Emmet told the camp director as he filled out the registration form. He signed them in as Leander Phelps and his wife, Rose.

"Rose?" Louise sniffed when Emmet returned with two white towels and a receipt. "I don't want to be Rose. I want to be Susanna."

"But I had to pick," Emmet said.

"I hate it. It sounds like someone's aunt."

"Well, I don't see how we can change it. It's written on the register. Besides, it's pretty. It makes you sound like a flower. You know, a part of spring. Like everything's beginning."

"It's the dead of winter," Louise said, stalking towards the cabanas of outdoor toilets at the entrance to the camp.

To appease her, Emmet offered breakfast at the local diner. She perked up as the waitress spread the three-page menu before them.

He ordered French toast. Louise studied the handwritten list of daily specials before shouting, "The blueberry pancakes look good—let's see, yes—and country sausages, two poached eggs, and a strawberry milk shake. Do you add malt? And a piece of wheat toast with butter on the side, and don't try to pawn off any margarine. I can smell it."

"Will that be all?" the waitress asked. Emmet saw her raise a plucked eyebrow at the cook behind the counter.

"How about tomato juice and one of those cheese Danishes if they're fresh today?" She slapped her hands together greedily.

When their food came, the sweet and meaty smells mingled in the air over their table so that Emmet stifled a gag. Louise cut the eggs and sausages with her fork. She slathered butter over her toast, even slapping the sprig of parsley set at the side of her plate. She swirled chocolate syrup over her pancakes. She stirred sugar into her malt with a straw. Her dishes ran blue, pink, yellow, and brown, bleeding with rivulets of grease and melted fat.

"Hmmm, yes," she mumbled as she stuffed forkfuls of food into her mouth. Parsley stuck to her teeth like bits of freshly mowed grass. "Lovely, yes . . . gosh," she said, like an incantation over every bite. She cleared her throat between swallows with a thick, gooey grunt as if she were gulping oysters. "Gosh."

Emmet concentrated on his plate. When he cut into his cooked bread, its interior oozed from the crust, mossy and gray, like the flesh of a creature living under the sea. The pats of butter sat stiff as faded plastic. "This is food," he told himself. "All natural ingredients." He tried to imagine the eggs picked that morning from a warm nest in a hutch; the bread hot from an oven and sealed tightly in a cellophane wrapper; the butter stirred in vats of freshly milked cream. But still the vapors choked him. He was parched with thirst. He called to the waitress for water, as a drowning person might call for help.

She brought it in blue plastic cups with thick rims. "I can't drink out of glasses that aren't clear," Emmet said, gazing longingly across the counter at the clear glass tumblers gathering dust on a shelf.

"Don't go weird on me," Louise said. "Here, drink." Syrup formed a fat, sticky tear on her lip. She ordered another malted, emptying the bottom of her glass with her straw. It made a sound like water being sucked down a drain.

Emmet pushed his plate away. To block the odor, he covered his mouth with his left hand, discreetly holding one nostril closed with his thumb. He pulled a notebook from his pocket and recorded each item of food they had ordered. He checked the menu to see if toast was included with Louise's eggs and if they charged for refills of coffee. As he listed the poisons they had eaten, he subtracted the cost of every morsel. In the upper-right-hand corner he recorded the total amount of money remaining in his pocket after their meal.

"I must put us on a budget," he announced.

"You worry too much. We'll have jobs soon." She smiled reassuringly. A blueberry bloodied her front tooth.

Emmet's pants felt baggy about him, like a scarecrow's. His arms jutted like sticks. "But who'll hire us?"

"Don't be so negative. You can be anything you want to be. You gotta have faith." She drummed her fingers on the table. "Faith. Faith. Faith."

"Ssshh," he said. "We have to make a list. We have to know the things we need and the things we can do."

"We can do anything we want. We can eat when we want to, sleep when we want to, play when we want to. It's ours to choose." Every word she uttered seemed blared over a loudspeaker. "Anything or nothing; anything or nothing. It's ours to choose." She rapped the table with her spoon.

Emmet did not want to do anything. He wanted something specific set before him, a boundary built around each day. He felt their freedom like a curse.

"Anything else?" the waitress asked, slapping the bill on the table like a subpoena. Emmet calculated a huge tip so that she might remember his generosity. His money felt like feathers in his pocket.

After breakfast they worked. They hammered the stakes of the tent into the ground with one of Louise's shoes. Their rental charge included a sooty circle of rocks for their fire and a splintered picnic table with a single bench. Emmet picked thrushes from a riverbed and stuck them in the long crack in the table as a centerpiece. He hung his sack on a string outside the tent for garbage. He wet a towel under the spigot and carefully wiped mud from the canvas floor of the tent. They gathered sticks in the woods and piled them as high as the back of the tent: the largest pieces at the bottom, the kindling on top. They had no blankets, but arranged their extra clothes in the shape of bodies on the floor for a cushion. Emmet bundled his jeans into a pillow. Inside the tent there was room for two only if they lay flat along the ground. They could rise no higher than balanced on their knees.

In town, they bought an aluminum pot, three bags of carrots, ten pounds of potatoes, and a plastic cylinder of sea salt. On a sale table, they found a box of plastic silverware and two packages of paper plates and napkins festooned with orange goblins and black witches on brooms, marked down since Halloween.

As they carried their purchases, Emmet heard a hush still the sidewalk and the racket in the stores cease the moment they stepped inside. Louise waltzed everywhere, oblivious to their strangeness, commenting on every object they saw. She greeted customers. She inquired after shopkeepers' families. She did not seem to notice when they refused to respond. Emmet felt as conspicuous as if he were lugging a dead body on his shoulder.

No one welcomed them. They were the only inhabitants of the camp except for the owner and a party of deer hunters dressed in fatigues the color of wintered bark and evergreen.

The first night Emmet made dinner. He set the table with

their paper plates. He folded the napkins into halves and weighted them with forks. He shaved the skins off the carrots and potatoes with the grooves of a plastic knife before he cut them into sections and dropped them into the pot. He made pyramids of wood, placing balled paper between every layer for their fire. They had no matches. For twenty minutes he rubbed two bowed sticks together as he had learned from scouting manuals, but he could not make a spark.

Across from their site, the hunters' bonfire was blazing five feet high. On a spit they prepared the carcass of a deer, its meat stripped of its hide and glistening wetly in the glow of the flames. Emmet considered bringing a stick to the hunters' fire to borrow a flame, but as he watched them prepare their meat with knives, they seemed bonded in a secret ritual. His nervousness would mark him as an intruder. If they had not noticed, he did not want them to realize who slept unarmed in the adjacent camp.

He borrowed a book of matches from the camp director. The sticks and paper burned, but never so strongly that the water boiled. Emmet was afraid to raise too large a conflagration in case he could not put it out. The hearth was two feet from their tent. He waited an hour as the sticks turned to ash and the water smoked, but its temperature grew no hotter than he could have gotten from a faucet. Louise ignored his efforts, studying her face in the round mirror of her powder compact. She applied coat upon coat of makeup, glowering from time to time at the partial moon as if to scorn its diminished light.

As he went about his business, Emmet pretended he was home in his old apartment, pulping carrots through the juicer and preparing to feed his dog. Outside it was twenty-eight degrees. Even with his hands directly over the pot, he could barely feel the steam. He saw the months ahead: December turning to January and then beyond into the most frigid days of the year. They would have no heat. They had no proper jackets. They had no gloves. They had not yet spent one night in camp and already he knew it could not last.

He spooned the food onto the plates. He doused it with sea salt until the vegetables were crusted with crystals. They ate in a silence heavy with resentment and blame that froze his body more rigid than the cold, a feeling he remembered from childhood dinners when his parents' breath flew across the table like blows.

Louise ate quickly, as if she were late for an appointment. When she had finished, she folded her plate in half and jumped into the tent. Emmet cleaned the pot under the spigot. He washed the plastic silverware and replaced it in its box. He carried the plates to the garbage dump at the far end of the encampment. In the tent, he shivered upon his clothes. As the temperature fell, they moved into each other's arms under cover of sleep, but impersonally, the way one might wrap within a blanket to hide from the cold.

For three days Emmet made the rounds. He applied for work at the local grocery store, at the newspaper, at an antiques store. Every place rejected him. He rang doorbells at house after house, offering to rake the last remaining leaves or shovel snow or cut dead limbs from trees. At each interview, he fought the tremor in his voice. He smiled disarmingly, hiding his hands in his back pockets to keep them still.

Every evening when he returned to the site he found Louise dozing in the tent where he had left her. She raised herself on one arm when he crawled through the flaps. "Don't worry," she told him as she settled back to sleep. "Something will happen."

She refused to eat. The second morning Emmet noticed four dollars missing from his pants when he awoke. He checked his records to be certain he had not made an error. That night while she slept, he buried his money at the foot of a tree. He marked the spot with a stick, like a makeshift grave. He kept a single dollar folded in his pocket.

He could not depend on her. Hidden in the tent, Louise could not see how the town turned against him at each place he stopped, so that it became no different from the city they had left. When his hope began to flag, he told himself, "Imagine you are pioneers." He pictured the cleared area of the campground as an uncharted western territory and he and Louise as settlers. He imagined they had arrived by covered wagon and claimed the circle of dirt as their homestead. He tried to begin from there, but all he saw around him was the desolate tents flapping in the cold, the remains of deer carcasses littering the dirt from the hunters' meal, and the outline of the town darkening the horizon with shadows. The world around them was already made. The only way to live there was to slip inside, and he could not break through.

He despaired of finding work. They did not have enough money to leave unless they hitchhiked, and he was afraid to set out onto the highway and be at the mercy of strangers. He considered calling his brother to ask to stay, but Emmet did not yet want to step so hopelessly into the past. He knew Jonathan's apartment would close around him, as if he were a prisoner returning on parole or a patient sent home to die. There would be nowhere to go from there. But even if they ceased to eat, Emmet could afford to pay for their campsite only until two weeks from the following Thursday.

On the fourth day it rained. They did not leave their tent. The rain beat upon them, denting the canvas roof as if someone were shooting nails from the sky. At first they felt secure inside, feeling the drops splash against their skin as they pressed their noses to the mosquito-netted window. But as the storm grew in force, water dribbled around the frayed area supporting the center pole, soaking their bodies. They huddled miserably together, ducking from each drop of water as the tent shrunk around them.

Emmet hung their pillows of pants and sweaters from a nail in the roof to protect them from the puddles forming on the floor, but still the rain ran off the legs and arms as easily as from skin. Outside, the trees swayed dangerously overhead, at first rustling like crinoline skirts, but then louder, like the rattle of snakes.

"Nighttime fucks me up," Louise said, holding her knees to her chest as if bent by cramps.

"It's just the rain," Emmet lied, knowing all too well how darkness unleashed his worst self. He recoiled from the smell of her unwashed body, as if it spread a contagion.

The flaps of the tent blew in at them. Their moorings shook. "Whoa," Louise repeated, as if she were flying too fast and needed to slow herself down. Emmet pressed his hand hard against the corner of the tent to hold it fast to the ground. "Whoa."

Louise reached across and stroked the flat bicep of his right arm, dispassionately, as if she were feeling a piece of sculpture. "If a tree fell on the tent and trapped me, do you think you'd have the strength to lift it? You know—like those women whose children are crushed by cars and they rush in and raise the whole thing by the bumper?"

"I would try," Emmet said, imagining the rain blinding his eyes as he struggled to heave the dead weight of the tree. In his mind, the branches held fast to the ground.

"No, no—trying isn't good enough. You've gotta just run over and grab it. If you stop to think, I'm doomed. I need to be sure, so that maybe I might sleep tonight and not worry."

There would be no sleeping. Emmet felt pebbles under his back and puddles sloshing beneath him. Water flooded from the hill behind their tent, rolling the floor like a boat bottom.

"Can you swim?" Louise asked.

"Sort of, but I never learned to breathe with my face in the water, so I hold my breath for as long as I can and then I give up."

"Do you think if the river overflowed its banks and I am swept away, you would jump in and rescue me? Not wait for the police to come, but really go for it, no matter the odds?"

Emmet did not know why Louise assumed he would be saved and so be free to save her. He did not want to be the one to dive into the current and reach for a drowning hand. He wanted to extend his own arm from the water and feel the firm grip of a swimmer pulling him to shore.

The air hardened with cold. Emmet heard Louise shift positions along the damp floor. Even in the dark, he could see his breath cloud the air above his face.

"I need to know," she said.

"Yes, I would jump in," he said, imagining their bodies dragged hopelessly along the white crest of the current. He patted the slick plastic of her coat reassuringly. Its fabric was wet and oily from the rain. He pictured the clean, starched sheets of the hospital and the woolen blanket folded at the foot of his bed. He should have eased himself out a foot at a time, as into cold water, until he had adjusted.

"It isn't working, is it?" she asked, her tone familiar again, as from the first afternoon they met.

"I don't know," Emmet hedged. He did not want to be the one to call it quits.

"We can't lose it, can we? Or I don't know about you, but I can't or maybe I don't want to. I wasn't lying, you know—I really did want to go. But now that I'm here, I don't think I can take a normal day—I don't even know what it is. You don't blame me, do you? I mean, when you're locked away, you lust after the wind hitting your face, as if you need it to breathe. But even out here I'm suffocating. Maybe I don't want to make the effort, or maybe I just don't have the imagination for anything that's good. I'd like to stick around to find out who the President will be and who'll die famous and who'll drop the bomb and what cities will be destroyed. And I wanna know if the glaciers melt or the planets collide and I want to know what'll happen to some people, like you. Basically I want to know who wins and who loses. But the rest is all watching, like turning on the television and not wanting to miss what's on next. But I don't care enough to be part of it, you know what I mean?"

Louise rose to her knees and peered into Emmet's face. He could see nothing but the shadows of her hair thick against the night. "I don't know what's gonna happen," she said. "Remember when you asked me back in the bin if jumpers think of something before they walk off a ledge, like if they spit on one particular face? I don't think it's like that. It's more like you're just stepping through another door, only this one doesn't have a bottom, but by then you don't care. You're nothing but paper flapping against the walls. You're that thin. I'm almost there. Who knows, maybe if I keep moving I might shake it, but there's nothing in it for you. God knows, I don't want you to leave, but how much further is there? I want to keep you with me, you know, partly to drag you down. It's nothing personal—just excess baggage to pile on more dead weight. I gotta admit that. But it's like we're off anyway and it's past anything to do with us. You know—like when your car is running out of gas and you're on a really hilly road and the register drags all the way down to empty, and when you climb each hill you think, 'It's gotta run out now.' But somehow you inch to the top and get enough momentum going to coast partway up the next rise and so you give the accelerator a little push and before you know it, you've cleared another one and start to coast again. Sometimes you can go for miles. Sometimes you even make it to the next gas station. But sometimes it runs out. The only thing left that fascinates me is waiting to see when it's gonna happen, because I don't know." She laughed. "But we're coasting, baby. We're coasting."

She rumbled "Zoom" deep within her throat, like an engine

warming. She hopped in circles on her knees, as if dancing on stumps, whirring "Zoom, zoom, zoom" about the tent until she toppled next to Emmet, laughing. He backed away, but even as he strained against the canvas walls, her hands were only inches from his body.

"Zoom," she barked on all fours. "Zoom." Then she dove towards the flaps of the tent and squeezed herself outside, as if wriggling through a pipe.

Emmet watched raindrops fly from her clothes as she shook her limbs dry. She paced around the circle of rocks, punching the air in front of her, addressing no one as the sound of her mutterings blew back at him with the wind.

"How do I know when it is over?" he wondered. Once his grandmother told him it was impossible to dream his own death. She said he might dream of falling from a cliff but he would awaken before his body hit the ground. Or if he dreamed he was tied to railroad tracks with an engine bearing down upon him, he might hear the whistle blowing, he might feel the vibrations shooting through the rails, but he would awake before he felt the wheels rip upon his flesh.

Emmet had always believed that somewhere inside of him lived the seeds of a last ace that would snatch him awake, as if from one of those dreams. But as he watched Louise run beyond the director's hut, he tried to imagine what was next for them, even the following morning, and he could think of absolutely nothing.

He slept, wrapped in her jeans, one sparkled stocking prickly as chapped skin under his cheek. And as he slept, he dreamed his car skidded on ice as he drove along a mountain pass, crashing through the railing and plummeting into the valley below, bouncing off the icy sides of the cliff: tumbling, tumbling in the air until the world outside was lost in the blur of blue white sky and snowy mounds of earth. Even strapped to his seat, he felt himself hurled unbearably about, round, round, and round, until the car straightened in the last ten feet of space and aimed at its target. He awoke to screams of splintered steel and shattered glass, the sensation of his body flying out the windshield into the chilly air before he slammed, dead, against the rocks dumped at the bottom.

Louise did not return until the following evening. Her eyes were bright with excitement when she pulled him from the tent. "I saw this sign for a carnival on the bulletin board by the post office. It's got everything: Ferris wheels, clowns, a roller coaster, even a shooting gallery. I haven't been to one in years. Let's smear our faces with cotton candy and get sick from dizziness. Let's forget all this shit. Let's go."

Before they made another move, Emmet wanted to discuss a new plan for their lives, but he was so relieved to have her safely back he could not deny her wish. Her happiness might herald yet another beginning. He zipped the flaps of the tent and fastened them closed with a piece of wire hanger. He placed the bench squarely against the picnic table. He stirred the soupy ashes of their fire with a stick.

"Come on, come on," Louise shouted. "I want to zoom over the earth like nothing's holding me back. I want to fly."

They raced through the city streets, as if nothing were amiss, as if they were a couple no different from the scores of people they found standing in line at the carnival's gate, ready for a diversion.

CHAPTER

SIX

One of the first days Emmet could remember was a trip he made to the amusement park with his family. His father ushered them to a ride that held them fast against a wall. Once the machine began to spin, the floor dropped out, keeping them there by nothing but the force of gravity.

"Relax, this is fun," his father murmured soothingly as they gained momentum and began to whirl and tip at a speed faster than Emmet had ever gone. When he tried to wriggle his feet, they did not feel part of him anymore. He flew as if his body had been lopped off and pieced together with Scotch tape. When he looked at the sky, he worried they might ricochet off the side of the trailers parked close to the wooden fence of the carnival, or further still, off into the deepest reaches of the galaxy.

Emmet prayed for it to end. Out of the corner of his eye, he saw his father struggle to raise his head to speak, but when he opened his mouth, he was slapped by a violent pocket of pressure. The wind swooped down and ripped his dentures away, sending the pink plastic gums and neat row of whites tumbling into the jaws of the machine. As they snapped against the pulleys, little pieces of crushed teeth splattered their skin like buckshot. Emmet still had an inch-long scar on his thigh from being struck by those teeth. It stood out whitely whenever he was tanned in summer. His father yelled for the conductor to stop, but no one could understand him. His lips slurped against his tongue, like an old man's. The machine continued to fly. At the end, the whole family and the circle of strangers lay flat against the wall, their mouths frozen in screams. When Emmet stood on the pavement afterward, his body blew in the air about him for hours. He did not eat for days.

"I am spinning that fast now," Emmet thought as Louise led him through the gates of the carnival. All around them were the fragrance of gunpowder rising from the barrels of plastic rifles and the crack of toy triggers becoming lost in the buzz of insects flying into neon-lit traps and melting into blue sparks. He heard the laughter of drunken girls as they leaned dangerously over the footbridge to a moat, and he saw the strings of lights blinking along a tent become entwined in their arms when they swooped forward to keep their balance. As the lights sank into the water, there was a zap of electric current before everything became dark. And everywhere were puffs of smoke and sparks that cracked and buzzed and zapped.

When Louise took Emmet's arm and led him into a tent off one side of the shooting gallery, it seemed as if mine fields exploded safely behind them each time they raised a foot to step forward.

When they lifted the flaps of the tent, they saw a computer with a glass-domed bubble rising from its center, half-buried by folded chairs and carousel ponies wrapped in canvases like shrouds. Under the glass lay the torso and head of a rubber witch wearing a sequined hat, but she was flattened and spread over the machine as if her flesh were made of warmed butter. "Morgana the Wonder Woman," a sign hung from the lid proclaimed; for fifty cents she would tell your fortune.

Louise blew the dust off the glass and put two quarters into a slot in the side of the machine. Morgana rumbled to life. Her face inflated as two pupil-sized bulbs flickered behind her eyes. She bolted upright, her head twisting from side to side and her tongue rattling against her teeth as if she had entered a trance. Her eyes snapped to a glassy stare and her rubber lips curled to a smile. From a speaker somewhere deep inside her, a muffled voice asked, "When were you born?"

Louise punched the numbers of her birthday into the panel. Seconds later, a slip of paper ticked from a slot and fell into her hand. Morgana deflated. Her eyes dropped into her lips and her lips slid into her chin and her chin fell forward, lolling against the shelf as if she were exhausted from too much seeing. Louise glanced at the paper and laughed, but when Emmet moved to read it, she balled it under her tongue.

Emmet wondered whether somewhere in the world every person born on the same day was punching numbers and receiving identical advice. But when Louise pressed the date of Emmet's birth instead of her own, Morgana ate the quarters without lifting her head. After that, each time the machine came to life they guarded it with their bodies, carefully tucking the papers in their pants without reading them. Emmet did not care how much they spent. They pumped Morgana with change until the rubber around her neck began to fray and their pockets were crammed with prophecies.

Louise led Emmet back outside. The night was loud with piped music, the grinding gears of the Ferris wheel, the squeals of people swinging in their cages high above, and the ting of bullets striking the metal rabbits that ran across the backdrop of watercolored trees in the shooting gallery. Strung along the roof of the tent were families of stuffed rabbits that peered down at them like pink, yellow, and blue gargoyles. Some had top hats sewn onto their heads and spectacles glued over their leather noses. Some wore aprons and carried little purses. Some were swaddled in diapers with mittens over their paws. Each had six whiskers stitched into a grin.

Emmet and Louise hovered by the tent, watching the people take aim and fire. Emmet could see dents gather at the rabbits' feet from the beebees as they rattled past with their painted, expressionless faces. The man behind the booth tapped Emmet's arm and asked, "Don't you want to take a bunny home?" He laughed as he held out a rifle.

Louise pushed Emmet aside. She took the gun and winked as she pressed the butt against her shoulder. She caught the first rabbit in the eye. It flipped over and then she moved quickly to the second, shooting it cleanly. She fired again. She turned to Emmet excitedly, opening her mouth as if she were short of oxygen, and wiped her finger along the barrel before she bent back over the gun. Each time she fired, a rabbit fell, but whenever one disappeared behind the screen, there was another running out of the bushes painted on the other side.

Louise pounded the counter for more ammunition. She quickly reloaded the gun, but by then the rabbits had risen again and were passing in front of her, ten hooked together on a chain, rattling forward in that one direction.

"Grab a gun," she called to Emmet. She pushed more money at the attendant behind the booth.

"Okay, you win, lady," the man said nervously. He unhooked a green rabbit from the back of the tent and walked towards her. The rabbit was so large it obscured him completely. All Emmet could see were his arms wrapped around the green fur in an embrace.

Louise refused to drop the gun. She had mastered the rhythm, each rabbit dropping effortlessly whenever it moved into her sight. For a few seconds she had got them all. She heaved against the counter, the rifle trembling on the wood, as she studied the empty black line clanking against the back of the tent. All they heard were the gears of the pulley and then ten pings of metal, like the sound of coins dropped into a can, as somewhere behind the tent the rabbits were propped up again and made ready to come back at them, alive, from the other side.

"There's no stopping them," Louise called breathlessly. The spectators pushed closer to get a better look, as if she were an exhibition at the fair.

"Let's go, Louise," Emmet said quietly. He tugged at her sleeve.

She crouched before the counter and prepared to fire. "Grab a gun, damn it. I can't stop them alone."

The man held out the rabbit. Emmet stepped two paces back, becoming almost part of the crowd. The gawkers encircled him in a wall of flesh. They left no exit through their bodies.

He heard snickers and snippets of conversations soar in the air around him: "Fat." "Crazy." "Clown."

Louise wiped her hands over her face to clear her eyes for a better aim, but she smeared her makeup, staining her skin a bright mask of colors, as if her features were melting.

To save them both, at least from that one moment bursting around them, Emmet tried to think of a way to reach her, but he felt as powerless as if he were praying to raise a body from the dead. For a moment he considered wrestling her to the ground. But even if he subdued her, anything he knew was useless to bring her back to safety: not only away from the carnival, but beyond its gates, through the next day and out into a life beyond.

Louise hopped onto a wooden box and surveyed the crowd below like a conqueror hailing her vanquished. She beaded Emmet with the sight of her gun.

"Let's go back," he whispered, because it was all he could think of doing. "Back in." But even as he spoke, he imagined cars on the highway catching them in their headlights if they hitchhiked, veering from Louise's wildness. No one sane would take them in.

Louise fired her gun into the air. Puffs of smoke crowned her head. She fired again. "Coward," she spat down at him, her face marbled with fierceness. She ran her hands through her hair until it stood about her head like flames.

The crowd backed off, but Emmet felt their hate regroup, forming a solid, angry mass behind him. "They think I'm like her," he thought, looking desperately around. He searched the strangers' faces for a sympathetic eye to help him, but all he saw was revulsion and fear. He felt their breath upon his neck: four feet, three, then only two. He heard a stampede of feet and a jangle of chains from a distance, as if the police were rushing towards them. They were nearly trapped.

"Get out, Louise," he shouted, hoping she might escape them. "Go."

He saw the force of the crowd's hatred register on her face as she took their numbers in. She stared at him bewildered for a moment before he shouted "Go" again, pointing his arm past the Ferris wheel rising up at the edge of the carnival, out beyond to the fields spreading far into the night. Louise jumped from the box and kicked the rabbit into his arms as she raced through the crowd. It parted from her like water.

Emmet saw her reach the last hurricane fence, stretching her legs like a hurdler and landing perfectly in stride. She hunched her shoulders and jabbed the air in front of her with the rifle. She must have decided the path was clear, for she started to run in loose, broad strides, jerking from left to right, like the lead runner in an ambush, until she made it over the last lit hill and was gone.

The crowd ringed Emmet with stares but did not move to grab him. He walked purposefully away, towards another section of the carnival, where he could hide himself from witnesses. He dragged the rabbit idly behind, as if intending to bring a present home for a child.

At the fence on the western perimeter, he sat down, gazing

over the meadow where Louise had run: the world out there dead and forbidding as the interior of a cave. If there was still a chance to see her, he knew he had to get to higher ground.

The cars of the Ferris wheel swooped above him. He purchased a ticket at the gate. The attendant strapped him to the seat. As the machine clanked to life, it drew him up and up, until he reached the top, only to descend, then quickly rise again.

He heard a screech of gears as he lurched to a stop at its highest point, the chair rocking as high as when he had been marooned above that dangerous space between mountains with his mother. He raised the safety bar over his head and felt himself float in his seat.

"Imagine yourself thin as air," he thought as he stood, feeling the wind sweep about him as if it might pick his body up and discard it like any piece of debris somewhere out among the stars. He leaned left, then right, drunkenly, even rising to one leg until his nerve endings prickled with sleep.

He could not help but think of leaning even further out, to feel his body tumble over the side as his mother's had done. He remembered reading from the police report that she had fallen 269 feet in 4.21 seconds. At the moment of impact, by their calculations, her velocity was 120 miles per hour. He must be higher than that now.

"Four seconds," he thought, astonished at the speed his body could summon in the blink of an eye, its weight gathering a force in the air that he had never found walking on the ground.

"Four seconds," he thought again, counting them one by one with a suddenness that filled him with terror. It seemed too quick to find an end, no time at all: so quick that no regret could flicker in his mind, so quick that he would feel nothing but the rush of the descent pound him down and down and down.

He dropped onto the seat, his chair swinging crazily in white clouds of snow. The sky seemed low and terrible, almost part of the earth. He felt the flakes melt on his face, fragile as forming cells.

"What was it that had pulled her down? What was it that still held him up?" he wondered, wanting to know their difference. He could not conceive how he would ever learn to move without fearing he stepped off into nothing; but as he looked out upon the crystals hardening like shards of glass on the earth below, he knew he lacked his mother's readiness to break free without wanting to catch hold.

"I am going down," he thought, as the machine rattled to life, sweeping in one last revolution before it settled at the gate. The attendant helped Emmet step onto the wooden sidewalk. When he stood on the ground, his body trembled, but he did not stop, feeling the rocks and dirt hard beneath his feet.

And as he walked, he remembered how he had wandered the city streets desperate for the night to end and had wished for nothing but a hand to touch him from behind and lead him back to safety. He imagined Louise crashing through the underbrush like a cat thrown from a car on a highway one hundred miles from home.

He had let her go too easily.

Emmet climbed the fence and set out in the direction Louise had run. He saw the whitened fields and hills ahead planted with thickets of trees, still black as masks. He did not know what was possible, but beyond the woods he saw the glimmer of town: tiny, radiant dots pricking the darkness like candles, reminding him of how the lights of the city had once beckoned. And although nothing he knew gave reason to hope, he wondered if they might beckon again if he made himself return. Maybe if he found her, one day together they might pack their things and go.